'Eight words the Wiccan Rede fulfill,
An ye harm none, do what ye will.'
–   The Wiccan Rede

'...It is evident that we are hurrying onwards to some exciting knowledge-some never-to-be imparted secret; whose attainment is destruction.' - Edgar Allan Poe Ms. Found in a bottle. 1833

'...The boundaries which divide Life from Death are at best shadowy and vague. Who shall say where the one ends, and where the other begins?' –Edgar Allan Poe, 'The Premature Burial.' 1844

Witches and Black Roses Series #1

Taming of the Vampire

By

Jaclyn Ciminelli-White

Chapter 1

Salem, Ohio

1983

An explosion rippled through the quiet town of Salem, Ohio.

Another building full of a rival mob family fell victim to the DeMarco Crime Family.

Bricks and molder from over a hundred years ago crumbled onto the main section of downtown causing a mountain of rubble blocking the town entrance.   The building once hid slaves during the Civil War era before becoming a speakeasy during the Roaring Twenties. From the end of Prohibition until now, the restaurant was a poplar mob hang out.

Red and blue lights danced on the old stone and brick buildings while bullets flew through the air.

The weretiger ran through the streets after a foot solider baring Godmother Marguerite DeMarco's tattooed mark on his left shoulder. In her Bengal tiger form, she pounced on top of him, knocking him onto his back, and dragging her claws down his throat. She quickly walked away watching a man throw fireballs at a group of mobsters as the battle died down.

The handsome Italian gypsy witch saw the weretiger approach him. He noticed the blood caked on her black and orange fur. His black tank top revealed the tattoo of the God symbol that was formed from a full moon with a crescent moon's horns pointed up.

Every male was marked, since birth, with the God symbol and the women were marked with the Goddess symbol a waxing crescent, full, and waning moons representing the three faces of the Goddess; Maiden, Mother, Crone. The Gods gave each family member an elemental power.

The weretiger paused a few feet away from him. Her feline body began to form into a beautiful half Indian and half Italian woman with dark skin that reflected her father's Indian ancestry. Her name bared her Italian mother's home country. Italia Astredo was a professional belly dancer as well as the family alchemist. She was dressed in a pair of lilac purple jeans and pink Indian design top. A purple hip scarf was around her waist. "Let's go to the club. The others may be waiting for us."

Markus's hand still held the warmth from his powers as a fire starter when he held her hand. "Are you ok?"

Italia wiped away the blood from her chin. "The blood belongs to the gangster. Are you holding up ok?"

"Getting there." He quickly escorted her across the street and onto the next block where his nightclub sat unharmed by the brief battle.

Deadly Nightshade was filled with the scents of a verity of food, incense, and candles.

Fake cauldrons with realistic flames hung from the ceilings while candles were placed on the dark green tables.

Plaster gargoyles sat along the dark wooden bar while pictures of Gothic painters, writers, and actors decorated the walls along with Gothic movie posters.

On one wall were a glow-in-the dark crescent moon with thousands of glow-in-the dark stars of different sizes and colors.

Vases of different sizes held dark colored flowers as well as black roses.

The rest of the nightclub had black walls, black ceiling, and the dance floor was painted deep purple.

The stage was painted black and maroon with black, maroon, and red veils draped over the dome-shaped doorway. Statues of Egyptian Gods and Goddesses decorated the floor and walls.

Markus wanted many types of food served from all over the world. He also employed belly dancers in every shape and size. Occasionally, Brenda, Michelle, and Charlotte Astredo would perform with Italia on special nights and private family parties.

They walked through the crowd of Goths dancing to Siouxsie and the Banshees.

Markus's brothers and sisters-in-laws sat at their booth. Markus was the oldest of three sons. He and his wife sat next to his younger brother, Jason.

Jason Astredo, like their father and youngest brother, he was telekinetic and controlled air. He, Markus, and their youngest brother, Caesar, resembled Giovanni

Astredo with their black hair and sexy Italian features. Jason and Caesar worked in the family theater owned by Giovanni.

Brenda Astredo was married to Jason. She had the power to control water. She was also the head physiatrist at the family mental hospital. In 1977, she and Jason adopted an abandon baby found on their doorsteps wearing a silver pentacle and wrapped in a gypsy's scarf. They named him Ari and recently the six-year-old was showing signs of being physic. Ari was born with the God symbol. He and his cousins were at the family mansion.

Caesar sat next to his wife, Michelle. They were local actors at Giovanni's Dragon Lair Theater. "Mom called while I was designing posters. Aunt Kathy and the other's plane arrived an hour ago."

"I thought they weren't coming in until tomorrow morning?" asked Italia.

"Aria had another vision of more attacks while she and Ahmed were at the museum," said Brenda.

Aria was Markus and the other's second cousin. She and their other family members lived on a small island in the Caribbean. Aria's husband, Ahmed, ran the DeMarco Crime Family museum. She was a nightclub singer like her mother, Barbara.

"Are they coming to Lotus's funeral?" asked Markus.

"They are. Gino has to do some undercover police work. Angelique has to work double shift at the hospital and Dominick has been on a spiritual retreat in Rome since the Winter Solstice," Jason said.

Italia looked at her watch and said, "Let's leave for the airport. I don't want to keep them waiting."

The ancient castle sat nestled in Ohio's country side in the small town of Salem. An ancestor of the Astredo family in 1803, brought it over from Basilicata, Italy, magickally. It's been the family home since 1509. Even the catacombs were brought over here.

Giovanni and Charlotte Astredo were the patriarch and matriarch. He was of Italian gypsy heritage. His short black hair had a few traces of silver. They were the High Priest and High Priestess of their family coven.   Giovanni was telekinetic and controlled air and Charlotte was a fire starter.

The wake for the slain gypsy woman was held in the large living room.

Octavia Latika was Lotus's baby sister. She shared her Egyptian features, long black hair, and psychic powers. Octavia was 23-years-old. She was dressed in a white sundress with a black shawl. Her eyes locked with the Astredo's butler, Charlemagne Asmodeus.

Charlemagne's icy blue eyes held hers. Like Giovanni, he was seventy-seven-years old. He resembled Tobin Bell from the *Saw* movies and had a low husky voice. His short hair was blonde and grey with a receding hairline. Despite a few lines across his forehead, framing his thin mouth, and a mass of crows-feet around his eyes, he looked handsome.

She quickly looked away and approached her newly widowed brother-in-law. "Thanks for staying with me since I'm alone now." She could still feel the old man's gaze on her.

Raven La Sorcère softly smiled at his innocent sister-in-law. He loved her as though she was his blood sister. Raven and Diana had been living with Octavia for a week after Lotus died. Since her ex-boyfriend was a mobster, he and the others wanted to protect her.   He gave her a tight hug. "Are you alright? You seem nervous."

"I'm ok." She glanced at Charlemagne and back at Raven. She slowly backed away.

Raven looked at Charlemagne and noticed he was watching them. Raven returned his gaze on Octavia. "Don't allow that creepy old butler to make you nervous. Your new family will protect you."

"How do you know my old boyfriend isn't around watching me?"

"He's not. He left the city and he's *never* coming back. If he returns, he'll be taken care of."   Raven left her for a moment when Jason called to him.

Octavia stood by a dark wood column and watched Charlotte feed Diana from a bottle. The other children played with various toys from the seventies and early eighties.

Octavia walked towards the bar where Charlemagne moved to as he began to make drinks.

On Charlemagne's finger, he wore a large ring with a secret compartment under a large stone that held a very potent memory-altering potion. Along the bar were wine glasses for each person in the room. The glasses were on a large pewter tray with dragons carved around the edges. Charlemagne glanced in the mirror and saw Octavia's reflection on the opposite side of the bar. He turned towards her and asked, "What would you like?" He softly smiled at her while gazing into her eyes.

Octavia's eyes fell to the glasses and to his ring with the stone half open. She moved her eyes towards the bottles of wine and hard liqueur that sat in front of the mirror. "Just a glass of wine. It doesn't matter what type."

Charlemagne opened a cabinet and pulled out a wine glass and filled it. He placed it on the bar.

Octavia reached for the glass only to have his hand gently grab her hand. She looked at him nervously.

"I don't believe we've met? Your name is Octavia, correct?" he asked. His eyes never letting go of her eyes.

"I don't believe we met and yes, my name is Octavia. Lotus's sister."

"My deepest condolences." He lifted her hand to his mouth and tenderly kissed the back of her hand. "Charlemagne Asmodeus," his low husky voice sending a shiver through her.

"Thanks." Octavia slowly removed her hand from his hold.

"If you don't mind me asking, Octavia, your sister was so young. Was she sick?"

"No. Raven and his friends told me she died in a car accident. Raven was so shaken up; he barely remembers that night. We all barely remember anything." Octavia took a sip from her wine glass and watched him lift the tray.

"You look like her. I can tell that Diana will one day take after Lotus."

Octavia shyly smiled. "She will."

"Diana is going to be beautiful like her aunt," said Charlemagne.

After taking another sip of wine, Octavia said, "I'm going to check on my brother-in-law now." She moved towards Raven. She turned her head to watch Charlemagne serve drinks. She stood next to a large fireplace. She spoke to a few people

While Charlemagne was serving drinks, his hand discreetly touched Octavia's butt. "Meet me in one of the parlors after everyone moves outside," his raspy voice whispered into her ear. He was tempted to kiss her along her neck. He looked down her white sundress.

Nervously, she moved away from him when Brenda moved beside her to have a glass of wine.

"How are you holding up?"

"I'm ok. I miss her so much," said Octavia feeling Charlemagne's stare on her. She wished he would stop staring at her. Feeling his breath in her ear had turned her on; he carried a type of sexiness that wasn't gorgeous just handsome although, now wasn't the time or place to allow an old man to flirt with her.

Brenda gave her a hug and noticed Charlemagne undressing Octavia with his lustful eyes. She pulled Octavia away towards the rest of the family. "You don't need to be around that pig." Brenda shared Charlotte's dislike for their new butler. There was something about him that made them cautious around him.

Briefly, Charlemagne moved his gaze to Charlotte and noticed she was gazing at him suspiciously. He returned his gaze towards Octavia. He hoped she would meet him in one of the parlors. He was already picturing the many erotic things he wanted to do to her.

Octavia's eyes locked with his for a moment before she watched the children silently play.

Italia and Markus's seven-year-old son, Viktor, played with his two younger cousins and their friends.

Ari's hair was black and his eyes were a grayish blue. His skin was pale although he had Egyptian features. His birth parents were a mystery. Ari was of gypsy heritage like his adoptive parents. In a letter, his gypsy aunt and uncle claimed they were hiding him after discovering his rare natural tattoo. Beside him was his best friend, Valentina Russo, also six. She had dark blonde hair and had the power to read minds. Her father, Aaron Russo, was Jason Astredo and Raven's friend. Jason and Aaron met Raven through Midnight Konstantine, a cousin of the Astredos.

Michael Astredo was four years old, an empath, and son to Michelle and Caesar. He moved his attention towards Charlemagne when he offered drinks to Michelle and her friend, Cassandra Russo. Michael looked at Charlemagne and said, "Out!"

Viktor was first to place his arms around his little cousin and softly rock him in his arms.

Caesar rose from the chair and knelt beside Michael. Taking his son into his arms, he asked, "Are you feeling our sadness?"

Charlotte and the others looked puzzled by Michael's outburst. Charlotte looked at Charlemagne. She thought about the mobster boyfriend Raven and the others mentioned after they introduced her to Octavia. Her memory of certain battles was hazy and it was beginning to bother her since Giovanni and the others began to experience memory slips. She kept her past as well as her maiden name a secret from her family, except Giovanni and his cousins for their protection and now she was wondering if her past recently applied for the job as their butler. If their butler was a certain serial killer from her past, she couldn't wait to vanquish him.

Caesar lifted Michael in his arms and carried him to the couch.

Michael clung to him and glared at Charlemagne.

After Charlemagne finished severing drinks, he sat the tray on the bar, looked at Octavia, and left for the kitchen.

Michelle caressed Michael's back.

"What do you think he's feeling?" asked Jason.

Charlotte said, "I don't know. It could be a mixture of emotions."

Cassandra looked at Valentina and asked, "Valentina, could you read the butler's mind?" She sat next to Italia dressed in a white dress with a black shawl like the other women. In her arms, she held her newborn son, Adrian Russo.

Valentina looked at her mother from playing with Ari and Viktor's action figures. "His mind is blocked."

"What about you, Cassandra? Can you read his mind?" asked Damian Aleister. His blonde hair was pulled back into a ponytail revealing his small dream catcher earrings. He was gay and helped Raven's sister-in-law run her tarot-reading parlor called Nefertiti's Tearoom.

"I can try. I wasn't focusing on him."

Charlotte hit the intercom and said, "Charlemagne, come here please." Saying the name *Charlemagne* struck her with an unscrupulous feeling.

Charlemagne entered the room and asked, "What do you need, mistress?"

"Is dinner almost finish? The children are getting restless," said Charlotte.

"It is."

When he left, Cassandra said, "I'm unable to read his thoughts."

Gathered around the large marbled dinner table, the Astredo's discussed various topics.

Before they dined, they agreed to cleanse their meal and drinks of any negative hex.

Octavia listened to the others talk briefly about Charlemagne.

Conversation ended when Charlemagne entered the room to fill drinks and to take plates away. He stood in a corner next to a gold and maroon column.

Octavia felt his stare while she spoke with Damian about her tarot reading parlor. Octavia said, "We can open it tomorrow. Lotus would've wanted us to carry on with our lives."

Damian tenderly squeezed Octavia's hand. "She would have. Lotus was a good person." When Damian released Octavia's hand, Octavia noticed Charlemagne was staring at Damian while he was giving her hand a comforting squeeze. Her eyes locked with Charlemagne's eyes before she noticed Cassandra was watching her.

"You haven't eaten anything, Octavia. Do you want to talk about it?" said Cassandra.

Octavia looked at Cassandra, softly smiled, and said, "I'm just drained. I spent last night crying after Raven and I picked out one of her favorite dresses. I don't know how I'm going to be able to deal without her."

"You're going to be alright. You have us to talk to. We would gladly help you and Raven with Diana and anything else," said Cassandra.

Octavia smiled and said, "Raven and I appreciate everything you and the others have done for us since we moved here."

The conversation moved to other topics as Charlemagne served dessert.

After dinner, everyone gathered outside.

They gathered at a picnic table and talked.

Octavia watched Charlemagne gather herbs in the large herb garden before turning her attention back to Raven and the others when Charlemagne walked inside.

The topics were mostly about Lotus, Lotus's job as a psychic detective, and moving onto past battles with mobsters and other criminals.

Octavia gazed at her glass of wine thinking about her sister. She watched as Diana and Adrian were being passed around to everyone at the table.

The other children were playing on the small playground next to the herb garden.

Octavia said, "May I be excused. I feel worn out."

"Go lie down in one of the spare bedrooms," said Charlotte.

Octavia thanked Charlotte and walked into the kitchen. Nervously, she walked down the hall. Her violet eyes found Charlemagne in one of the parlors gazing out the window. She entered the parlor, closed the door, and asked, "Why have you been staring at me all afternoon?"

Charlemagne watched the witches and said, "I wanted to make sure you were safe. This is your first undercover assignment."

Octavia softly smiled at him. She gathered him into her arms. "I don't want our cover blown."

Charlemagne began to cover her body in deep passionate kisses.   His aged hands caressed her under her sundress.

Octavia back away and said, "Not here."

Charlemagne drew her close again. "I can't refrain from touching you." He held her against the wall while his hands explored her body. "Don't worry about anyone hearing us or catching us." He kissed her along her neck and throat.

"I read their minds, Charlemagne. They are suspicious. We should leave. Charlotte *still* hates you. You aren't safe here."

Charlemagne caressed her arms, softly smiled, and said, "For the past few years, they have allowed a dangerous serial killer to walk among them. They are the ones who aren't safe. I could've murdered them all the first day I entered this castle." Charlemagne had his face close to her face. His psychotic stare burned into her eyes. "It would have been over. Marguerite would've won."

"Why didn't you?"

"Marguerite's orders. There has to be balance, according to the Gods. Even though we are Mafia, we have to be mindful of the other side. Too much evil and too much good could destroy us all. Besides, Marguerite likes to play mind games. She's allot like what your mother had been. Both love to torture their victim's slowly."

Octavia softly smiled at the memory of Esmeralda Latika. "Do you think she would've been proud of me?" Her arms circled around his neck. She couldn't wait until they were alone.

"Very. I wish she was still alive so she could've watched you grow into the powerful mobster you've become. *I* am very proud of you." Softly, he kissed her mouth.

Octavia hugged him tightly as she returned his kiss before she asked, "What do you think she would've thought about us getting together finally?"

"She would've been pleased. She didn't want you to stay in Egypt with your father. She didn't care how old you were as long as you were with me and away from Amari."   In 1975, Esmeralda threatened to kill him if he allowed Amari to hurt Octavia.

She wanted to see Octavia married to Charlemagne since Esmeralda never had the choice to marry the man of her choice. She wanted both Lotus and Octavia to have that choice. Out of all her husband's friends, Esmeralda was pleased Octavia fell in love with Charlemagne. He was the only mobster Esmeralda trusted, despite him being a serial rapist.

Octavia smiled. Her mother was always dressing her like an adult and encouraging her to seduce Charlemagne. Esmeralda wanted *friends*, not daughters. Mob boss Marguerite DeMarco was the only friend she was allowed to keep after being forced to marry Amari after he got her pregnant. Octavia gazed into her beloved's eyes, and couldn't imagine her life without him. He saved her life when she was a young teenager. She recalled that night he cried thinking she died of a drug overdose from her kidnapper. It was the first time she'd seen him cry.

His hands moved to her thighs and caressed the old self-inflected scars she caused when she wanted the pain to replace the hurt from her father's betrayal. Charlemagne removed her underwear after he unbuttoned his pants.

Octavia moaned with his fingers thrusting inside her. She kissed him along his neck and caressed his back. "I love you," she whispered.

"I love you," he whispered kissing her gently on the neck. He moaned and softly cried out when her hand reached through his pants and began to stroke him. His fingers brought her to a climax which caused her to stroke him faster. He exploded onto the wall.

Octavia sank to her knees and took him into her mouth.

"Oh Octavia, Octavia. Massage my balls...oh yes, yes!"

After she swallowed him, Octavia lay on the couch and watched him quickly remove his pants. From Outside, she heard the Astredos talking and laughing somewhere among the tall labyrinth of bushes. Her eyes moved to the parlor door.

Charlemagne opened her legs and mounted her in hard thrusts.

Her moans mixed with his moans. She loved hearing his voice in ecstasy.

Charlemagne's face was buried in her chest while his tongue slid over her breast towards her nipple before sucking her deeply.

Octavia moaned and gripped his grey hair with her fingers. "Charlemagne, oh yes Charlemagne." She began to spasm around his penis.

Charlemagne lifted his head to give her other breast the same affection. His eyes locked on Damian's surprised expression before Damian quietly scurried out of the room.

Charlemagne turned his attention back to his Octavia.

#

An hour later, the family was gathered in the living room. Damian just returned from discovering Octavia in Charlemagne's arms. He was sent to look for Jason so they could have a family meeting about their new butler.

The elders in the Astredo clan were beginning to suspect their old rival, The Gypsy Killer, was back. Charlotte, Giovanni, Kathy, Leonardo, and Luca sat next to each other speaking coded Italian.

Leonardo Astredo sat beside Giovanni. He was born in 1905. He controlled earth. Giovanni was his younger cousin. Leonardo's daughter, Marigold, was married to Midnight.

Luca Astredo was Leonardo's youngest brother. He was born in 1915. He was a screenwriter and was an empath who could control water. His and Leonardo's older brother, Russell, was a fire starter and read minds. His daughter, Aria, and her husband, Ahmed, were seated next to Brenda and Jason.

Kathy Astredo was Luca and Leonardo's windowed sister-in-law. She was born in 1910. She and Russell were detectives. She was telekinetic, alchemist, and control the earth. Kathy and Russell's daughter, Lia, sat next to her.

"Octavia realizes he's evil now. Why didn't you *stop* him, Damian?" Raven asked.

"I heard her cry out: 'don't stop, Charlemagne' and when he paused to look at me she demanded he continue. She sounded irritated that he *stopped* kissing her," said Damian.

"She's working with him," said Brenda.

"No, Octavia's different now. She's innocent," said Raven.

Jason placed a brotherly hand on his shoulder. "We all thought she was Charlemagne's prisoner, but there've been traces of memory-blocking potion in our drinks and food, Marguerite seems to know our every move, not to mention other things that have occurred."

"But she's my responsibility. She's my baby sister-in-law."

"Your baby sister-in-law has been helping a serial killer attempt to kill us," said Markus.

"Raven, we're sorry about this. Giovanni and I want you and Diana to move in right away," said Charlotte.

Raven sighed. "Diana and I will move in this weekend."

"Tonight," said Giovanni.

Conversation stopped when Octavia entered the room. The after-glow on her face, her erect nipples revealed through the light cotton of her sundress, her slightly messed up hair, and the small red mark on the side of her neck betrayed her fabricated story that she needed to be alone since the memory of her sister was still depressing her. Octavia noticed everyone was studying her. She planned to revise Elizabethan DeMarco's recipe for memory-blocking potion so it would work faster. She had Charlemagne slip the potion in all their drinks and food earlier again after Michael screamed at him.

"Feeling better, Octavia," asked Brenda.

"Much. I needed that nap." She was a little sore from Charlemagne's passion. She didn't like making love whenever the family would gather out of fear of being caught, although Charlemagne's kisses and caresses were difficult to resist.

"You needed to fuck your dirty old man," corrected Markus. Markus resembled his mother's side of the family.

With a poker face, Octavia said, "I *wasn't* with anyone."

"I lifted the identity shielding spell from our new butler. We'll know the truth soon," said Giovanni.

The poker face faded and was replaced with fear for Charlemagne's life.

"Don't lie to us, Octavia. I can read minds and Raven is psychic," said Cassandra.

"Charlemagne is a *good* man. He has helped me through so much. *Don't* kill him."

"He has poisoned your mind," said Raven.

"No. He's..."

"He's a murderer and a rapist," interrupted Charlotte.

"You *can* find a better man," said Leonardo Astredo.

"There are no better men. They're all liars, but Charlemagne."

Charlemagne entered the living room. "You asked for me, Mistress Astredo?" His eyes moved to the knowing expressions on each family members face. His eyes locked with Octavia's eyes for a moment before he looked at Damian.

That son of a bitch ratted him out.

Charlotte rose from her regal position on one of the Gothic style chairs and said, "You're fired, asshole."

Charlemagne withdrew his gun and aimed it at Charlotte.

The others stood; ready to defend the matriarch of the family.

"Raven, Midnight, Damian go protect the children," said Charlotte.

The three gypsies obeyed and left for the nursery.

Charlotte conjured a fireball in her hand. She threw it at Charlemagne.

Octavia knocked Charlemagne to the floor.

The fireball hit the wall and quickly died when Brenda conjured a water ball to extinguish it.

Octavia placed her arms around Charlemagne protectively. "Leave him alone."

Charlemagne sat in front of her with his hand on her arm.

"Move away from him," said Giovanni.

Jason and the rest had guns drawn and aimed at them.

"Obey, Octavia. I can handle this," said Charlemagne. He and Octavia rose to their feet.

Tightly, Octavia held his hand.

Charlemagne refocused his gun on Charlotte. "You will allow Octavia and me to leave quietly."

"I can't allow you to leave, Charlemagne. We can't allow a killer to run free. Octavia will be placed in one of the rooms in the psyche ward until we figure out what to do with her," said Charlotte.

"I won't be separated from him."

Another fireball was conjured in Charlotte's hand. She was about to throw it when Midnight called from upstairs,

"There's a car full of mobsters out back."

"Giovanni and I will take care of Octavia and Charlemagne, go battle the mobsters, we'll join you later."

Charlemagne ducked out of the fireballs path. He fired a few rounds at Charlotte.

The bullets struck the dark woodwork.

Giovanni fired twice at Charlemagne at the same moment Charlotte fired at him with her gun.

The bullets struck Charlemagne's chest and stomach.

Octavia was at his side. She embraced him just before Charlotte's nozzle was placed on her head. "Don't let him die. I need him." Tears filled her eyes.

"Step away from him. You can have a better life. His death will save many people," said Charlotte.

Holding him tightly, she said, "I have a wonderful life with him. He has been taking care of me since I was fifteen." Magickally, Octavia took Charlemagne and herself away as bullets sailed through the air.

Chapter 2

In Octavia's apartment, she laid him on the bed after she removed his blood soaked clothes.

Blood continued to flow from his chest and stomach.

While she gathered towels and bandages, she called for Marguerite. Her heart was breaking. She wished she had her mother's power to heal. She couldn't take him to the hospital. He'd be arrested soon after his recovery. They wouldn't put him in jail this time, they would execute him.

Her hands trembled as she used pliers to remove each bullet. The first two weren't that deep. The bullet lodged in his stomach was in deep. She dug through skin and muscle to try to retrieve it.

He screamed when she carefully extracted the last bullet. His hands gripped the sheets. The pain was unbearable.

After she was able to stop the bleeding, she began to sew the holes. Heavy tears fell from her eyes.

Charlemagne was drifting in and out of consciences.

While Octavia worked on removing the last bullet, Marguerite appeared in their bedroom.

"Let me finish, Octavia. You've done well. Hold him for now."

Octavia crawled in bed beside Charlemagne. Tenderly, she took him in her arms and cried on his shoulder.

Marguerite looked at Charlemagne and tenderly placed her hand on his cheek before tending to his wounds.

Two hours passed before Octavia felt Marguerite's hands on her arms.

"He's going to live. It's going to take a while for him to recover." Affectionately, she squeezed her arms. "I'll stay so I can help you with him."

"Thanks." Octavia was talked into taking a warm shower.

Octavia stepped out from the shower, dressed in a nightgown, and lay next to Charlemagne. She lay on her side and watched him sleep. On his left shoulder, was Marguerite's crest tattooed on his pale skin. A black rose with blood dripping from the thorns and detailed leaves was worn by the members of the DeMarco Crime Family. She kissed the center of the rose. Her hand caressed his thigh and snuggled beside him. Charlemagne drifted off to sleep.

Octavia continued to watch him sleep. New tears filled her eyes realizing how close she came to almost losing him. Caressing his chest, she looked at her bare left hand and thought about the last assignment that ended with him being shot by Giovanni Astredo. She kissed his wrinkled cheek and stepped out of bed.

She approached her dresser and opened a jewelry box where one of her old dolls sat.

An assortment of rings sparkled from the lights.

Octavia slid a gold band on her left finger with the words: *Charlemagne loves Octavia 1975* across the top. Next, she placed her gold band engagement ring next to her wedding band. Engraved on her engagement ring were the words: *Charlemagne and Octavia 1973*.

1973 was the year they became engaged. They waited until she was fifteen before they made love.

Before closing the jewelry box, Octavia removed his wedding band with the words: *Octavia loves Charlemagne* engraved across the top.

Returning to the bed, she lifted his left hand and slid his wedding ring on his finger.

"I missed wearing that," he said, his voice sounding weak and tired. He held her hand in his.

"Me too. I'm glad we no longer have to pretend we're not together. Should I continue to pretend your middle name is our last name?" Octavia kissed his hand and each knuckle.

"There's no need to. They know who I am."

Octavia said, "I was getting used to the name 'Asmodeus.'"

"They know about you now, *Mrs. DeMarco*. I want you to be careful."

"Raven is moving out soon. Marguerite wants us to hide in here. She doesn't want anyone to see you." Octavia cuddled beside him still holding his hand. In her other hand, she held onto his black satin robe.

Charlemagne nuzzled her neck and slid his other arm around her. Softly, he kissed her forehead. He wished she wasn't a part of the battle, sometimes. He just wanted her to be safe in his arms.

#

Marguerite stood in Octavia and Charlemagne's living room.

Candles of every shape and size were lit around her. With an athame, she drew a pentagram in the air.

Purple light formed the doorway between the physical realm and the realm of Ancestors.

"Nephthys, Hades, Persephone, Anubis, Osiris, Gods and Goddesses of the Underworld, permit my six children to join me while my oldest son recovers. So Mote It Be."

Marguerite sat the grimoire on the coffee table.

The room began to chill and many scents belonging to six ghosts filled the apartment.

A woman in her early thirties appeared bringing to fragrance of coconuts. She was dressed in a 1930's style suit dress. Delilah DeMarco looked like her mother. She was a fire starter. Her ghostly body was riddled with bullets. She was Marguerite's first daughter born in 1907 and died in 1938.

A black wolf appeared next to Delilah. The woodsy scent remained with him until he turned human. Frank was turned into a werewolf at sixteen. He was Marguerite's oldest son born in 1899 and died in 1935. His face was sliced up from a windshield.

Nikkolas DeMarco appeared in a dark suit and his body riddled with bullets. He was born in 1920 and died in 1944.

Lucian Phoenix appeared with the seductive aroma of sandalwood. He was Delilah's husband and an incubus. He was born in 1906. He hung himself in prison in 1946.

The seductive scent of ylang-ylang accompanied Molly DeMarco. Frank's wife and succubus. Molly was dressed in a gold lame blouse and black pants. Her chestnut colored hair was short and in the style of 1940's. Her hair covered the spot in back where her head cracked open in 1946. She was born in 1906.

Roses surrounded the ghost of Jacqueline DeMarco-Tortelli. She was twenty-six when she died in 1946. A long scar divided her face from her hairline to her chin. A knife scar ran along her throat, shoulder, and thigh. A bullet hole was on her chest. She wore a grey suit dress. She was an empath and Marguerite's youngest daughter born in 1922.

Jacqueline's schizophrenic husband, Tony, appeared next to her in an aroma of pineapple. A long scar traveled down his face matching Jacqueline. He resembled Anthony Perkins from the movie *Psycho*. His body was riddled with bullets.

Marguerite smiled at her sons and daughters. "I need you to guard Charlemagne and Octavia while he recovers."

Delilah said, "We will gladly help."

Frank and Nikkolas were placed outside their brother and sister-in-law's bedroom while Lucian and Molly stood outside the apartment door.

Delilah, Jacqueline, and Tony assisted Marguerite and Octavia with whatever they needed.

#

Opening an oak dresser drawer in his bedroom, Raven removed his light green T-shirt, which bared a picture of a wizard enchanting a dragon. He placed the shirt in the suitcase that sat on his bed.

Raven and the others didn't see the gangsters' ghosts from a spell Octavia casts.

He couldn't wait to leave Octavia's apartment. He was surprised she didn't give him any trouble.

She kept her bedroom door locked anytime Jason and the others would come over to help Raven move. She would close the door and pretend to cry heavily. Pretending to be in mourning worked.

Through his bedroom wall, Raven could hear her cries for Charlemagne. He felt sorry for her, although her lies broke his heart. He wanted to save her from the life Charlemagne gave her.

A heavy rap behind his bedroom door startled him. He asked in a surprised voice, "Octavia?"

"Raven; Jason and the others are on their way to help you move the rest of your things."

"I'll be out in a moment." Raven opened the door and stepped out from his bedroom. He followed her towards the living room. He sat on a chair and she sat on the couch.

A stuffed animal sat at one end of the couch and another one on the back of the chair where Raven sat. She had a verity of stuffed animals in different places in the apartment as well as dolls from the 1950's, 60's, and 70's.

A small dollhouse from the 1960's sat in the corner beside the television stand.

Octavia wore a green and tan dress. The dress was a gift from Charlemagne.

"Octavia, how could you turn your back on The God and Goddess?"

"Charlemagne was the only person who helped me whenever I needed someone to talk to."

"Lotus and I have always been there for you."

"You and Lotus were always trying to break Charlemagne and me up. I'm still angry at you and her for calling the police on him when we lived in Cairo. Do you have any idea what they would do to him if they caught him? He would be executed."

"He's dead now, Octavia. You're free from whatever hold he had on you. Brenda would like to have a psychiatrist examine you."

"Examine me for what? Finding a decent man who would do anything for me? Charlemagne murdered many people, but he was *good* to *me*. He would never hurt me. He loved me." Tears filled Octavia's eyes. Real tears for the thought of Charlemagne dead tore her heart apart.

"You need someone, like a psychiatrist, whom can help you get over what he has done to you."

"He has done *nothing* to me. He cared for me."

"He molested you. You were too young to be his girlfriend."

Octavia slapped Raven's face. "How can you say that? Mom and dad were delighted when they found out that Charlemagne and I were dating."

Raven rose from the chair and stepped back. "Where *did* you bury that asshole?"

Octavia turned towards a shelf and lifted an urn filled with ashes stolen from the Astredo's fireplace. She held the urn close against her and said, "I cremated my beloved. I miss his tender kisses and the feel of his hands caresses my body. How could you allow them to kill your baby sister-in-law's boyfriend?"

The innocent little girl expression no longer worked on Raven. "You can find a better lover. I'm glad that monster is out of your life."

Octavia hugged the urn, kissed the top of it, and said, "Leave!"

Raven wished she would join him so he could give her a better life. Help her get over Charlemagne's death. He hated to see her heart broken, although, she *didn't* need a dangerous man like Charlemagne in her life. "If you need me, call."

The doorbell rang.

Raven answered as Octavia left for her bedroom and slammed the door.

Markus and the rest of the Astredo clan were there to help Raven and Diana move into the castle. Midnight was driving his in-laws to the airport and planned to return after Leonardo, Kathy, and Luca were on a plane to a small Italian island called Medea in the Caribbean Sea off the coast of Jamaica.

After Raven and the others left and the DeMarco ghosts were in the bedroom with Charlemagne, Octavia stepped out from the second bedroom and walked down the dark hall. In her hands, she carried a small box she hid in the back of her closet. Over her arm, she carried his black satin robe with his name written in red letters.

Charlemagne was asleep from pain pills. The old serial killer requested to lie in bed naked. He felt too warm for the Ohio heat.

Octavia entered the living room and sat the box on the coffee table. Her argument with Raven brought back too many bad memories. She had to erase them. She removed the lid while tears fell from her eyes. She almost lost Charlemagne again. She gazed down at the knife and the joints that were forbidden to her by Charlemagne. He spent years trying to get her off the pot her kidnapper hooked her on and to stop cutting herself. She had gone two years without the cutting and the drug.

The knife was removed first after she pulled up her sundress.

Heavy tears flooded over her cheeks.

Her mind replayed the evening the Salem Police arrested him for making love to her in his car while they were parked in one of the parks downtown.

She was fifteen, just learning English from Charlemagne, and not understanding why everyone was treating her like a child. Esmeralda told her she was *never* a child. Just her best friend. For years, everyone she was told to trust lied to her about many things. Lotus, with Raven's help, was the only one who wanted to protect Octavia from Charlemagne and their parents.

While Charlemagne sat in an interrogation room in handcuffs, she sat in a small office with a woman from child services who spoke Arabic.

The knife cut into her skin.

Another memory surfaced. Her father giving her away to another mobster as payment for a debt Amari couldn't pay. She fought both men while Charlemagne was away from the house. If Charlemagne were there, despite Amari being his close friend, he would have saved her from being kidnapped and fed an assortment of drugs to keep her quiet.

After making the second cut, she set the knife on the coffee table and picked up a joint. She lit a few incense sticks hoping Charlemagne wouldn't smell the pot. He hated drugs. She tried to calm herself with things Charlemagne told her in the past. *'Think about waking up in my motel room as I nursed you. I found you starved and near death. I fought for your life. You almost died as I carried you into the motel room from the car. I cried the entire three days you slept. If Dante hadn't have briefly given me the power to heal, I would've lost you. I would've been alone. Amari's betrayal hurt me but losing you would kill me.'* Octavia leaned against the couch and smoked. Her eyes fixed on the dollhouse she used to play with when she was a child. She held the black satin robe as though it was a security blanket.

Over the years, Charlemagne raped and murdered many women although, he never hurt Octavia. He was the first and only man to treat her with respect and *not* like an object.

Her tears stopped and she softly smiled.

He took care of her while she was recovering from her kidnapper's abuse.

Now it was her turn to take care of him while he recovered.

After she finished the second joint, she closed the box and got rid of the evidence. Her clothes, she quickly threw in the laundry hamper so he wouldn't smell the marijuana. Next, she brushed her teeth, rinsed her mouth with mouthwash, and took a shower.

After she stepped out from the shower, she stepped into a short nightgown since her ghostly brothers-in-law were standing outside their bedroom door.

"Octavia," Delilah said seated at the small dinette table.

Octavia walked down the hall and sat between Delilah and Jacqueline.

Jacqueline was seated on Tony's lap with his arms around her waist.

Delilah reached for Octavia's hand and Jacqueline softly touched her arm. "Octavia, we care about you and as your spirit guide it's my job to protect you."

Octavia looked at Delilah and Jacqueline and said, "I know I shouldn't cut myself, but the memories of Amari still haunt me."

"Just remember Charlemagne's words: he loves you. Amari's betrayal hurt him, but, losing you would *kill* him," said Jacqueline.

"You can always call on me, Jacqueline, or Molly. You mean a lot to this family."

Octavia spoke with Delilah and Jacqueline for another hour before returning to her bedroom.

Octavia laid beside Charlemagne after she placed a few stuffed animals on her night stand beside a picture of him. She undressed since she wanted to feel him near her. In her arms, was his robe.

Octavia watched him sleep running her hand through his grey chest hair. Her fingers played with his hair. Her leg lay over his leg. She kissed his cheek and mouth. She lay her head on his chest and listened to his heart. As her ghostly sister-in-law suggested, she began to think about the happier times with him.

#

A few months ago

Charlemagne changed out of his butler's uniform into a white sleeveless shirt and blue shorts. He entered the smoke-filled bar wearing dark sunglasses.

He slipped through the late night crowd towards the back.

'Hotel' by Tori Amos pumped through the speakers.

Charlemagne entered a dark hallway where the kitchen, restrooms, and a private meeting room were located. He knocked on the private meeting room door.

A small window slid open.

A pair of violet eyes stared at him.

Charlemagne softly smiled and said, "Can you hear the drums, Fernando?"

"I remember long ago another starry night like this. In the fire light, Fernando."

Charlemagne entered the room as Octavia locked the door behind them.

The paneled room was medium-size and had a round oak table and a secluded booth.

Octavia was disguised in a black summer blouse and black leather skirt. Lying over a chair was her black and gold shawl and her black sunglasses lay on the table.

Charlemagne removed his sunglasses and placed them beside Octavia's sunglasses. His desire-filled eyes scanned her out-fit.

"After eight-years of marriage and working undercover, I still can't get use to these types of clothes."

"I know, Charlemagne. We have no choice."

Charlemagne placed his hand on her thigh as he placed his arm around her waist. "I love that out-fit on you." He kissed her cheek.

"I wore it for you." Octavia pulled him closer. "Just for you, I'm not wearing underwear."

Charlemagne smiled picturing many ways he could please her.

"I ordered your favorite." Octavia grabbed his hand and brought him towards the booth. She sat beside him. Her hand caressed his thigh.

On the table sat a double cheeseburger, fries, and a glass of beer for Charlemagne.

Octavia's plate held a chicken fajita and a glass of tea.

Charlemagne placed his hand on her thigh and moved it up her skirt. His eyes followed his hand. "I love what you ordered, but I would rather eat you."

Octavia smiled. "After dinner."

He kissed her neck and said, "I can't wait."

During dinner, Octavia listened to him tell her everything the Astredos did that week so she could tell Marguerite. Octavia felt his foot rub her foot. After she finished eating, she leaned back into his arms. "I miss living with you."

"I know. I miss it also. At least we are able to spend nights together."

"I always look forward to screaming your name." Octavia kissed him deeply and passionately on the lips. Her tongue explored his mouth.

Charlemagne returned her kiss while he held her close. His fingers touched her shaved genitals. He began to rub her.

"Oh Charlemagne. Rub me harder."

He kissed her along her neck. Charlemagne rubbed her harder after his fingers kneaded the bottom of her underwear.

Octavia placed an arm around his neck, laid her head on his shoulder, and stroked his cock with her other hand.

Charlemagne kissed her along her neck and shoulder slipping his middle finger into her. His other hand squeezed and massaged her breast. He moaned instructing her to stroke him faster.

Octavia moaned. She kissed the side of his neck and rode his finger. "Oh Charlemagne, Charlemagne, Charlemagne! I want you."

Charlemagne removed his hand from under her skirt. He combed his fingers through her long black hair. He hugged her. "You mean everything to me, Octavia."

"You mean everything to me, also." Octavia moved to her knees and pleased him with her mouth.

He moaned as he slid in and out of her mouth.

Octavia brought him to his climax before laying on the padded bench.

Charlemagne kissed her mouth and removed the rest of his clothes before he pleased her orally.

"Oh, oh, Charlemagne, Charlemagne. Deeper. Yes, yes, yes."

After her second orgasm, Charlemagne mounted her gliding into her.

Her mouth caressed his cheeks, lips, neck, throat, and shoulders. She caressed his back and the back of his thighs.

Charlemagne pushed her harder and faster. His psychotic eyes gazed into her eyes. His wrinkled hand caressed her breast.

Octavia looked at her sixty-one year old husband as ecstasy washed over her. She ran her fingers through his blonde and grey hair. She softly moaned as he continued to grind into her.

Charlemagne kissed her deeply along her throat and along the side of her neck. He nibbled on her ear. "I love you Octavia," he said before licking the inside of her ear causing her to scream passionately. He moaned and went deeper inside her.

Octavia's legs tightened around his waist as her intense orgasms began. "Yes, yes, yes! Charlemagne, oh Charlemagne." Her hand gripped the back of the leather bench.

Charlemagne's wrinkled mouth hungrily caressed her breast before sucking and biting her nipple. Their moans, cries, and groans weren't drowned out by the music playing in the next room.

"I love to make you scream. I love you, Octavia."

Octavia gently smiled. "I love you, Charlemagne."

Charlemagne watched her ecstasy-filled expressions. He hugged her tightly as he continued to make love to her.

#

Their undercover work was exciting. She almost hated to see their days of sneaking out to see each other were over.

In his sleep, he lay his arm around her and caressed her arm, waist, and back.

Octavia slowly fell asleep nestled against him.

#

Outside in the warm spring air, Giovanni planted more herbs in their garden. After he planted another lavender plant, he noticed Charlotte sitting on a lawn chair in deep thought. He sat across from her.

On the table was a glass of herbal ice tea and a mystery novel.

"What's wrong?"

"I want to bring Octavia in. Lock her in one of the rooms in the family asylum for a while. I don't like how calm it's been these passed weeks."

Giovanni reached for her hand and said, "I agree. We killed Marguerite's son and head assassin. She wouldn't leave us alone like this. Octavia's been too quiet."

"Octavia *is* grieving," said Charlotte.   "I *still* don't think it's over. I hate having been under all those mind altering potions. There are many past battles I can't remember and I know it's *not* from my age."

"We'll bring our memories back," said Giovanni.

"Do we need servants? Your mother never had any," said Charlotte.

"I suppose we don't. I just figured we could use extra help."

"I don't think we do. You love cooking all the meals and we could split the chores amongst the kids as we have done in the past," said Charlotte.

"You wouldn't trust anyone applying to be our butler again, would you?"

"No. Not with what has just happened," said Charlotte.

"Whatever you desire," said Giovanni.

#

A few days later

Marguerite stood at the foot of her son's bed. "Perhaps if you weren't preoccupied with Octavia, you wouldn't be in this situation," said Marguerite.

Charlemagne lay in bed in his underwear with a bandage over his chest. His recovery was still slow. He was in pain.

Marguerite paced the bedroom. "Since you insisted to think with your dick, I have to hide you for a while."

"I wasn't thinking with my dick. I just wanted to make sure Octavia was ok. She looked nervous."

"She was nervous because she was afraid you would blow her cover."

Octavia entered the bedroom carrying a tray with food.

"Being caught making out with Octavia in the parlor while the entire family was outside was not a smart move. Couldn't wait until you brought her home?"

Charlemagne smiled and said, "I'm irresistible. Octavia can't keep her hands off me."

Octavia moved a few stuffed animals off her bed before she sat next to Charlemagne. She placed her arm around his waist and rested her head on his shoulder. Her hand caressed his chest. His robe lay over her.

Charlemagne looked at Octavia and softly smiled. He kissed the top of her head.

"Octavia, you are too old for pigtails," continued Marguerite.

"I like them, said Charlemagne.

"Your relationship with her disturbs me." Marguerite looked at Octavia and said, "Take care of him. Allow the Astredos to believe he's dead. Keep him hidden until I'm ready for my serial killer to roam the streets."

Charlemagne watched her leave and said, "Do you want to sit on my lap?"

"No. Marguerite instructed you to rest." Octavia pulled away from him and placed his dinner over his lap.

Charlemagne watched her enjoying her in the pink baby doll nightgown he bought her.

Octavia lay beside him. She watched him eat not understanding why Brenda and the others thought of him as a sex offender. Octavia innocently laid her head on his lap. Her hand caressed his thigh.

"What's wrong with my little girl?"

"Quit calling me that! I'm 23," she said without thought.

Charlemagne finished his dinner and sat the tray on the night stand. "Sit up and talk to me."

She recoiled from his hand touching her back. Again, it was an involuntary reaction. "I don't want to."

Charlemagne let out an irritated sigh. He stared at their wedding photo taken next to the sphinx in 1975. She was 15 and he was 69. He wasn't irritated with her; he was irritated with Charlotte and the others. "Octavia, come here."

After she sat up, she was pulled onto his lap. She didn't understand why she didn't want him to touch her. At the same moment, she wanted to cling onto him. Her legs were around his waist and her arms were around his neck.

"What did that bitch say about me?"

"Charlotte told me to stay away from you. Everyone says you're a pervert."

"You know better Octavia. You've seen my crimes before we dated. You know I would *never* hurt you. Don't listen to them. I love you." He held her close to him. His fingers combed through her long black hair. "Perhaps mom is correct: you are too old to wear your hair like that." Charlemagne pulled the ponytail holders out from her hair.

Her hair fell over her shoulders and down her back. Octavia looked into his ice-blue eyes. She felt foolish for recoiling from his touch. In her eyes, he was the only man worthy enough for her to talk to. No one else could be trusted.

Charlemagne tenderly kissed her forehead and said, "Can I still call you my little girl?"

Octavia smiled and said, "Yes." Her hand caressed his chest touching the places were the bullets entered. "I don't want anything to happen to you."

Charlemagne softly kissed her and said, "I'll be alright."

Octavia hugged him. "Did someone catch us making love the evening of Lotus's wake?"

"Their friend Damian Aleister walked past the parlor searching for Jason."

Octavia held him tightly and trembled at the memory of Giovanni shooting her Charlemagne. Tears filled her eyes. She couldn't picture her life without him.

Running his fingers through her hair, he said, "I'm alright. I'm not going to leave my little girl." He kissed her hard and passionately. "While I'm in hiding, you can be my eyes and ears."

"I'll do anything for you."

#

After their dinner, Octavia carried their plates into the kitchen.

Frank and Lucian were now standing outside the apartment door and Molly and Nikkolas were outside the bedroom door.

Octavia was unloading and loading the dishwasher while Delilah, Jacqueline, and Tony stood in the kitchen.

Delilah leaned against a cupboard and said, "I'm glad everyone left. I hate hiding."

Tony was leaning against the opposite cupboard with Jacqueline leaning against him. His arms were around her.

Octavia said, "Raven was getting on my nerves. I wish I could have killed him too."

"It was wise that you didn't. Let them think you are finished with the mob," said Jacqueline.

Octavia rinsed off a plate and placed it in the dishwasher. "I enjoy your visits. You are the family I've always wanted."

"I enjoy being your spirit guide," said Delilah.

"We love having you for a sister-in-law," said Jacqueline.

After Octavia finished loading the dishwasher, she sat with Delilah, Jacqueline, and Tony at the dinner table.

The next morning, Octavia woke finding Charlemagne sleeping on his back. Octavia kissed his receding hairline before getting a shower and dressed.

Before she left, she kissed Charlemagne's cheek. He was able to get out of bed and fix his own meals now. He was limited to how much he could move around and was restricted to their bed. He didn't mind that either. He enjoyed his and Octavia's talks. He always liked the many hours they shared just talking.

She entered her tarot-reading parlor at the corner of North Ellsworth and State Street. She planned to slip more memory-altering potion in their food and drinks since Giovanni and Charlotte were searching through old grimoires for a counter spell. That idea had to be cleared away. She needed to have Damian and the others work for her since she needed to report the Astredo's activities. She loved the power to read minds.

In the small Egyptian style tarot parlor, Octavia watched Damian shuffle a deck of cards while Raven wiped off a counter and Midnight filled the tea and coffee machines that were behind the turquoise counter.

The walls were lilac and the large display window showcased the eight Pagan holidays.

Midnight Konstantine was Markus, Jason, and Caesar's cousin. His father-in-law was Leonardo Astredo, Giovanni's cousin. Leonardo's coven hived from Giovanni and Charlotte's coven. Midnight's coven stead was in Italy until he moved his coven members to help their family with the DeMarco Crime Family, in 1975. Midnight was a medicine man for his small caravan of gypsies. He was in medical school and considering psychiatry so he could work in the Astredo Institution for Mental Health with Brenda.

After moving to America, he mixed Native American spiritually with Wicca. He was widowed and bisexual.

Raven looked up from the counter and asked, "How are you holding up?"

"Still hurt. Sleeping alone sucks."

"Tell me about it," said Raven.

She was pleased the memory-blocking potion made him forget about the conversation they had as he moved the last piece of baby furniture out from her apartment as well as Damian catching her with Charlemagne. She softly smiled at her brother-in-law and said, "I know he was the enemy, but I miss him so much."

"We still think it's a good idea for you to seek counseling. He put you through allot," said Midnight.

Octavia tried to hold her temper in. *'I fucking don't need to see anyone! Charlemagne was never abusive to me. He loves and respects me.'* She wanted to say it, but instead said, "I'll think about it." She entered her office. Closing the door, she sat at her desk. She looked at a picture of Charlemagne in a light purple frame on her desk. A small doll from the 1960's sat beside the picture. His black satin robe was draped over her chair. She hoped he was managing being on his own. Her thoughts changed to Damian. She knew she wouldn't be trusted to enter the castle again and the crystal ball didn't show allot of detail. She called Damian into the office. When he entered the parlor, she asked, "What are Raven and Midnight doing?"

He said, "Raven is with a customer and Midnight left to get more coffee filters. What do you need?"

Octavia smiled. "I'm going to make you do my bidding."

"Sorry?" He noticed Marguerite's crest on her left shoulder.

Octavia rose from her seat and approached Damian. "Do you remember what happened the evening of Lotus's funeral?"

"Yes, we sat around and talked. You left for one of the spare bedrooms to take a nap. Charlotte suggested that."

"Do you know why Raven and Diana moved out?"

"Giovanni and Charlotte wanted to keep the kids together. And to protect everyone. They didn't want Raven and Diana to be alone."

"What did they say about me?"

Damian's head became clear. "They don't trust you." He was suddenly hit with a mind control spell. He fought it.

"You are going to help me, Damian. I need you to tell me everything that goes on in that castle. You must convince them that I'm slowly being rehabilitated from being a mobster. Charlemagne's death has left me devastated. I miss him so much. He's apart of me."

"I won't betray my friends."

Octavia noticed Damian wore charms that protected him from being controlled. She snatched them off him and hit him again with the spell. "When you approach anyone in the Astredo clan about me or Charlemagne, you, like Raven and Midnight, will become mute. Damian, you alone, will slowly have no control of your thoughts and actions. I want to see you suffer guilt each time you betray your new gypsy family. That is your punishment for turning Charlemagne and I in. You caused someone I care deeply about to get hurt. He's gone. Someday, I hope you feel the same unbearable pain of loss death can cause."

"I'm telling Charlotte."

"Go ahead. It won't do you any good. I need a special ingredient for Elizabethan DeMarco's memory-altering potion. I need to make it stronger."

Damian trembled. "Do you need an article of clothing? An herb?"

Octavia brought out a pewter heart-shaped box lined in blue stones. "My hex does not need something from the living."

"I won't kill for you."

"Bring me Diana's heart before morning."

Damian's own heart sank. "No, Octavia! I cannot kill her. She's my friend's only daughter. She's only a child."

"Diana will grow to become a powerful witch, more powerful than me. I don't want competition."

"I won't hurt a child."

"Do it! I want her dead and so does Marguerite." Octavia looked in his eyes and saw her mind control hex was beginning to control Damian.

"I shall do it."

Damian felt himself grow sick with the thought of killing an infant.

#

Damian parked his tiny sports car among a grove of trees near a farm. He carefully stepped out from behind the bushes and approached a fence that ended near the woods where he was. He spied a lonely pig chewing on a blade of grass near the woods. His palms began to become sweaty as he reached for his pocketknife. He never harmed another living thing. It was against his Wiccan religion and not in his heart to cause pain and death on another creature. He was a strict vegetarian. But, he figured his God Osiris and Goddess Isis would excuse this slaughter of an animal for the sake of saving a child's life.

Damien pulled out his wand and aimed it at the pale pink pig. He whispered a spell that caused the pig to disappear and reappear in front of him. He hypnotized it commanding it to lie on its side. Damian squatted in front of the pig opening his pocketknife. His hand trembled as he began the laceration down the pig's stomach.

The muscles in the animal quivered as the blade lightly touched the skin. Blood began to emerge from under the blade, as the cut was made deeper.

Damian felt his stomach turn looking at the guts and muscles. He felt his vomit rise up in his throat. He held it in as he reached through the wet slimly fat and skin. He couldn't understand how some people could eat something that was once living. He shuttered as his hand grabbed the beating heart pulling it out of its chest.

Next, he placed it inside the pewter box closing the lid. After he gave the pig a proper burial, he left the woods driving towards Salem.

#

"That fucking faggot!" Octavia placed the pig's heart on the kitchen counter and stared at it. She left the small kitchen, entered the small dinette, and stepped in the sunken living room. She enchanted the TV to show her Castle Olympia. Anger filled her eyes as she watched Raven rock his baby to sleep in the nursery. Next, she changed the image to Damian. She hit him with the strongest mind control hex in Elizabethan's grimoire. Now, his thoughts and actions were hers. He no longer had control.

"Octavia, what's the matter?" Charlemagne carefully walked down the hallway.

"Nothing now. I took care of it."

"The heart didn't work?"

"It's the wrong kind. The fag gave me a pig's heart."

"So. Use it."

"I need a *human* heart."

"A pig's a mammal also. Don't worry about it," said Charlemagne.

Octavia approached him and took his arm when she noticed he seemed unsteady on his feet. "Why are you out of bed and don't you want me to make a stronger potion?"

"I'm tired of lying in bed all day. My legs weren't filled with bullets."

"No but you lost allot of blood. You still have to take it easy."

Charlemagne permitted her to escort him to their bedroom. "I want you to make a stronger potion. I don't think we should kill anyone yet. It's too soon. Just continue to use what we have. I don't want anyone getting suspicious. Italia is an alchemist and Michelle makes the potions, they will know what the heart was used for. Use the pig's heart. Don't murder anyone unless Marguerite instructs you to." Charlemagne stopped in the hallway and said, "I want to sit on the couch. I'm tired of sitting up in bed. I don't feel as weak."

She had her arm around his waist. She began to walk him towards the living room. "When I finish the potion, I'll snuggle beside you on the couch while we watch a movie."

Charlemagne softly smiled. "I like cuddling with you."

Later, they sat cuddled together on the couch with a pizza and a 2-liter of Coke on the coffee table.

The DeMarco ghosts remained another week before returning to the realm of Ancestors.

Chapter 3

1999

Salem, Ohio

Dragon's Lair Theater

Dusk fell over the small town casting a red-orange light over the century old buildings.

The black and purple marquee was switched off after the last play finished for the evening. The theater was built to resemble a castle with a statue of a forest green dragon placed in front of the building. The theater was built and owned in the early 1800's by one of the Astredo's ancestors.   It sat a few stores down from the Salem Community Theater.

The scent of popcorn still lingered throughout the lobby, stage, and dressing rooms.

Ari Astredo sat in his adopted father and uncle's office with his cousin, Michael Astredo.   The twenty-two-year-old witch was a playwright when not fighting Marguerite's crime family. Ari's psychic and elemental powers of air matured as Michael's empathic power and his ability to control water. His shoulder length black hair was pulled away from his pale handsome face. His bluish-grey eyes were now grey and looked very sexy. As with all males in the Astredo family, Ari and Michael bared the natural tattoo of the God symbol with a pentagram in the center of the Circle. Around his slender neck, he wore the silver pentacle his gypsy aunt left with him.

Michael was the family alchemist, trained by Italia, who crafted silver bullets to use on some of the criminals they engage in battle with.

After they left the short meeting, Ari and Michael began to clean, stock the concession stand, and close the theater while Jason and Caesar Astredo worked on paperwork before Caesar would return to his office to gather the new programs he designed and place them in the lobby.

Ari and Michael cleaned the lobby before moving to the snack area.

"I love the part you wrote for me, Ari."

"I figured you would."

"I always wanted to play the bad guy in your horror plays. It was a nice change from playing the hero."

Ari laughed. "Since we battle real criminals, I figured you would want to play the bad guy."

"I love both roles."

"Let's lock up. I need to meet Valentina at the library."

Michael looked at his older cousin. His smile was ornery.

"What's that look for?" Ari caught himself smiling and quit.

"Your new found desire for her *isn't* wrong. You grew up together, you're not related."

Ari walked towards the snack counter and began to turn off the popcorn machine and other equipment. "I don't have any desires for Valentina. She's my best friend."

Michael lifted a trash bag from the garbage can, leaned over the counter, and said,

"I can *feel* your emotions. Why are you denying it?"

Ari stocked the cups and straws. "What if it doesn't work out? Her mom and my adopted mom are best friends. It would be too awkward."

"She bares the Goddess's mark and she's *not* blood. Do you know what that means?"

"That she is to join us in the battle against the DeMarco crime family. And if anyone *not* of our family is born with the mark, which is rare, they have a choice weather or not they want this life. If someone *doesn't*, the mark disappears. What does this have to do with my feeling for Valentina?"

Michael said, "It also means she's the type our ancestors married. Our Great-Great-Great Grandmother Olympia made it so that *not* only are we born with it, but that is how our ancestors chose their mates."

"Even though we have dated women who didn't bare the mark? Dad had a few girlfriends before he married mom."

"Why do you think those relationships didn't work out."

Placing a package of nacho trays on the counter, Ari filled the empty space by the cheese dispenser.   "You think our ancestors have something to do with that?"

"Why not." Michael carried the trash out before he helps Ari finish stocking shelves.

#

After washing the dishes from breakfast, Octavia began to make more mind-altering potions. She was glad the charade of the loving aunt was over. Octavia was now 39-years-old. She hated covering the tattoo that she was born with. A mark that showed she was one of Marguerite's mobsters.

Octavia walked towards her bedroom where Charlemagne was wearing nothing but a towel.

His grey hair was damp and he smelled of men's cologne.

Among the clothes in her closet, hung some article of clothing worn by Charlemagne. Even though it was sixteen years later, she still had to make people believe he was dead. His other personal things were discreetly hidden in Octavia's bedroom.

She removed her nightclothes and waited for him on their bed. She could still smell his cologne on the pillow where his head lay last evening. Softly, she closed her eyes and anticipated his sensual touches. "Don't get dressed."

Charlemagne dropped the towel and joined Octavia on the bed.

Gently, she smiled when she felt his wrinkled hands caress her young bare thigh. She gazes into his eyes as he opened her legs with his aged hands. She moaned when he teased her with his finger.

Charlemagne covered her mouth with his mouth before moving down towards her stomach.

Octavia moaned when his head spread her legs before he pleased her with his tongue.

While he performed oral sex on her, he slipped his fingers into her.

"Charlemagne!" she gasped as he continued to lick her and thrust his fingers into her. She reached her climax twice and was about to come again when he sat on his knees, wrapped her legs around his waist, and roughly entered her. She screamed his name savoring his every touch as though this was their last morning together.

His 94-year-old mouth caressed her shoulder, throat, chest, before he covered her breast and hungrily caressed her. While inside her, he grinded heavily. His arms and legs held her in a tight embrace like a steel trap.

She moaned and softly cried out for him. Her hands caressed his back while she kissed his handsome but aged face.

His passionate kisses traveled all over her body. He stroked her hard and fast.

Their headboard slammed against the wall.

Octavia's legs wrapped around his waist and screamed.

He moved in and out of her enjoying the feel of her rising toward her climax.

After a few hours of passionate love making, they lay in each other's embrace. She watched him sleep noticing for the first time a soft wheezing as he breathed. Her fingers combed through his hair. Grey hair strands clung on her fingers in small clumps. She watched his beautiful grey hair join the rest on their green silk sheets. He didn't have trouble making love although she began to notice on occasion that he would become drained performing the smallest chores around the house. She didn't want to admit or even think about him finally showing his age. She wanted him to live for as long as she would live.   Her hand caressed his chest while she continued to watch him sleep.

His hand tenderly caressed her back.

Octavia kissed his cheek and asked, "How are you feeling?"

Charlemagne pulled her closer and said, "Stop worrying about me. I was once a feared serial killer. I'm *not* planning to die peacefully in my sleep."

"I don't want you to die and leave me alone."

"When my time comes, you will be taken care of." He softly kissed her and held her for the duration of the afternoon.

#

Astredo Institution for Mental Health

A large statue of the Goddess Isis stood in front of the Victorian Hospital on East Pershing Street.

The Astredo Institution for Mental Health was built in the 1800s by Autumn Astredo. Her Pagan Hospital mostly had Egyptian, Greek, and Roman Gods and Goddesses statues and other Pagan imagery. She made one wing a family practice before the Salem Community Hospital was built across the street from the three story asylum on East State Street. Autumn and her family continued to keep a few rooms for internal medicine.

Each room was designed like a small apartment, sans kitchen.

In a room overlooking the parking lot and Southeast Blvd with the castle towers in the far distance, Damian lay in bed while a psychiatrist examined him.

After the psychiatrist left, Brenda entered the room.

The hex to cause him, Raven, and Midnight to turn mute was lifted by Michelle a month after Octavia had cast the hex. Damian suffered a mental breakdown from Octavia. When Charlemagne recovered, she didn't need Damian anymore to pull jobs for her. For the past sixteen years, he lived in the hospital.

"The psychiatrist tells me you're improving," said Brenda.

Damien smiled and said, "When am I going to be released?"

Brenda placed a sisterly hand on his hand and said, "You get to go home in a few days. Whatever Octavia did to you was very traumatizing. I'm happy to see you recover.

We all are.   I wish you were able to tell me what happened so I could help you."

"Me too. I can't recall talking to Octavia after Lotus's funeral."

"I know."

Brenda and Damian spoke for a while before she left to do her rounds.

Later that night, Damian opened a letter from a friend in Cleveland. He had been keeping contact with another friend of Midnight. The witch's name was Panther. Panther lived in Cleveland. He and Panther wrote to each other. They made arrangements for him to move to Cleveland after he was released.

Damian left the hospital with the knowledge of his betrayal to the people he loved. He left to protect them.

Chapter 4

Castle Olympia

In the North wing of the castle, Valentina Russo just returned to the castle from investigating a haunting.

On her right shoulder was a tattoo of the Triple Goddess symbol. She was dressed in a black summer shirt and a black leather skirt. Around her neck was a pewter ankh.

After Valentina graduated high school in nineteen ninety-eight, she entered the field of paranormal research to help others with restless spirits and wronged ancestors.

Michelle Astredo companied Valentina to study her techniques for a play.

Valentina set her ghost hunting equipment on a table before she wrote in her journal about their recent ghost hunt. "I'm disappointed the ghost was harmless. I love slaying the bad guys."

"You're just like your mother. She embraced her destiny as the mother of a chosen warrior for the Gods. We Astredos wear their natural tattoo with pride," said Michelle.

"As do I." Valentina reached for her purse.

Michelle began helping her put away their equipment before they began to browse through the journals written over the centuries by members of the Astredo family.

#

After Valentina returned home, Valentina entered her bedroom carrying a tiny piece of paper with a love spell. She had another hour until she had to meet Ari at the library.

Ari.

The thought of his sexy grey eyes and handsome Egyptian features made her shiver in ecstasy.

He was in her fantasies at night when she would take herself while she pictured him making passionate love to her.

Valentina had a large three-wick pillar candle in her bedroom that was dark red and mulberry scented. The candle melted down causing a deep creator within the wax. Her love spell needed red candles and a cauldron. The round fat candle sat on an altar next to a statue of Venus.

Valentina placed two red candles on either side of her pewter altar pentacle. After Valentina lit the candles, she closed her door and shut off the lights. She sat Indian style in front of the candle. Next, she placed the spell against her DVD collection using a small pewter unicorn to prop it up so she could read it. Valentina poured holy water her mother had in a tiny bottle into a small dish. She also had one of Ari's senior pictures in her hand.

Holding Ari's picture over the flames, she whispered, "Goddesses Isis, Hathor, Venus, and Aphrodite this is the man I desire!" With the holy water, she made the sign of the pentagram over Ari's picture. Next, she whispered, "Goddesses of lovers, I pray that a vision will tell Ari I love him."

Valentina placed his picture beside the candle and took the paper in her hand and tore it into small pieces. As she burned the spell and Ari's picture, she whispered, "Since smoke symbolizes prayers being lifted into Summerland, let the words and my lover's image be carried into the realm of Summerland to be looked upon by The Father God and Mother Goddess that my desires are granted! So Mote It Be."

Valentina closed her eyes for the third part of the spell. She cleared her mind of all thoughts. The three yellow flames finished eating the objects thrown into the candle and began to flicker. Valentina concentrated on Ari lying in his king size wrought iron bed decorated in black and deep purple satin sheets and blankets. She pictured his head resting on a deep purple satin pillow with his gorgeous grey eyes gently shut. Valentina touched her arms and legs causing Ari to feel her erotic caressing on his body. Valentina astral projected herself into his vision causing him to see her lying beside him on her side wearing a long black nightgown that matched his black satin pajamas.

'Ari saw her beside him running her fingers threw his raven black hair. He became hard as she encaged him in her arms caressing his pale skin with her lips.'

Valentina softly whispered his name and softly told him to open his eyes.

'Ari opened his eyes. He pulled her closer to him as she slowly unbuttoned his nightshirt. He parted his lips meeting hers in a passionate kiss. His hands explored her

body strongly caressing her.

Valentina gently took him in her mouth and sucked him deeply until he cried out her name. Valentina mounted him and grinded slowly loving the feel of him growing inside her. She kissed him along his shoulders and neck. She softly whispered, "I love you Ari!" She quickened her pace on him causing him to moan with passion.

Valentina ended her vision opening her eyes. After she blew out the candle, she left to meet Ari at the library.

\#

The scent of musty books mixed with the fresh scent of newly published books perfumed the library as if the yellowed and white pages were incense.

Valentina read a book of spirit communications while Ari researched ancient Roman culture for his next play.

Ari's sexy gray eyes lifted from a book and watched Valentina take notes. Slowly, he brushed his foot against her foot. When he first climbed into his car, as it sat in the theater parking lot, he received the erotic vision Valentina sent him. Now, he couldn't remove the image of them making love out of his thoughts. Not that he wanted to. He decided it was time to remove the stick out from his ass and not worry about his heart breaking again.

Her hazel eyes met his eyes. Softly, she smiled. Desire grew within her when he lifted her hand towards his warm soft mouth. His warm breath on the back of her hand sent erotic sensations through her. Valentina briefly pictured what he would look like naked and in her bed among her black satin sheets.

Ari gently kissed her hand and said, "Valentina..."

A crash came from the stacks.

Next was gunfire before the large window broke distributing shards of glass across the library.

Rising to their feet, Valentina and Ari withdrew their pistols loaded with silver bullets.

Marguerite's foot soldiers slaughtered the entire library staff while searching for Valentina and Ari.

Bullets entered the mobsters.

Soon, there were only four mobsters.

Valentina sought shelter behind a bookcase. She loaded her gun.

Movement from the corner of her eye caused her to glance up.

A nozzle was jammed on her throat.

From behind the bookcase, came Ari's rapid gunfire blending with the other mobsters.

Valentina fired the gun into the mobster's stomach and quickly searched for Ari. She followed the sound of gunfire as she descended the long staircase. Her eyes rested on her handsome witch and watched him battle the last mobster.

Ari fired a few rounds at the mobster before joining Valentina who stood at the bottom of the stairs.

#

On the large stage, Italia danced to live Arabic music dressed in black harem pants, a black top with a silver beaded dragonfly covering her small chest, a matching dragonfly hip scarf was wrapped around her waist. She danced with a black veil with silver sequins. In front of Markus, she performed a series of hip rolls before she draped the sheer material around his neck. She returned to the stage. As she remained in one place with one leg out, toe pointed, her arms moved like serpents while she rolled her hip a few times. After her belly dance routine, she joined her husband at their table.

Markus welcomed his wife on his lap as another belly dancer appeared on stage. "I ordered the usual."

"After we close, dad asked us to pick up a few things at the store." Italia ran her hand down his red silk shirt. She kissed him across his shoulders while his hand caressed her thigh.

Markus tenderly kissed her mouth before she moved off his lap and sat next to him.

Italia gently placed her veil next to her and said, "Brenda, Michelle, Cassandra, and I discussed what you guys are doing."

Markus waited until a waiter wearing a black mesh shirt and black leather pants served their drinks: two banana daiquiris. He thanked the waiter and asked, "Are you with us."

"No."

"No? Italia, this is important."

"We understand why having the knowledge of mom's past may benefit us, but she's *not* ready."

"*Not* knowing the entire story can get us all killed. Is Aunt Kathy on your side?"

"Yes. She says the same things dad says: give mom time."

"It's been sixteen years."

"Mom's early life must've been hell. You and the others shouldn't be making it worse."

Markus played with his straw making a small whirlpool in his glass. "I haven't thought about it like that. We won't bother mom anymore, but Jason, Caesar, and I are still investigating."

"You men can do it without us. I'm sorry, but it's *not* right."

"We know. We are only trying to prevent situations like Charlemagne using identify shielding spells again."

"We understand, although, things happen for a reason. Perhaps the Gods don't want us to know yet."

Their dinner arrived silencing them until the waiter left.

While they talked and dined, songs by Tori Amos, Rob Zombie, and others played.

After he closed the restaurant, they walked towards their car.

Chapter 5

A group of Oak trees shielded the Victorian mansion from the rest of the farms that inhabited the mountain valley.

The mansion was painted a pale yellow with cotton candy pink fretwork, arched trim along the gables, and cupolas.

Some vampires kept the fashions and décor of the era they were born and some mixed the old fashions with modern.

Marguerite dressed in the fashions of the Middle Ages and the Victorian era. She was born in the Middle Ages and loved the fashions of the Victorian era.

In Marguerite DeMarco's private chamber, tall blue candles were lit giving off a soft glow throughout the room.

Her bedchamber was circular with arched windows. Thick heavy black curtains hung over the windows shielding the vampires from the sun's deadly rays.

Her ebony coffin was placed along a wall with green and blue roses wading in crystal vases on either side of the coffin. The coffin was open showing off the blue velvet lining and sea-green satin pillows. Gold marbled pillars held long and wide white candles stood among the flower arrangements.

In a parlor, Marguerite stood by a fireplace gazing at a picture of her oldest daughter, Delilah DeMarco. With her third lover, during the early years of the 1900s, she had five children who became ruthless mobsters. Her lover Armand was an French and Italian mobster. Her children died during the 30's and 40s. Among her three lovers, Dante was her favorite. Marguerite placed the photo back on the shelf above the fireplace. She would give up her immortality to have them with her and *not* just as ghosts. Even her sons-in-laws and daughters -in-laws she loved as though they were her own. She sat on a bench that stood in front of the fireplace. In the yellow and orange flames, Marguerite watched Valentina and Ari battle the mobsters and an assortment of thugs, she summoned, to kill the witches.

Gerard DeMarco stood in front of a window. He was dressed in a white pirate shirt and black pants. His silver hair reached the middle of his back and his silver goatee was short. In 1723, Marguerite made her pirate lover a vampire. He watched her scry in the fire.

Marguerite lifted her deadly eyes staring into Gerard's gentle but concerned eyes.

Her tiny European Shorthair climbed on her lap curling herself into a ball. Marguerite began to stroke Saturn's soft gray and black fur.

"Are you ready?"

Marguerite walked towards Gerard and tenderly placed her arms around his neck. "Tonight is my night to be with Dante. Tomorrow, you're all mine."

Gerard sighed deeply, turning away from her. He watched a stream of blue wax run down a thick candle creating a distorted design on the side of the candle. He was beginning to understand why Armand no longer wanted to be a part of her harem of men. "Why do you bother with me when you are only in love with Dante?" He said watching the yellow and blue flame dance in the center of the candle.

Marguerite said, "I love you too, Gerard. You and Dante are the only men for me."

Gerard gazed into her eyes wishing he were able to hate her and leave her as Armand did. He was still in love with the Italian bandit he accidentally set free from her coffin while looting mausoleums. Marguerite was staked in 1717 by the Astredos. She was imprisoned in a coffin unable to move from the stake that paralyzed her. He wished she would return her love to him, as she had done when they were first married. Over the centuries, he was beginning to see that she loved Dante more than him.

Marguerite tenderly kissed his lips while her hand caressed his inner thigh. "You can always join us."

"I'll wait until tomorrow night."

"I wasn't giving you a choice. You don't make the decisions," said Marguerite as Dante entered the room.

Gerard withheld his jealousy as he backed away from Marguerite.

Dante placed his arm around Marguerite's waist and kissed her along her neck and shoulders. He watched Gerard leave as he asked, "Is everything ok?"

"Everything is good. I just miss my girls. Delilah was the perfect underboss. I wanted to turn her, but she would've had syphilis for eternity."

Dante gave her a gentle hug and said, "You still have your youngest son and your daughter-in-law."

Marguerite softly smiled and said, "Charlemagne and Octavia has made me proud."

#

Ari walked Valentina to her front door.

The early autumn air was cool.

The scent of decayed leaves perfumed the yard.

Valentina slightly shivered. Ari's gentle embrace warmed her when he pulled her into his arms. She snuggled into his arms. "What were you about to tell me before we were attacked?"

Ari pressed her closer to him. His satiric eyes were burning with desire. "I want to ravage you."

Valentina moved her hand down his back and touched his butt before she moved her hand towards the front of his pants. "Ravage me."

Ari caressed her back before he moved his hand between her legs. His two fingers teased her through the bottom of her underwear.

Valentina began to softly moan. "Do you love me, Ari? I don't want to make love unless it's for love."

Continuing to tease her with his finger, he said, "I agree with you. I love you."
His mouth passionately caressed her mouth.

Valentina read his mind and his erotic intentions. She escorted him inside.

In her bedroom, Ari stripped her after he undressed. He continued to kiss her.

Valentina moved her hand from his waist towards his warm penis. She massaged
his testicles before her hand stroked him.

Ari moaned thrusting into her hand. "You've always meant a lot to me,
Valentina."

Valentina kissed his shoulder and tattoo. "I've always loved you wishing you
were my lover."

Ari softly smiled before he moaned and cried out from her swift strokes.

Valentina covered his pale chest in deep passionate kisses. Her mouth caressed
his stomach before she moved to her knees, kissed the inside of his thigh, and took him
into her mouth.

"Oh, oh, Valentina, Valentina!" He felt she was doing well for her first time
giving oral sex. He loved the way she teased him with her tongue. "Don't stop doing *that*.
Valentina, Valentina, Valentina."

After she swallowed him, she rose from the floor and took him into her arms.
"Make me scream." Her mouth caressed his a few times. She savored the taste of his lips.

"Can I tie you?" Ari bit into her shoulder after he kissed her. His hand caressed
the inside of her thigh.

Valentina moaned when his finger entered her. "Bind me." She was laid down on the bed.

After Ari tied her hands to the headboard, he reached for her vibrator. His mouth and hand caressed her body.

Ecstasy washed over her with his gentle strokes. She couldn't wait to experience his penis stroking her. She had always dreamed that he was her first lover.

Ari deeply sucked her nipples. He stroked her faster bringing her to climax. His teeth bit her erect nipples.

In passion, Valentina screamed when he placed the tip of the vibrator on her clit. "Oh Ari, Ari! I love you, I love you." After her multiple orgasms, he placed the vibrator on her nightstand, kissed the inside of her thighs before he stroked her clit with his tongue. She continued to scream.

Ari continued to lick her enjoying the taste of her in his mouth. He moaned when he replaced his tongue with his penis.

She almost came when he penetrated her.

Seated on his knees with her legs around his waist, he stroked her. His moans and cries mixed with hers. He felt her climax rise.

After her climax, her moans softened. "Lay on top of me. Ari, Ari."

Ari's body covered hers. He was still inside her heavily stroking her.

"Untie me so I can caress you. I want to hold you."

His hands moved up her arms and released her. His kisses travel down her throat.

"Oh God Ari! Yes, yes, yes." Her nails racked across his back.

He loved her screams of passion. Harder and faster, he pushed her. When he kissed her several times on her lips, an erotic vision came to him, *'He was on his knees grinding into her on his den floor. They appeared older."* He was still heavily pushing her when the vision ended. She was his chosen lover. He hugged her tightly.

"What did my lover see?" she moaned.

"You and I in the future. Locked in each other's embraces." He kissed her several times on the lips. "I love you, Valentina."

Valentina's hands explored his body as she moved him onto his back and slowly grinded on top of him.

"Faster, Valentina. Yes, yes!"

Their passion lasted throughout the night.

Chapter 6

The vision showed *'Marguerite leaving a vet's office. A pool of blood grew around a friend of Valentina and Diana's. Lisa Stoker.*

Next, a dozen gypsy women were murdered by an unknown killer.' The vision was shown to her in grisly detail.

She gripped her maroon velvet pillow tightly in her arms. The sixteen-year-old witch stepped out of bed, opened her heavily decorated bedroom door, and walked down the ancient hallway. Diana la Sorcère was new to understanding her psychic gift and the natural tattoo of the Triple Goddess she wore on her right shoulder.

As she walked down a heavily decorated staircase, the fresh sent of pancakes and blueberries muffins mixed with Giovanni's cigar and incense smoke flowed towards the large foyer.

Throughout the large castle, cats and kittens of every breed roamed the ancient building. In the 1800's, Bertha Astredo wrote in her journal and Will that no one living in the castle is to spay or neuter any cat. She felt that it was an act of blasphemy to alter the Gods' creation. Also in her Will, she requested that the first black and white cat in a litter be named after her favorite cat, Jingle bells. Jingle Bells was born on Yule.

Giovanni and sometimes Charlotte were the first ones up and the last to go to bed. Like his mother, Athena, Giovanni prepared meals and made sure his children and grandchildren completed their chores. After Charlemagne, they never hired another butler or servant. Athena Gaia Astredo *never* had hired help. She was a widowed single mother who was a belly dancer by day and a powerful slayer at night.

Diana entered the large living room and entered the dining room.

Her father was the first one seated at the maroon marble table. She sat across from him.

Raven la Sorcère was dressed in a black T-shirt with a purple pentacle on the front and a pair of black pants. His black hair was cut short, but his goatee reached the center of his neck. On his left hand, the handsome widower still wore his pewter wedding ring and on his right hand, he wore two Gothic style rings. He continued to work in Octavia's old palm reading shop which had been her cover for her dealing with Marguerite. The store was now owned by Midnight and Raven. He gently smiled when he saw Diana. "You look so much like your mother when she was sixteen. I miss her so much." His eyes became misty for a moment remembering his late wife. He still mourned her death heavily.

Jason and the others soon entered the dining room and took their seats.

Giovanni and Charlotte began to set the table with Viktor, Ari, and Michael helping.

"I think I had my first vision."

"Tell us about it," said Charlotte.

Diana explained her vision to them.

"Your vision is advanced for someone your age. Mom didn't receive her first detailed vision until she was eighteen," said Giovanni. His 75-year-old skin was wrinkle free except for a few crow's feet in the corner of his sexy eyes. He resembled Christopher Lee.

"Don't worry. It's rare, but it happens. If you receive any more visions, call my cell. I want Viktor and me to be updated in case we are needed," said Charlotte. Charlotte and Viktor were working on a murder case in Beaver Falls, Pennsylvania. They were staying a month in a motel. This was to be their final case before they retired. Charlotte and Viktor wanted to focus on their scared birth rite.

Giovanni took Charlotte's hand and said, "Will my lady keep in contact with me?"

"Every night. I'll have my lap top. We can send instant messages." She smiled at him. Out of her past lovers, Giovanni treated her with respect and taught her how to love and be loved.

Feeling his grandfather's arousal, Michael quietly smiled.

Giovanni nudged her foot with his foot and said, "I can't wait for our instant messages."

"I bet," said Michael. He and Ari softly laughed.

Giovanni softly kissed the back of Charlotte's hand while the conversations turned to other subjects. He was going to miss her.

After breakfast and the family left for their careers, Giovanni tenderly held Charlotte in the large dark grey hallway while Viktor carried their luggage to Charlotte's car. His eyes scanned the black suit dress and silver pentacle around her neck. It was his favorite outfit on her. He was happy she was about to retire so they could enjoy retirement together. Although, he would sometimes miss making sure he packed her lunch before she left every morning for work. He used to arrive at the theatre later in the afternoon, worked for a few hours, and made sure he had time to prepare dinner before everyone returned home. He loved being a stay-at-home father and later grandfather when he retired five years ago.

Charlotte snuggled into him as he softly kissed her neck. Her hands slid under his shirt as she caressed his back. Her mouth tenderly caressed his mouth savoring the taste of his mouth.

Giovanni returned her passionate kiss feeling tempted to carry her to their bedroom and allow Viktor to take care of the trail. This was their first time traveling away from home and he already missed having her near him.

Charlotte kissed him again before she said, "You've made my life so much better." He rescued her from a nightmarish life many years ago. She continued to pray to the Gods that her past stayed buried and no one *ever* discovers who she was *before* learning what the tattoo she was born with meant. Giovanni, Athena, Stefano, Stefano's husband, Roman, and their cousins on the Island of Medea were the only people who knew her secret past. She couldn't tell their children. It was safer for them that they *never* find out.

Giovanni gazed into her eyes and said, "You deserve *this* life." Tightly, he hugged her.

Charlotte returned his hug before kissing him again. When she pulled away, she noticed Viktor standing by the large door waiting for her. *"Au revoir, Je vous aime. Vous étes ma vie,"* she said.

"Arrivederci, Ti voglio bene. Vous étes ma vie," he said. He slowly released her from his embrace before he gave their oldest grandson a hug goodbye.

#

Shadows hung over the slightly dim temple room forming grotesque shapes on the marble floors.

Statues of Egyptian, Greek, Roman, Celtic, and Norse Gods and Goddesses filled the temple as well as other rooms in the castle. The Astredos during the 1500's worshipped the Roman Gods until later on when the family grew.

Black, purple, and silver candles burned on carved shelves and pewter pillars beside statues of various sizes.

Incense carried the scents of myrrh and frankincense throughout the old castle.

Drums and chants echoed throughout the large vaults from a stereo.

Ari sat in the lotus position before a shrine to Isis and Osiris. He was dressed in a long black robe with his clothes draped over an Egyptian designed chair.

A cryptic vision interrupted his meditation.

*'In 1934 Italy, ten-year-old Charlemagne DeMarco gazed at the corpse of a gypsy woman while holding a blood covered chef knife. The look in his young **grey** eyes was jealousy.*

Next, the vision showed Charlemagne at twenty-years old seated at a poker table with Dante, Amari and Esmeralda Latika, Charlemagne's brothers and sisters: Frank, Nikkolas, Tony, Jacqueline, Delilah, and Frank's wife, Molly, Delilah's head hit-man Lucian Phoenix, Marguerite, Gerard, and Esmeralda.

Marguerite took a third lover, Armand, in the early 1900s. He broke away from Marguerite's mob family to form his own mob becoming a rival mob boss. The vision was showing a time after Armand and Marguerite split up since he wanted her to have only one husband. Delilah, Frank, Jacqueline, Charlemagne, and Nikkolas were Armand and Marguerite's children. Marguerite sat in-between Dante and Gerard. Dante had his arm around her waist while Gerard had his hand on her thigh and was nuzzling her neck.

Charlemagne and Nikkolas were laughing and joking around with their friends, mother, and siblings.

Marguerite was bragging how Charlemagne is becoming her number one assassin.

Charlemagne smiled as a waitress refilled his glass of beer. His satiric eyes undressed her.

Nikkolas whispered to the waitress, "China, would you like to meet my friend and I later?"

China was Nikkolas's girlfriend of two years. This was the first time he introduced her to his close friend and brother. Her red hair was pulled into a ponytail and clashed with the blue and yellow uniform the casino made their employees wear. She looked at Charlemagne, shyly smiled, and asked, "Is he Charlemagne? The one you're always talking about?"

"It's him. He's my whores' favorite john. You still interested? It would be his first *threesome."*

Amari and Gerard laughed. Amari said, "Are you serious?"

China sat on Charlemagne's knee, gently caressed his chest, and said, "Don't pay attention to them." In his ear, she whispered, "It'll be my first threesome too."

Amari and Gerard traded crude comments aimed at Charlemagne. They laughed harder when Charlemagne gave them the middle finger in a sarcastic manner.

Charlemagne turned his attention to China. "We'll have a good time tonight trying something different."

China touched his leg, gently caressed his inner thigh, and said, "I can't wait. I heard you were a good lover."

"I'm a killer in the bedroom." He and Nikkolas laughed. Charlemagne placed his arm around her waist and caught the same look in Nikkolas's eyes that Delilah gives to her gunmen.

The vision moved forward to show Charlemagne reaching his climax before he lay next to China.

She cuddled close to him anticipating bragging to her co-workers how she got to sleep with mobsters Nikkolas and Charlemagne DeMarco. They'd be jealous.

Nikkolas lay behind her caressing her arm. "Did you enjoy it, China?"

"I didn't think I would, but I did. I love bad boys." China gazed into Charlemagne's grey-blue eyes and saw why women couldn't wait to have him.

Charlemagne softly smiled and said, "You find dangerous men attractive." He moved to his side and ran his fingers through her red hair. He exchanged glances with Nikkolas before looking at her. "Do you realize you're in the arms of two of the most dangerous men on this island?"

Nikkolas kissed her along her shoulder as she said,

"Why do you think I agreed to have you spend the night? I've always wanted to sleep with a serial killer."

Charlemagne asked, "Don't you find it strange that your boyfriend has agreed to help you fulfill a fantasy after he caught you sleeping with one of his sister's gunmen?"

The excitement suddenly faded and was replaced with fear.

Nikkolas turned her face towards his face not caring if the position was uncomfortable. "I ask Charlemagne to do favors for me."

"Favors?" she asked.

"Like disposing of cheating girlfriends."

Charlemagne forced her to look at him. "I've wanted to experiment with a new killing technique for my boss Delilah for a while now."

China was locked in Nikkolas's arms. She screamed and struggled to break free.

"I thought you liked bad boys." Charlemagne kissed her forehead and mouth before he tied her to the bed with Nikkolas's help.

Nikkolas stepped off the bed and watched Charlemagne beat and rape China until she lay lifeless on the bed.

Time advanced to show Salem, Ohio in the 1970s. Sixty-nine-year-old Charlemagne was in a crowded disco dancing with fifteen-year-old Octavia to ABBA's 'Fernando'. He gently held her in his arms as they danced around the dance floor.

After their song ended, they were cuddled together in a dark booth.

Octavia sat on his lap with her arms around his neck and his arms around her waist. In the dim light, she gazed into his eyes loving him despite all the stories of his violent crimes told by his friends and her parents. Octavia knew Charlemagne would never hurt her.

Amari loved what Charlemagne did to China. Octavia occasionally heard her father threaten Esmeralda he would punish her that way if she ever got out of line. Esmeralda would pay no mind to his threats. He never carried them out. He was afraid her.

Octavia kissed him a few times on the mouth before she kissed him along his throat and neck. Her hands slipped under his shirt and caressed his chest and back.

Charlemagne softly ran his fingers through her hair. To him, she was precious. For the first time in his life, he didn't want anyone else.

Octavia rested her head on his chest. She gave him a gentle hug.

Charlemagne softly kissed her and said, "You've made me very happy." His hand moved towards her stomach and felt the beginnings of a tiny bump. Tears of happiness filled his eyes.

The vision ended leaving a perplexed look on Ari's face.

Giovanni entered the temple room through the cloakroom where the robes and headdresses for Sabbaths were stored. He waited until Ari was finished with his meditation before he said, "Did you have a vision?"

"I did. I don't understand why I saw parts of Charlemagne's life. He's dead. He can't come after us." Ari explained the vision.

"Sometimes psychic visions are like dream symbols. Certain things can mean the opposite. The imagery and the people you meet may not necessarily mean the dream was about that person or situation. In some cases, it can be. Analyze the vision in your journal the way Raven and Midnight had shown you."

"I will. Was Octavia ever pregnant?"

"She was. Under Esmeralda's order, Charlemagne moved Octavia to the United States from Cairo. A week prior to his first arrest in Salem, Octavia slipped on the icy parking lot at their apartment building and fell down two flights of steps. While in the hospital, Charlemagne was mistaken for her father when he was informed of her miscarriage. Their hospital visit raised too many questions and his identity was discovered. Charlemagne was devastated at the loss of their baby."

Ari said, "She was too young to go through that. Who was the woman he murdered at age ten?"

"His step-mother."

#

The scent of Mexican food mixed with the scent of autumn at a small outdoor café in the center of Main Street.

Diana was on her lunch break and was seated across from sixteen-year-old Adrian Russo, Valentina's brother and Diana's boyfriend of four months. She walked towards the restaurant to meet him.

Adrian worked at the Dragon's lair theatre training as a director from his father. His brown hair was short and his eyes were almost copper. Like his parents and younger brother, he *didn't* bare the Astredo's scared tattoo. Valentina and her two baby sisters bared the mark. "Have you told Valentina about your vision?"

"I just hung up with her. She's going to call Lisa. Before Ari left for the theater, he told me he was researching a vision he had earlier and suggested I do the same. He's going to show me how to analyze dreams and visions tonight." Diana cut her vegetarian enchilada.

"Do you think there is a correlation between your vision and his vision?"

"I've thought of that when he drove me to work. I'll see how the vision parallels with his. His was cryptic and revealed things we already knew."

Their conversation moved to other topics before Adrian drove her to Nefertiti's Tearoom on his way to the theatre.

Chapter 7

The sun slowly sank behind the town covering it in a pale pink and orange light.

Guns sounded through the computer's speakers as police sirens screamed down a computer-generated street.

Valentina was in the dark blue and silver kitchen placing dirty dishes into a dishwasher listening to her brothers play a computer game in Aaron's study.

An island sat in the center of the large kitchen with Scarlet laying in a Gothic style bassinette in the corner of the island.

Carrying a black dishtowel, Valentina stood at the archway and said, "Our sister just fell asleep, could you turn the speakers down, please?"

"No problem," replied Adrian. He turned down the speakers just as her thirteen-year-old brother gunned down a group of mobsters.

"Thanks," she said before she returned to cleaning the kitchen.

Cassandra Russo entered the kitchen carrying Rosa in one arm and the family cat in the other. She had just given Rosa and the kitten a bath. Setting both on the floor, Rosa reached for Angel and drew her into her arms.

"What did Ari want?" Cassandra helped her daughter with the last of the plates.

"He told me Diana phoned an hour ago saying she had a vision of Lisa being attacked at work and a series of murders reminisce of Charlemagne's killings."

"Sounds more like a nightmare than a psychic vision. Psychic visions are normally not that graphic for someone her age. It's probably from studying all those journals and watching past battles with you and the others."

Aaron entered the kitchen from the living room as Valentina said,

"Ari asked me to tell Lisa about the visions when I take Angel for her shot. We feel it wouldn't hurt to warn her, just in case."

Aaron's long black hair reached his shoulders. A silver pentacle hung around his neck. At work he wore dark colored poet shirts and when he was with friends and family, he wore T-shirts with sci-fi or fantasy themes. Aaron walked behind Cassandra wrapping his arms around her waist. He nuzzled her neck as she helped Valentina put a glass in a cupboard.

Adrian stepped out from the study. "When are we going to the Dragon's Lair, dad?" He looked like his father and even began to dress like him. Around his neck was a pewter dragon holding a crystal ball. It matched the ring on his finger.

Aaron kissed Cassandra along her neck. "As soon as you pick out the next play *you* want to direct."

Adrian glanced down at a pile of plays on the island. He glanced back at his father who was watching his surprised face suddenly brighten.

"Do you mean it? *You* want *me* to direct."

Valentina and Cassandra had an arm around Aaron's waist looking proudly at Adrian.

"Yes, I think you could use the experience."

"Thanks dad!" Adrian searched through the plays. When he selected one, Adrian said, "*A Street Car Named Desire.*"

"Beautiful Choice," His father said. He approached Adrian grabbing his long black coat from the landing leading down towards the basement.

"Good luck," Cassandra said giving Adrian a hug and kiss.

Valentina had done the same before she picked up the tiny black cat. She held the cat close to her and reached for her purse that hung on a chair with her mother's purse.

Rosa walked towards her big sister. "Can I go with Angel, Valentina?"

Valentina got eye level with the two-year-old. "I don't mind as long as it's ok with mom."

Cassandra said, "I don't mind."

Valentina tenderly lifted her sister in her arm and held the kitten in the other arm. Her mother opened the door for her as she stepped out into the garage.

After Valentina strapped Rosa into her car seat, Valentina placed Angel in her lap. Next, Valentina climbed into the driver's seat and pulled out of the garage.

Chapter 8

Lisa Stoker worked with veterinarian, Dr. Carolina, in downtown Salem. Like Valentina and Diana, she bore the natural tattoo of the Triple Goddess. Her dark blonde hair was tied in a ponytail. Lisa was a were panther, like most lycanthropes she could turn into a panther at will.   Unlike the others in the Astredo family, she has yet to discover her inherited powers. Her earrings bore the image of the Goddess Sekhmet and her necklace was the image of the Goddess Bastet. She worked as her nurse and secretary in the tiny one floor animal clinic. She gave Angel a shot and a quick check up. She reacted the same way Ari, Valentina and Cassandra had, believing the vision was only a nightmare since Ari, Midnight, and Raven didn't begin to show that they were psychic until they were eighteen. Nevertheless, she reassured Valentina she would be vigilant.

The veterinarian's office was dark except for the tiny leopard lamp, which sat by Lisa's desk. Angel was the last patient of the day and Lisa was working on files to take back to her boss.

The sun sank further behind the small town leaving the earth in a robe of darkness until morning where light replaces twilight. A full bright harvest moon hung in the sky as stars began to map the sky.

A tiny radio on Lisa's desk played a little Gothic metal and dark wave music.

 Hearing something fall over in the back room startled her. She rose from her chair and began to walk down the hall passed operating rooms. Walking passed Dr. Carolina's office she said, "I'm taking care of it, doctor." Lisa opened Dr. Carolina's office door when she didn't hear a reply. Lisa's eyes fell on Dr. Carolina's desk.

Dr. Carolina sat behind her desk staring lifelessly at Lisa. Her ginger hair was pulled up in a bun. On the side of her neck were two bloody puncture holes. Two wide lines of blood ran down her neck onto her white lab coat.

Lisa removed her cell phone from her uniform as she walked towards the dead vet's desk. She pressed an arrow key that automatically dialed the young witch's number.

"Ari, it's me Lisa, Diana was right, my boss is dead. Marguerite is here."

She watched as a light blue mist entered from under the door.

"Lisa, are you alright? Lisa!"

The above light busted as the mist settled transforming into Marguerite wearing a long blue velvet cape.

Lisa trembled unable to see the vampire in front of her. She screamed as Marguerite placed her cold undead hands around her throat causing her to drop the cell phone. She heard Ari call for her. Lisa placed her hands on the vampire's wrists trying to pull her hands away from her throat.

Marguerite pinned her against the wall squeezing her neck. She was forced to let go after Lisa kicked her.

An arm snaked around Lisa's waist and a large chef knife was brought up to her throat.

Marguerite approached Lisa and her second attacker. "Start with her and then stalk the streets as you had done in Cairo, Rome, and Paris."

"She's *not* my normal victim. I want my gypsies," said a low husky voice.

"I want to use her as an example for Charlotte. She hasn't discovered her inherited powers, so she'll be easy for you to fight. I don't want her dead. Just beaten enough to send a message to Charlotte and Giovanni."

Lisa felt his hot breath on her neck. Her fist jammed into his side.

Marguerite said, "Don't struggle. A very dangerous serial killer has you in his embrace."

Lisa trembled as a sick feeling erupted in her stomach. Several years ago, when she and this generation had gathered in the castle's living room with Charlotte and the others, they watched past battles and learned the history of Marguerite's crime family. They were instructed to read old journals from their ancestors. Most of the battles Charlotte fought in at the time when she was new to the family were mysteriously clouded on the crystal ball. One mobster was the focus of Charlotte's obsession to educate her children on various ways of self-defense. Mostly the female members of the family. He was the only mobster who angered Charlotte by just his mere mention. Lisa's voice betrayed her nervousness, "He's *dead*. Giovanni and Charlotte killed him." She felt him laugh.

Marguerite softly smiled before opening the door to allow the hall light to blanket Lisa and the 94-year-old serial killer. "Don't forget to tell Charlotte I've sent my favorite serial killer to target two of her girls." Marguerite left in a cloud of mist.

He moved his hand down her waist and onto her thigh where he caressed her. "I faked my death. I've been in hiding. My Octavia has been protecting me."

Lisa kicked his leg, turned, and broke out from his embrace. She ran from the office and towards the front of the clinic. When she reached her purse that sat on the desk in the waiting room, she reached in to retrieve her gun.

The cold steel of the blade smacked the gun out from her hand and onto the floor.

The skin on her hand tore apart. Quickly, she ran towards the door. She collapsed onto the floor when he threw his knife at her leg. She landed on her stomach. She lifted her head from the cool tile. Her eyes locked with his pale blue psychotic eyes. She screamed. Before she could reach for the knife stuck in her flesh, he pulled it out creating a light sprinkle of blood to fall on the floor.

He kicked her ribs forcing her to lie on her back. He stabbed her arm to prevent her from striking him. His hand touched her cheek and turned her face towards his face. He straddled her. "You should be thankful I promised my girl I would *never* rape my victims anymore." He removed the knife from her arm and slid it under her shirt. "You being a part of Charlotte's family makes it worth breaking that promise." His knife tore her shirt open exposing her leopard printed bra.

Her arm and leg were in too much pain to move. She screamed when he began to caress her breast with his hand. Her mind replayed watching the many times he used to torture and rape his victims during the 1960's and 1970's. The loss of blood began to weaken her. Lightheadedness followed, she passed out on the floor.

#

After he left Lisa lying in a pool of blood, he hunted his favorite prey among the streets. He fled the animal clinic when he heard Giovanni, Jason, Ari, and the other Astredos approach the front door. He *didn't* have the chance to rape Lisa. Even if he had, Octavia would *kill* him.

Octavia was the only person he feared. She was also his weakness.

Entering a palm reading parlor, he began his slaughter of gypsies.

His large knife was embraced in blood as well as his clothes. He took to the allies where he would chase his victims before mutilating them.

Screams carried through the night.

He walked down an alley and stopped suddenly.

Standing under a street light was a young gypsy woman. Her arms were crossed over her chest and she was staring at him. Her violet eyes revealed her irritation.

He approached her with his knife in his hand. His eyes looked at the way she was leaning against a building. "I've obeyed you, Octavia."

Octavia removed the bloody knife from his hand and returned it to his pants pocket. "I've told you before; I watch you through the crystal ball and read your thoughts."

"You married a..."

"I know, I know. I married a dangerous man. You were a serial rapist for most of your life. You still have urges...I've heard it all before." Octavia was unnerved by the blood that covered her beloved Charlemagne Asmodeus DeMarco. "You are as threatening to me as a newborn kitten."

"I *don't* frighten you?"

"You *never* have. You are the only man I feel safe around and who I can trust. Stay away from the woman in the Astredo family. Charlotte *will* kill you." Octavia's mood shifted from being irritated with her lover to fearful of him dying. He was human, not a vampire like Marguerite.

"She doesn't scare me," said Charlemagne.

"You are all I have. You are the only man who ever cared about me." Like a child, Octavia threw her arms around his waist and pulled him close to her.

Charlemagne caressed her back and slowly rocked her in his arms. Softly, he kissed her along her neck and shoulders. "You're the longest relationship I've ever had." He gently backed her against the wall and began to explore her body with his hands.

Octavia returned his passionate kisses. She cried out when he penetrated her with force as though he had to force himself on her. She moaned loving his rough lovemaking.

His strokes were heavy and quick.

"Charlemagne, Charlemagne!" She held him tightly. Her head rested on his shoulder. It was her favorite place to rest her head. He took away all her pain from her past. She used to drag a knife across her thighs to stop all emotional hurt until he made her life better. He scolded her for cutting herself, took away her drugs, and saved her from dying. She hasn't cut herself in sixteen years. That time in 1983 was the first since they moved to America. Charlemagne discovered the box and threw it away after scolding her again. Octavia listened to his rapid heartbeat, moans, and cries. The sounds were soothing to her. With her legs, she squeezed his waist.

He pushed harder during his climax.

She buried her face in his chest and repeatedly screamed his name until her climax faded. She continued to hold onto him. She lifted her head to look at him. "Stay in me for a moment. I love this feeling."

Charlemagne softly kissed her cheek and remained holding her for a few moments longer.

#

After he brought her home, he made love to her again.

When they finished making love, a few hours later, Octavia stood on the balcony wearing only a turquoise satin robe that matched her baby-doll style nightgown that lay on the bedroom floor, and holding his black satin robe. She lifted her arms and nuzzled her face in his robe becoming intoxicated with his scent. She looked at the city of Salem and thought about Marguerite's promise to her. '*My casinos shall be yours someday.*' Octavia respected Marguerite and grew to love her as another mother. She was honored to be her daughter-in-law.

"How did my son do?"

Octavia turned to the other side of the balcony and saw Marguerite at the other end. "Well. He's in the bedroom. Sleeping."

Marguerite approached her and caught Charlemagne's scent all over her. "You've done well hiding him. Does Raven and the others still think you are innocent?"

"No. When they brought me into their hospital to rehabilitating me a few years ago, Valentina read my mind and Michael felt my emotions. They were shocked to discover that Charlemagne and I honestly love each other. They didn't think he would care for anyone. If Charlemagne hadn't have broken me out, I might still be in there. They think I was too young to be his girlfriend."

"You *were* too young. I've told Charlemagne that he was stupid for seducing a girl that young. He's lucky he didn't make me lose you to a foster home and get himself executed. You *do* know that's what will happen to him if he ever goes back to Paris or Cairo?"

Octavia shuddered at the memories of the many times the Salem police arrested him as the Cairo police had done in front of her. She was too young to see that the Cairo and Salem police were trying to help her escape a very dangerous serial killer. Her parents raised her to view the police as the bad guys and they as well as her father's best friend were the good guys. She wasn't born when he was in jail for multiple murders in Pairs, although, she heard stories and had psychic visions that told her more then she needed to know about the psychopath her parents encouraged her to date. "I know Marguerite. I'm an adult now. I don't have to worry about the Salem Police anymore.

They think he's dead and I'll make sure it stays that way." Octavia glanced through the window and looked in on Charlemagne asleep under the covers. She turned her attention towards Marguerite. She said, "Charlemagne is ninety-four years old. He may not be with me for long. He gets exhausted quicker. I've noticed he's moving slower. That's one of the reasons why I followed him tonight. I'm surprised he could still make love as much as usual. Could you make him a vampire so I'd *never* lose him?"

Marguerite softly smiled and said, "He and I were recently discussing something like that. I've told him I would like to turn him as a reward for everything he has done for me. More importantly, I don't want to bury another child. He asked me to wait."

"What for?"

"He wanted to see how *you* would feel about having a vampire for a lover. Charlemagne cares for you very much. You are the first and only woman he has loved and cared for. He *wasn't* going to permit me to turn him if *you* didn't approve."

Octavia smiled and said, "I approve."

"I'll return after he's awake and we can talk more about it."

After she left, Octavia remained on the balcony. She held the robe tighter in her arms as she tried to block out the painful memories of the police taking him away from her. He was all she had and the only one who cared about her. He was always around when she needed to seek his comfort. Tears began to fall from her eyes when she began to think about Amari. He was a waste. Octavia turned towards the bedroom window to make sure the window was closed before she knelt beside a table and removed a loose brick from the wall. From the hole, she withdrew a plastic bag. She removed three joints and a lighter. Sitting on the chair, she lit a joint to erase her abusive father from her mind.

Amari *didn't* go away.

She tried to think of the many times Charlemagne would come to her aid.

1973

Cairo, Egypt

Esmeralda stood behind a kitchen counter loading her pistol. She was dressed in a black pinstriped suit. She and Amari were dealers in lycanthrope trafficking. They exploited humans with lycanthrope by making them perform in their illegal carnival and sell them as sex slaves.

Lotus was cleaning the kitchen from the dinner she prepared. It was her duty to cook meals, clean the one-level house, and raise her baby sister. Lotus and Octavia resembled their mother.

Octavia was thirteen and playing with her dolls in the living room. The bedroom door slamming behind her startled her as Amari entered the living room and then kitchen.

"Lotus! You fucking ruined my shirt. What the fuck am I supposed to wear tonight?" Amari was dressed in a pair of dress pants and no shirt.

Lotus stepped away from the sink and took his dress shirt from him. She looked at the sauce stain that appeared on the beige fabric. "I'm sorry dad. I tried to soak it."

Amari slapped her across the face and said, "Get your ass in the laundry room and get me another shirt."

Lotus threw the shirt at him and said, "Don't ever hit me again."

"I don't take orders from women. Do what I tell you."

Lotus turned to Esmeralda and said, "I'm going out with Raven and Morning

Glory, is that alright mom?"

"Go ahead," said Esmeralda.

Amari said, "Charlemagne is babysitting you and Octavia. You're not going anywhere."

"That's why I'm leaving. I hate Charlemagne and I really hate that Octavia likes him."

Esmeralda said, "Let her leave. I don't feel like hearing her and Charlemagne bitch at each other."

Amari watched Lotus give Esmeralda a hug and kiss before she left. He approached Esmeralda.

Esmeralda looked at his stained shirt and at him. "I'm not cleaning it. I'm not your fucking maid."

"Don't talk back to me."

"You don't own me."

"Lotus is too much like you. Why couldn't you have given me sons? I never wanted daughters. Women are useless. Lotus is a horrible daughter. I think you had girls just to piss me off. I told you the only children I want are boys. I didn't want girls."

"If you hate women so much go fuck a man," Esmeralda said.

Amari's hand struck her face.

Esmeralda fought back. She hit him with the back of her gun. "Stop it. We have to meet Marguerite and Dante in a few moments. They want to give us a new load of werewolves. I don't want to be late." She turned away and entered the dining room to gather more bullets.

Amari threw the shirt down and entered the living room. His cheek was beginning to turn red from the gun. Without care, the edge of his shoe stepped on Octavia's toes. When she cried, he kicked her leg hard and said, "Next time get out of my fucking way, bitch." He sat on the chair just as Charlemagne entered the door.

Forgetting about the slight pain in her foot, Octavia dropped her doll, ran to Charlemagne, and hugged him tightly.

Charlemagne returned her hug and walked her towards the couch. When he sat down, she climbed in his lap. Noticing tears in her eyes, he asked, "Is my little girl ok?"

Amari said, "Ignore that whiny little bitch. These girls have no fucking respect for their father. Lotus left with those hippies again and that one is starting to be just like her. Sons would have been so much better."

Octavia held onto Charlemagne as Amari's words were hurting her. New tears filled her eyes. She nuzzled her face into Charlemagne's chest to hide her tears from her father.

Charlemagne caressed her back. "You shouldn't speak that way in front of your children. You love them."

"I don't love them because they weren't what I wanted. What am I going to do with girls? They're nothing."

Charlemagne covered Octavia's ears and said, "Have a little respect."

"What the fuck happened to you, Charlemagne? Since when do you care how they feel? Women are not even human."

"Octavia changed me. I like being her companion. Gerard, Armand, and Dante have always treated their lovers with respect."

"Women are only good for one thing." Amari watched Esmeralda enter the living room. He grabbed her arm and forced her on his lap.

The more Amari bashed women, the tighter Octavia held Charlemagne. Innocently, she buried her face in Charlemagne's neck and clamped herself around him as though hoping his body would protect her from her father's verbal abuse.

Charlemagne caressed her back and slowly rocked her in his arms. He was the only one, besides Lotus, to give her real affection.

Esmeralda looked at Charlemagne and said, "Octavia wanted to wait until you arrived before she had dinner. Have fun."

"We will," said Charlemagne giving Octavia a comforting hug.

Esmeralda rose from her husband's lap and grabbed her guns.

Amari followed after he said to Octavia, "Be good for Charlemagne. Remember I gave him permission to slap you around if you don't obey him. He could beat someone senseless."

Charlemagne watched them leave wondering what turned his friend into such an asshole towards his family. Charlemagne would love to have a wife and a few kids. He didn't believe in hitting children.

Octavia trembled nervously until her parents left.

"Where do you want to order in dinner at," asked Charlemagne.

"Can we go to a restaurant? Like Raven and Lotus do?"

"No. We have to have it delivered. You know the rules. Amari and Esmeralda don't want you and I to be seen together. We can only be here or Marguerite's place."

Octavia sighed. "I want Chinese. We had pizza last time." She lifted her head *from his shoulder and gazed into his eyes. "Did I do something wrong to make dad hate me?"*

Charlemagne returned her loving gaze. "No. Amari is an asshole. Pay no mind to him. You'll always have me. I care about you allot."

Octavia hugged him tightly.

Charlemagne rose from the couch after moving her off his lap. He kissed her cheek before he left for the kitchen to order their dinner.

Octavia looked at the diamond engagement ring on her finger. She couldn't wait to marry him. When he returned to the couch, she asked, "When we get married, will you take me away from him? I feel safer with you."

"I will."

1999

Salem, Ohio

Octavia finished her last joint and entered the apartment. The robe trailed over the floor as it hung from her arms.

"The first cutting and drug session in sixteen years will be your last."

Octavia looked at the couch where Jacqueline stood with Tony looking at one of Octavia's stuffed animals.

Tony was softly rambling to the stuffed dolphin in an odd mixture of English and Italian.

"Jacqueline, I'm worried about Charlemagne. Like I told mom, he's beginning to show his age and it scares me."

Jacqueline smiled and said, "I understand. You need your thoughts clear especially after he turns into a vampire. Our ghosts will take turns guarding him during the day."

Octavia softly smiled. "Thank you. I appreciate it."

Jacqueline approached her and said, "Let's perform a spell to help you resist the urge to cause harm to yourself." Jacqueline looked at Tony and said, "Bring us some candles."

Tony set the dolphin on a chair and removed four candles from a drawer in a cabinet. He placed them around Jacqueline and Octavia forming a circle. When he passed Jacqueline, he gently ran his hand down her back, butt, and thigh.

Jacqueline nuzzled his neck and said, "Guard your brother-in-law while I help Octavia."

Tony obeyed after kissing her tenderly on the mouth.

Jacqueline and Octavia stood in the center of the circle. They worked a spell causing Octavia to lose desire to cause herself harm.

After the ritual, Octavia thanked and exchanged hugs with her sister-in-law and brother-in-law before they left.

When she entered their bedroom, she lay next to Charlemagne and tenderly ran her fingers through his hair. As she combed her fingers through his hair, grey hair broke away from his scalp and clung to her fingers. She turned on a night stand light and looked at her hand and his head. She didn't mind the bald spot. He still looked handsome even with his receding hairline. She couldn't wait until Marguerite made him a vampire. He would have the body of a 94-year-old man forever. Even his wrinkles would remain. As long as the vampirism keeps him with her, she didn't care if he remained old forever. She caressed his back as he placed his arms around her and laid his head on her stomach while he slept.

Chapter 9

Demonique de Obscuritè slowly pulled a pair of cream skintight shorts over his thin thighs. Next, he slipped on a matching blazer revealing his hairless chest. Gold chains hung around his neck and an assortment of rings was on his fingers. He used half a bottle of cologne throughout his body. On his left shoulder was Marguerite's tattoo.

Demonique looked at his street-clothes and decided against all the jewelry. He knew if his widowed mother saw all that jewelry, she would make him remove it anyway. She *didn't* want any of her men to look cheap. He was the highest paid hooker in Salem.

For three years, Charlemagne has been training him to become an assassin for Marguerite.

When Demonique first began to sell himself, he enjoyed it. It was exciting. He loved posing nude in front of a camera.

Recently, he began to prefer working for Marguerite over being a male escort. He paid more attention to Charlemagne's stories on how he became the infamous killer he was now and on past battles.

To be one of the mobsters. That was much more appealing than being a whore.

In the other two bedrooms and attic, emerged the sounds of love making.

Outside, a few cop cars passed the house with their sirens turned on creating a dancing red and blue light to shine on the houses.

Demonique glanced out of his dirty window glad the cops went up the street instead of pulling into his driveway. After being arrested for drug charges and drunk driving, he did not want to spend another night in prison.

Demonique returned to his beautiful reflection in a long mirror. He wished his mother would allow him to retire from hooking and focus more on being a mobster.

His reluctant towards the oldest profession irritated his mother. They no longer had the close mother-son relationship. She treated him like one of her whores instead of the Mafia royalty her close friend, Marguerite, wished him to be. She was still proud of him for that although, she hoped he didn't turn Marguerite down and embarrass her if something better came up.

Demonique rose and walked over to his bedroom door. As he opened his door, he heard his mother sell drugs over the phone to one of her returning customers.

He walked out of his two-story century old home and onto a street corner where he had been standing ever since he quit school. He desperately wished he could get out of this. He was tired of selling himself. He wanted more action. More danger. He only wanted one lover.

Demonique could see an ankh standing on Castle Olympia's highest towers from the other side of town. Demonique's house was located on Ellsworth Avenue only a few blocks away from downtown Salem.

A long white limo pulled up to the curb. A woman opened the passenger door for Demonique.

He slowly walked towards the car wanting this night to end.

Chapter 10

Ari was sitting in his room reading his notes on herbal remedies while listening to London After Midnight's 'The Black Cat' when Jason walked in knocking on the doorframe. Ari looked up. "Hi, dad." Ari closed the book before setting it on his nightstand. He rose off his double bed.

"I just arrived from the hospital."

Ari turned off his CD and radio. "Is Lisa alright? Can I see her now?"

"She's fine. She's just a little shaken up. Valentina and Diana are on their way over. Valentina phoned Brenda at her office saying that she would pick Diana up from the store."

Ari grabbed his book. "Do they know who did it?"

"Brenda told me that the police informed her it was a supernatural attack; we can begin our investigation," Jason replied.

"Investigation? You mean it wasn't Marguerite's usual MO?" Ari asked walking out of the room with his father behind.

#

Astredo Institution for Mental Health

Doctor Brenda Astredo placed her stethoscope back around her neck. "Can you remember what your attacker looked like?"

With Brenda; were Giovanni, Caesar, Markus, Italia, Jason, Raven, and Michelle Astredo.

Lisa was sitting in the hospital bed. She said a Wiccan prayer for her late boss once she woke up finding Brenda and her nurses checking on her. Tears came to her eyes. "It was Charlemagne. Even before he said his name, I recognized his low husky voice and his face."

Ari, Valentina, Michael, and Diana entered the hospital room as Brenda asked,

"Charlemagne *DeMarco*?" She tenderly placed her hand on Lisa's hand.

Michael stood next to Valentina.

Lisa caught herself softly smiling as Michael asked Brenda about Lisa's progress.

Giovanni sat on the opposite side of the bed and said, "That's impossible. *I* was the one who shot him."

Lisa explained the conversation between Marguerite and Charlemagne.

"Perhaps not, dad," said Jason.

"I was in the middle of analyzing my vision when Lisa called me. I feel the Gods are telling me he's still alive and Octavia is still hiding him," said Ari.

"Did you see Charlemagne in your vision also?" Valentina asked Diana.

"I only saw Lisa lying on the floor."

"If it was Charlemagne, then why hide all these years and wait until now to attack? Those murder victims from last night, did they have his trademark, Brenda?" asked Giovanni. *If* Charlemagne was still alive, he'd kill him for touching one of his girls.

"The forensic pathologist and I only had time to examine one of the ten victims since Lisa was brought in. I wanted to get to Lisa first to make sure she was alright. The woman she examined was a gypsy. Among her corpse was the king of hearts placed in the same area Charlemagne used to place his calling card on all his victims. So far, the only difference is that there was *no* sign of rape."

"Could it be a copycat," asked Caesar.

"I won't be sure until I speak with the pathologist."

Ari looked at Diana and asked, "Mom, would it be faster if one of us could get a psychic vision off the card?"

"I could have a nurse bring it up." Brenda left the room.

A moment later, Brenda returned with a blood soaked card in a plastic bag.

In a brotherly gesture, Ari placed his hands on Diana's shoulders and said, "Diana needs to practice gaining a psychic vision through touching an object, give it to her." He tenderly squeezed her shoulders.

With a pair of tweezers, Brenda pulled the card out from the bag.

The sharp smell of blood wafted into the room.

Diana stepped close to Brenda and touched the card.

A vision quickly came.

'The gypsy was attacked after she finished locking the door to her bookstore. At first, the knife was seen moving in and out of the bookstore owner. Next, a handsome man in his middle nineties appeared with grey hair and some wrinkles on his forehead and a little around his eyes.'

Still in the trance, Diana whispered, "Charlemagne."

Protectively, Ari placed his hand on Diana's shoulder and coached her through the vision. Raven had trained Ari on his psychic powers and now it was Ari's turn to help train Diana. "Don't be freighted. We're here to help you. Don't lose the vision." Ari went silent as he went into the trance and together, he and Diana saw,

'Charlemagne stood in the alley with Octavia pinned to a brick wall. He was roughly making love to her. The blood on his clothes rubbed off on her making it appears to the two young gypsies that Charlemagne was attacking *Octavia.'*

They woke from the trance finding the others looking at them with concern.

"Charlemagne was attacking Octavia. I don't know if it already happened or if it's about to. It took place in this time period." Diana looked at Ari.

"Octavia's face was nestled in his shirt. We couldn't see her expressions."

"Did either of you hear any protest?" asked Brenda.

"No. I only heard his moans. The vision didn't last," said Ari.

Giovanni looked down at Lisa and asked, "You heard him mention his wife was hiding him?"

"He said that, yes," said Lisa.

Giovanni looked at his children. Ever since his last battle with Charlemagne, after discovering he went undercover as their butler, he and Charlotte have been forgetting the times before the 1940s. That battle, right after Lotus's funeral, seemed as though he and she fought Charlemagne years before instead of just meeting him. He needed to call Charlotte.

"When did she marry that pig?" asked Michelle.

"Better question, *why* did she marry him?" said Michael.

"I don't recall. Although, with the vision Ari and Diana had may suggest that Octavia *wasn't* being attacked by Charlemagne," said Giovanni.

#

Never before had the feeling of Deja vu bothered him as he paced through his hallway. Giovanni knew his lapses in memory were *not* from old age. He knew he had argued with Charlemagne before a long time ago. Before Jason was born. He and Charlotte were still on the Island of Maeda. Giovanni couldn't wait until Charlotte arrived home so they could work on finding out why certain battles were a blur.

In his den, Giovanni dialed Charlotte's cell phone. Giovanni and Charlotte's den was decorated in blacks, gold's, and reds. His walls were deep red velvet with black and gold vines reaching from the ceiling to the deep red carpet.

In glass cases were his hunting supplies. His den and bedroom, like other parts in the castle, displayed his and Stefano's hunting trophies.

Giovanni sat at his dark cherry desk while he spoke with Charlotte over his black candlestick phone.

"Hello. Attorney Charlotte Astredo speaking."

"Charlotte, it's me Giovanni. We think Charlemagne faked his death."

There was a long pause, a deep breath from Charlotte, before she said, "Are you sure?"

Giovanni told her about the visions, the murders, and Lisa's attack.

Charlotte's voice sounded irritated. "Is he a vampire now?'

"I'm not sure. Brenda is now examining the other corpses to see if there are any fang marks."

"Keep me updated. I'll gaze through my travel crystal ball whenever I get the chance."

"I'll keep you notified."

#

Like the other rooms in the Gothic castle, Jason and Brenda's bedroom was decorated with black and other deep colors.

Jason held Brenda tightly on their blue satin sheets. He covered his wife's body with deep passionate kisses as he pushed her. At the hospital, he lured her away to make love to him during her lunch break.

Brenda's hand tenderly caressed his back and paused over his natural tattoo of the God symbol. She moaned as her climax began to rise. Her nails sank into the natural tattoo.

Jason kissed her forehead, cheek, and neck. His moans mixed with her moans and cries. He pushed her faster and harder as she began to spasm around his penis.

"Oh, oh, oh, Jason! Jason!" She bucked under him during each climax.

Jason moved in and out of her while he kissed her along her neck down to her chest. He sucked on each breast before he returned to her mouth and along her neck. "Brenda, Brenda, oh God Brenda."

Brenda's legs tightened around his waist. Her hand clutched his hair while her other hand gripped his pillow. She began to scream when he placed his finger on her clit when he continued to push her.

After they finished making love, Brenda dressed in her doctor's uniform and left for the hospital while he returned to the theater.

Chapter 11

Pulling into the castle's long driveway, Valentina stepped out of her car.

Valentina walked passed the many statues of gargoyles, Gods, Goddesses, and mythical beats towards an arched door that led into the North wing.

The early autumn air was crisp although warm with the sun in the darkening sky.

Feeling an arm coil around her waist, Valentina said, "Are you looking forward to accompanying me on this paranormal investigation?" She was turned until she was looking into Ari's sexy grey eyes. She was lost in them.

Ari led her deeper into the tall labyrinth until they were away from any view from the windows.

"Ari, I have to go to work." She tried to resist his hands caressing her back and butt.

Ari softly kissed her mouth.

Valentina's body relaxed against him and returned his kiss. If they had time, she would take her handsome witch. "I love you, Ari. I promise, when we return from tonight's investigation, I'll slowly pleasure you anywhere in the castle you want."

Valentina stepped back and watched Ari's form turn into Demonique.

Demonique grabbed her shoulders and shoved her against a bush. He was happy the transformation spell worked.

Valentina kneed him between his legs again.

He doubled over holding his crotch.

Valentina approached him. Valentina kicked his side.

Demonique attacked.

With their fists, they battled in the secluded area.

Valentina held her arms in the Goddess position.

The breeze began to blow stronger creating a small cyclone of leaves to circle in front of her.

Demonique backed up and was sucked into the cyclone. He was tossed onto the cobblestone walkway. He slowly rose to his feet swaying and feeling sick from dizziness.

Valentina approached him calming the air between them.

Demonique was about to deliver a left hook onto her face when she grabbed his wrists and pinned him against the thick green wall.

"Where *is* Charlemagne? Is Octavia hiding him?" She read his mind and found he had blocked his thoughts. Valentina tore him away from the bush and tossed him on the ground. "Where is he? Is he a vampire?"

Demonique rose to his feet quickly and backed away.

Valentina turned around and saw Ari approaching. She turned back to Demonique to find that he was gone. When Ari joined Valentina, she told him about the conversation between her and Demonique.

Ari placed his arm around her waist and began to escort her towards the north wing.

#

When they returned from the investigation, Ari brought Valentina to the castle.

Their clothes lay among the cool grass in a room made of tall hedges.

First, he went down on her, teasing, torturing her slowly with his tongue and finger. He loved fingering her while he licked her clit with his tongue.

Valentina's moans and cries mixed with the night time sounds from the woods. "Ari, oh Ari!"

Ari made her climax a few times before he mounted her. His mouth covered her body in deep passionate kisses while he pushed her deeper.

Valentina returned his kisses. She caressed his back, thighs, and butt. "Ari, Ari, oh Ari." She moaned louder when his hand cupped her breast, caressed her while his thumb caressed her erect nipple.

Ari kissed her along her neck. His tongue mixed with his passionate kisses across her skin. He moved in and out of her.

Valentina lifted her breast to his mouth.

Ari's mouth covered her nipple and sucked her as hard as he was stroking his penis.

Her legs tightened around his waist while she bucked under him. "Oh God Ari! Yes, yes!"

Ari continued to suck each breast until she was aching.

After her fifth climax, Valentina caressed his back before she moved him on his back. Her mouth moved along his chest and stomach. She sat guiding him into her. Slowly, she rocked on him before she began to grind heavily on him.

Ari caressed her thighs. His fingers caressed her clit and caused her to convulse in many orgasms.

#

Seated on their couch, Octavia was snuggled against Charlemagne with his arm around her waist.

They were speaking with Marguerite and Dante when Demonique entered. Charlemagne softly smiled and nuzzled Octavia's neck before he kissed her.

"They know Charlemagne is still alive."

"Are you certain, Demonique?" asked Marguerite.

Demonique told them about the battle between him and Valentina.

Dante said, "He's a vampire now, it doesn't matter."

The conversation changed from the Astredos to Marguerite's casinos and her side business of trafficking lycanthropes.

Marguerite said, "I want to begin preparing Octavia to become my underboss."

Octavia quickly smiled. Her face was turned towards Charlemagne's face with his wrinkled hand.

"I would love to see my little girl sit next to Marguerite as the next boss."

His touch and his low husky voice still excited her. "As long as you continue to be at my side, my love," said Octavia.

Charlemagne smiled and said, "I'll always be with you." He kissed her forehead.

Marguerite softly smiled at Octavia. The young mobster reminded her of herself when she was Elizabethan's underboss. Octavia would make her proud. She wished she had the chance to turn her other children, although Armand did everything to keep her from them. She also wished she could have turned Charlemagne into a vampire when he was younger instead now that he was an old man. She did give him a choice many years ago, but he was always indecisive.

Demonique's eyes looked at Charlemagne and Octavia. He liked the two mobsters and secretly wished he was their son. Octavia wouldn't force him to sell himself and having the Gypsy Killer for a father would be awesome. Demonique admired Charlemagne.

Reading Demonique's mind, Octavia looked at Charlemagne and noticed he carried the same thoughts. She was consumed with guilt, but quickly hid it not wanting her face to betray her.

Charlemagne felt Octavia's stare and looked at her. "Are you alright?"

"I'm ok. I'm just afraid they'll find you."

Charlemagne laughed, "If they do, I'll have the pleasure of killing them." He kissed her mouth before they turned their attention to Marguerite.

"Soon, I want to conduct a ceremony that will make Octavia my underboss."

Charlemagne squeezed Octavia's hand and said, "You've made me proud."

"I will take the title of underboss with honor." Octavia looked at Charlemagne and said, "Your sisters are wonderful spirit guides." Octavia nuzzled his neck taking in his cologne.

#

Charlemagne closed the door after Marguerite, Dante, and Demonique left. He turned and watched Octavia clean off the round glass table. Approaching her from behind, he placed his hands on her arms and softly caressed her. "Was that the only thing that was bothering you? You fear that the Astredos would find and destroy me?" His hands touched her breasts and began to caress her. His chest pressed against her back.

Octavia stared for a moment at the clean glass and the cream carpet. "Mostly that." Tears of guilt filled her eyes. She never intended to hurt him. "I'm sorry I lost the baby."

Charlemagne tenderly hugged her. Tears filled his old eyes. "It's *not* your fault. You shouldn't feel guilty. We can try again," Charlemagne kissed the side of her neck.

"I don't want to disappoint you. You made my life better."

Charlemagne moved his hands under her shirt and cupped her soft warm breasts in his hands. "You *never* disappoint me. I'm very proud of the woman you became. I was looking forward to being a father. Technically, I am *still* a father and you are *still* a mother. We just couldn't keep him and I wish we had. I miss him." He removed her shirt and bra.

"I know you do." Octavia just turned fifteen when she discovered she was pregnant after her first miscarriage. She and Charlemagne were happy. Marguerite was furious. She didn't want her son and best serial killer thrown in jail and her newly trained mobster sent to a foster home. Octavia leaned against him realizing he quickly stripped before he encaged her in his arms. His hardness brushed against her thigh. The longer he continued to massage her breast, the more she desired him. "I also *don't* want them to find you. I *don't* want to be away from you." Softly, she cried out when he entered her. She was bent over the cool table. The scent of lavender dish soap rose from the glass. Her arms were folded under her head. Her forehead touched her arm and her eyes looked at his pale feet on the cream carpet.

Charlemagne slowly stroked her while his hands caressed her back and thighs.

"Oh Charlemagne, Charlemagne!" Her body moved with his as he pumped harder and faster into her. She screamed when his fingers touched her clit and stroked her.

"Oh Octavia...you mean everything to me...oh yes, yes...Octavia!"

Octavia gasped for breath. Her thighs were struck by his fast moving thighs. Her climax began to raise.

He moaned when he felt her tighten around him. "Oh, Oh Octavia."

Octavia screamed in passion before his arm wrapped around her waist and pulled her against him. In ecstasy, Octavia trembled. "Don't stop. I want more of you."

His husky laugh turned her on. "I'm not finished with you." He turned her towards him, entered her, and carried her to their bedroom. Charlemagne laid her on the bed and covered her in deep passionate kisses.

Her hands explored his slim but aged body. She moaned and her nails dug into his back.

Charlemagne pushed her. "Scream for me."

Octavia screamed as another wave of ecstasy rolled over her. She bucked under him violently. "Charlemagne, Charlemagne, Charlemagne."

Charlemagne rolled onto his back. "Ride me, Octavia." He lay on his back with Octavia sitting astride him.

Octavia rocked on him before she began to grind. Her hands caressed his chest while Charlemagne caressed her breasts.

"Oh, oh, that's perfect...Octavia....Octavia!"   Charlemagne moved in and out of her until she climaxed with a long scream. He loved her moans and screams.

Octavia gazed down upon her lover and enjoyed his moans and cries. "Hold me beneath you."

Charlemagne held her under him while he continued to make love to her.

Chapter 12

The outdoor altar was placed around a hedge deep into the Gothic garden.

The sun was about to set over the small town.

Ari lit a candle in one of the votive hearing footsteps approach him. He brushed it off thinking it was one of the cats. When he finished with an evening ritual, he placed the athame and wand on the altar. Ari turned around feeling someone watching him. His eyes fell on Demonique's short, skintight leopard printed shorts and matching tight shirt.

Ari covered the black scrying bowl with a piece of cloth. He approached Demonique.

Demonique noticed the scrying bowl. "Charlemagne has been a good role model for me. I love him like a father. I won't let you find him." Demonique attacked Ari.

Ari kneed Demonique in the stomach and pushed him off him. He went to his side and placed his hand around Demonique's throat. "Where *is* he?"

Demonique refused to answer.

"Where is that mother fucking son of a bitch?"

Despite the pain Ari's hand was causing his throat, Demonique remained silent.

"Where's Charlemagne? Where has Marguerite stashed that asshole?"

"Charlemagne is a good man."

"He's a dirty old serial killer." Ari screamed when Demonique drug his nails down his face. Ari punched his jaw several times before Demonique tore Ari's hand away from his throat.

Demonique knocked him on his back before he was thrown against a bush. Ari's fist landed in his stomach.

His hands clasped around his throat. "Tell me where Charlemagne is."

"Fuck you!"

"Start talking."

Demonique quit struggling and said, "You're the psychic, you find him."

Ari concentrated on Demonique and tried to get a vision. A quick vision came to him. *'Valentina was held against the garden wall after Demonique had tied her hands together. Demonique intended to copy the way Charlemagne murdered his victims. He loved the idea of being a sexual predator. Before he had a chance to remove his pants, Ari punched his face.'* Ari looked deeper. Another vision came forth. *'Charlemagne led Octavia to a spare bedroom with his hand over her eyes. His hand was on her arm leading her towards the room.*

Octavia wore a brown maturity sundress. She was six months. She was led into the room. Her eyes fell on a 70's style wooden cradle when he removed his hand. She smiled. "You bought it!"

"I did. Look inside." Charlemagne softly kissed her cheek.

Octavia approached the cradle and peered inside.

A cream satin blanket lay inside with the name DeMarco embroidered in the center in red. Seated on top of the blanket was a tiny white and grey stuffed cat.

Charlemagne approached her and placed his hands on her arms. "I also picked up a book on baby names." He hugged her tightly.

"I love it, Charlemagne." Octavia turned and tightly hugged him.

Charlemagne nuzzled her neck and gently kissed her a few times.

When the vision ended, Ari gazed into Demonique's nervous eyes.

Demonique hoped he didn't see where Charlemagne was.

"You're their son? I thought Candyce was your mother."

"I *wish* I was their kid. Charlemagne would make a terrific dad."

"Yeah everyone wants a sadistic killer for a father," said Ari. "Where is Charlemagne?"

Demonique softly smiled. "I'm *not* ratting him out. *If I am* their son, I wouldn't want to place the best father in the world in danger."

"You stupid fuck! He's killed many people! How could you love that asshole?" Ari shoved him onto the ground.

Demonique attacked.

They fought again among the statues and plants.

Demonique wrestled Ari onto the ground. "Perhaps I should ask Charlemagne to finish what he began on Lisa and attack Valentina and Diana." Demonique saw the hatred and the fury in Ari's grey eyes. He backed away.

"Never threaten my family." Ari delivered a right hook into his chest.

"They're *not* your real family. You're adopted."

"Get the fuck away from my castle." Ari rose to his feet.

"This isn't over." He left.

"Fucking coward," said Ari. He returned to scrying for Charlemagne. Taking a few deep breaths, he gazed into the black water.

A soft meow from the bushes didn't distract him.

Ari's concentration was broken when a tiny kitten leaped at him. Gently, he picked up the grey tabby. He stroked its soft fur before the kitten jumped out of Ari's arms and stood away from the altar.

Ari watched the kitten change forms.

Marguerite stood in the kitten's place.

Ari backed away out of shock.

Marguerite attacked pinning him against a Roman style column with morning glories trailing down the dark marble. She caught Valentina's scent on him as well as his own masculine scent.

Embraced in her arms, Ari fought her but her vampiric strength render him motionless.

Her fangs sank deep into his neck. She drank enough to make him faint when she heard leaves crunch under someone's shoes.

Ari coughed and slid to the ground. His eyes closed.

#

"Ari!"

Hearing his name, he looked up into Valentina's eyes. He was laying in her lap while she sat on the ground.

"Should I get Aunt Brenda?" said Michael.

Valentina ran her fingers through his black hair. "He's waking. Do you need to go to the hospital?"

Michael knelt beside his older cousin. "He's feeling...I'm not sure...neutral."

Valentina looked at the fang marks on his neck. "He was attacked by a vampire."

"Marguerite. After...after Demonique and I fought. He didn't want me to find Charlemagne." Ari slid from his lover's lap.

"Let's take him inside and notify the others," said Valentina.

Michael and Valentina helped Ari to his feet.

Inside the castle, they informed the rest of the family.

Giovanni and Diana were the only ones present when Ari was sat on the couch.

Brenda was at the hospital and Jason, Markus, Raven, and Caesar had gone out for the evening.

Michelle was at Cassandra's house practicing their lines. Italia went along with Michelle before she had to be at Deadly Nightshade.

Ari began to feel better as he explained the battles between him, Marguerite, and Demonique. After he told them about the visions, he said, "I think Demonique is their son."

"What do you think made them give him up?" asked Michael.

"The only explanation I can think of is perhaps Octavia was under eighteen and Marguerite didn't want anyone to find out," said Valentina.

"That doesn't make sense," said Giovanni.

"Demonique is the same age as Diana and Adrian. Octavia would have been 23," said Valentina.

"The visions could have meant something else. I should ask Raven and Midnight's opinion," said Ari.

"We mustn't rule out all those years of Charlemagne and Octavia slipping us mind altering potions," said Michael.

Ari considered it and said, "Perhaps my cryptic visions have been real memories trying to surface."

"That's a possibility."

#

Beaver Falls, Pennsylvania

The thundering noise from a machine gun woke her after helping her experience another nightmare. Her eyes were still closed as she screamed. She moved around as though someone was attacking her. "Get the fuck away from me! Giovanni!"

Feeling a hand clasp over her mouth and someone pull her close after the bedside lamp was turned on, caused her to open her eyes.

"Grandma, it's ok. I turned the TV down." Viktor now had his grandmother in his arms as he tried to soothe her. He had been watching *Mobsters* on the second bed.

Charlotte became fully awake and watched a few moments of four mobsters gunning down a rival mob. She shuddered and noticed she had been crying. She turned her attention to her grandson.   "Why did you place your hand over my mouth?"

"I didn't want the neighbors to call the cops. You were acting as though you were being attacked. Did you dream about Charlemagne?"

"Did I say anything in my sleep?" She *wasn't* dreaming she was being attacked by Charlemagne.

"You said, 'get the fuck away from me.' You screamed for grandpa. Who was attacking you?"

Charlotte hesitated. She finally said, "Secrets in our family shouldn't be kept. Although, I am being forced to keep my past silent."

"Why? Does it have to do with Charlemagne? What *can* you tell me?"

Charlotte said, "Viktor, I made some mistakes when I was younger. Terrible mistakes. Giovanni, Stefano, your Great-Aunt Kathy, Great-Uncle Luca, your Great-Uncle Russell and your Great-Aunt Barbara, Great-Uncle Leonardo, Great-Uncle Roman, and Great-grandmother Athena are the only ones who know my past since they were the ones who helped me through it. While a gun was aimed at your father's head when he was younger, a person who I once trusted told me that if I reveal anything about my past he would murder everyone I love beginning with Giovanni. I have to keep silent to protect our family. Please understand. I wish I can tell everyone."

"I understand."

Charlotte tenderly ran her fingers through his black hair and said, "You and the others don't even know my maiden name. I was so happy to escape and to take the name Astredo."

Viktor stayed next to her until she fell asleep again. When he was sure she wasn't going to wake, he removed himself from the bed and walked towards his briefcase. He was in his black satin pajama pants and no shirt. His pentacle necklace was pewter and had a Roman design to it. Opening his briefcase, he removed his laptop. Quietly, he stepped onto the balcony.

Seated at a chair, Viktor opened his laptop and logged onto the internet.

One of his file folders under internet favorites was given the pseudo moniker 'pornography.' His cousins and his uncles had the same folder. They also shared a jump drive.

Viktor searched through his collection of genealogy web sites and sites pertaining to search engines for background checks. Not knowing Charlotte's maiden name caused the search to be impossible. Although, with their new knowledge of Charlotte and Charlemagne being longtime enemies gave them something to work with.

There was a connection.

The first four letters of their names were the same. They were both born in France around the same time. Maybe that meant something.

Viktor looked at a web page he saved a month ago of Charlemagne's criminal profile and mug shot. Going on Jason's theory, he studied Charlemagne's face after he brought up family photos taken on his digital camera in another window.   Next, he searched for a picture of Charlotte that showed her facing the camera. After going through his Samhain folder, he clicked onto the folder marked 'Adrian's sixteenth birthday party,' Viktor found a picture of her with her black hair pulled back by a purple head band as she sat next to Giovanni and Raven. He zoomed in on Charlotte's face and placed the window next to Charlemagne's face.

Next, he compared the pictures searching for any similarities.

In a separate window, he wrote, "Jason's twin theory is inconclusive. They don't look alike. Although, twins don't always look alike. And that doesn't mean they still couldn't be related."

Viktor studied Charlemagne's mug shot. He read his birth and 'death' date 1906-1983. Viktor picked up his cell phone and called Michael. "What year was grandma born?"

"1923."

"He's not her twin brother. I don't see any family resemblance." Viktor told Michael about the nightmare she had.

"Too bad grandma doesn't talk in her sleep," said Michael.

"I know. I've been watching her. Could we have Brenda or you run a DNA test?"

"I asked Jason but he told me Brenda won't do it. She and the other girls think we should give grandma some time. Grandma wants to tell us everything and like you said our lives have been threatened if she says anything."

"Our lives are threatened everyday by the mob. What's the difference?" asked Viktor.

"We think the hit will happen at once. One big mass murder when we aren't expecting it. Should we still pursue this with our fathers and uncles?" said Michael.

"I don't know. If there *wasn't* a connection between Charlemagne and grandma, I'd suggest we obey our aunts and mothers and allow grandma to have a chance to tell us when she feels fit. However, a dangerous killer may be involved with grandma's past.

We need to know everything about him. I intend to search his background more tonight. I'm hoping through this research I'll stumble upon something the crystal ball *won't* show us."

"Good idea. Keep us posted."

"I will."

"Are Valentina, Lisa, and Diana on our side with this?"

"They feel that we have the right to know especially since Charlemagne has returned. Although, they do agree that grandma should be the one to confess," said Michael.

"*Confess*. You make her sound like a criminal or something."

"Anything is possible. Grandpa just entered the room." There was a pause before Michael said, "That's awesome, Viktor. A 1934 porno magazine is all I need to complete my vintage porn collection. I still can't believe of all the porn stores in Alliance, Youngstown, Boardman, and Salem, not one of them carries *all* of the good vintage porn from that year. I'll talk to you later, goodbye."

After he hung up, he wrote a note to purchase a vintage pornography magazine to help Michael's cover. Michael did collect vintage porn, claimed it was better than some of the new stuff. Knowing this, Giovanni would assume Viktor must have told him about seeing a small adult video store and asked if he and Ari wanted him to pick up a souvenir. Viktor and the others hated to sneak around their grandparents, although, with a serial killer loose they didn't want to pursue him blindly. Also, what if Charlotte Astredo wasn't who she claimed to be?

Viktor read Charlemagne's profile with Ari's visions in mind. When he read that

Charlemagne is a registered sex offender in Cairo, Paris, and Salem, he wondered if their child had been taken away from them because of Charlemagne's record. It would make sense. After a few hours of reading articles about Charlemagne's criminal history, he was disappointed to discover nothing mentioned a child being taken away from him. Octavia was mention once and it was the night of his first arrest in Salem after Octavia had a miscarriage.

Viktor ran a background check on Octavia in Egypt, France, and Ohio.

Nothing.

He typed in her maiden name.

Nothing.

Not even a speeding ticket.

Unlike her husband, she has *never* been to prison.

Her record was clean.

As though she didn't exist.

Viktor gazed at Charlemagne's picture taken the night he was arrested for statutory rape with Octavia's picture beside his picture. He refused to believe she *hadn't* followed behind him after she grew older. She was too much like her mother. Michael could feel her evil vibrations. Charlemagne covered for her. He has sheltered her from the police and for a while even them.

After he e-mailed the information to the rest of his family, he logged off the internet and closed his laptop.

When he placed the laptop in the briefcase, he stood in the middle of the room and watched his grandmother sleep. He hated to think she could be a mobster in disguise.

There was a quick way to test. He removed his wand from their travel alter case and lightly touched Charlotte's forehead.

Charlotte fell into a deeper sleep.

Next, Viktor turned on the other lamp causing light to fill the room. He pulled down the covers just enough to reveal her bare left shoulder. Hovering his wand over his grandmother's body, he said, "Goddess help reveal any scars that may reveal an old natural tattoo. May I obtain a sign, a clue even as to what my grandmother had endured in the past? So Mote It Be."

The spell worked quickly.

To his relief, her left shoulder remained unscarred by the natural black rose tattoo.

She didn't bare Marguerite's mark...although...

Something began to materialize along her upper arm, shoulder, neck, and face. Her skin turned black, blue, yellow, and purple.

Viktor sat the wand down and threw off the covers. Next, he removed her maroon nightgown and stepped back. Tears filled his eyes as he kept reminding himself that it was only a spell. She *wasn't* in pain and the marks *weren't* really there.

Her body was covered in scars, bruises, deep cuts, and other wounds. Her right arm was twisted and at closer inspection showed at one time in her life, she had been shot either before or after her arm broke. The Triple Goddess symbol on her right shoulder appeared as though someone took a knife and attempted to rip it off.

Her face was black and blue.

Around her neck were finger marks.

Her chest and stomach were riddled with bullet holes.

Viktor studied the bullet holes and wondered if they were added over a period of time or if she was gunned down by a machine gun. There were too many to be collected over the years. If she was gunned down her chances of being alive were slim. Carefully, he looked at her back and was surprised to see the same bullet-hole pattern.

His eyes moved towards her legs. More knife wounds. A few more bullet holes. Her inner thighs bared bruises mixed with fingernail scratches. Her genitals looked the same.

Without adverting his eyes from her heavily battered body, he fumbled for his cell phone. He didn't want to call the land line phone in case Giovanni answered. Instead, he dialed Ari's number.

"Hi Viktor. What's going on?"

Words escaped him. Perhaps he was panicking for no reason. She was in her eighties. She's endured many battles with mobsters and other criminals.

"Viktor? Is everything ok?"

"I don't know. I cast a spell to see if there were any marks that showed she once bared Marguerite's mark." He explained the different wounds to Ari.   "Could they be from past battles? If I would do the spell over everyone in our family would *we* be this battered?"

"Maybe. Although, we aren't always injured too badly. If she was gunned down by a machine gun, there's no way she would be alive. Are there any signs of supernatural attack?"

Viktor studied the wounds and said, "I don't see any fang marks. If a werewolf bit her, large chunks of skin would've been torn away."   His hand shook as he matched his fingers with the nail marks on her inner thigh. "The scratches are human. A werewolf would've been deeper, longer, and larger. There's no sign of supernatural creatures."

Ari said, "It sounds as though she was beaten by a human. Multiple times."

"I was thinking the same thing. After she woke from that nightmare, she told me she made some mistakes when she was younger. What had she done?"

"She didn't tell you what the nightmare was about?"

"No. I can't tell if this was from a single person over time or more. With the way her genitals have been bruised and scratched, it appears as though she may have been raped." Viktor looked at the marks on her left arm. Needle marks were visible. "She's had heroin. It looks as though she tried it once."

"I wish I was there. I could get a vision."

"You don't want to see her under this spell. I realize she didn't receive them all at once like this, but it's still a disturbing site."

"I'll inform the others."

After Viktor hung up, he lifted his wand and removed the spell. Next, he dressed her, and pulled the covers back around her shoulders. He sat on the edge of the bed and looked at her unmarked face. Tenderly he combed his fingers through her black hair. "What happened to you? Who were you?"

Chapter 13

The next evening

While reading a fantasy novel in the large Gothic living room, Diana went into a trance.

The vision began to get hazy.   Diana tried to see what the warning was, but her mind was too clouded. She felt herself tremble a little as the vision left. She sat the novel on the coffee table and tried to bring the vision back.

She was the only one home. Raven was still out with Jason, Markus, and Caesar bowling and later, to Taco Bell. Valentina and Ari were on a date. Michael and Giovanni were at the hospital with Lisa and Brenda.

Lisa will be released in the morning.

Diana reclined on the couch, closed her eyes, and began to breathe deeply. "Goddess, help me gain the vision back. So Mote It Be."

The vision slowly came.

Octavia was at a stove placing a teaspoon of oregano and other seasonings into a small pot of spaghetti sauce.

Charlemagne approached her from behind and placed his arm around her waist. He kissed her along her shoulder as he said, "I set the table. What else do you want me to do?" His hands caressed her back, waist, and thighs.

"I'm almost finished. Just continue to touch me."

Charlemagne smiled and continued to caress her.

Diana lost the vision. She tried again.

Nothing.

Diana tried for a final time. When nothing came, she resorted to the scrying mirror that sat next to the TV.

The scrying mirror was a flat and the size of their large screen TV.

Moving a wand in front of the mirror, she searched for Charlemagne and Octavia's apartment.

The image was clear and revealed Charlemagne caressing and kissing Octavia while she stirred the sauce.

Next, Octavia and Charlemagne moved to the dinette area before the image faded.

Diana tried again. "Damn it!" she said.

The room filled with the sweet scent of lavender before a ghost of a 46-year-old gypsy woman appeared in front of Diana.

Diana rose from the couch and said, "Grandma Athena."

Athena Gaia Astredo was dressed in a maroon 1946 style dress with a black hip scarf around her waist. Gold coins dangled from the scarf. She was Giovanni's mother and the woman Charlotte loved and admired as though Athena was a Goddess instead of a spirit guide. "Diana, your visions were controlled by Octavia."

"Should I trust my visions then?"

"Not all. Octavia has recently began giving you false visions." Athena approached Diana, placed her hand on her cheek, and looked into her violet eyes. "You look so much like your mother."

"Where *is* mom? Is she with you or has she been reincarnated?"

"She's with me, Stefano, and the others." Athena removed her hand from her cheek and said, "You also look like Octavia."

Diana softly smiled and asked, "Where *is* Charlemagne? What does Ari's vision of Octavia's pregnancy mean? Is Demonique their son?"

Athena said, "My duties as a spirit guide are to guide my family, protect, to send messages from the Gods, and to act as counselor. Your questions, I cannot answer. I came with a message from the Goddess. Marguerite's successor has joined her consort on his killing spree. She will become twice as powerful as Marguerite. And for that reason, I've decided to give you advice and help you through some of your visions."

#

Charlemagne sat at the table and watched Octavia turn their crystal ball on after receiving a vision of Diana using her psychic powers to find Charlemagne.

Octavia prevented Diana to receive any more visions or images on the scrying mirror.

"What did she see?" asked Charlemagne.

"Us in the kitchen and that's all." Octavia joined Charlemagne at the table. She watched him soak his garlic bread into his sauce before consuming it. "I don't know if I can do this any longer," said Octavia.

Charlemagne looked at the plate of meatballs and said, "They weren't bad. You're improving."

"Not that. Hiding you here. Someone may follow you."

"You took care of that with that spell that made this place look empty. If someone would be foolish enough to follow the Gypsy Killer, they would deserve to die." Charlemagne reached for her hand and said, "You've hid me for sixteen years. They are *not* going to find me."

Octavia looked at her elderly husband and asked, "Are you going out tonight?"

"After I help my Octavia wash the dishes." Charlemagne tenderly nudged her foot with his foot.

"I'll watch over you."

"Don't worry; this is my last night of stalking and killing gypsies. Marguerite wants Charlotte to preview the death and destruction that will befall over those she loves." Charlemagne rose from his seat and helped Octavia unload and load the dishwasher. Next, he took her in his arms while he held her against the wall. His fingers entered her.

Octavia moaned enjoying the sensations his fingers was giving her. She cried out when his finger moved to her clit and his penis entered her.

His low husky voice whispered, "This is a preview for later tonight after we take a long sensual bath together and I carry you to our bed." He softly bit her neck.

Octavia's legs tightened around his waist as she screamed in ecstasy.

Charlemagne kissed her, reached his climax, and pulled away from her.

Octavia continued to keep her arms around his neck and her head on his shoulder. "Am I to accompany you some time?"

Charlemagne softly smiled and said, "Some night."

"Will you be taking Demonique, tonight?"

"Not tonight. He's working. Candyce and Marguerite doesn't think he's ready."

"What do *you* think?"

"I think he's ready for the small stuff. His performance while he battled Ari could've been better. I'll let him know during his next lesson," said Charlemagne.

Octavia caressed his back. While gazing into his eyes, she read his mind. "I love him like a son also. Charlemagne, you won't let me kill with you because you're afraid of me getting killed."

Charlemagne tenderly ran his fingers through her long black hair. "It would kill me if something ever happens to you. I want to protect you."

"You act as though I've *never* killed anyone. I butchered my kidnapper when he finally found me after you saved me. You can protect me all you want as long as I can join in the fun."

Charlemagne hesitated. From 1975 to 1997, she murdered eight people. She was brutal and enjoyed torturing her victims. After he healed from being shot, she was instructed to kill again. It had been awhile. He was fearful that she'd get hurt. He stepped away from her and withdrew his chef knife from the counter.

Octavia watched as he withdrew another knife from the knife rack. She smiled.

"Let's see what my little girl can do."

Holding his hand, she walked out of the apartment with him.

Chapter 14

Candyce entered his bedroom. "A new client just called. I want you to meet her at this address wearing your blue silk suit."

She handed Demonique a piece of scrap paper with a name of a motel downtown.

Demonique took it from her. "Why my blue silk suit? What is wrong with this one?" He was wearing a pale green silk suit that revealed his chest.

"She told me she preferred her hookers in blue."

"Mom, can I ask you something?"

"What?"

"Are you my *real* mother? Did you sleep with Charlemagne?"

Candyce stared at Demonique as though he grew a third eye. "Are you serious?"

"Yes."

"You *are* my son and Charlemagne is *not* your father. I've *never* slept with him.

I've *never wanted* to sleep with him. Charlemagne is a handsome man, although, he is nothing like your father. Your father *died* a few months before you were born. Besides, Octavia would mutilate me if I ever *touch* him."

"Honest?"

"I'm honest. I have your birth certificate."

"*Anyone* can fill out a birth certificate."

In irritation, Candyce said, "I don't want you to be late. *Never* accuse me of sleeping with that old pervert!"

Demonique walked behind his changing screen to put on his light blue silk suit. He kept his gold jewelry on and applied more cologne. He decided to ask Charlemagne. Sometimes, Candyce wasn't always truthful.

#

As he drove two blocks to the motel, he thought about the conversation between him and Candyce. He wasn't sure if he should trust her answers. He hoped she was lying and Charlemagne *was* his father.

In the backseat sat two body guards.

When he finally reached his distention, he left the two-armed men outside the motel door. Demonique walked into the semi-dark room wishing he was at his criminal training. Battling the good guys was more exciting then hooking. He loved the fight between him and Ari. He couldn't wait to hear Charlemagne's opinion on it.

Only one lamp was lit. Demonique announced his arrival thinking his client must be in the bathroom getting undressed. He sat down on the couch awaiting his client. He leaned his head on the back of the couch with his eyes closed. He pictured what it would be like to be a sexual predator like Charlemagne. Perhaps Charlemagne could show him how he used to tie his victims up before he raped them. Perhaps he'd practice on Valentina. Or Diana? Lisa? Whichever one crossed his path first.

"Your mother was right. You are a handsome boy."

Demonique opened his eyes and stared at the ceiling surprised by the old-world accent his client used. He felt himself tremble as he slowly rose from the couch. He could not see his client since the light was so dim, but he knew who *he* was. He backed towards the wall searching for a light switch.

"Keep the lights off!" he ordered.

He was standing in front of him now blocking the light.

He could see the outline of the man's body.

"What are *you* doing here Gerard? I'm straight and I thought you were too. I don't fuck men."

"I am straight. Bedding you *wasn't* my intentions when I set my trap. I want to prevent you from rising as Marguerite's hit man when you are old enough."

Demonique backed away. "I thought you *were* one of us."

"I don't want anything to do with Marguerite anymore. She cares more for Dante then me. My only purpose is to make sure her plans blow up in her face."

"If you kill me, Marguerite will *kill* you."

"I don't care anymore. I'm tired of being just one of her men."

Demonique screamed when Gerard sank his fangs into his throat.

For the first time in 300 years, Gerard tasted human blood and flesh. When he first became a vampire, he feasted on cattle, bags of blood from blood banks, and other legit sources.

Demonique fell limp in his arms. His blood was slowly drained from his body.

After, he drained the blood out of him; Gerard let him fall onto the bed. He walked towards the door. He opened the door on the unsuspecting bodyguards, leaving them with broken necks.

#

Charlemagne watched Octavia while she slit the throat of a small grocery store owner who was a gypsy. Before he permitted her to enter, he destroyed the security cameras. He didn't care if he was ever caught, he didn't want her to experience jail and taken away from his protective sight. He knew she wouldn't survive a night in prison. He couldn't live without her. He stood with his back towards the wall.

Octavia turned towards Charlemagne and said, "Well?"

Charlemagne smiled. "You've made me proud, as always." He stepped towards her. Charlemagne carefully wiped away her fingerprints off the counter, the victim, the murder weapon, and any place she may have touched.

Octavia smiled and said, "Do you still wish to take a bath together?"

"I'm looking forward to it." He took her by the arm and led her from the store.

While in the car, Octavia snuggled beside him with his arm around her waist.

In their bathroom, Charlemagne bathed Octavia after she bathed him. He sat behind her with his legs on either side of her.

She leaned against him and savored his sensual caresses. She said, "I enjoyed accompanying you this time."

He hugged her tightly. "I enjoyed having you by my side."

Octavia gently caressed his leg as he kissed her along her shoulder.

His mouth caressed her shoulder while his hands caressed her butt and her breast.

Octavia softly moaned.

Charlemagne kissed her shoulder and tenderly held her in his arms. His hand moved towards her clit and stroked her.

She gasped and softly cried out when he slid into her with his finger still stroking her clit.

Slowly, he stroked her. He nibbled on her earlobe and whispered, "I love you." He moaned when he felt her muscles contract around his penis.

After her climax, she was carried from the tub to their bed.

Charlemagne continued to make love to her.

#

The catacombs sat under the temple room and half of the bedrooms in the ancient castle.

Along the walls were shelves with glass covering the skeletons and bone dust of ancestors past.

Coffins of many sizes, colors, and shapes lined the floor.

Rooms with bars separating the room from the coffins line the other side. There were jail cells for mobsters and other evil creatures for interrogations before handing them over to the police.

Carrying a five candelabrum, Raven walked down the winding staircase. He walked towards the newer coffins.

Like other tombstones, theirs had a pentacle, their powers, and a brief description on the cause of death.

The 'in-law' was always dropped since every generation treated new family members as their own.

Raven approached a glass coffin with a tombstone on the wall that read: LOTUS LA SORCÈRE 1957-1983 PSYCHIC DETECTIVE. UNDETERMINED. BELOVED WIFE, MOTHER, DAUGHTER, SISTER, NIECE.

Raven placed the candelabrum on a Roman style column and placed his hand on her coffin. He gazed at her face, which had a subtle hint of decay from being in the catacombs.

Raven's mind replayed the many times he and Lotus shared together.

#

1975

Four days later

Egypt

Darkness covered the Egyptian sky glittering it with stars as the bright crescent moon hung above the pyramids and the Sphinx enveloping them with its pale light.

Lotus nervously watched him lower her sundress strap as a bonfire blazed beside them.

Raven tenderly placed his hand on her cheek, drew her face closer to his face, and kissed her passionately. His other hand removed his pants. Parting his lips away from hers, he finished removing her sundress and his shirt and underwear.

Lotus scanned his beautiful body. She loved the way the moonlight fell over him.

Enjoying the way, he respectively removed her bra, she wished her chastity belt could be that easily removed. Amari forced his daughters to where the chastity belt so they would stay a virgin until he found an appropriate mate of his choosing.

Together, they cast spells to thank The God and Goddess for bringing them together after he had made a magick circle with white candles. They danced around the campfire chanting their praises to the Gods in between the two large pyramids.

After their worship, Raven pulled her in a close embrace caressing her soft bare back. He pressed her tightly against him. They explored each other's bodies with their hands gazing into each other's desire filled eyes.

Lotus sat on a black blanket and pulled him down with her. She lay on her side combing her fingers through his shoulder length black hair while her arm circled around his shoulders.

Raven lay on his side with his arm around her waist and playfully traced her breasts with his finger. He nuzzled her neck as he moved his hand away from her breasts to her back and along her side. He laid his head on her shoulder while her hand touched his warm penis and then his backside. Raven gently rolled her on to her back laying his upper body over her. His goat-tee brushed against her chest and throat as he rested his head on her shoulder.

They remained snuggled together for hours before they dressed and he brought her home.

#

Raven stared at Lotus's coffin and tried to recall the night she died. His mind was clouded by the use of memory altering potions throughout the years. He even had trouble having psychic visions to help sort out the events that led to her death. His only memory was holding her in his arms and crying on her shoulder. Raven looked at the word 'undetermined.' It bothered him.

Footsteps walking down the stairs didn't break the widowed gypsy's concentration.

Jason approached Raven. "Do you want to talk?"

"Jason, I *can't* remember how she died."

#

Seated at his large wooden desk, Giovanni logged onto his instant massager. He was pleased to see that Charlotte was online.

In a tortoise shell ash tray, sat his cigar sending a light cherry scent around the room.

Giovanni explained the battle between Demonique and Valentina, Demonique and Ari, Marguerite and Ari, Diana's vision; her visit from Athena, and Ari's visions about Charlemagne.

"I agree with Ari's theory that some of his visions *may* be his and our real memories. When we return, you and I should go through our old grimoires for any counter spell," Charlotte wrote.

"I find it disturbing how Demonique thinks Charlemagne is a good father figure," said Giovanni.

"That's very disturbing. Do you think Demonique *is* their son?" asked Charlotte.

"I don't know. I may have Brenda check hospital records from the 70's and 80's."

"Good idea. Why the 70's?" she asked.

"I have my theories." Giovanni and Charlotte exchanged their theories concerning Ari's prophecy of Octavia's and Charlemagne's child and other things concerning the elderly psychopath and his very young gangster bride.

"I had another nightmare, Giovanni. I know our children should know. But if I tell them, we'll lose them. I don't know what to do anymore." She told him how the movie brought on the recent nightmare.

"Perhaps you should seek mom's advice," said Giovanni. He was glad Viktor was there to comfort her. Giovanni wanted to tell everyone. He hated to lie and he didn't like the way their children were 'secretly' researching her family history. He and Charlotte weren't stupid. They knew the code word among their files. Giovanni discovered the file on Ari's computer after Ari gave him his jump drive with his play so he could read and approve it. Ari forgot to delete the transferred file marked 'genealogy.' One of the file names under genealogy was marked 'pornography.' He and Charlotte spent one evening searching through the shared files. Last night, he watched Viktor through the crystal ball while he spoke with Ari and Michael. He wasn't happy about the spell he casts to expose any scars or tattoos. He was debating telling Charlotte. He never kept anything from her. He decided to tell her when she returned.

"I've considered it. Mom is a very wise woman. That's awesome how she appeared to Diana to give her some advice." She liked the way her daughters and granddaughters didn't approve of the men researching her family without hers and Giovanni's knowledge. They were a family. They researched together and shared information with *everyone*. She wanted to set a good example, although their lives were in her hands. There had to be a way around that.

"Indeed it is." Giovanni wrote next, "If you like, I can give you a good fantasy before you go to bed."

"Seduce me."

"I'm giving you a sensual massage with scented oils made from rose, ylang-ylang, and other herbs that invoke sexual desire on our gold and red satin sheets. Next, I'm spreading your legs and going down on you. I've made you cum several times before I drive my cock deep into you and make you scream my name all night." He continued to describe a passionate evening between him and Charlotte in French.

In Italian Charlotte replied back with the erotic things she would do to him. She and Giovanni made love on line for an hour before saying good night to each other.

#

Goth music blared on stage at Deadly Nightshade. Italia was scheduled to perform after the local band.

The walls were black with pictures of Gothic writers in Victorian frames.

Valentina and Ari sat across from each other in a booth.

He had his arm around her waist and was softly kisses her. Ari's hand was moving up her maroon peasant blouse towards her breast before he caressed her.

Valentina returned his passionate kisses before she asked, "Why is that vision still bothering you? So what if Demonique is their son. Enjoy yourself tonight." Her hand dropped between his legs and caressed his genitals through his pants.

Ari softly moaned and said, "It doesn't make sense. The time frame. The love they had for their baby. Who gives up a child they've *planned*."

Valentina softly kissed his neck and said, "We'll figured it out. Kiss me, Ari."

Ari tenderly kissed her as their dinner arrived.

A bottle of dark red wine sat on the table.

After dinner, they danced together.

Ari held Valentina in a tight embrace. He nuzzled her neck breathing in her perfume and the scent of her blood. While he nuzzled her neck, he felt her pulse and her blood flow through her veins. He looked at her neck puzzled by the new urge to bite her. His arms tightened around her as his sex drive increased.

Valentina rested her head on his chest and caressed his back under his black poet shirt.

Softly, he nibbled her neck. His gums above his canines began to hurt. As he gazed into Valentina's eyes, a vision came,

He was making love to Valentina on his bed. During Valentina's climax, long fangs broke through the skin and buried deep into her neck.

The vision switched to Charlemagne seated in an old wooden rocking chair holding an infant in his arms.

The baby was only a few hours old.

He looked down at his newborn with tears in his eyes.   Tenderly, he kissed the baby's forehead. "I love you," he whispered. For a while, he held the baby before he rose from the rocking chair. Next, he left the nursery and entered their bedroom.

Octavia lay in bed asleep from the pain pills Marguerite gave her after she delivered their first child.

Charlemagne placed their newborn in Octavia's arm and took a few pictures. Next he lay beside Octavia with an arm around her. He took a picture of the three of them. Charlemagne placed the camera on the dresser and lifted their baby in his arm for a little while longer.

Ari came out of the vision.

"What did you see?"

"I had two visions. I'll explain them to you when we go to my house."

#

In Ari's bedroom, Ari told Valentina about the two visions.

They were laying in his bed with their clothes scattered over the floor.

After they finished talking, Ari slowly performed oral sex on her. His tongue teased her as it moved around her clit before he began to caress it.

Valentina lay on her back moaning and gripping his purple and black sheets with her hand. She cried out when he inserted his fingers into her while he continued to please her with his mouth. "Faster Ari, faster." She began to scream when her climax finally surfaced.

Ari sat on his knees and slowly entered her and slowly pulled himself out. After a few times of moving in and out of her, she said,

"Go deeper...oh yes, yes! Don't stop Ari, don't stop."

Ari held Valentina tightly in his embrace while he pushed her. He covered her body in deep passionate kisses. He entered deep inside her causing her to cry out. His mouth circled her nipple and sucked her deeply. His teeth softly bit her nipple before he moved onto her other breast.

Valentina's nails drug across Ari's back. Her legs tightened around his waist. "Oh my God Ari! Ari, Ari, Ari!"

Ari kissed her along her throat and cried out from her muscles contracting around his penis. He continued to push her after he reached his climax.

She trembled in ecstasy as his erection returned.

For the rest of the night, they made love in a verity of positions.

Chapter 15

Salem, Ohio

Salem Animal Clinic

The door to the waiting room swung open as Lisa rushed passed a couple who were crying on each other's shoulder. Lisa had been paged ten minutes ago.

Lisa quickly entered the emergency room dressed in her black leather pants and a white poet shirt. A silver pentacle hung around her neck.

"A dog has just arrived. He has a gunshot wound to the head."

Lisa put on a pair of latex gloves as the vet explained how the dog was injured by a hunter while his owners were camping.

"Hold his head Lisa while I try to retrieve the bullet." The vet began to remove the bullet.

Another nurse said, "He's dying."

Blood began to spill onto the operating table and onto Lisa's shirt as she tried keeping the frightened dog's head steady. She began to scratch him behind the ear while her other hand held his head.

The heart monitor stopped.

The palms of her hands began to warm as serge of energy grew from her hands.

The bloody hole sealed magickally and the dog began to breathe again.

Lisa stepped back. She glanced at her hands and tried to hide her shocked expression. She couldn't wait to tell Valentina and the others. After she removed the gloves, Lisa left the animal hospital after the couple was reunited with their dog.

Lisa drove towards Castle Olympia.

Horse and unicorn farms were spread out along the back country roads.

Loreena Mckennitt played through the speakers as she drove her 1997 maroon Lincoln Town Car against the sinking sun.

Her front tire hit something. Her hands bounced off the wheel as the car swerved into a U-turn on the country road and smacked against a pole on the passenger side. Lisa stopped the car and saw blood stream down the windshield. She stepped out from the car. Her frightened eyes fell on a large blood soaked animal. She rushed to its side with a stream of blood under her white shoes. Tears filled her eyes as she gazed upon a bobcat.

The bobcat's organs were forced out from the tear in its stomach.

Lisa carefully knelt in front of it and planned to bury it. Tenderly, she placed her hand under its neck and the other hand under the bobcat's hindquarters. She stood with the bobcat in her arms and began to walk off the road and into the fields. As she searched for a place to bury it, the split torso sealed and the bobcat sprang to life.

Lisa screamed and dropped the animal. She stood in silence as the bobcat raced towards a patch of woods. She gazed at her hands and thought about the natural tattoo on her right shoulder.

Goth music blared from her pocket. She let out a startled scream before she pulled out her cell phone.

"Lisa, is everything alright? Giovanni has dinner on the table."

"I'm ok, Valentina. I hit a bobcat."

"Do you need someone to pick you up? Are you hurt?"

"I'm not hurt. The car's passenger side sideswiped a pole. A window broke."

"I'm just glad you are alright. I'll have someone pick you up."

"Valentina, the bobcat was dead, but when I touched it, I healed it."

#

Ten minutes later, Ari and Adrian picked up Lisa and her car. The car was attached to the trailer hitch on Adrian's truck.

Lisa sat in-between Ari and Adrian.

At Castle Olympia, they gathered in the dining room. Sundays, Giovanni and Charlotte gathered their family together for dinner. Charlotte carried on the family tradition of teaching the women in the family to belly dance after dinner. Italia was to take over for Charlotte until she returns. The tradition began with Olympia Astredo. After the lessons, they would practice fighting techniques in the gym across from the dance studio.

While they ate the veal parmesan, they discussed Lisa's newfound power.

"So it's official," said Michael. "You're one of us."

"She's been one of us. She just wasn't sure what she could do to help defeat the bad guys," said Caesar.

Lisa softly smiled as her eyes locked with Michael's eyes. She felt his foot brush against her foot.

"You do know what else it means to bare the Goddess mark? There're two Astredo men who are free," said Michael.

Brenda said, "Lisa doesn't *have* to date any of you. There have been ancestors whose mates *weren't* marked. It was rare that the relationships worked out, but it can happen."

"Look at Adrian and I. Adrian *isn't* marked," said Diana.

"I'm *not* in a hurry to find a husband yet," said Lisa.

Michael watched Lisa dine and speak with the others. Ever since they met in third grade, he's had a crush on her. He almost hated that he had to leave for his last semester of collage in a couple weeks. He wouldn't mind helping her through her new power.

Michelle said, "Roman Astredo left a journal as did a few others in the family who processed the power to heal. You should study it."

"I can't wait to learn more," said Lisa. She glanced at Michael and back at Brenda. "While I was waiting for Ari and Adrian, I was thinking about a career change. I would like to work in the hospital with you so I could use my powers to help more people."

Brenda smiled and said, "I'd be happy to train you as one of my nurses and give you a good reference at the hospital. Like Midnight, you could even study to become a doctor. The hospital can always use more magickal witches to help sort out the supernatural causes from the more mundane causes."

Later that evening, Jason and Raven looked at Lisa's car while the ladies were practicing belly dancing.

Her car was totaled.

Since he'll be away at collage, Michael loaned Lisa his car until she could

purchase a new one.

The men were helping Giovanni in the kitchen cleaning the dishes from dinner.

Chapter 17

The sun rose warming the city of Salem.

In the autopsy room, a forensic pathologist trained Lisa by examining

Charlemagne's newest victim.

"Why the king of hearts?" asked Lisa as she carefully pulled the Gypsy Killer's

calling card from the victim's torn body.

"That card depicts the Medieval French King Charlemagne."

Moving onto the next victim, a male store owner, they soon discovered Octavia's

finger prints. Charlemagne forgot Octavia had grabbed the store owner's wrist to prevent

him from escaping.

#

Lisa entered a vaulted hallway towards a room at the end of the hall.

The nameplate read BECKY STOKER.

Becky's long brown hair turned grey. A stroke left her paralyzed on the right side

of her body. She was English and Irish. She followed the Celtic pantheon and was a

Gardnerian Witch. She trained under Stefano and Roman Astredo after Stefano and

Roman hived off from Giovanni and Charlotte's coven to form their own in America

while Giovanni and Charlotte remained on the Island of Medea a few years to help their

cousins fight Marguerite 's crime family. She was human unlike her husband who was a

werewolf. Her daughter-in-law was a were panther and her son was human. Becky met

Charlotte after Giovanni saved Charlotte from her past.

Lisa approached her grandmother's as the old crone said,

"I see Michael was correct. A nurse's uniform complements you," said Becky. Her English accent was thick whereas Lisa's English accent faded over the years. Sometimes it was there.

Lisa softly smiled and sat next to her. "I want to use my powers in the mundane world as well as my calling."

Becky gently reached for Lisa's hand and said, "I'm proud of you. Your grandfather would be too."

Lisa lived with her grandparents since she was eight.

Becky said, "Michael, Viktor, and Ari have grown into striking young gentlemen. Which one do *you* fancy?"

"I don't want to think about men right now."

"Not every man is like your ex-boyfriend. Viktor is of stable mind. Very protective of his family. Must be the dragon spirit that surrounds him.   Ari is very passionate. Exotic. Thinks too much with his heart. Michael has an ornery strike. He's flighty although he has a good heart. Any of the three Astredo men would be a good match for you."

"Ari is Valentina's boyfriend."

"So? It's not wrong to have multiple lovers as long as it's a mutual agreement with everyone involved. One of the Astredo ancestors, a great-great grandmother, had a harem of men. One of the great-aunts had two husbands at the same time."

"I know. I only want one lover." She visited with her grandmother for a while before bringing her dinner and moving onto her other patients.

#

When her break came, she ate dinner in the small picnic area next to the parking lot.

A grey cat joined Lisa on the balcony and was soon joined by a few other cats. They rubbed themselves against her legs purring and softly meowing.   Lisa was the only nurse the cats were drawn to even if she didn't have food in her hands.

Lisa pet a longhaired black cat with a white mark under his chin that had crawled on her lap. When she finished her sandwich, she stroked the cat's fur while her other hand scratched under his chin.

At the end of her break, she returned to work.

#

After hours of passion, Charlemagne lay on his side and gently caressed Octavia's arm.

Octavia played with the blonde-grey hair on his chest.

They talked for an hour before he fell asleep.

Octavia continued to gently touch him. She slowly traced his black rose tattoo with her finger before she caressed his shoulder. Her hand touched his face after she moved to her side and placed her leg over his leg. Softly, she kissed his balding forehead. She remained in bed for a few moments before getting up for a drink of water.

Throwing on her robe, she walked out from their bedroom, down the hall, and into the kitchen.   From the cupboard, she pulled down a glass and turned on the facet.

Octavia lifted the glass to her mouth and was struck from behind by a club. She fell to her knees as the glass fell from her hands and shattered on the floor. Her scream was muffled by his foot striking her throat. Octavia fought back once she was able to stand. Her throat exploded in pain. She was unable to scream. She threw her attacker against the wall upsetting pictures and other wall ornaments.

He swung a large frying pan at her after he picked it off the floor.

She fell into the dinette area and landed on the chair. The frying pan hit her chest again. She kicked his stomach and was finally able to scream for Charlemagne. She stepped away from his strikes and heard Charlemagne remove himself from the bed.

He quickly threw the pan onto the floor and tackled her. They fought on the carpet. Kicking. Punching. He pinned her to the floor using his hands as shackles. He sat on top of her.

Octavia screamed when he revealed his fangs to her.

A rifle blast stopped him from tearing her throat apart. Gerard was knocked off Octavia by the bullet striking him.

Charlemagne stepped into the living room wearing his black satin robe. He focused his gun on Gerard.

Gerard rose to his feet and waited for his arm to heal.

"It was a silver bullet, Gerard. The poison will be coursing through your veins soon." Charlemagne approached him and stuck the gun under his chin. "Octavia, are you alright?"

Octavia carefully moved herself into a seated position. Her chest hurt worse than any place else. "I think so."

"Sit on the loveseat." Charlemagne turned his attention to Gerard. If he had killed

Octavia, Marguerite would've found pieces of him throughout Salem. Charlemagne jammed the barrel onto his throat. "For attacking Octavia it doesn't seem fair if I just shoot you. I think I'm slowly going to torture you."

Octavia pulled a thin blanket off the back of the loveseat and worn it like a shawl to cover her nakedness. She was in too much pain to walk. Once the pain ceased, she wanted to torture Gerard.

"I can't allow Octavia to rise as Marguerite's successor. This has to end."

"Sit."

Gerard slowly sat on the couch. His arm was covered in blood. The barrel was now level with his eyes. "Charlemagne, don't kill me over some woman. We've been friends longer then you two been together."

Anger flashed in his eyes as well as Octavia's eyes. He sounded too much like Amari.

"Octavia, do you feel strong enough to help me tie this asshole up?"

"I do. Can I get my robe first?"

"You can."

Gerard watched her leave for the bedroom and return a second later wearing a black satin robe that matched Charlemagne's robe. The silver was making him feel weak. "I didn't think you cared that much about her. You told us you would never stick to one girl."

"Remove his shirt and pants. I want him to feel what I felt when he hit me," said Octavia.

Charlemagne ordered him to obey Octavia. "Remove your underwear."

Gerard slowly obeyed.

Octavia tied his hands and feet together as Charlemagne said,

"That was *before* I met Octavia. I don't want anyone else. She loves me more than anyone else ever did."

Charlemagne lowered the rifle, leaned it against the wall, and gently placed his hands on Octavia's arms. "Are you still in pain?"

"It's subsiding. I'll be back." She softly kissed Charlemagne's mouth.

"What is she doing?" Gerard looked at Charlemagne nervously.

Charlemagne watched Octavia enter the kitchen. He turned his attention to Gerard. "Remember how sadistic Esmeralda was? My Octavia would make her proud."

Gerard screamed for Marguerite.

Charlemagne softly smiled and said, "I'm discovering allot of interesting things as a vampire. A wooden stake won't kill us, only paralyzes us until the stake is removed. Sunlight could destroy us. My wounds heal although I can still experience pain. Mortal weapons can't kill us, but the pain will linger for a while."

From the kitchen, came the scent of grease from a fryer.

"Marguerite won't allow you to torture me. I'm one of her lovers."

"Dante is her favorite."

Gerard suddenly prayed Charlemagne would never find out what he did to Demonique.   Gerard nervously watched Octavia enter the living room with the frying pan in her hands.

"Hold his hands above his head," Octavia said.

Charlemagne obeyed.

Gerard screamed when the hot fraying pan slammed onto his stomach after Octavia dumped the boiling oil onto his exposed penis. He was struck again. And again.

The oil burned the flesh off his penis and balls.

Large circles appeared on his chest from where the frying pan burned him.

He continued to scream when Octavia hit him again.

Charlemagne watched with a proud expression on his face. He sat on the arm of a chair and watched.

"Charlemagne control her!" screamed Gerard.

"I don't believe in dominating women. Octavia is my equal. Whatever Octavia wants I'll give to her. When she becomes mom's underboss, I am going to give her the best body guards and spoil and pamper her."

"Enough Octavia," said Marguerite when she appeared magickally in the living room.

Octavia stopped and sat on Charlemagne's knee when he sat in the chair.

"Marguerite, he was allowing her to torture me."

Marguerite approached Gerard and slapped his face. "That was a foolish thing to do. You know he's *very* protective of Octavia."

"I intended to attack Charlemagne next.   Don't you think this has gone on long enough? Can't we die normally? I hate out living friends and family."

"The legacy *will* continue and I will have my warriors. If you want out I'm *not* stopping, you. I don't need you. I don't take the opinions of men seriously." She turned to Octavia and Charlemagne.

Octavia was cuddled against him with his arms around her waist.

Charlemagne nuzzled her neck and softly kissed her. He was relieved she was alright. Gently, he hugged her.

"You may finish what you started on him," said Marguerite.

Octavia rose from Charlemagne's lap after she kissed him.

Charlemagne followed Octavia to the couch while Marguerite sat on a chair to watch Gerard slowly become tortured by the two mobsters.

After Gerard's body was dumped into the Ohio River, Charlemagne slowly removed Octavia's robe after he removed his.

She was already showing bruises on her stomach and chest. Her breasts were swollen, yellow, blue, and black from the fraying pan. She winced from Charlemagne's gentle touch after he cleaned her wounds and made her an ice pack. She lay in their bed with the ice pack on her chest.

Charlemagne lay beside her and placed his arm under her and tenderly pulled her closer. Tears filled his eyes. It reminded him too much of the morning he found Octavia near death.

Octavia brushed his tears away with her fingers. "I'll be alright. The ice and your touch are helping. Mostly your loving touches." She rested her head on his shoulder.

Charlemagne combed his fingers through her hair as he watched her fall asleep.

In her sleep, she snuggled against him. She remained in his arms when he fell asleep.

#

Brenda waited for Jason in their private place in the Gothic garden.

Jason opened the vine covered door before he sat on the stone bench and pulled her on his lap.

She placed her arms around him. "Cassandra just called. She's picking Michelle, Italia, and me up in an hour to have dinner in the new Mexican restaurant downtown. Ari is watching Scarlet, Dario, and Rosa since Valentina had to work and Adrian is rehearsing lines with Michael and Aaron." She passionately kissed his neck and shoulders while his hand traveled up her black leather skirt caressing her leg. She couldn't get enough of him.

Jason kissed her a few times on the mouth. "Do you want me to wait up for you?"

"Only if you want to. Caesar and Markus has no plans for tonight, so maybe you guys can do something." Brenda brushed her lips across his forehead touching him everywhere.

"Maybe I will see if they want to watch a movie or something." He gazed deeply into Brenda's desire filled eyes while his hands explored her body.

Brenda ran her fingers through his short hair before moving her hand down his back. Her other hand touched the crotch of his pants.

"I may wait up for you," he said smiling.

They made out in the garden until Cassandra arrived at the castle.

\#

Cassandra ordered another margarita as live Mexican music played on a stage.

A mixture of Aztec and Inca Gods and Goddesses statutes and pictures decorated the restaurant.

Italia sat next to Cassandra drinking a long island ice tea.

Brenda and Michelle sat across from her. Brenda drank a strawberry daiquiri while Michelle drank a glass of peach ice tea, no alcohol.

They continued to talk and have a few drinks until the restaurant closed.

The small town grew silent as they walked to the car.

Cassandra handed Michelle the keys to the car. She, Italia, and Brenda weren't drunk, only a little tipsy.

Michelle opened the driver's side just as a few foot soldiers approached them.

There were only three with long swords.

Brenda grabbed her sword from the backseat. Her sword bared turquoise stones on the handle. Her turquoise tinted blade held the Goddess chant Isis, Astarte, Diana, Hecate, Demeter, Kali, Inanna. The blade caught the glare of the moonlight.

Michelle's sword bore the image of the Goddess Nekhebet with moonstones. The mother-of pearl tinted blade bore the Goddess chant.

The pewter handle on Italia's sword bore Alchemy symbols. The Goddess chant ran along her rose-colored blade.

Cassandra withdrew her sword. Her sword wasn't made by the Gods as the others. Her sword was made into a Greek design with pearls on the handle and the Goddess chant along the sea-green blade. She didn't bare the Astredo's mark, although, she carried weapons in case she would be attacked for having friends and three daughters who were marked by the Gods.

Around the parking lot, they fenced with the mobsters.

Cornering a mobster, Michelle swung her sword at his arm that held his sword.

The mobster's hand severed from his body and dropped to the pavement.

Michelle impaled the mobster.

Italia decapitated a mobster with one swing of her blade. When she saw a mobster sneak behind her little sister-in-law, she quickly impaled it.

Brenda looked at the black top between her and the gangster. She moved her hand over the ground.

Water pooled between them before it turned into ice.

Brenda delivered a left kick into a mobster's side causing him to fall onto the ice dropping his sword. Her turquoise blade sliced the mobster's head off. She joined her sister-in-law just as Cassandra defeated her mobster.

With Michelle in the driver's seat, they left for the castle.

Chapter 17

A cold breeze blew over the city as Salem began to wake.

Aaron stepped out from the car with Dario. He arrived at the theater before the others.

Adrian was taking Diana on a breakfast date before he drove her to the palm reading parlor.

Dario wanted to try out for a small role in Ari's horror play.

The scent of popcorn, pizza, and nachos still lingered in the air from last night's production.

Dario left his father's side to check out the costume room and hang out in the large prop room until Ari and the others arrived.

In his office, Aaron looked through his directorial notes while he sat in his black leather chair.

When the clock reached eight, Aaron set the script on the desk and walked out of his office. He was expecting a delivery for new props. As he walked down the hall and down the stairs, he heard Dario playing with the cap machine guns where the props from the 1930's were stored.

He entered the lobby and towards the double stained glass doors that led into a foyer before the outdoors. His hand touched the decorated doorknob just as his arm was grabbed. He was forced against the glass with a large knife under his throat. He kneed his attacker in the stomach before escaping to protect Dario. He made her chase him upstairs so she wouldn't attack Dario.

Octavia pursued after him holding Charlemagne's knife.

Terror filled him when he no longer heard Dario play in the large room. He knocked a small column over.

Octavia stepped over the column and continued to pursue him. She followed him into his office where he opened his desk drawer for his gun.

Aaron's hand was slammed in the drawer. He screamed the harder she pressed the drawer onto his wrist. His other hand grabbed a letter opener and stabbed her with it.

Octavia backed away. Blood trickled down from her shoulder.

His hand throbbed and it almost made him scream when he tried to lift it out from the drawer. He was about to use his other hand to reach his gun when her knife sliced his wrist. Blood gushed out onto the desk and the floor. He backed away. His hands bursting with pain. "Where's Dario?" he asked hoping the thirteen year-old was quietly playing downstairs. The loss of blood weakened him. He backed against the wall.

"He's visiting with Marguerite."

"Marguerite," his voice grew weak.

Octavia held the knife to his face and teased him with it. "She's a very powerful vampire. Unlike Charlemagne, she can be out in the sunlight." She drug the blade lightly over his cheek and down his neck.

A thin line of blood appeared over his cheek and down his neck.

Aaron screamed when she stabbed him in the shoulder before she drove the knife deep in his chest.

Octavia pulled the knife out of him and pushed him onto the floor. She watched him chock on his own blood before he lay still on the carpet.

#

Cassandra laid Scarlet in her crib before she walked downstairs to the kitchen. On the counter, she wrote Valentina a note explaining she needed to go to the theater early.

The ride to the theater was quick since most of Salem hasn't woken yet.

When she drove in the parking lot, she noticed only Aaron's car in the parking lot. It would be another thirty minutes before the others arrived.

She entered the backdoor and was surprised to find it quiet. Normally, Dario would be making some type of noise. Cassandra set her purse on one of the lobby chairs and left for the prop room.

The prop room could be a full apartment. The props were arranged by time era. The furniture and other items were designed from ancient times to the present.

Cassandra passed the different styles of props until she saw Dario lying on a Victorian era couch. She ran to him and knelt beside him.

He appeared to be sleeping but his stillness mirrored the old-fashion Victorian post mortem photos.

Tears filled her eyes as she placed her hand on his cheek and turned his face towards her. Her eyes fell on the two fang marks on his neck. Her tears fell heavier as she held her son close for a few minutes. A part of her died. She laid him down again.

Anger coexisted with her heartbreak. She searched the prop room for something she could use as a wooden stake. The wooden stake used in the play 'Dracula' was collapsible. She walked towards an area that held ancient Roman props. She broke one of the spokes in a chariot. Quickly, she rushed towards Aaron's office with the stake in her hand.

Her scream echoed throughout the theater when she discovered Aaron covered in his blood. In shock, she stared for a moment at what was left of her husband. She turned to find Marguerite standing in the doorway. She attacked her with the stake.

Marguerite fought back. She grabbed her wrist that held the stake.

Cassandra kicked her knocking her into the hallway. She sat on top of Marguerite and stabbed her with the stake.

Marguerite softly smiled and grabbed the stake with her hand. "I'm too old for this to have any effect on me."

Cassandra grabbed the top of the stake and pressed down so it could go deep enough to have its paralyzing effect. She felt the nozzle of a gun rest on her temple.

"Let go of the stake," said Octavia.

"I'm ending this," said Cassandra.

"I *don't* want to kill you like this. I *don't* like a quick death. But, if you stake Marguerite, Jason and the others are going to discover your brains splattered on the wall."

Cassandra released the stake and slowly rose to her feet. The gun followed her.

Marguerite rose from the floor. She held the stake in her hand.

Cassandra backed away.

"Stop her Octavia."

Octavia fired a bullet into her knee sending Cassandra against a wall.

Blood flowed down Cassandra's knee as pain shot through her body.

Marguerite approached Octavia and said, "She's yours. I want you to have more practice with your victims."

Octavia approached Cassandra. She grabbed her arm and said, "I'm not killing her in the hallway. It won't be any fun."

Cassandra struggled. With her good knee, she tried kicking her. Octavia overpowered her since the pain almost made her immobile. Before she could scream, Octavia placed her hand over her mouth.

"Normally, I love to hear my victims scream, although, I don't need you drawing any more attention to us." Octavia forced her downstairs, down the lobby, through the carved double doors, down the aisle, and onto the stage. She threw her in a chair that was to be used in a 1940's crime-drama.

Terror filled her eyes when she noticed shackles were attacked to the chair. A gag was suddenly stuck in her mouth. She fought her.

Octavia struck her with the gun before placing her hands and feet into the shackles.

Cassandra screamed hoping to alert anyone walking passed the theater. She watched Octavia pick up a thread and needle off a tray.

"Charlemagne once told me how he hates the way gags only muffle screams. His torture stories gave me inspiration to experiment with a way to keep a victim silent if need be," said Octavia.

Cassandra noticed Marguerite standing at the entrance acting as look out. Her terrified eyes locked with Octavia's innocent seeming violet eyes. She screamed when the needle first penetrated the corner of her mouth.

"Don't jerk. You don't want me to mess up. I'll just have to start again." Octavia tightly sewed Cassandra's mouth closed after she removed the gag. Octavia looked at her work, pleased. "I can't wait to tell him my idea worked." Octavia picked up her knife.

The knife was covered in Aaron's blood.

Cassandra watched helplessly as Octavia stood before her staring at her husband's knife. She wondered if Charlemagne forced her to kill.

Octavia lifted her gaze from the blade, stepped closer to Cassandra, and swung the knife at her chest causing a line of blood to appear. "I'm tired of everyone thinking I can't make my own decisions! Charlemagne has *never* forced me to do anything. I grew up with parents who were Marguerite and Dante's head assassins! I've watched many hits when I was younger. I've always wanted to be like mother." Octavia set the knife down and picked up the gun. Beating Cassandra's face, she said, "I'm *not* a child! I'm *not* innocent! I committed my first act of murder when I was *fifteen*!" Octavia broke Cassandra's nose and gave her a welt across her eye. She replaced the gun with the knife.

Blood seeped from the places were the gun struck. Her eyes socket was a puddle of blood.

Octavia touched the tip of the knife onto Cassandra's wrist and began to slice deep into the skin. "Do you *still* think I'm innocent...No? Good...During Lotus's wake, were you surprised to learn that I was working with Charlemagne?" Octavia smiled and continued to read her mind. "So everyone thought Charlemagne left town and I was his prisoner. Everyone thought I was acting nervous because he creped me out. No, I was nervous because it was my first undercover job and I was afraid Charlemagne, with him being so protective of me, would blow our cover. That's why he was staring at me. He wanted to make sure nothing happened to me."

Cassandra's thoughts became clouded. She was too weak to scream. '*Just kill me. End my suffering,*' she thought.

"You call this suffering? You have no fucking clue what suffering is! You *didn't* have a father who sold you to a mobster to cover a debt. You *weren't* kidnapped on your wedding day and fed a verity of drugs and beaten to keep you quiet. I spent four months away from Charlemagne not knowing if I was going to see him again."

Cassandra read her thoughts and found she was thinking about the evening she and Charlemagne planned to elope after Esmeralda instructed them *not* to wait another week to get married. Octavia chose a white sundress from her closet and waited for Charlemagne on her balcony. She was only fifteen. Cassandra couldn't understand why Esmeralda was so determined to allow her daughter to marry a sixty-nine-year-old serial killer.

Octavia changed her thoughts to how Charlemagne's loving embrace made her feel loved and protected. She tried not to need a joint or to mutilate herself to erase those bad memories. Charlemagne always told her just to think of happier memories. She thought of him. The only happy memories she had were of him and everything they've done together.

"Octavia, hurry. I don't want them to find us," said Marguerite.

Octavia slit Cassandra's throat before she left with Marguerite.

Chapter 18

Viktor was dressed in a black poet shirt and black leather pants. A pewter ankh hung around his neck.

Charlotte entered the castle after her grandson. Her suit dress was black with a red blouse. Her gold pentagram necklace had a ruby in the center of the star.

Giovanni met his wife and grandson in the large hallway. He gave them a tight hug.

"We were excused, but after the funeral the judge wants us to return," Charlotte said.

Giovanni tenderly nuzzled her neck as he pulled her into his embrace again. "I missed you."

"I missed you." She kissed him a few times on the lips before they entered through the living room and into the dining room where the others sat.

Viktor said, "I can't wait to retire. I want to be available in case you and the others need me."

"Charlotte can't wait either."

Later, Charlotte and Giovanni dressed in white robes while the rest of their coven dressed in black and white.

Charlotte and Giovanni delivered the Wiccan funeral service in their outdoor garden temple.

When Aaron, Cassandra, and Dario's bodies were brought to the hospital, Raven received a vision of their attack as well as Marguerite attacking Dario and the conversation Octavia had with Cassandra before she killed her.

Dario was discovered with two fang marks on his throat after Jason and Caesar found Aaron in his office and Cassandra on stage.

Valentina stood in the circle closest to the caskets holding Scarlet. She leaned against Ari listening to Caesar, Markus, Jason, Raven, and Giovanni talk about Aaron, Cassandra, and Dario with tears in their eyes.

Brenda held Rosa.

Lisa and Diana stood beside Caesar and Michelle. Diana's gypsy dress was white trimmed in silver. Raven wore a black poet shirt with wide sleeves and medieval style paints. They wore a pentagram with three crescent moons around the circle representing the Triple Moon Goddess.

After the triple funeral, Ari, Viktor, Michael, Lisa, Caesar, and Raven carried Dario's small coffin and Michelle, Brenda, Jason, Giovanni, Midnight, Adrian carried Aaron's double silver coffin with Cassandra lying next to Aaron with his arm around her waist and her head on his shoulder.

After the coffins were placed in the catacombs, Ari found Valentina in the garden.

Valentina approached a wrought iron gate that encircled the outdoor entrance to the catacombs. She looked at the castle not noticing Ari approaching her from behind. Ari placed his arm around her shoulder. "Valentina, is there anything you want me to do?"

Valentina placed her arms around his waist and cried on his shoulder. She could no longer hold it in. She hated crying in front of people. But, Ari was different. He knew she was a strong person. "Just hold me," she whispered.

Ari held her tightly as he ran his fingers through her hair. His embrace was relaxing and soothing. He told her he would do anything to help her with Adrian and her younger sisters. He placed his hand on her cheek lifting her face to make her tear-filled eyes gazed into his.

Ari softly kissed her cheek as a tear run down his cheek.

She gave him a gentle hug.

Ari hugged her back tightly as they cried on each other's shoulders.

The air was cold making the rain feel like ice as it blew on Valentina and Ari. Ari unbuttoned the small round buttons on his black trench coat allowing her to snuggle inside his coat. His body heat kept her warm as the wind blew harder and the sky grew darker.

Ari rested his head on her shoulder as he held her in a brotherly way.

She did not want out of his arms. She felt protected and relaxed. She watched their family return into the castle. Valentina did not want to leave the garden yet. She was too comfortable in his arms.

She buried her face in his warm chest.

Ari nuzzled her neck and slowly rocked her in a close embrace. Around him, the sights, smells, and sounds of the garden and the country air were heightened. He suddenly caught the scent of vampire.

It was in the mid-fifties although to Ari, the sun felt hot as though it were a scorching summer day.

Valentina noticed his mind was expressing many thoughts. "Are you alright?"

"I don't know. I smell vampire."

"You don't have that type of power. You're human."

"Can we go inside?"

"I suppose. Are you sure you're ok? You know you can tell me anything."

"I know I can." He told her about the strange sensations he'd been experiencing since he was attacked by Marguerite.

"Did you drink her blood?"

"No. That's why I don't understand why I'm showing symptoms of vampirism."

"Let's go inside and talk about it with the others. This shouldn't be kept from the rest of the family," said Valentina. She escorted him into the castle.

#

Octavia and Marguerite watched from a tower.

Marguerite was pleased with Octavia's performance lately. She noticed Octavia was staring at Ari.

"Why is he slowly turning into a vampire when Charlemagne's transformation was quick?" asked Octavia.

"I didn't get the chance to finish it. I will."

"Why don't you just kill him?"

"It'll hurt Valentina more having a lover she'll have to vanquish when he starts feeding off her family."

Octavia smiled and said, "I love your mind games."

#

Hours after the wake, Viktor, Ari, Michael, Jason, Markus, Caesar, and Raven gathered in Ari's den.

Viktor said, "Those bullet wounds bother me the most. As a lawyer, I've seen many gruesome crime photos but this was nothing." He paced the room while the others sat on Ari's black leather office furniture. "At some point in her life some asshole raped her. I hate sex offenders. They all deserve to have their dicks sawed off! I wish Aunt Brenda and the other women would side with us."

Ari said, "Did you bring anything of grandma's so I can receive a vision?"

Viktor handed him a tube of lipstick from her purse.

Ari held the lipstick and received a vision.

1940s

Island of Medea

Dressed in a lilac suit dress, Charlotte stormed through an office of a casino. Her long black hair was styled like Veronica Lake's peek-a-boo hairstyle. In Italian, she was yelling at a man behind a desk.

The man was older, mid-fifties. Built like Al Capone. Black suit. Black fedora hat. In Italia, he argued back.

Charlotte seemed to be pleading with him at the same time telling him to fuck off. She stood behind his desk and watched him rise from his chair. She back away when he gently reached for her arm. Still in Italian, she said, "Get the fuck away from me! I hate you! I don't want anything to do with you!"

The man forced her into his arms and gently wiped her tears away with the back of his hand. He spoke to her softly.

Charlotte struck his chest several times with her fists. She argued with him. Her arms hung around his neck involuntarily.

He tenderly rocked her in his arms caressing her back. He kissed her cheek. "Charlotte, you belong to me."

"I belong to no one."

He moved his gaze to another mobster who entered the office.

Charlotte stopped struggling when she saw a foot solider. Her eyes fell on the machine gun he held in his hands. She looked at the senior mob boss and said, "Let go of me."

He smiled and shoved her into the center of the room and into the gangster's gun fire.

She screamed before she collapsed onto the floor.

The vision showed Giovanni, aged in his early twenties, carrying Charlotte into a bedroom in the old family castle in the jungle along the small island. He laid her bullet-riddled body on the bed and called for Stefano and Roman. He held her on his lap crying on her shoulder.

A 25-year-old man entered the room with his boyfriend following behind. Roman Astredo recently married Stefano in a private handfasting ceremony performed by Athena. Roman rushed to the bedside and said, "I can't heal the dead, Giovanni. I'm sorry."

"She's not dead yet. Roman, please try," said Giovanni.

Stefano placed his hand on Roman's back, softly caressed him, and said, "You can do this."

Tears filled Roman's eyes. Recently, he discovered he had the power to heal. "Lay her on her back."

Giovanni obeyed. His clothes were covered in her blood. He held her hand tightly.

Roman held his hands over the wounds and concentrated. Heat flowed from his hands and a blue light surrounded her.

Bullets dropped out from her skin as her body healed.

Charlotte began to breathe again.

When she was completely healed, Roman, Stefano, and Giovanni tears of relief fell from their eyes.

Stefano tenderly took Roman's arm and said, "We should leave them alone. Charlotte will need space from what they did to her."

Roman quietly stepped out of the room with Stefano.

Charlotte woke finding Giovanni next to her. She sat in the bed. Heavy tears fell from her eyes. "Why did you save me? I'm not worth it. I'm not worthy to bare the Goddess's mark. Why didn't you let me die?"

Giovanni gathered her into his gentle embrace and said, "You are worth everything to me. I love you."

Charlotte held him close and cried on his shoulder.

Giovanni caressed her back and softly kissed her forehead. "You're with us now. This is where you belong."

"Help me. I feel so lost."

Giovanni hugged her tightly while she cried on his shoulder.

Ari woke from the vision with his cousins, uncles, and father watching him. Tears were in Ari's eyes when he told them about the vision. "I couldn't understand what they were saying. It was all in Italian. Grandpa, Roman, and Stefano spoke English. The men Charlotte were with, their features were a blur."

"She *was* gunned down," said Viktor.

"By who?" asked Jason.

Ari's door opened and Giovanni stepped in causing conversation to arrive at a halt. "I'm glad to see that my boys are gathered in the same room. You wouldn't be discussing your shared 'pornography' file, are you? I found that file to be quite interesting. It contained *no* porn. Care to explain why my boys are acting like a group of manipulative mobsters instead of the honest witches I thought Charlotte and I raised? At least our girls have the decency and the *respect* to allow Charlotte to tell her secret when she's ready," said Giovanni.

A mask of guilt covered their faces.

"Dad; Markus, Caesar, and I started the investigation. We have the right to know. How do you and mom expect us to protect the world from evil when we don't know who or what we are fighting," said Jason.

"Do you think your mother is a mobster?" asked Giovanni.

They hesitated before Viktor said, "I was beginning to think she was which is why I cast the spell to reveal any scars. I wanted to see if Marguerite's mark would appear."

"And did it?" asked Giovanni already knowing the answer.

"No. But every wound she'd ever had appeared."

Giovanni said, "Charlotte and I watched you, Viktor, through the crystal ball. She's not happy."

"Why can't she tell us?" asked Ari.

"You mustn't concern yourself with your grandmother's past now. It is unwarranted at this time since we have a serial killer to capture."

"What is stopping her from telling us?" asked Jason.

"You know why. Charlotte is working on a way around the threat. She wants to inform you. But there are forces preventing her from doing so. Promise me you will stop this. Give her time. Through Ari's vision and the spell, you've had a small preview of the tormented life Charlotte had before she discovered what the tattoo on her right shoulder meant. So now, just back off."

Jason said, "We promise. We didn't mean any disrespect. We are just concerned."

"The truth will be out soon," said Giovanni.

Later, they gathered in the living room where the rest of their family sat.

#

Dusk slowly crept across the corn fields and the ancient castle.

Among the red and gold satin sheets, Giovanni brought her to her final climax. He remained laying above her holding her in a gentle embrace.

Charlotte softly caressed his back and turned her head to look at the alarm clock. They had another ten minutes before she and Viktor had to leave.

Giovanni rested his head on her shoulder after he kissed her mouth again. "Are you sure you can't talk the judge into allowing you and Viktor to return tomorrow?"

"I'm sorry, I can't. I would like to. We all have to stay together." She caressed his back wishing they had time to make love again. After the wake, they returned to their bedroom to change out of their ritual robes. When she began to tell him about the nightmares of her past, his comforting kiss led to him carrying her to their bed.

Giovanni gazed down at her. "I love you, Charlotte."

Charlotte smiled. He was the first to have ever say 'I love you' and mean it. She kissed him and said, "I love you, Giovanni." She hugged him tightly as Viktor knocked on the door.

"Hey grandma, we have to go. I'm getting impenitent."

"You were *born* impenitent," said Charlotte.

Giovanni hugged her, moved off her, and said, "Just like his grandmother."

Charlotte climbed out of bed and quickly dressed, "I'm improving."

Giovanni joined her at the door after he dressed. He gently held her in his arms. "I'll miss you."

"I'll miss you." After she kissed him, she and Viktor left.

#

After Charlemagne rose from his coffin, he entered the spare bedroom they used as a temple room. He was in his underwear. Opening the closet, he looked at the wooden crib he had purchased. Tears filled his old eyes. He reached in and lifted the cream colored baby blanket. He looked at it and wished it still held their child. Setting the blanket back in the crib, he walked towards the window and looked at the city. Tears fell from his eyes deeply regretting giving him up. He was stupid for finally listening to Marguerite.

He also missed Demonique. His protégé.

The door to the apartment opened and closed and soon he felt Octavia's arms around his waist and her head on his bare back.

"Marguerite told me I did an excellent job with Aaron and Cassandra's murder."

Charlemagne softly smiled and said, "I wish I was there to see it."

Octavia hugged him, kissed his back, caressed his chest with her hands, and read his thoughts. Now that she is older, she was beginning to understand why her mistake hurt Charlemagne. She said, "Marguerite has been more of a mother figure to me than Esmeralda was. I did what I did to impress her. I wanted to please Marguerite so I could receive the motherly love Esmeralda *never* bestowed upon Lotus or me. I didn't realize what I was doing."

"It's *not* your fault. I was *never* angry with you. It's more my fault. I should have waited until you were older before we had a baby."

"I'm 39; we have time to try again. I promise Charlemagne it will be different. We could keep it this time. We wouldn't have to get rid of it." Octavia moved around him and stood in front of him. She held his hands in her hands.

"We can although, I'm 94. It won't be easy. We *can't* adopt. Not with my criminal record."

"I've never meant to hurt you."

"I know. I forgive you." Charlemagne placed his arms around her and pulled her closer to him.

Octavia looked into the eyes of her beloved. His ice blue eyes seemed almost grey in the dim light. The crow's feet framing his eyes added to his sexiness.

"Our son is *still* out there, Octavia. I want to find him and bring him back to us," said Charlemagne.

Chapter 19

Dusk began to settle over the Gothic garden and the ancient castle as well as the small town.

Brenda walked down the hallway in the hospital.

Above each door were call lights in shapes of pentacles and ankhs. One side pentacles and the other ankhs.

Statues of Gods and Goddesses were placed throughout the hospital as well as Pagan themed pictures and shrines.

She met her head nurses outside a door.

Nurses Collins and Bernadette worked in the hospital as long as Brenda had. They were humans.

"How is he?" asked Brenda.

"He's still in a coma," said Nurse Bernadette. She and Nurse Collins followed their doctor into the room.

Brenda approached the hospital bed. "Has anyone came to visit him?"

"No. We contacted his mother at her brothel," said Nurse Collins.

Looking at Demonique's pale and fragile body, Brenda said, "I'm surprised Candyce hasn't been here."

Nurse Bernadette said, "She was arrested for drug trafficking and running an escort service a few hours ago. She's in jail."

Brenda examined the fangs marks on Demonique's throat and planned to have Diana, Ari, or Raven try to gain a vision to see if the marks were from Marguerite or some other vampire.

"What caused those marks, doctor?" asked Nurse Collins.

"Vampire. It's clean. A lycanthrope would've destroyed his entire throat. I'll have to run more tests." Brenda looked at her nurses and said, "Visitors to this patient is restricted to anyone, except the Astredo family. No one else."

#

Lisa entered her small apartment she shared with her grandmother until she had to live at the hospital. She hung her keys up on a dragon shaped rack.

She walked down the hall and entered her bathroom.

The walls were turquoise with black shelves and a black shower curtain.

Black flowers sat in turquoise vases.

After her shower, she wrapped a black towel around her and stepped out of the bathroom. She changed into a brown satin leopard printed nightgown. She left her room, walked down the hallway, and entered the living room, before entering the kitchen.

She made a glass of ice tea and opened the freezer where she had a few frozen dinners.

Lisa reached for a chicken parmesan dinner and stopped. Her feline hearing picked up a car slowing in front of her house. She dropped to her knees as bullets penetrated her living room window.

When the shooting stopped, she listened to the car door opening and footsteps hurrying up the bricked walk.

Lisa crawled through her kitchen to the dinette where her sword hung. She rose to her feet just as two mobsters broke through the door. Lisa sat her sword aside and used her power to conjure water. She threw an icicle into the first mobster's chest and another icicle through the second gangster's forehead.

The mobsters collapsed onto the floor.

Lisa took cover under the table when the machine gun fell to the floor spraying bullets. When the gun emptied, she rose to her feet.

Ten minutes later, the cops arrived with Diana, Valentina, Ari, and Michael.

Lisa sat in the living room with her friends.

"Italia and the others talked with grandma and grandpa. They feel you may be safer living with us," said Michael.

Lisa was wearing a black satin robe over her nightgown. She leaned back against the couch while Diana tenderly caressed her back and Valentina held her hand.

"You don't have to move everything right away. Just stay a few nights and think it over," said Ari.

"I will."

"Diana and I will help you pack an overnight bag."

Lisa led Diana and Valentina towards her bedroom. She changed into a black sundress placing her nightgown and robe into her suitcase.

Ari and Michael boarded up the living room window.

When the packing was complete, she drove her car with Diana in the passenger seat, towards Castle Olympia.

Arriving at the old castle, Lisa repeated her battle with the Astredo elders. She was still a little shaken. "Thank you for letting me stay here."

Giovanni smiled and said, "You're family."

Chapter 20

The nursery was dark purple and had been unchanged since Valentina was born.

A black wrought iron crib sat under a window and a small twin bed sat at the other end of the room.

Ari rocked Scarlet in the rocking chair softly singing slow heavy metal songs and a few Celtic songs from Enya to help the infant sleep.

He gently caressed the baby's back. He loved the fatherly feeling he received each time he was with Scarlet and Rosa. Ari loved helping Valentina with the children. Valentina had to investigate a haunting in a restaurant at the other end of town. She received the call while Michelle was showing Lisa her room. Adrian and Diana were at a friend's house, Giovanni had to take care of business at the theater, and Jason was at the movies with Caesar and Raven.

Scarlet rested her head on his shoulder playing with his silver pentacle. She slowly fell asleep as footsteps were heard coming up the hall quietly.

#

Valentina stood in the doorway listening to Ari sing to Scarlet. She loved his deep seductive voice. She watched him gently stand as he placed her in her crib. She smiled as he bent down to kiss her forehead goodnight.

When Ari looked at Valentina noticing her for the first time, Valentina whispered, "You have a beautiful voice Ari. Everything about you is beautiful."

"Perhaps my real father was a stripper," he said smiling at her.

Valentina approached the crib and gazed at her little sister. She placed her arm around his shoulders. "Have you ever wanted to find out who your real parents were?"

Ari shrugged, kept his grey eyes on Scarlet, and said, "Sometimes. Perhaps someday I'll search for them. It might be interesting to know my heritage." His eyes fell on her black wide sleeved blouse with her black leather pants. He noticed how lovely her face was with her dark golden hair falling around her shoulders. He tenderly touched her hand as he asked, "Was the case real?"

Valentina held onto his arm as she escorted him out of the children's room.

They walked down the stairs as Valentina said, "It was. The original owners just wanted to make sure their building was in good hands."

At the bottom of the stairs, Ari gave her a big hug.   He could not get enough of her. "Are you disappointed you couldn't fight a monster tonight?"

Valentina returned his hug and savored being in his embrace. She could not get enough of him either.   "A little. Perhaps a good cuddling session with a certain witch will make me feel better."

"I can arrange that." Ari smiled at his best friend and lover. He began to wish she and her parents lived at the castle with him.

Valentina said as they walked towards the kitchen, "Have you experienced more vampiric symptoms?"

Ari reached for her hand. "Nothing new. We didn't exchange blood, so perhaps grandfather is right, I'll be ok." He tenderly kissed her mouth and said, "Let's sit on the back porch. It's a nice evening." Ari placed his arm around her waist as he walked her through the kitchen. He grabbed the baby monitor off the counter and took it outside with them.

She softly smiled when she saw a bottle of wine on a table. A few citronella candles were also lit on the glass table.

Ari sat on a glider at the end of the long porch. He placed his hand on the empty spot beside him. "Valentina, sit by me."

Valentina looked at Ari through the amber glow of the candles. He looked handsome in his black poet shirt and black leather pants. She loved the way he allowed his black hair to grow longer. She undressed him with her eyes wanting him to take her on the back porch. She pictured him making love to her on the glider. Valentina sat beside him. She leaned back into his arms resting her head on his shoulder. The scent of his cologne seduced her. She caressed his thigh while he kissed her along her neck and shoulder. Feeling his warm breath gently blow on her shoulder made her desire him even more.

Ari thought about the talk he had with his family during Aaron, Cassandra, and Dario's wake. He played with Valentina's hair and asked, "If I do become a vampire, will you still love me?"

"Of course. Not all vampires are evil." She sat on his lap with her arms around his neck. She unzipped and unbuttoned his pants before slipping her hand through the zipper. She began to stroke him after she massaged his balls.

"Oh Valentina, Valentina!"

Valentina slowly stroked him enjoying listening to his moans.

"Take me in your mouth," he moaned.

Valentina moved to her knees, ran her tongue along his erect penis, before she took him in her mouth. She stoked him before he reached his climax. She climbed on his lap and kissed him deeply and passionately on the mouth.

Ari gazed into her desire-filled eyes. His hand slid under her blouse and caressed her breast. His mouth passionately caressed her mouth while he stripped her before he stripped himself. He laid her on the glider and entered her.

Valentina caressed his back and cried out as he began to stroke her.

He kissed her everywhere while his hands explored her body. "I love you so much, Valentina."

Her cries, screams, and moans were her response. She held him in a tight embrace as she bucked under him.

He pushed her harder and deeper.

"Ari, Ari, Ari!"

When he released himself into her, he remained on top of her. He hugged her and said, "We better get dressed before Adrian returns."

"I hate to leave your arms."

"I'll still hold you. I'm not ready to pull away from me."

Valentina had taken Ari to her bedroom so they could finish making love.

#

Giovanni sat behind his giant solid mahogany desk with his deep burgundy curtains pulled back away from the long and wide sainted glass windows.

"I can't wait until this trail is over Giovanni."

"I can't wait either. We miss you and Viktor."

"We miss everyone also."

"How are things between you and Viktor?"

"Fine. He just gets a little overprotective."

"He inherited your hot temper."

"Mixed with your stubbornness. He apologized for yelling at me earlier. And since the deaths, I think he is just stressed out and it is hard to focus on the trail and not mourn. During our break, he apologized and cried on my shoulder."

"I know. He cares for us. I am glad he apologized. You are right, he is just stressed out."

"Giovanni; Markus and Italia were thinking about breaking the binding spell they placed on his powers. They gave me the potion for him."

"I don't know, Charlotte. He still hasn't learned to control his temper yet."

"You tell me I've never learned to control my temper and we have the same powers."

Giovanni gently laughed and said, "Have you spoken to Viktor about this?"

"No and I haven't told him about his gift."

"Why not?"

"I haven't have had the chance. He has been too busy sheltering me to listen."

"When you guys have a moment to yourselves tonight, tell him. Unbind his powers also. Brenda told me the police found Gerard's body in the Ohio River. After she examined him, she discovered Octavia's fingerprints."

"Octavia?"

"She's committing murders with Charlemagne now.   Just unbind his powers."

"I'll talk to him when we go to our hotel tonight. Nevertheless, don't you think it's dangerous for him to have his gift considering the mood he is in?"

"That may help calm his attitude down. You and Markus have controlled your gift each time you both would get angry."

"That is true. I'll tell him before I unbind them. I don't want him to accidentally set fire to the courthouse. Have you found where Octavia is hiding Charlemagne?"

" Not yet. Michelle and Diana are scrying for him in the living room. They're using a crystal and a map of the city," said Giovanni.

"I want him found and brought to me so I can slowly torture that perverted fuck."

"We'll capture him."

"When we do have him, I'll roast his nuts off."

Chapter 21

Beaver Falls, Pennsylvania

In a hotel suite, Charlotte waited by a table for her grandson to return with dinner.

The room had a Southwestern motif with pink walls, pale blue ceiling, and lavender carpet.

The pale pink door opened and Viktor entered carrying two fast food bags. He was still dressed in his dark suit with a gold pentacle around his neck.

He sat the drinks on the table after he placed the straws through the lids. Next, he pulled out a cheeseburger and fries for Charlotte and a double cheeseburger and large fry for himself.

Charlotte smiled at her grandson and said, "I told you I would be alright while you were gone."

Viktor kissed her on her cheek and said, "I'm glad. I was worried." He sat across from her and began to eat his meal.

"Viktor, I need to talk to you about something."

"Did another relative die? Is grandfather and everyone else alright?"

"Everyone is alright. No one died. I was speaking with Giovanni while you were gone."

Viktor smiled. His eyes were filled with tears earlier from repressing the mourning state he had been in. "What did grandfather and you talk about?"

Charlotte dipped her French fry into a ketchup container and played with it. "Viktor, do you remember the talk Giovanni and I had with you and your cousins a few years ago?"

"Yes. You said we were chosen by the Gods to fight evil. I love our destiny. I find it odd that out of the six of us; I am the only one who can't tap into my power. Ari called while I was waiting in the drive-thru and told me about Lisa's new found power to heal. I think that's cool."

Charlotte said, "Your parents decided to bind your powers."

Viktor smiled slightly. "Why bind them?"

"Out of the many gifts in our family, yours is the most dangerous. Since some of our powers are triggered by our emotions, we wanted to wait until you were old enough to handle it. We had to bind Markus's power as well."

"Unleash the dragon within me."

Chapter 22

Salem, Ohio

On second night of the Full Moon, Giovanni performed the Full Moon Ritual with his family.

Since Charlotte wasn't there, Italia filled in as high priestess.

After the quarters were called, prayers offered, chants sung, Giovanni and Italia blessed their weapons as everyone thanked the Gods for their powers.

After the ritual, Michelle walked through the garden thinking about Cassandra, Aaron, and Dario.

The others had gone inside.

Valentina and Ari left for their date.

Michelle sat on a bench and gazed at the moon. Silently, she cried for her best friend. She felt a tender hand on her shoulder. She looked up at Caesar.

Caesar sat next to her and placed his arm around her waist. "We miss them also." Tears filled his eyes.

Michelle snuggled close to her husband and said, "I wish we could have seen that Octavia was evil sooner."

"She's Raven's sister-in-law. Our first instincts were to protect her. We learned from our mistake." He softly kissed her.

Michelle slowly broke away from his kiss and said, "He's such a horrible man. I don't understand what she sees in him."

Caesar caressed her thigh and said, "Unfortunately, he was the only one who cared for her since her parents were a couple of assholes. We'll catch them."

"I know we will." Michelle tenderly kissed him while her hands explored his body.

Caesar laid her on the grass after he removed their clothes. Holding her in a tight embrace, he glided into her in slow strokes.

She covered him in deep passionate kisses. Her moans and cries began to blend with his moans and cries.

#

"Oh Ari, more, more," moaned Valentina. She was sitting on Ari's lap with her legs around his waist. She stroked him as she grinded on his lap.

They were in the back seat of his car along the back roads.

She rode him until she climaxed. She placed her head on his shoulder.

Ari kissed her along her shoulder and thrust against her until he became hard again. He began to stroke her again with his new vampiric sex drive rising higher. His hand gently cupped her breast before he sucked on her nipple.

The car shook violently from their passion.

Ecstasy began to rise in her again. Her legs tightened around his waist. She kissed his shoulder and his tattoo. She began to scream his name as he pushed her faster.

Ari kissed her along her shoulder and up her neck before he laid her on the backseat of the car.

#

Diana remained in the temple room.

The scent of sage and Nag Champa still lingered.

Diana walked towards a small waterfall and gazed at the statues of Sobk and Hapi. She pried for a moment before she walked towards a shrine dedicated to their ancestors.

On a wicker table stood a statue of Osiris and a statue of Anubis, Gods of the Underworld. A painting depicting the weighing of souls was painted onto the wall. Photos of ancestors hung on the wall forming pyramids with the matriarchs at the top. Recently added to the wall were pictures of Cassandra, Aaron, Dario, and Lotus.

Diana looked at her mother and noticed how much she resembled Octavia and her. She wondered if Lotus knew that she and Raven moved into the castle a week after she died. Diana wished she knew her mother. Diana stepped away from the wall and began to walk towards the entrance.

Diana passed the main altar to leave the room. As her hand brushed against the altar cloth Giovanni had laid over the large tree stump, a vision came to her:

Island of Medea

1942

The ninety-five square mile islet sat west of Jamaica in the Caribbean Sea. The oval shaped island was seventeen miles long. Only twenty-thousand people lived on the jungle-infested island.

The village was primitive with only one apartment building that housed nine hundred people where the rest of the population lived on jungle plantations.

A small farm that produced bananas, mangos, papayas, and sugarcane sat next to a grocery store and a movie theater.

The hot sun rose, looking as if the giant ball of flames were rising out of the ocean waves. The sun lit up the square miles of warm tropical paradise.

The cool, pale blue saltwater crashed onto the beach creating a soothing and relaxing sound that was heard throughout the dense jungle.

The tropical wildlife began to awaken; their calls mixed with the sound of the pounding waves.

Most of the population was Pagan. Many Pagan temples and shrines were dedicated to the Greek and Roman Gods and Goddesses.

A younger Giovanni Astredo fired a silver bullet into a mobster's head as a twenty-two-year-old Charlotte Astredo threw fireballs at a group of mobsters belonging to Marguerite 's oldest daughter, Delilah DeMarco.

Marguerite's youngest daughter, Jacqueline DeMarco-Tortelli was training to become a lady mobster. Jacqueline and her schizophrenic husband, Tony, were the deadliest mobsters in the tropics.

They were in Marguerite's mansion that sat in the middle of a dense jungle where the backyard dropped off a cliff.

Charlotte delivered a right hook and then turned to throw a fireball at another mobster.

Giovanni's four cousins, Kathy, Russell, Barbara, and Luca were fighting using their elemental powers alongside Giovanni, Charlotte, Stefano, and Roman.

Giovanni, Stefano, and Roman were staying with their Aunt Scarlet and Uncle Mariano with their mother.

After the last mobster was defeated, Giovanni and Charlotte held hands as they entered the mansion.

"Charlotte, Giovanni; I got him!"

The witches fallowed the voice of Stefano.

In a dark grey and maroon living room, Stefano Astredo held a 45-year-old man at gunpoint.

Charlotte smiled. She picked up a machine gun and aimed it at Delilah 's underboss. Charlotte's words were in Italian.

Another battle broke out when a dozen mobsters appeared.

Charlotte instructed Stefano to help Giovanni, Kathy, Russell, Barbara, Luca, and

Roman to battle the DeMarco Crime Family. Locking eyes with Delilah's underboss, Charlotte filled his body with bullets.

The vision showed the next morning.

Charlotte and Giovanni were speaking with a few cops at the small police station.

Kathy and Russell Astredo entered the police station with Jacqueline DeMarco-Tortelli and Tony Tortelli in handcuffs.

Jacqueline and Charlotte locked eyes as the policeman escorted her and Tony passed Charlotte and Giovanni.

Tony gave Charlotte and Giovanni a cold stare.

Next, a nightclub belonging to Diana's ancestors appeared in the jungle's clearing.

Delilah and Python arrived at Astredo's and found it empty except for a couple standing by the craps table. The couple had their arms around each other's waists and held their Fedora hats in front of their faces.

Python led Delilah towards the Roulette table and embraced her.

Delilah asked, "Are they opened?"

"Does it matter? I want us to be alone." Python kissed her forehead.

"I love being alone with you."

Python began to sway her in his bulky arms as the couple behind the crap table lowered their Fedora hats just so they could watch Delilah and Python. Delilah laid her head on his shoulder, feeling him softly nibble on her neck and shoulder. Delilah opened her eyes in time to spy Detective Kathy Astredo's 1931 white Chrysler parked beside a table.

Kathy stepped out, holding a rifle in her hand. Russell Astredo was behind her holding his rifle. Kathy and Russell stood beside the car waiting for the mobsters to face them.

When Python turned her around on the dance floor, she noticed the couple was Barbara and Luca Astredo, who now wore their hats on their heads and rifles in their hands. Delilah held onto Python as the first bullet pierced through her leg and through Python's leg. Delilah and Python faced their assassins realizing they were trapped in the ambush. Soon, the witches began to fire at the two mob bosses. A shower of bullets went into Python's back and out the other side, spraying blood and organ tissues on the table, floor, and Roulette table. A bullet went through his head and sailed through Delilah's face. The force of the bullets crumbled the side of their heads causing blood to flow from their heads like a waterfall. Another bullet shot through Delilah's left eye and shot out the back of her head. The bullet and her eye landed on the Roulette table. Barbara's bullet shattered Delilah's heart at the same time Kathy's bullet shattered Python's heart. Fifteen bullets filled Delilah's chest and back. Fifteen more filled Python's massive chest and stomach. His brains scattered over the tables and palm trees. Parts of the pink and gray mass fell on the Roulette table. His large hand was nearly blown off. A hail of gunfire covered them both like a thick blanket of steel and sulfur. The bullets entered their bodies. When the police ran out of bullets, they walked towards Delilah and Python.

Delilah and Python collapsed on the ground beside the Roulette table. Blood flowed from their bullet-riddled bodies and trickled down from the table beside them. They were in each other's arms.

Next, the scene disappeared to be replaced by darkness.

Diana left the temple room.

#

Ari woke after his short nap.

The first draft of his horror play lay on the Gothic designed coffee table beside a pen.

Sitting on the couch, the handsome playwright slowly rose from the couch and walked over to the bar. He poured red wine into a shot glass. He and Valentina returned from their date two hours ago.

Ari sat the shot glass on the black marbled bar as Diana entered the living room.

"I had a vision of grandma gunning down an underboss and Marguerite 's oldest daughter being gunned down by our great-aunts and great-uncles. Why did I have a vision of the past? We already know grandma killed an underboss when she, grandpa, and our great-uncles were helping grandpa 's cousins battle the mob. I just wish it wasn't in Italian."

"Did you touch something of grandma's just before the vision?"

"Yes, the altar cloth."

"Grandma was the last person to touch it. I think the Gods want us to know about grandma's past."

"Grandma Athena told us to give her time."

"She told me the same."

"The DeMarco crime family must be connected to grandma's past," said Ari.

"The look Jacqueline gave her was of betrayal and Tony's look was unsettling," said Diana.

"Unsettling?"

Diana shivered and said, "It wasn't as though he was angry he was arrested. It just looked as though his thoughts were somewhere else."

"That doesn't surprise me. From Great-Uncle Luca, Great-Aunt Kathy, grandpa, and grandpa's stories, he practically *lived* in asylums."

As they spoke, Valentina entered the room.

Valentina wore her favorite black V-neck blouse with a black leather skirt with a pewter chain around her waist. Two large pewter dragons hung from her ears and a dragon and snake rings wore on two of her fingers. A pewter ankh with a tiny pentagram beside it hung around her neck and a silver ankle bracelet was wrapped around her ankle. Her heels were clear with a black bow above her painted black toenails. In her hair was a headband made to look like real braided hair. Her eye shadow was black and dark purple with black eyeliner and mascara. Her lips were a deep shade of purple to match her eye shadow.

After Ari explained Diana's vision to Valentina, Ari said, "We should speak with

grandpa."

#

Charlemagne entered their spare bedroom and approached a shelf that held many different pictures of them. His eyes looked lustfully at a picture of Octavia that sat in the bottom shelf.

Charlemagne removed the five by ten photos in a sapphire blue frame and stared at Octavia's image. He gazed lovingly into her deep violet eyes, which was surrounded by her blue Egyptian style, make up complete with a black line drawn under her eyes and out from the corner of her eyes as the ancient Egyptian's did. His mind

drifted back to the many evenings when she would sneak into a guest bedroom to carry

out Marguerite's plan and to make love to him at Castle Olympia.

As he placed the photograph on the shelf, he felt Octavia's hands tenderly caress

his shoulders.

"Dinner is ready."

He turned to her and placed his arm around her waist.

They walked out of the room and down the short narrow hallway that led into a

small dinette area.

On the glass table sat a casserole dish with pieces of meat in a red spicy sauce.

Next to the dish were small bowls filled with green peppers, cheddar cheese, cubed

grilled chicken, and onions. A plate of tortilla shells sat next to the bowls.

Charlemagne sat across from Octavia as she poured their drinks. He watched her

place the items on a flour tortilla before he scooped a large piece of meat from the

casserole dish and placed it on his plate. His stake knife cut across the raw meat causing

blood to flow onto the plate. Stabbing the meat with his fork, he placed it in his mouth.

"Do you like it?" asked Octavia after she had taken a drink of wine.

"Yes. Would you like to try it?"

Octavia shuddered and said, "No thanks."

Charlemagne laughed as he took another bite.

"Charlemagne, I think we should move."

"Why? I like this apartment. I've been living here since the 40's."

"I love this apartment also. This was the first decent place I have lived in before I married you."

"Why do you want to move then? We have wonderful memories here."

"We do."

"Is it because you gave birth to our son here, in our bedroom?" He looked at his plate and briefly thought about the evening when he sat by her side guiding her through her contractions as Marguerite began to deliver their son. He hoped once Octavia held their baby she would want to keep him.

"No. Charlemagne; Esmeralda and Amari were not loving parents. Mom treated Lotus and me as if we were her best friends while dad treated us as if we were his salves. He sold me to another mobster since he could pay off a loan. I don't know how to give a child love. That's why I don't have the same feelings you do."

"I could've taught you. Octavia, I made your life better."

"I realize now that you could have taught me. I appreciate everything you have done for me since we met. I was fifteen when I was pregnant. I was not mature enough to have a baby even though I was happy about the pregnancy."

"Could we give it another try? You just turned forty a few weeks ago."

"I'll think about it."

Charlemagne smiled softly as he placed another piece of meat on his plate. "Why do you want to move?"

"We can't stay here because you're a vampire. There're too many people around."

"I have to get my food somehow."

"If we could live in a secluded place in the country it would be easier for me to stalk your meals. I don't want anything to happen to you while I'm carrying out orders from Dante and Marguerite. I would feel better about leaving the apartment while you rest in your coffin if we didn't live in this type of surrounding. I'm glad your meals don't leave any incriminating odors."

"I'll think about it."

Octavia rolled her eyes before she rose from her seat. She sat on his lap and placed her arms around his neck. On his breath, she smelled the coppery sent of his meal. She kissed his forehead. "I want you to be well protected. You're weak during the day."

Charlemagne hugged her. "I'm so glad I found someone like you. Not many women would have wanted a man like me."

Octavia smiled and kissed his wrinkled mouth. "I think I made a wonderful choice. You have been good to me. You have always treated me with respect. That's why I fell in love with you." She returned his hug.

Someone knocked on the door.

Octavia rose from his lap. She walked a few feet from the table and answered the door.

Marguerite and Dante entered. They sat at the table as Octavia sat on Charlemagne's knee with his arm around her waist.

"How are you adjusting to your new lifestyle?" Marguerite said as she smiled.

"I love it. I shouldn't have been so stubborn, mom."

Marguerite held his hand and tenderly squeezed it. "I understand why you hesitated. Your father didn't like his children being vampires. It's his fault your brothers and sisters aren't here with us." She released his hand.

Octavia nuzzled Charlemagne's neck and played with his grey hair as Dante said,

"We are going to take Charlemagne downtown to practice his new powers. Octavia can watch the Astredos through the crystal ball while you pack."

"Pack?" asked Octavia.

"Marguerite and I think it may be a good idea to have you and Charlemagne move in with us."

Octavia laughed as Charlemagne looked at his mother and step-father before he looked at Octavia.

Octavia said, "I was just saying the same thing to Charlemagne. It's not safe for him to live here."

"We agree. Soon, the stench of rotted human flesh will begin to rise from your refrigerator and leak into the hallway. Your neighbors will begin to complain to the police. I can't have my serial killer sent back to prison."

"Fine," Charlemagne said as he nuzzled Octavia's neck before he kissed her neck.

Chapter 23

Valentina stood on the nursery's stone balcony overlooking the East end of the Gothic garden. She wore her black satin nightgown with matching robe. Since it was Ari's favorite, she kept it in his bedroom and wore it on the nights she spent the night. The memory of her parents, and brother's deaths still lingered in her mind. She wanted to cry, but couldn't summon the strength to cry anymore. Her thoughts were interrupted hearing someone enter the nursery. She turned to see Brenda enter the balcony.

"Valentina; Cassandra and Aaron named Jason and I legal guardians for you and your brothers and sisters. We, as well as the rest of the family, don't want you and the others to live by yourselves. We're safer, if we stay together."

Valentina said, "I don't know what I want to do. I do know that I want to adopt my baby sisters. I'd adopt Adrian, but he's too old."

Brenda softly smiled and said, "That is a wonderful idea, although, why don't you wait awhile before you make that decision. You shouldn't make rash decisions like that while you're in mourning."

"Athena became a single mother after Alexander died and still fought evil."

"That was different, Valentina. They were her children. Dad was barely seven and Uncle Stefano was ten. You'd be adopting an infant and a two-year-old."

"*If* I decide to move in the castle, I'll have you and the others to help me."

Brenda softly laughed before she said, "That's true. Although, that won't make it easy. Jason and I didn't decide that night we found Ari on our doorstep to adopt him. We thought about it. Seeing that he was born with the God's mark helped our decision."

Soft tears came down her cheeks. "I love them and I know I'll make a good parent. But, I will think about it. You may be right. My judgment may be clouded."

Brenda cried as well. "We just don't want you to make any rash decisions. Give yourself time to heal and then decided if you want to adopt Rosa and Scarlet. If you still want to be their mother, we'll support you and we'll be happy for you and the girls. Have you mentioned this to Ari?"

"I have." Valentina softly laughed. "He was anxious to adopt them right away until Viktor gave him the same talk you just gave to me. He wants to wait."

Brenda tenderly embraced Valentina and allowed her to cry on her shoulder. She caressed her back. "After you move in, use this time as a trail to make sure you and

Ari want to do this."

Valentina tightly hugged her.

They talked for another ten minutes before they returned to their rooms.

Valentina entered Ari's bedroom and laid next to him. She cuddled in his arms and told him about the conversation she had with Brenda.

#

Lisa packed the last box before walking around her apartment. Pleasant and sad memories surfaced.

Lisa stood in the doorway of what used to be her grandmother's room.

#

1995

17-year-old Lisa Stoker placed a red sweater over her black blouse that matched her knee length skirt. She walked out of her bedroom and into the living room where her grandmother sat in her favorite chair reading a mystery novel.

"How do I look grandmother?"

Becky Stoker lowered the book from her eyes and scanned her letterman sweater and the tasteful black blouse. Placing the glossy hardcover novel on the coffee table, she asked in her heavy British accent, "You are wearing that *to the play auditions?"*

Lisa shrugged. "Yes. Everyone else who are auditioning are so much older than Michael and I that we figured to dress mature and business like for the theatre's choir director. We figured that we would have a better chance if we dressed wholesome."

Becky rose from her chair. "Lisa, you and Michael need to dress like the mature young adults you are. You don't *have to dress to impress anyone. Just be yourselves. You look as though you are about to meet your friends at the public library. Come darling, allow me to pick out one of your Goth gowns you and your companions wear to Markus 's nightclub." Becky escorted Lisa back into her bedroom where Becky went to Lisa's closet. Becky pulled out a long red skintight gown. "I think your black fishnet gloves will look good with your gown. You and Michael need to forget about everyone else and be* yourselves.*"*

The doorbell rang as Lisa said, "That's Michael. Would you let him in, please?"

Becky left the room as Lisa slipped into the red gown that had a slit traveling up to her thigh. She sat at her vanity applying her black and maroon eye shadow and black eyeliner hearing her grandmother show Michael in. She heard Becky suggest that Michael take off his maroon sweater and just go to try outs in his black shirt and black pants. Lisa set her dark purple hand mirror on the dark cherry surface of her vanity and gazed at her newly painted face as she fashioned her long garnet earrings into all four holes in her earlobe. She thought about what her grandmother had said earlier and admitted they would be more respected being themselves. After Lisa put on her tear shaped garnet necklace, she met Michael in her living room.

Michael felt his heart melt as she walked into the room with her grandmother holding a brush to her hair. He watched as Becky took out Lisa's tightly wrapped bun and transformed her hair into a peek-a-boo hairstyle modeled after most of the screen sirens of the forties. His desire-filled eyes focused on her half exposed leg as it stuck out from under the satin opening in the dress. His loving gazed moved up to her face and wished she would give him a chance. He was so glad her grandmother had talked her into changing. Michael approached her. "You look lovely."

"Thanks. You look handsome as well," Lisa said as her grandmother stated, "You kids have fun on your date. Good luck."

Michael shyly blushed as Lisa said, "Oh, bloody hell grandmother! I told you, Michael and I are just friends. He, Ari, and Viktor are the only men I trust. I have no desire to date because men can 't be trusted."

Becky watched her granddaughter exit the room to get her long velvet cloak and purse wishing she could convince her that not all men were assholes.

As if reading Becky's mind, Michael said, "She'll get over her mistrust of men, Mrs. Stoker. I promise I will help her see that not all men are assholes."

Becky smiled at him. "Do you love her?"

"Yes. But, I don't want to tell her until she is ready to try dating. I'll wait until she is ready to trust men again," Michael said wishing Lisa would allow him to help her get over her rape from an abusive boyfriend.

Becky gently took his hands. "I can tell you will treat my Lisa right when the time comes. Michael, I do not mean to push her into a relationship, I just do not want her to grow up a bitter old woman because of an asshole."

Michael returned the smile, "I won't let that happen to Lisa. I'll honor her and respect her."

When Lisa returned to the living room, she and Michael left in his car towards the Dragon's Lair Theater.

#

The car ride was silent as Michael drove his late uncle's '79' brown impala *towards the Gothic theater. At a stop sign, he glanced at Lisa and noticed a nervous look on her face. He, also, began to get butterflies in his stomach as the lit marquee came into view over the trees and the buildings down town.*

"Are you nervous Lisa?"

Lisa nodded her head. "Yes. Grandma tells me that Thor is a big Frank Sinatra fan, so instead of singing 'Gypsies, Tramps, and Thieves,' I am going to sing 'Witchcraft' since I know all the words."

"I guess I will do 'Chicago' instead of 'Sabbath Bloody Sabbath' then. Lisa, in case he only chooses one of us, I do not want it to hurt our friendship."

Lisa smiled. "It will not. You know I am not the jealous type."

Michael laughed pulling the car into the parking lot on the left side of the building.

Once they were in the long lavish lobby, they sat in the front seats and waited for their turn. Lisa was called before Michael feeling nervousness and excitement wash through her. She took a few deep breaths and then walked towards the microphone. Lisa waited until the few seconds of music played before her sultry soprano voice was heard throughout the theater.

Michael listened to her voice becoming enchanted by her mesmerizing voice as she sang 'Witchcraft'. He hoped Thor, the choir director, would choose her for the lead, for he loved the thought of hearing her voice in every scene. He hoped that one day she would fall in love with him. Michael wondered if Diana or Ari could teach him to perform a love spell.

When she finished singing, Michael, as well as Thor and the other actors, applauded her. Lisa sat in the chair, watched and listened to Michael's sweet alto

voice carry through the stage. She found him to be very handsome.

Ten minutes later Michael and Lisa sat beside each other and waited for the

results.   Excitement filled them when it was announced that Lisa and Michael had

been accepted as the leads. They gave each other a congratulating hug.

#

Lisa felt Michael's hands on her shoulders. She leaned against him.

"The car is packed. We can go whenever you're ready." Michael felt her sadness.

He, Raven, Caesar, and Jason helped her move. An hour later, it was just him and Lisa.

"I know this day would come, packing up grandmother's things. Grandmother

told me she's happy I'm moving on. She told me I could keep the money from the house.

I'm going to use it for medical school and become a nurse and maybe a doctor someday."

Michael gave her a brotherly hug. "I like that idea."

Lisa turned towards him. "I was thinking about that night we tried out for that

play. I heard you and grandmother talking about me."

Michael looked at her nervously. "I've always cared about you."

Lisa softly smiled. "I'm sorry if I seemed standoffish. I trust you, Michael."

Michael felt her sadness turn into desire. "I would *never* hurt you. I 'm proud of

you."

Lisa looked at the floor and returned her eyes towards him. "Thanks." She began

to walk towards the door.

Michael tenderly took her arm and pulled her close to him. He softly smiled when

he felt her desire rise. "If you're *not* happy living in the castle with us, no one will be hurt if you got a place somewhere."

"I'm sure I'll like it. I know I'm *not* being forced into anything." Lisa pulled him closer and gently caressed his mouth with her mouth.

Michael returned her kiss before he said, "I want you to be my girlfriend, but if you want to take things slow, I'll understand."

Lisa caressed his back with her hands. "I've kept you waiting long enough." She kissed him again finding that she missed being held. This time, she knew she had one of the rare good guys.

Michael's hands explored her body wanting to hold her against the wall and make her scream his name. His mouth found hers again while their clothes fell onto the red carpet. Feeling her desire heightened his desire. He held her against the wall and said, "Are you sure you want this now?"

"I do. I've been afraid to admit how much I love you."

Michael placed her legs around his waist and began pounding into her. His kisses traveled down her neck where his mouth caressed each breasts before sucking hard on her nipples.

"Michael, Michael, Michael!"

Michael continued to push her during her climax before he lay her on the floor. He opened her legs and penetrated deep inside her with her hands holding her hands above her head.

Their moans and cries echoed throughout the empty house.

Michael reached his orgasm crying out her name. He remained on top of her gazing into her ecstasy-filled eyes.

Lisa ran her fingers threw his hair. "That was wonderful."

Michael kissed her mouth and said, "I couldn't wait to hold you."

"You can hold me every night." Lisa hugged him before they rose off the floor and dressed.

When they returned home, Michael held her among her leopard printed sheets in her new room.

His room was across from her room.

Michael looked down at her. "No regrets?"

"Only that we *didn't* get together sooner." She moved him onto his back and rode him.

Michael moaned. His hands caressed her thighs. He fell into rhythm with her movements.

They made love in many positions for a few more hours before falling asleep in each other's arms.

Chapter 24

The next evening

Charlemagne sat in his old car and watched her close the tiny palm reading shop. He'd been stalking her for a few days.

He anxiously waited until she was alone in the store.

#

The purple neon sign reading Nefertiti's Tearoom matched the turquoise walls and Egyptian style store.

The display window was decorated for the Pagan holiday of Lughnasadh. The gold statues of Isis and Osiris were surrounded by images of the sun and the first harvest until Mabon.

Stocking the shelves with tarot decks, Diana emptied the last box.

Raven left with Midnight after Diana reassured them Adrian was arriving anytime to pick her up.

Next, Diana wiped off the counter.

The antique bell on the door rang.

With her back turned towards the front of the store, Diana said, "Have a seat, Adrian. I have to stock the coffee and tea."

Silence was her reply.

Slowly, she turned and quickly backed against the counter where the coffee maker and teapot sat. Her violet eyes locked with his icy blue eyes.

"How's my favorite niece?" His low husky voice broke off in a short laugh.

Diana's eyes moved to his hand that lay on the counter holding his knife. Quickly, her hand moved under her purple gypsy skirt to withdraw her knife.

Charlemagne's eyes scanned her body noticing how much Diana has grown into the mirror image of his beloved Octavia

"You're my uncle?" she asked looking for a way out from behind the counter without him attacking her.

The tiny half door was one side of the counter and on the other was the front window. Charlemagne stood a few inches from the door.

Charlemagne smiled. "I've been married to Octavia for twenty-four years."

"Why would she want to marry you?"

"She loves me." Charlemagne approached the half door and walked behind the counter.

Diana started to climb over the counter.

His arm clasped around her waist and his knife was held at her throat. He nuzzled her neck. "You look so much like my Octavia. Killing you is going to be difficult." His hand caressed her side. The desire to rape again returned. He tried to repress the urge since he didn't want to break a promise to Octavia. However, she looked so much like Octavia. He softly kissed the side of her neck. He screamed when she stabbed his leg.

Next, she hit his face with her elbow and hind kicked his other leg. She tore away from him and ran towards the Dutch door.

Charlemagne leaped over the counter and blocked the door.

Their blades struck as they fought.

Charlemagne's blade was wider and longer then Diana's knife. He swung his arm knocking Diana's knife from her hand.

She ran towards the back of the store only to be knocked towards the floor when he tackled her. She screamed while she struggled to get away from him.

He sat astride her with his hand holding her wrists down over her hand. His other hand held his knife. He teased her with it as he lightly touched the blade along her neck and throat.

She was unable to move her wrists from his tight hold. "Adrian!" she screamed when she felt his hardness through his pants.

The blade lightly touched her blouse after he used his powers to tie her hands to a table leg. Her blouse was ripped open.

Diana screamed when he removed her skirt and underwear after he tore off her bra.

Charlemagne, still clothed, lay above her, and began to thrust on top of her. He kissed her across her shoulders picturing her as his Octavia.

Diana prayed he didn't rape her. She didn't want her virginity stolen by the old rapist. She continued to scream for Adrian.

Charlemagne touched her thigh just as the parlor door opened.

Relief overwhelmed her when Adrian entered. Tears filled her eyes when Charlemagne rose off her.

Adrian removed his gun and fired at Charlemagne.

The bullet entered his chest only to be pushed back out as his body healed.

Adrian and Diana watched in surprise as another bullet had no effect on Charlemagne.

Charlemagne quickly attacked Adrian.

Adrian fought back. His gun slammed against Charlemagne's face.

Charlemagne threw him against the wall.

The table and a few chairs were upset from the impact of Adrian's body.

Diana watched helplessly as Charlemagne picked up Adrian and sank his new fangs deeply into his throat. She screamed as large tears began to fall from her eyes.

Charlemagne drank deep savoring his first taste of human blood. He raised his eyes towards Diana and watched her cry. She even had the same build as Octavia.

Adrian became limp in Charlemagne's arms.

After Charlemagne removed his fangs, he tossed Adrian's bloodless body onto the floor; he approached Diana and returned to lying on top of her with his arms around her.

Adrian's blood smeared on her from Charlemagne's mouth and hands. Heavily, she cried.

Charlemagne softly kissed her mouth and said, "Don't cry, Octavia."

Diana spit in his face before she said, "Get away from me." As she struggled, a vision came to her, *'Charlemagne and Octavia were in a large apartment a block from Nefertiti's Tearoom. They were snuggled on the couch watching a movie.'* When the vision ended, Diana screamed when he began to kiss her.

Charlemagne moved his hand down to his pants and unzipped the zipper. Next, he grabbed her legs, forced them apart, and as he was about to place her legs around his waist, he was quickly pulled off her by Octavia.

Octavia watched as Charlemagne rose to his feet. She had her arms across her chest and she was glaring at him.

"I'm sorry, Octavia. It's this new vampiric sex drive. Mom warned it may be uncontrollable at first."

Octavia continued to read his thoughts. Marguerite did warn him that his new blood lust could cause his natural instincts as a rapist to resurface. It wasn't an excuse.

Charlemagne said, "She looks so much like you. I wanted her to be you."

Octavia struck him across the face before she grabbed his throat and said, "Learn to control your blood lust. You are mine."

Charlemagne trembled in her presence and said "It won't happen again, I promise. I'm sorry. Forgive me."

Octavia released his throat from her hand. "I forgive you since this is the first time you almost broke a promise to me. Don't do it again. It would hurt me if you started to rape again."

Guilt infested in him. He didn't want to hurt her.

She read his mind and discovered that he was feeling guilty. She took his hand and said, "Let's leave before they find us with them." She walked him out from the door. She was too hurt and angry to do anything with Diana.

When they arrived to his car, she sat in the passenger seat and cried.

#

Charlemagne parked the car in Memorial Park's parking lot and tenderly touched Octavia's hand. "I told you a long time ago I may revert to the rapist I used to be. I didn't rape her. You stopped me. I told you, it's my new vampiric powers. I'll try to control myself." Tears filled his eyes. He wanted to tell her what he done to her in the past was wrong, but was afraid of Octavia rejecting him. He felt guilty for touching her when she was younger. He didn't understand why he had done so.

Octavia continued to cry. In her arms was Charlemagne's black satin robe with his name written in red. She looked at the gate that leads into the duck pond. "You're so fucking stupid. You tried to rape Diana. Raven isn't the only person in that castle who is protective of her. I understand the vampire in you has brought out old and new desires you have to learn to control, but why couldn't you have just killed her?"

"What difference would that make? I honestly feel terrible about hurting you. It was a mistake. Stop being so protective of me." Charlemagne placed his arm around her waist and drew her near. "Rape *isn't* about sex. I don't want to sleep with anyone else but you. Not only would it hurt Raven if I had raped Diana, it would hurt the entire family.

Charlotte would get what's coming to her. She's the one who sent me to prison back in the 40s. She used magick to prove that I was a killer. She took five years of my life. She is the reason I'm a registered sex offender in Salem, Paris, and Cairo."

"Is that all she's done to you to make her hate you so much?"

Charlemagne softly smiled and said, "No."

Octavia looked at him in the light from the street light. "Were you lovers?"

"No! No." He began to laugh at the idea of him and Charlotte romantically involved. Whereas he found the notion funny, it would make Charlotte sick. "We have been enemies for a *very* long time." Charlemagne told Octavia *everything* Charlotte *couldn't* tell her family.

For a few moments, they sat in silence.

Octavia continued to look out the window. "Do you love me?"

"Yes! You mean the world to me." He softly kissed her mouth as his hand moved under her shirt while his other hand guided her hand towards his open zipper.

Octavia pushed him away and said, "Do you think a hand job would fix what you just did?" She opened the door and stepped out from the car.

Charlemagne stepped out from the car. "Octavia! Get back here."

"Leave me alone!" Octavia walked through the park.

"Octavia!" he called. He began to run after her.

Octavia ran along the sidewalk that winded through the trees, benches, and the play yard. She stopped when he grabbed her arm and held her against a tree so she couldn't struggle. Her wrists were held by his hands in a tight grip.

"*Never* run away from me again. We talk. You have every reason to be angry with me. I almost broke a promise to you. I deserved you slapping my face and probably more. I made a mistake and I'm sorry. I wasn't trying to make love to you for the sole purpose of making you forget what I done. I'm *not* like that. I *don't* want you to forget what I'm capable of for your own protection now that I am a vampire."

Octavia calmed and read his thoughts. Everything he said to her that night and during their long relationship was the truth. "Never touch her again. I'll fucking castrate you if you ever do that again."

He released her wrists from his tight hold and said, "I sometimes think you deserve better than me."

Octavia combed her fingers through his blonde and grey hair. "You've always been there for me. You've always treated me with respect. That's what I love about you."

Charlemagne slowly pulled her closer to him and held her.

Octavia rested her head on his chest. The sound of his heartbeat soothed her. Her arms were around his waist. "Why do you do it, Charlemagne?"

"Do what?" His arms were around her neck. His face was close to her face.

"Rape. You've told me how you used to stalk your victims. But *why* do you do it?"

"My older sister, Delilah, was the most feared and respected mob boss during the nineteen thirties. She controlled our every thought and action. I loved her although she is the only person I've ever been afraid of. It was my way of rebelling against her strict ways and to have control over my victims. Rapist don't do it for sex. I began when I was fifty-four years after she died." He told her about his beginnings as a serial killer and what lead to him to become a sexual predator. As he spoke, he noticed she wasn't frightened off. She was taking it as though he was telling her how he came to enjoy action movies instead of being a killer. He was relieved she took the truth so nonchalantly. Although, it worried him. What if he *couldn't* control himself with his new vampiric blood lust? He didn't want to place her in danger. He would gorge out his own eyes before hurting her.

"Would you ever rape *me*?"

"No! I would *never* hurt you. You know better." He tried not to become insulted. It was a good question. He hoped she'd never have to experience what he puts his victims through.

Reading his thoughts, she said, "You'd *never* do it. I know you too well. You'll find control before anything happens. Besides, I can protect myself. I'm *not* weak or innocent as many people believe me to be."

"I know you're not weak or innocent. Do you forgive me, Octavia?"

"Should I?"

"If I had raped her, no. Although, since this was my first offense, I think you should."

Octavia moved her hands under his shirt and caressed his back. "I'll give you another chance."

Charlemagne softly smiled and said, "I would *never* do anything to purposely hurt you. You have been a good companion and lover all these years. I don't want to lose you." Tenderly, he kissed her.

Octavia returned his kiss. Her caresses became heavier. She gazed deeper into his eyes and read his mind further. She wasn't surprised she infested his thoughts more than anything else. She was the first and only woman he cared about besides his sisters. After meeting her, he stopped treating women like an object.

With her still in his arms, he walked her behind the trees and laid her among the grass. His mouth explored her body in deep passionate kisses. He lay above her grinding heavily inside her.

#

A vision sent Raven back to Nefertiti's Tearoom. After he discovered Diana and Adrian, he called an ambulance.

Adrian was brought to the morgue and Diana was examined in the emergency room.

A few hours after she was released, she told her family about her vision.

They were in the living room.

Ari and Valentina were on their date before they would bring more of Valentina's things to the castle.

"You didn't see the name of the apartment building?" asked Michelle.

"No. I think it may be the apartment dad and I lived in before we moved here. It was a block from the tarot shop." Diana was still bothered by the experience of being attacked by her uncle.

Michael sat beside her and placed an understanding arm around her shoulders. "You're going to be alright. You survived."

"He told me he was my uncle. He *married* Octavia."

Giovanni was pacing in front of the large fireplace. He couldn't wait to gather the family and hunt Charlemagne down. Along with everyone else in the room, he wanted to tear him apart for what he did to Adrian and Diana. He couldn't wait to notify Charlotte. He said, "Brenda, Markus, Jason, Raven, Caesar, Lisa; we are going after him. Michael, Italia; make more silver bullets. Michelle stay with Diana."

They gathered their weaponry.

Giovanni's pewter sword bared the images of the Scorpio glyph and the God Geb with maroon stones. Along his maroon tinted blade ran the God chant: Osiris, Pan, Poseidon, Dionysus, Cernunnos, Apollo, Mithras.

Jason's pewter sword bared his zodiac glyph with multicolored gemstones on the handle. The dark blue handle held the God chant: Osiris, Pan, Poseidon, Dionysus, Cernunnos, Apollo, Mithras.

The pewter handle on Markus's sword was black and red, the color of lava. Engraved on the blade were dragons. The God chant: ran along his black and red blade.

Lisa's sword handle bared the images of panthers on a silver leopard print pattern with onyx and tiger-eyes in the eyes of the leopard. Along her black tinted blade was the Goddess chant: Isis, Astarte, Diana, Hecate, Demeter, Kali, Inanna. On her pewter dagger was the Goddess Bastet.

Caesar's pewter Celtic designed handle bared the images of the Virgo glyph and sardonyx. The God chant, was on his earth-tone blade.

Giovanni and the others left to search for Charlemagne.

Michael tenderly hugged Diana and said, "We're not going to allow him to hurt you."

Diana softly smiled.

He left for the alchemy lab while Diana took a shower.

After her second shower, Diana stood in front of a pewter framed mirror with a pair of scissors in her hand. Tears continued to ran down her face.   She was in the living room gazing into a mirror with gargoyles carved into the pewter.

"Diana, what are you doing?" asked Michelle entering the room.

"I don't want to look like *her*."

Michelle removed the scissors from her hand and placed an arm around her waist. "Cutting your hair *wouldn't* matter."

Diana cried on her shoulder with her arms around her waist. "He called me Octavia as he was kissing me. He attacked Adrian before he had the chance to rescue me."

Michelle softly caressed her back. Her tears returned.   She sat her on the couch and they talked.

#

Beaver Falls, Pennsylvania

The cell phone in her hand snapped closed and was tossed onto the table.

The balcony doors swung open as Charlotte stepped outside. Fire burned in her eyes and her hands were beginning to warm as she placed them on the black wrought iron bars.

If they weren't under orders to stay, she'd hunt down Charlemagne and set the asshole ablaze.

Charlemagne.

Out of all the *monsters* from her past to plague her family...

Now the mother fucker was a vampire.

He allowed Octavia to kill Cassandra and Aaron.

He killed her godson.

And almost raped her granddaughter.

A tree grew beside the balcony.

Its leaves began to wither and the tips of the branches began to burn slowly.

The wrought iron railing began to turn red where her hands rested.

Viktor stood in the doorway. He was seated on the bed going through his notes when Giovanni called. Charlotte was silent during the conversation until the end when she said, "Kill the prick." He watched Charlotte not knowing what to do. She looked as if she was about to release her inner dragon on the city of Beaver Falls. Sometimes, his grandmother's temper scared the hell out of him and he was glad he wasn't the only one who felt that way. He gently said, "Grandma, what happened?"

Without turning around, she told him. Her eyes were focused on a trash bin.

Flames roared out of the trash bin.

"You know grandma, we can ask to be excused from this trial, go home, and help the others barbeque Charlemagne."

"And allow *another* murdering son of a bitch to roam the streets! I became a lawyer for a reason. The judicial system is corrupt. We are the only lawyers who will *refuse* to be bribed."

"I understand that grandma, but after these deaths and now this, we shouldn't be here. This is why we are retiring. Why can't we just cast a spell to make time freeze for the trail, help our family, and return when it's over." Viktor could no longer hold the tears in for Adrian and Diana. Just the thought of Charlemagne touching Diana and Lisa made him want to burn off body parts slowly.

Charlotte began to calm as a fire truck arrived to put out the fire in the dumpster. She sighed deeply and said, "You're right. We'll cast a spell. Get the ritual supplies; I'll call Giovanni."

She entered the room and withdrew her sword. Charlotte's sword was pewter with the images of phoenixes and the Goddess Maat. The gems were red, yellow, and orange. Her blade was tinted red, yellow, and orange to resemble fire with the Goddess chant engraved on the blade.

Viktor's sword had bats and lions engraved on the handle with topaz stones in the eyes of the bats and lions. Along his brown topaz blade was the God Chant: Osiris, Pan, Poseidon, Dionysus, Cernunnos, Apollo, Mithras. The handle on his pewter dagger bared the image of Horus.

Chapter 25

Giovanni sat in his long black limo and informed the rest of his family about Charlotte and Viktor's plan. Next, he instructed them to search the many apartment buildings in Salem in pairs. Their meeting place would be Markus 's nightclub.

After they split up, Giovanni walked to a small sitting area in the center of downtown Salem where Charlotte said she and Viktor would meet him. He ordered a hot cup of strawberry tea and anxiously waited for his wife and grandson.

Five minutes later, he saw them walk up the street.

Viktor walked next to Charlotte as they passed the Dollar General Store.

A few cars slowly passed on Viktor's side while stores closed for the evening.

A fireball passed them hitting the side of a brick building. The flames caused the bricks to char.

Viktor pulled Charlotte back, raised his hand up where a ball of fire began to form on the inside of his palm. His other hand held her arm protectively.

A woman dressed in a 1930's purple suit dress appeared blocking their path. The scent of coconuts replaced the odor of charred brick. Delilah DeMarco glared at Charlotte and said, "Stay the fuck away from Charlemagne. Next time, I will not miss." She disappeared just as Viktor's fireball sailed passed the gangster's ghost.

"Who was that?" Viktor asked.

"Later. Let's find your grandfather."

When they approached him, they exchanged hugs. Charlotte remained in his arms little longer. She buried her head among his shirt. "We should have stayed home when Aaron and Cassandra died."

Giovanni caressed her back and said, "Don't worry about it. Let's get the bad guy." He hugged her tightly before they began to search for Octavia and Charlemagne.

#

The apartments around Nefertiti's Tearoom were searched as they split up in pairs.

Jason, Markus, and Brenda searched a building; Raven and Caesar; Viktor and Lisa; Giovanni and Charlotte.

They used spells to allow themselves access into different apartments that matched Diana's description.

A two-story apartment sat across from a tanning salon and a vegetarian restaurant.

Viktor and Lisa searched the rooms for Octavia and Charlemagne.

Down the hall, five mobsters approached them.

Swords clashed together as they fought.

Lisa rammed her sword into a mobster's chest before delivering a hind kick to a mobster who was about to attack her from behind. She quickly impaled the mobster before turning another into ice and kicking him in the stomach.

The mobster shattered into big and little cubes of ice.

"Not bad," said Viktor as he conjured a fireball and threw it at a mobster.

"Thanks. Michelle was correct, this is fun."

They continued searching apartments.

#

When Octavia and Charlemagne returned home, Charlemagne took a shower.

Octavia sat in the living room and turned on the crystal ball. His robe was draped over her arm while she was brushing one of her doll's hair. She watched as Raven entered Nefertiti's Tearoom discovering Diana and Adrian. Fear swept through her when she heard Giovanni make plans to search apartments for Charlemagne.

Charlemagne entered the living room with a towel around his waist. "Care to dry me off?"

Octavia looked at Charlemagne. It was tempting. "Diana had a vision of us in the apartment. They're looking for you now."

"I can handle them."

"Charlotte and Viktor returned to Salem. I can't wait to hide you in Marguerite's secluded mansion."

Charlemagne approached her unwrapping the bath towel. He closed the towel around them and said, "I love the thought of us hiding somewhere secluded." He held her in a tight embrace and kissed her. "I enjoyed the way we made love in the park," he whispered.

Octavia nuzzled her face in his damp chest hair. She loved his cologne. "So did I. Let's go."

Charlemagne quickly dressed and helped Octavia pack some of their things.

#

Cardboard boxes were stacked throughout Octavia and Charlemagne's apartment.

After Octavia packed the last of their clothes, she approached their walk-in closet to make sure she packed everything.

A shoebox was recently uncovered where his suits were hanging above in the far corner.

Octavia picked up the box, stepped out of the closet, and sat on the bed. Curiously, she opened the lid and discovered a tiny stuffed cat and a book of baby names dated 1976. The items were once in a wooden cradle that was now with their other furniture in Marguerite's mansion. Charlemagne refused to get rid of their baby items. Octavia glanced through the book and noticed he circled some names. Octavia remembered when he bought the toy and the book. She was six months pregnant. She set the items aside and looked at a stack of Polaroid pictures that lined the bottom.

The first picture showed her lying in bed sleeping with their newborn in her arms.

A vision showed her Charlemagne placing him in her arms after she fell asleep from the painkillers Marguerite gave her. Next, she saw Charlemagne and Marguerite argue after Charlemagne told her he wanted to keep the baby.

Octavia gazed at a picture of her sleeping with the baby. Charlemagne lay beside her with his arm around her waist. His other hand held the camera on the baby, Octavia, and him. She studied the look of pride on his face. An unfamiliar pain twisted through her heart as if someone had stabbed her. She placed the pictures in the box with the toy and book before she closed the lid.

She rose from the bed and walked down the hall towards the kitchen. Octavia opened a cupboard beside the sink and looked at the row of glasses before she grabbed a pink packet of pills. She opened the pale pink circular disk and noticed she had a few weeks left. She also had two more refills. She stared at the tiny white pills as she thought about the things Charlemagne had done for her. She felt guilty for hurting him.

"What are you doing?"

Octavia looked at Charlemagne. Her eyes filled with tears.

Charlemagne placed his hand on her cheek and wiped a tear away with his thumb. "Do you want to talk?"

"I found your pictures. I didn't realize how much you loved him and that I hurt you when I agreed with mom. Mom was acting out her jealously towards her daughter and didn't want our child to betray us since her daughter betrayed her. She was protecting me. I was confused then. I wanted to give you a family but I also wanted to show mom that I could be a good mobster."

"I understand Octavia. I don't hate you for it. Mom was also afraid that if the wrong people found out that you were only fifteen when you married me I would be sent back to prison for statutory rape. If I'm ever sent back to prison-especially if I return to France- I'll be executed." He moved his hand from her cheek to her arm.

"Maybe you were right Charlemagne. We could have worked it out. We made a mistake and we have to live with it."

Charlemagne looked at the case of pills and back at Octavia. He said, "What are you going to do with those?"

"I've been thinking about what you said the other night. Charlemagne, I owe you for giving me a better life. I would be dead if it weren't for you."

"You don't owe me anything. I did it out of love."

"I know. If we try again we don't have to tell mom until we are sure they will leave us alone this time."

"Are *you* willing to try again?"

"Yes." She tossed the case into the trashcan.

#

Caesar won against a few mobsters before he joined Raven inside an apartment building that sat a block away from Octavia's old store.

Raven wanted to see his and Octavia's old apartment to see if he would have a premonition of their exact location. In the lobby, Raven finished vanquishing a mobster with a spell from his wand.

The witches searched the apartments on the first floor before going to the second.

On the fourth apartment, Raven touched the doorknob and received a vision of the many times he, Octavia, and others have walked through the door. "I found it." He kicked the door opened. He and Caesar stepped into the apartment and noticed it hadn't changed too much.

They checked the bedrooms and the bathroom as well as the closets.

Raven approached the closet in the spare bedroom that was used as a temple room. When he opened the closet door, he discovered the baby blanket, stuffed cat, and the name book. He lifted the baby blanket and looked at the name DeMarco. A vision appeared,

Octavia sat on the couch wearing a pink lace teddy, as with all her nightgowns and teddies, it was in the baby-doll style. It was the only thing that she was comfortable wearing. She was almost nine months.

Charlemagne sat a television tray in front of her. He softly smiled at her while he served dinner. He cooked whenever she didn't feel up to it. He didn't mind.

After dinner and he washed the dishes, Charlemagne returned to the couch. He knelt in front of her and placed his arms around her waist and softly kissed her stomach. "I love you, Charlemagne," he whispered.

"Charlemagne? Don't you think that's a little cliché?" Octavia placed her hand on his back, caressed him, and with her other hand, ran her fingers through his newly grey hair.

"If we have a boy, what do you want to name him?"

Octavia softly smiled and said, "I don't know. How about Robert, Scott, James, Sunflower, Mars, Star-shine..."

Charlemagne looked up at her and said, "We're mobsters. Our child won't be a flower child. I won't name any child of ours after those hippies."

Octavia laughed and said, "Moonbeam? Rainbow?"

Charlemagne laughed. "You weren't serious, were you?"

"No. Although, I do like Rainbow. Maybe we can name the baby Rainbow if we

have a girl."

Charlemagne looked at Octavia's stomach and said, "Rainbow, daddy's going to teach you to torture your victims and later teach you how to load a machine gun."

Octavia said, "I see your point."

Charlemagne kissed their unborn child a few times before resting his head on her stomach to feel the baby kick. "We have to make up our minds, Octavia."

"I can't. I'm seriously trying to think of a name."

Charlemagne caressed her side and said, "Don't allow what mom said upset you. She could be wrong. We are *keeping this child."*

The vision moved ahead in time to Charlemagne rocking their newborn in his arms while Octavia lay in their bed from the pain killers Marguerite gave her.

Raven stared at Caesar. "She carried it full term. We should remember that. Why did they remove that memory from our minds?"

Caesar asked, "Demonique?"

"Could be. It was late seventies early eighties judging by the clothes, hairstyles, and furniture."

Raven and Caesar looked at each other and examined all visions he, Ari, and Diana had received over the past weeks.

"Demonique is still in a coma, correct?" asked Raven.

"He is."

"Go into the kitchen, grab a sandwich bag, and meet me in the bedroom," said Raven. He left the room and entered Octavia and Charlemagne's bedroom. He approached Charlemagne's dresser and picked up a comb.

Grey and blonde hair weaved through the teeth on the yellow plastic comb.

Raven searched for Octavia's comb or brush among her jewelry boxes. When he couldn't find one, he walked towards the bed. A disturbed feeling crept through him when he saw a few stuffed animals on the bed. It wasn't as disturbing as the doll on her dresser and the dollhouse in the living room. The stuffed animals and the doll didn't mesh well with the thirty-nine-year-old psychopath that was his sister-in-law.

Caesar entered the bedroom as Raven was searching the pillows for Octavia's hair. Caesar took the brush off Raven and placed it in the bag. "Where would we send this for a DNA test where we would receive the results very soon?"

"Brenda may know someone at the hospital. We should ask her or Lisa to examine Demonique's blood." Raven carefully pulled the blankets back and with Caesar, searched for a piece of Octavia's hair.

Chapter 26

Valentina was cuddled beside Ari while he drove towards the castle.

His arm was around her waist with her head on his shoulder.

Valentina caressed his thigh.

When they arrived at the castle, Valentina and Ari carried a few suitcases as well as the baby carrier into the castle.

Setting the baby carrier and a suitcase on the floor in the hallway, Ari said, "I'll see if someone could help us."

Rosa let go of Valentina's hand and ran to the step to play with an orange cat. She had Angel in one arm and now held the orange cat in her other arm.

Valentina sat a box on the floor as Italia entered the hallway.

"Can you guys come in the living room for a moment?"

Their stomachs twisted at the tone of Italia's voice. They followed the witch into the living room.

Diana sat on a couch her eyes red from crying.

Valentina and Ari sat on the loveseat as Michael and Michelle walked into the room.

Michael sat in a chair as Michelle sat in Giovanni's black leather chair.

"What happened?" asked Valentina. She tightly held Ari's hand.

Italia told Valentina and Ari the events beginning with Diana's attack, Adrian's death, and Diana's vision.

Valentina and Ari cried on each other's shoulders. After a few moments, they sat in the living room with Diana while Michael, Italia, and Michelle helped unpack the car.

Michael gave Valentina a brotherly hug and said, "We can get the rest tomorrow."

Valentina said, "That's fine." She was released from his embrace. She placed her infant sister into a bassinette that was black satin with dark purple lace. Seeing Diana by the large window, Valentina gently placed her arm across her shoulders.

Diana leaned her head on her shoulder.

"Valentina, Diana; there are mobsters out back," said Michael holding his sword. The pewter handle on Michael's sword bared the images of wizards, ravens, and gargoyles. Along the grey tinted blade was the God chant. On his dagger was the image of the God Aker. He handed Diana her sword as Ari gave Valentina her sword.

Ari's pewter sword bared ankhs and bats with rubies in the center of the ankhs and bats engraved on the handle. On the deep red tinted blade was the God Chant.

Valentina's sword was pewter. Engraved into the handle were bats and dragons with amethysts in the eyes. Her pewter Celtic knot dagger bared the image of the Goddess Isis. The sword's blade was purple tinted and bared the Goddess chant: Isis, Astarte, Diana, Hecate, Demeter, Kali, Inanna.

Diana's sword bared unicorns, pentagrams, and ankhs with emeralds in the center of the pentagrams, in the loop of the ankhs, and in the eye of the unicorns. Along the green tinted blade was the Goddess chant. Her dagger bared the image of the Goddess Sekhmet.

After placing the children safely in the nursery, they battled the mobsters.

Michael rammed his sword into two mobsters while Diana fought beside him vanquishing her share of mobsters.

Michelle's mother-of pearl tinted blade struck against a mobster's sword before she impaled him. Quickly she turned to slice another mobster in half.

Valentina fought a few feet away from Michelle.

Italia quickly impaled a mobster who tried to impale Valentina before slaying three more mobsters.

Ari fenced with a mobster before decapitating him.

As the battle reached its climax, the witches separated.

Ari's sword lay on the ground beside a mobster's sword while they fought with their hands and feet.

Ari kicked him a few times before he was knocked against a hedge. He delivered a right hook onto the mobster's jaw. As the mobster fell onto the ground, Ari moved to reach for his sword. Before his hands touched the handle, he was pinned against the hedge with Marguerite holding his wrists. He struggled for a moment, before his eyes locked with her hypnotic gaze. He fought to move but was unable to.

Marguerite's fangs buried deep into his neck. She didn't stop drinking until he was weak. She let him fall to the ground.

Chapter 27

A chill swept through the woods as Octavia moved her and Charlemagne into one of Marguerite's spare room.

Octavia moved her arms around his neck and drew him near.

Charlemagne gazed into her eyes and said, "We *never* had a honeymoon, did we? We *never* had the chance to have that large wedding we planned."

Octavia tenderly caressed his back. "No, we didn't. It's too late now. We've been married for twenty-four years."

Charlemagne smiled. "It's never too late. You *are* mom's underboss and knowing mom she'll throw a large party to show off her favorite mobster."

Octavia stared at him puzzled at where he was going with this.

Charlemagne pulled away from her, dropped to one knee, and took her hand into his hand. "When we first became engaged, I seriously wanted for us to have a large wedding and go somewhere for our honeymoon. You deserve to have everything. I want to continue to pamper and love you. I don't think mom would mind if we renewed our wedding vows as part of your coronation as underboss."

Octavia smiled and asked, "Renew our wedding vows?"

"Would you marry me again?"

"I will."

Charlemagne rose from his kneeling position and tightly embraced her.

Octavia softly kissed him along his neck and on his mouth. She placed her arms around his neck again when he lifted her in his arms and carried her to their bedroom.

#

After the battle, Valentina, with Michael's help, laid Ari on the couch. Valentina knelt on the floor beside Ari while Michael, Diana, Italia, and Michelle sat on chairs.

Valentina cleaned the last of the blood from Ari's neck as Giovanni and the others returned home. She informed everyone about the battle and Marguerite attacking Ari.

Ari's eyes slowly opened. While regaining consciousness, he had the same vision Raven had while in Octavia and Charlemagne's apartment.

Valentina helped him sit up while Diana gave him a hot cup of chamomile tea.

"I just had another vision of Octavia and Charlemagne. They were discussing what to call their baby." He told them what Raven had already told them.

They sat in silence thinking about their many theories about Octavia and Charlemagne's child and why they had to give him up.

"With all the memory-altering potions Charlemagne and Octavia fed us, their child could be *anyone* or perhaps we are seeing the future. Their apartment still carried the late seventy early eighties motif," said Caesar.

Brenda said, "That was a good idea for you and Caesar to collect DNA samples from their apartment. Lisa and I will examine the samples with Demonique's blood. I've also considered taking blood samples from each of us."

"Why us?"

Ari felt ill. He had his own theories he *never* wanted to voice.

"Because our memories on certain things are still clouded. Raven, you're *not* the only one who *can't* remember *how* Lotus died. What *other* important events in our lives have we forgotten? For all we know Ari may be mine and Jason's *real* son and *Michael* may be the one who's adopted. Or Viktor? Or even Jason? *No one* could've been adopted. The child may *not* even be in this state or country or even be alive. We *do* have a record of Octavia having a miscarriage. These visions may also be planted to throw us off, to confuse us," said Brenda.

"For all we know, Ari could be Diana's big brother or *I* could be Giovanni and Charlotte's fourth son," said Raven.

"I don't understand why none of the counter spells in our Book of Shadows have a spell to break any mind control spell. I may have to research the grimoires of our ancestors," said Michelle.

Charlotte said, "Let's all do this soon. If none of us match with either of them, then we can explore other possibilities. Although, I think the most important thing to do is to find where Octavia hid him." She would rather them focus on Charlemagne, Octavia, and Marguerite more than their hazy memories. She didn't want them to know anything about her side of the family. Not until Charlemagne was dead.

"I'll try to put together my own memory gaining potion while I look through those old books," said Michelle.

Ari took a drink from the tea and studied his family. He shared their raven black hair although where did his grey eyes come from? When he was a child, his eyes were blue. There were blue eyes in the Astredo family. Charlotte's family was a mystery, perhaps that's where he got the grey eyes from. The only two people who shared his

Egyptian features were Raven and Diana. He softly smiled. He thought, '*Could Raven be my father? Is Diana my sister? With grandma's past being a mystery, does that mean we have family members we haven't met or* did *we meet them? What* is *she keeping from us? Who were those men who tried to kill her? Why are we having visions of past battles with the DeMarco Crime Family?*"

Valentina read his mind and noticed the others harbored the same questions pertaining to Charlotte and her suspicious past. She read Charlotte's mind and noticed she was blocking certain things.

As Ari drank the tea, his canines began to ache. He sat the mug down and placed his hand over his mouth to discreetly feel his tooth. They were changing shape.

Feeling his cousin's tooth ache, Michael asked, "Are you ok?"

"I think my teeth are turning into fangs."

"That can't be. You *didn't* drink her blood," said Jason.

"Perhaps he doesn't have to. Every time she attacked him, she was interrupted and wasn't able to finish the process. Besides, they're different ways to become a vampire," said Caesar.

"Why would she want me to be a vampire?"

A vision quickly came to Diana:

'*They were battling Marguerite and her mob. Using his vampiric powers, Ari destroyed more mobsters and others then a human was able to. He was just as powerful as Charlemagne.*'

When Diana woke from the trance she said, "Marguerite *doesn't* want him to be a vampire. The Gods do. They want our side to equal theirs."

"But, we wouldn't equal them. We outnumber her head assassins," said Lisa.

They discussed Marguerite and her small team of assassins while Brenda and Lisa took blood samples from their family members including themselves.

#

After everyone retreated to their bedrooms, Ari dressed in his black satin pajamas he lifted from the floor beside Valentina's black satin nightgown.

Valentina was asleep on her side of the bed. On her night stand, sat the baby monitor.

Ari carefully closed the bedroom door, before he walked down the hall towards the large temple room.

He walked across the room towards the vaults where the door to the catacombs sat. He opened the door and walked down the spiral staircase. With a candle stick in his hand, he read each tombstone and wall hanging searching for clues to his past and his newly discovered vampirism. If he would happen to get a vision exposing his grandmother's secrets that would be an added plus.

An old tombstone caught his attention. Under the name Alexander Astredo was the years 1483-1778.   ALCHEMIST WITH THE POWER TO HEAL. BELOVED HUSBAND, BROTHER, UNCLE. CAUSE OF DEATH DECAPITATION BY MARGUERITE'S HEAD ASSASSIN AND THIRD LOVER MATTHEW DEMARCO.

For a moment, Ari was relieved that Alexander was on his side.

He moved onto the next coffin and continued to read the years.

So far, Alexander was the first and only vampire in the family.

Ari approached his great-grandmother's glass coffin. On the wall, the tombstone

read, 'ATHENA GAIA ASTREDO.   1900-1946. MURDERED BY CHARLEMAGNE
DEMARCO, GYPSY KILLER. SHOT FOUR TIMES.

Through the glass, Ari gazed upon one of the bullet holes revealed by her decayed
gypsy style blouse. He and the others saw how she died while battling a group of
mobsters on the crystal ball the evening Giovanni sat the new generation in the living
room with the others to teach them the family history. She fought with Charlemagne for
five minutes before he shot her. Ari placed his hands on the coffin to have a vision of the
battle in case it had something to do with Charlotte's mysterious past. Through his vision,
he saw Giovanni and Charlotte in their late teens battling criminals and monsters. Next,
he saw Athena fight and win against a crowd of mobsters before fighting Charlemagne.
He heard his great-grandmother say,

"Ari open your eyes."

The vision was quickly wiped from him by Athena's ghost.

Ari turned to find her next to him with Stefano and Roman Astredo's double
coffin behind her. "Why did you take away my vision?" His voice was nervous as though
he were standing before The Goddess.

"Charlotte's past is no concern *yet*. It is *she* who needs to tell you and the others
not by seeking the information without her knowledge. Obey the words of your
grandfather. It would be too dangerous for her past is very complex. Your focus should
be on Charlemagne and Octavia. Octavia has the potential to raise as a powerful ruler of
organized crime. More powerful then Marguerite."

"What about Charlemagne? Is he going to be her partner?"

"Traditionally yes. Charlemagne will become her most devoted follower, willingly.   He will care not for the title. He wants it all for Octavia. This will cause him to become extremely protective of her."

Ari asked, "Why am I having visions of them expecting a baby? Is that in the future or was that in the past?"

"The answer shall come to you when the time is right. I'm a spirit guide. I'm *not* permitted to give the answers to all questions. Only certain questions. There are some things a witch must find out on their own."

Ari looked around at the coffins and the corpses of deceased witches. He moved his gaze on Athena. "Am I an Astredo? Am I where I belong?"

Athena softly laughed and said, "You *are* an Astredo. That should tell you where you belong."   She disappeared.

Ari left the catacombs and walked down the North wing hallway towards the library.

In the library, he scanned the spines of journals dating back to 1509 to the present. Finding Alexander's journals, he brought them to a table, and began to read.

After the eighth journal, he discovered how Alexander shared the same concerns when he first became a vampire. The further on he read, the more relaxed he became. He had someone he could turn to. An ancestor he could summon in case he needed guidance.

His concentration was broken when Valentina entered the library dressed in her black satin nightgown. Placing her arms around his neck, she asked, "What are you reading?"

Ari told her about the visit from Athena and the things he read in Alexander's journal.

Valentina tenderly kissed his shoulder before sitting down next to him. She took his hand into her hand.

"If Marguerite completes the transformation, would you *still* want me?"

"Yes. Nothing is going to change the way I feel about you."

Ari softly smiled and caught the scent of her blood. He returned to reading the journal with his hand still in her hand.

With her free hand, she picked up a journal and began to read about Alexander's life as a vampire so she'd know what to expect from her vampiric lover.

Chapter 28

The Next Morning

The September sun dried the multi-colored leaves that fell off the tree where Valentina laid a black satin blanket under a tall tree.

Valentina had Scarlet lying on the blanket with her as she read a novel by one of her favorite mystery writers. Valentina dressed in a black gypsy style sundress.

Ari was in his den rewriting a scene in his play. Jason requested he make it more suspenseful. He told her he would join her outside when he finished.

Rosa was playing with Angel by a small pond watching the insects and frogs jump in and out of the water.

In the center of the pond stood a life size statue of a centaur.

Cats and kittens were in various parts in the garden.

"Valentina! Valentina!" screamed Rosa.

Valentina dropped the book and ran towards the creek. Fear swept through her as her eyes fell on Rosa holding Angel tightly and screaming loudly.

Rosa looked at Valentina and screamed, "Snake!"

Valentina almost stepped on a harmless black and dark green garter snake. She let out a sigh of relief as she bent down to pick up the snake.

"It's ok Rosa. It will not hurt you. See."

Rosa approached her older sister as she watched the serpent twist itself around Valentina's arm as if it were an ancient Egyptian armband.

Valentina wanted to cry in relief. At the same moment, she wanted to hold her in her arms and never let her go. She allowed Rosa to examine the snake.

Rosa bravely touched the soft leathery scales.

Angel sniffed the snake and licked Rosa's chin afraid that she might like the snake more than her.

Rosa kissed Angel on the lips, and let the snake go.

Valentina pulled her in her arms trying to stop from trembling. She held her sister vowing to protect them with her life.

"Valentina, Angel and I are hungry."

"Alright. I will fix you something." Valentina took her hand and walked towards the blanket to pick up Scarlet. When Valentina entered the kitchen with the children, she found Ari in the kitchen refilling a glass of herbal tea.

Rosa sat at the kitchen corner table while Valentina placed Scarlet in a bassinette.

Valentina tenderly placed her arm around Ari's waist and reached into the refrigerator for the left over lasagna Giovanni made a night ago.

After lunch, they put Rosa and Scarlet down for a nap.

Ari escorted Valentina towards his den. He closed the door, passionately kissed her mouth, before he lay her over his desk. From behind, he entered her pushing her slowly at first.

Valentina moaned as he moved in and out of her.

His hands caressed her breasts, her waist, hips, and her thighs before he touched her clit with his finger.

She moaned as her climax began to raise.

"Call out my name...oh my God Valentina!"

She screamed before she began to call out his name.

Ari placed his arm around her waist, lifted her from his desk, and lay her on the black leather loveseat. His mouth explored her body as his thrusts became heavier.

She caressed his back loving the feeling his penis gave to her as he stroked her. She began to buck under him.

He pinned her to the couch cushions and pushed deeper into her. His mouth caressed her skin.

Valentina screamed his name repeatedly. "Yes, yes, Ari! Ari, Ari!"

"I love you, I love you, Valentina," Ari moaned.

Valentina's nails raked across his back. "I love you, Ari," she moaned. They continued to make love.

#

Midnight was filling a querent's mug with meridian orange herbal tea while Diana prepared the tarot cards.

While Diana began the reading, Viktor entered the tearoom. He greeted Midnight and accepted a cup of tea.

Midnight said, "I'll send positive energies your way and if I could be of any help, let me know."

"I will." Viktor sat at a table and watched Diana before Midnight joined him after cleaning the teakettle. He talked to the old hippie for thirty minutes before Midnight said,

"I have to go to class. I'll talk to you guys later."

After Midnight left, Viktor continued to watch Diana as she turned up another card. As he gazed upon her Egyptian features, he noticed how much she looked like Lotus. He also realized how mature she became since he left for his business trip. His eyes focused on the way her gypsy style blouse and skirt accented her newly developed female form. She recently turned seventeen and because of that, he tried not to enjoy the sight of her leg slightly peering out from her black and gold skirt.   He wasn't sure if he should allow himself to fall in love with the young gypsy. She did bare the Astredo's mark and traditionally since it was rare for someone outside the family is born with the Triple Goddess symbol that someone was to be their chosen lover. Perhaps he should seek Raven's permission to pursue her. Viktor suddenly looked down at the cover of a Lynsay Sands paranormal romance vampire novel when her violet eyes locked with his dark eyes. He opened the book and pretended to be interested in the humorous antics between the vampire and the heroine.

Diana watched him for a moment before continuing with an old woman. She studied the last card and said, "The ace of cups. Cups represent the element water. Emotions. Love. Intuition. The cup or chalice represents the Goddess. After you overcome your obstacles, your home life will once again be at peace and happy. Your husband will pull through with his surgery. It will be a long recovery but he'll bounce back."

After a few exchanges, Diana and the old woman rose from their seats.

"Thank you and Blessed Be," she said before she left.

"Blessed Be," said Diana. She neatly stacked the cards and joined Viktor at the table. She watched him read a page before she said, "Michael likes her too. He enjoyed the 'Buffy, the Vampire Slayer' reference."

Viktor softly laughed, set the book down, and said, "It was good. Although I'm more of a Dean Kootnz and James Patterson fan."

"Kootnz isn't bad. Valentina's got me hooked on Kim Harrison and I may try one of Lisa's Galenorn and Hamilton novels," said Diana. A short vision struck her.

"What did you see?" asked Viktor.

"I saw Marguerite holding Charlemagne as an infant. Next I saw grandma and Charlemagne as young teenagers."

"Strange," he said.

"I think they are related somehow. Cousins?"

Diana rose from her chair to clean the store before closing it.

Viktor stood up to help her. "Do you think it could've been one of those abstract visions?"

"Could be." Diana wiped off the counter and tables while Viktor washed his mug and set it with the others. She stepped away from the table and looked at the floor where her boyfriend died. Her eyes moved to the place where Charlemagne tied her and shuddered at the lingering feel of his hands on her legs. She felt Viktor's hands on her upper arms softly caressing her.

"I won't allow him to hurt you," he said.

Diana softly smiled and found herself leaning back in his arms. "Do you think he'll try again?"

Truthfully, Viktor said, "I'm not sure. He didn't taste your blood so that's a good sign. He's afraid of Octavia. She would maim him if he raped anyone. Octavia would have to wait in line though." He gave her a brotherly hug.

"It bothers me that he called me Octavia. He told me I look so much like her."

Viktor said, "You're in a safe environment now. Besides, I've watched you battle mobsters. You've kicked some serious ass."

Diana laughed and said, "I have."

Viktor released her form his protective-brotherly embrace. "Let's lock up. I don't want grandma and the others to worry about us."

#

Sunlight filled the large living room in the mansion.

Octavia sat in front of a TV she enchanted to be used as a crystal ball. She prevented them from gaining any results with any divinatory tool they would use. She'd even led them in the wrong direction.

After a while, she backed off some.

Octavia entered the bedroom and placed her hand on Charlemagne's coffin. She wished she was able to climb in with him and just snuggle in his arms.

To her, he was perfect.

She kissed the coffin and returned to the living room. Sitting on the couch with his black satin robe over her arm, she began to look through a bridal magazine. She was too tall now to fit into the white sundress she originally planned to wear the night she and

Charlemagne were going to elope. The sundress hung in their bedroom closet. It was

yellowed and the yellow roses that circle her head with a long white veil had faded and

dried. Some of the rose pedals were beginning to brake off. Octavia marked a page with a

picture of a tiara made out of pearls and some sequins. The veil was framed in white

beads and white sequins. She excitedly smiled over the thought of purchasing an adult

size wedding dress this time. The seventies style sundress was made for a young

teenager. She was marking a few dress choices when Marguerite entered the room.

Marguerite watched Octavia leaf through the magazine. "What are you doing?"

Octavia looked up at Marguerite and said, "Charlemagne and I are renewing are

wedding vows the day you make me your underboss. We want our 24th wedding

anniversary to be special. He's taking me on a real honeymoon, too."

Marguerite smiled and said, "I'm glad you told me before I made out invitations."

Octavia said, "Will Demonique be ok?"

"I don't know. He's *still* in a coma."

"When could Charlemagne and I see him?"

"It's still too risky. Brenda had faeries patrol the hallways and there is a police car

stationed by the front entrance. I'll work on sneaking you in."

After Marguerite left, Octavia left the magazines open on the coffee table so she

could ask Charlemagne his opinion on the cake, his tux, and whatever else.

After sunset, Octavia and Charlemagne dined in the living room making

arrangements.

When they finished for the evening, a few hours later, they stepped into the hot tub.

Their robes hung on hooks that were made from deer hoofs.

The water was scented with ylang-ylang oil.

Lights were built in the hot tub changed from blue to red to green to yellow, and to purple.

Octavia sat next to him while they gazed at the moon and the constellations. They talked for a while before he pulled her onto his lap. She placed her legs around his waist and her arms around his neck.

Charlemagne kissed her along her neck and shoulders before he slowly licked her nipple before he sucked her. When he became hard, he entered her in slowly strokes.

Octavia grinded heavily on his lap while her hands caressed his body. She nibbled his neck before kissing him along his throat. "*Je vous aime! Charlemagne! Amoureux. Amoureux.*"

"*Vous êtes ma vie,* Octavia. Octavia!"

Octavia moaned as he moved in and out of her in a fast pace. She held him tightly while she rode him. Her head tipped back as he kissed her along her throat. She screamed in passion for Charlemagne.

Chapter 29

Astredo Institution for Mental Health

Finishing her last office call, Brenda walked down the hallway with Lisa. She wanted to look in on Demonique.

Distant humming from breathing machines and the smell of oxygen tanks lingered through the arched hallways.

"Has Marguerite, Dante, Octavia, or Charlemagne attempted to visit Demonique?" asked Lisa.

"No and that surprises me."

"What are we going to do when he wakes up?"

"Place him in one of the cells in the catacombs." Brenda opened the door to Demonique's room.

Demonique lay with tubes attached to his body. His skin was beginning to gain the color back. Blood began to refill his body.

Brenda brought out a needle and stuck it in Demonique's arm.   As she drew blood, she said, "This is a good sign that he's healthy enough to give blood.   Cut some of his hair. I want to include that as well."

Lisa cut a lock of his raven black hair and slipped it into a bag.

"Let's begin testing the blood and hair samples," said Brenda.

Chapter 30

Dusk settled over Giovanni's Gothic garden revealing the quarter moon.

Silver moonlight blanketed the statues and the small fountains.

Ari and Jason were strolling down the cobblestone path passed large statues of Egyptian Gods and Goddesses.

"Dad, did my real mother ever come for me?"

"No."

"It doesn't matter. I was only curious. Dad; you, and mom *are* my real parents as far as I am concerned. You two scarified a lot for me. If I had known who she was, I would have stayed with you and mom. She means nothing to me, but you two mean everything to me. I love you both very much."

Jason gave Ari's hand a tight squeeze. "We fell in love with you the moment I brought you inside the castle. You were a gift from the Gods to us. We had to adopt you. After we reported it to the police and went through the adoption process, we knew we did the right thing and vowed to always love you and be there for you. Brenda wanted to name you after one of our ancestors."

"Thanks." Ari thought about the conversation they had the other evening. "Do you think there's a possibility that you discovering me on your doorstep was *not* our real memories?"

"I do. Mind altering potions are dangerous and mustn't be used unless there's an emergency and it's your only option.   Octavia and Charlemagne abused the intent of the spell."

Ari softly smiled and said, "I could be anything from your real son to your nephew. Lisa and Diana could be my sisters or Viktor could be my brother. *You* could turn out to be my brother."

Jason softly laughed.

They walked towards their car and drove to the hospital where they waited for Brenda and Lisa so they could escort them to the castle safely.

Chapter 31

After tucking Rosa into bed, Valentina walked into the living room where Ari had placed an Alice Cooper CD, an Inkubus Sukkubus CD, and a Black Sabbath CD into the big stereo system.

Soft yellow candlelight flooded the dining room where Valentina and Ari shared an erotic dinner.

The rest of the castle was dark.

Giovanni and Charlotte went out to eat.

Jason, Michael, and Michelle were at the theater performing. Brenda, and Caesar were with them.

Markus and Italia were at Deadly Nightshade.

Raven was working late at Nefertiti's Tearoom.

Diana was in her room scrying for Charlemagne's location.

Viktor and Lisa were downstairs working on fighting techniques in the private gym.

Valentina moved from sitting across from him to his lap with her legs around his waist. She kissed him along his neck and shoulders while she unbuttoned his black pirate shirt.

Ari caressed her back and thigh as he softly nibbled on her shoulder. He unfastened the two shiny black buttons that closed her corset at the bottom. Ari slipped her blouse off her shoulders. He tossed it beside his shirt as he gave her long passionate kisses across her shoulders. He rose from the chair silently inviting her to dance with him. Ari pulled her into a tight embrace as they danced to some of the slow songs that were on the *School's Out* album and the *vampire Erotica* album. Ari seductively danced close to her moving his hand under her long black skirt stroking her thigh.

Valentina placed her head on his shoulder breathing in his cologne. She loved the scent. It was warm, fresh, and inviting. She kissed him a few times on the lips and nibbled on his neck.

Ari removed her bra. He kissed the side of her neck and lightly nibbled her earlobe. His hand caressed her breast, playing with her nipple. His warm breath excited her as he whispered how much he loved her. Next, his hand heavily caressed her thigh before entering her with his fingers. He thrust his fingers inside her roughly while his thumb circled around her clit. He kissed her along her neck and hungrily sucked at her breasts licking the nipple with his tongue.

Valentina softly bit his shoulder before caressing his neck and chest with her tongue. Her hand moved along his waist, thigh, and towards his penis. She massaged his balls before stroking his large penis. Ecstasy filled her from his fingers. She moaned before she screamed.

After she rode his fingers, he kissed her passionately on the lips before he laid her on the carpet. After he had removed their underwear, he entered her heavily pushing her. The vampire in him wanted to ravish her. Her screams of passion made him more sexually aroused. He sat on his knees grinding deeper and harder into her.

Valentina's fingers dug into the thick carpet. She reached her climax more than once.

Ari caressed her thighs as he moaned and called out her name. He lay on top of her continuing to stroke her. He kissed her along her throat before he sank his teeth into her skin and bit her.

She scratched his back when he broke through the skin. She moaned feeling his tongue lick the small amount of blood.

Ari kissed her neck before moving onto her shoulder. He remained inside her enjoying the feel of her wetness caressing him.

Marguerite watched from the large dining room window.

#

The cool night breeze blew the arched window open causing the deep purple and black curtains to dance around the Gothic window like faeries dancing in the pale moonlight.

Valentina left the bedroom to give Scarlet a bottle.

Ari lay beneath his black and maroon satin sheets with sensual dreams of Valentina running through his head. He couldn't wait until she returned. A photograph of Valentina stood beside a black marbled lamp and his deep purple alarm clock. His black ankh hung over the picture just above his lover's head. A black candle stood in a crystal candleholder in front of the picture.

A tiny tabby cat leaped onto the stone window ledge from the outside. The cat's dark green eyes stared hungrily at Ari's exposed neck creeping out from under the covers. The first bite left her craving for another piece of the handsome man that occupied the bedroom. Marguerite jumped from the ledge onto his bed. She rubbed her feline body against his form feeling the warmth of his body under the satin covers. Her paws walked up his leg and up to his waist flicking her tail from side to side. She gazed at Ari's peaceful face. Marguerite changed from her feline form placing her legs on either side of his waist. She wore a blue corset dress with flowing blue velvet cape around her shoulders.   She wrapped her arms around his back staring into his closed eyes.

Feeling Marguerite above him, Ari began to think he was in Valentina's arms. He slowly placed his arms around her waist seeing Valentina in his thoughts.

Her cape fell over him like a blanket as she whispered, "Ari."

In his sleep he whispered, "Ride me again, Valentina. I love it when you do that."

Marguerite gently caressed her lips with his giving him small pelvic thrusts feeling him begin to harden under his satin sheets. She nuzzled his neck searching for the right place to bite him.

"Oh Valentina, I love you so much!"

Marguerite pulled her lips away from his after she kissed him again.

Ari quickly woke. His eyes widened in terror as Marguerite placed her cold hand over his mouth as she scratched his bare chest. He screamed trying to push her away, but his scream was muffled from the pressure of her hand that stayed clamped over his mouth. Ari reached for his ankh that hung over the picture of Valentina on his nightstand. He shoved the ankh in her face.

Marguerite laughed taking the ankh from him in the hand that was scratching his chest.

"Ankhs, pentacles, pentagrams, and any other religious symbols *do not* have any effect on me.   I am much too powerful and old."   She tied Ari's hands together with the chain attaching it to the bedpost.

Ari struggled to get his hands free as he screamed for Valentina. He tried kicking her, but she overpowered him with her legs still on either side of his waist.

"Valentina!" Ari struggled to escape the vampire's torture.

Marguerite led a trail of burning passionate kisses from his lips to his pale neck. Her fangs felt like two needles being driven into his skin.

Ari screamed in pain as she drank from him satisfying her thirst for his blood. His head fell back onto his black satin pillow as his arms fell limp at his side. Next, he tasted blood as it ran down his throat.

Just as the bedroom door opened, Marguerite shape-shifted into a bat and flew out the arched window.

#

Dragon's Lair Theater

Brenda watched as Jason sang and danced between a roulette table and a blackjack table. She was mesmerized by his seductive voice as he sang, 'Luck Be a Lady Tonight.' She undressed him with her eyes as he rolled a pair of dice in his hands as if he were shuffling cards.

Later, she met him in his office. Brenda sat on the edge of his oak desk.

Jason had his hand on her thigh as he tenderly caressed it. He laid his head in her lap with his arms around her waist. "Have you tested the blood yet?"

"We're still working on it. So far Caesar, Michelle, Italia, Michael, and Viktor are negative. Tomorrow morning, Lisa and I are going to the police station to take samples from Candyce and see if they match with Demonique. For all we know, she could've just taken care of Demonique."

"What are we to do about mom's mysterious past?"

"We are going to obey dad and Athena by giving mom the chance to tell us in her own time and we are going to focus on finding Octavia and Charlemagne." Brenda ran her fingers through his hair.

"But this has gone on too long."

"Jason, please give her time. She's been through allot."

Jason rose from his seated position and tenderly pulled her in his arms. "I'll try to be a little more patient." Softly, he kissed her.

Charlemagne held Octavia tightly beneath him as he pushed her deeply. His mouth caressed her neck, throat, and shoulders as she gave him a series of moans.

Earlier, they stepped out from the hot tub, dried each other off, before Charlemagne carried her into the mansion and into their bedroom.

Her legs were wrapped around his waist as she caressed his back with her hands. She kissed him across his shoulder and his lips. She gazed into her husband's eyes. She couldn't wait from them to renew their vows.

Charlemagne let out a soft moan before he kissed her again.

Octavia hugged him tightly.

Charlemagne gazed down at her as his hands caressed her legs. He kissed her along her throat whispering, "I love the way you moan my name." He felt her spasms begin.

Octavia pressed him tight against her as pushed her harder and deeper. Her multiple orgasms began as his mouth caressed her body. Her legs tightened around his waist as she began to gasp for breath.

"Octavia, Octavia!" he softly cried wanting her to scream his name. He hugged her tightly as he caressed her back while he kissed her along her shoulders.

"Oh Charlemagne!" She wanted him to push her faster. Her nails dug into his shoulder and stabbed at his black rose tattoo. "Charlemagne, Charlemagne, Charlemagne!" she screamed in passion.

Charlemagne brought her to another orgasm before he reached his climax. He slowly pulled out of her and laid next to her.

Octavia held him close to her. "Don't stop."

"Mom will be here. After she leaves, we can continue." Charlemagne kissed her across her youthful skin.

Octavia kissed his wrinkled forehead.

He kissed her a few times on the lips before he climbed out of bed and dressed.

Octavia watched him dress before she got dressed. She approached him. She placed her arms around his neck and drew his face close to her face. "I cannot get enough of you."

He didn't want to leave her embrace. "I've never thought I'd ever hear anyone say that to me." With an arm around her waist, he escorted her out of the bedroom and into the living room in time for Marguerite to appear.

"They searched your apartment," said Marguerite.

He sat on a chair pulling Octavia onto his lap.

"Raven and Caesar took pieces of your hair and now they are examining Demonique's blood and Raven had a vision when he saw the crib. Soon they are going to know everything."

"So, I can just hit them with the memory blocking hex," said Octavia.

"What difference does it make now? Octavia's over eighteen. You both have to stop trying to protect me. Just because I'm in my nineties, doesn't mean I'm fragile."

"I *wasn't* trying to protect you in regards to Octavia getting pregnant. I was protecting *her* feelings."

Chapter 32

The warm afternoon sun poured into the castle's nursery lighting the dark room with its natural light.

A couple hours later, the sun sank behind the ancient castle.

Valentina sat on the couch as she fed Scarlet while Ari was giving Rosa a bath. Like, Scarlet, she was asleep.

Ari walked down the stairs holding Rosa in his arms. He walked into the nursery setting her in her playpen to play with her toys. He sat on the edge of the couch and watched Valentina sleep. He gently brushed her dark blonde hair away from her neck wanting her to stay home from work. Ari carefully removed Scarlet out of Valentina's arms giving her a kiss on the cheek.

"I hope you and Rosa call us dad and mom soon." He kissed her again before he laid her in her maroon and black bassinet. Ari embraced Valentina gently nibbling on her neck. The attack the other evening had left him feeling aroused wanting to be alone with Valentina more than ever. After Valentina found him lying on the bed with his wounds reopened, they hung black velvet curtains around the bed to keep the morning sun off him.

Valentina woke quickly feeling someone's cool breath blow on her neck. "Ari you startled me."

"I'm sorry. I thought I would wake you up so you won't be late." Ari held her tightly kissing her across her shoulders. His hand found her thigh and began caressing it heavily. He leaned her back into the back of the couch with his leg over hers.

Valentina hated to make him stop kissing her, but she did not want to be late. Her eyes closed in satisfaction as his mouth caressed her throat.

"What time is it?" she asked feeling him pressed her tightly against him. She placed her arms around him glancing over his shoulder. She noticed that Rosa was slowly falling asleep in the playpen.

"Ten till seven. Why don't you stay home?" He gazed into her eyes with his lips inches away from hers. His hand moved further up her thigh while his other hand began to unbutton his shirt.

Valentina was tempted to stay home from his gentle embrace, but she needed to go. His touch was making her aroused, she tried to overcome it. She hugged him tightly saying,

"Spending the entire evening in your arms sounds like paradise. One of these nights we will lay cuddled together on a blanket either down here or outside."

"I would like that," he said kissing her lips long and lovingly. His tongue explored her mouth. His hand heavily stroked her inner thigh causing her to moan softly. He added almost out of breath, "I want to take you into our bedroom and make love to you all day." He began to gather her on his lap with her legs on either side of him. He led a trial of burning passionate kissing along her neck and throat.

Valentina tried to move, but he held her in a tight embrace. "We will finish this later Ari. I have to go." Valentina gently pushed him away. Alexander's journal spoke of him having difficulties controlling his lustful desires at first.

Ari placed his hand under her blouse touching her satin bra while he nuzzled her neck. He stood lifting her in his arms and carried her into their bedroom.

Valentina found herself lying on her back with him above her slowly thrusting himself on top of her. He seduced her into calling her client to tell him she would be an hour late due to Rosa requesting they both get her ready for bed. Ari hung up the phone for her as he continued to caress her covered breast with his mouth.

Valentina caressed his back heavily as his hand slipped between her legs. She watched him kiss her chest and before he looked up at her.

His finger went into her slowly, moving in and out of her.   Ari kissed her lips a few times and whispered, "I want to make love to you." Ari kissed the corner of her mouth before kissing her passionately on the mouth. Ari nuzzled her neck. "I want you to be my wife. I want Rosa and Scarlet to be our daughters. I want to adopt them."

"I want to be your wife and I want my sisters to become our daughters." She kissed him deeply on the lips as he pleased her with his finger. She called out his name as her body climaxed.

After they made out, they held each other close with him lying above her. He gently kissed her cheek as he reached into his shirt pocket with drawing a tiny black velvet box. He opened it revealing a two-karat diamond ring. He slipped it onto her finger. "I love you."

Valentina tenderly caressed his back feeling his warm breath on her neck. "I love you."

#

Rosa was playing on a leopard-printed blanket while playing with toys and a few kittens and Angel.

Ari pulled a deep purple picture from the refrigerator and poured apple juice into a deep burgundy spill proof cups before carrying them to the nursery.

From the tiny black radio fixed below the changing table, came the sound of heavy metal and Goth rock music.

Ari changed Scarlet's diaper before sitting on the blanket next to Rosa.

A few more kittens ventured over to play with the young witch and the vampire-witch.

Scarlet smiled at him. She placed her tiny arms around his neck hugging him and talking baby talk to him.

Ari gently hugged her whispering in her ear, "I love you so much." He played with a grey and white kitten while holding Scarlet around the waist on his knee. He realized why Viktor and Brenda wanted him and Valentina to wait a while before they adopted Valentina's sisters. He liked that their family was giving them a chance to experience what it would be like if they would become Scarlet and Rosa's parents. It was a lot of work. Although, he found himself loving it. He loved the parental responsibilities.

It took a while anyway for the adoption process to go through so it would still give them more time.

After a while, she started to fuss wanting to join Rosa with the cat and the kittens. Ari carefully sat her down giving her a bottle of apple juice.

"Rosa, I would like to talk to you and your sister about something," Ari said as if the toddler would understand everything he was about to say.

Rosa lifted her head at the sound of his voice and giggled quietly. She gently smiled as he tenderly took her small hand into his.

Ari tenderly caressed her smooth finger with his as he asked, "Rosa, your big sister Valentina and I love you and Scarlet with all of our heart.   I want to be *more* than just your brother-in-law."

Rosa watched as he used his other hand to pull another ring box from his black shirt. Her large brown eyes grew large viewing a shiny sapphire stone on a pewter band.

Ari tenderly slipped the ring on her finger. "Rosa, Scarlet, will you be mine and Valentina's daughters?"

Rosa gazed into Ari's loving eyes. "I love you, daddy."

Tears of joy filled Ari's eyes as he walked over to Rosa and lifted her in his arms. He held her tightly not wanting to let go.

Chapter 33

Nefertiti's Tearoom carried the scent of sage as Raven cleansed his tarot deck. His last appointment was due any moment. He laid the tarot cards down when Diana entered the room from the office.

Diana poured a cup of water into the tea kettle and filled the trey of shortbread cookies.

"Diana, I need you to go back to the castle right away."

"Why?" Before she could turn around, Raven placed his arm around her waist and with his free hand; he held a wand to her head. Diana slumped forward in his arms.

Raven nervously kissed her cheek and sent her by magick to Castle Olympia. He quickly turned when Octavia entered the store.

Octavia said, "Are you alone?"

"You're my last customer for the evening."

Octavia browsed through the tarot decks that were for sale and the verity of Pagan and Wiccan books. "Where's my niece?"

"Tell me how Lotus died and who your and Charlemagne's baby is."

Octavia approached Raven and said, "I can't believe you and the others haven't figured it out yet. I want Diana."

Raven suddenly felt his mind become unclouded as a short vision showed him Michelle, Charlotte, Italia, and Michael finally discovering a potent spell that would unlock their memories. He remembered *everything*. Tears filled his eyes.

Octavia grabbed his hand. "I see our latest memory blocking spell has been broken. You know now how Lotus died now. I'm not satisfied with you just remembering. I want you to feel the hurt death can cause again."

A vision flashed in his mind:

1983

Salem, Ohio

Charlemagne and Octavia were in Lotus and Raven's apartment. Charlemagne tore open the dresser drawers allowing the clothes to fall onto the floor. He searched through the closet and dumped its contents all over the floor.

Octavia and Lotus fought with their knives while Charlemagne left to go into the next room. Lotus sliced Octavia's arm before punching her in the face to knock her to the floor.

Charlemagne tore open the closet door as he searched for the infant. He was about to remove the blanket, when he was stabbed in the side by Lotus who pushed him into a stand of candles.

Lotus was about to reach for Diana when she felt a sharp pain enter her through the center of her back. She turned to find Octavia standing in the doorway as she held a gun with a silencer. She felt Charlemagne's arm encircle her waist and stab her in the stomach.

Charlemagne let her fall to the blood soaked carpet while Octavia aimed the gun at the lump under the blanket.

Octavia fired the gun at the blanket. She watched Charlemagne lift the blanket. Their eyes fell on a pile of dirty clothes. Octavia gazed down at her dying sister and looked at Charlemagne. "A faerie must have stolen her and now is hiding her from us."

The sound of a car stopping in front of the apartment building caught their attention. Charlemagne looked out the window and saw Raven, Damian, and Midnight race towards the apartment. The sound of police sirens sounded in the distance.

"The Gods have giving them a warning through the tarot cards and gave one of them a vision that Lotus and Diana were in danger!" Charlemagne said.

Octavia gazed down at Lotus. "I'll work on a memory blocking spell for Raven, Damian, and Midnight and give them a different memory. Let's get out of here before we are discovered."

They left hearing Raven enter the apartment calling out Lotus's name.

In the corner of the closet, invisible, stood a faerie dressed in a long burgundy robe safely holding Diana in his arms.

Lotus saw him and knew he was there to escort her to Summerland.

The faerie laid Diana in the basket before he escorted Lotus to be with the Gods. He watched as Raven ran into the room and Damian picked Diana up into his arms.

Raven held Lotus close as Midnight and Diana stood behind him waiting for the police to come with tears in their eyes.

Lotus gazed into Raven's eyes. "I love you, Raven."

Raven kissed her forehead. "I love you, Lotus." He kissed her passionately on the lips before her head fell on his chest dying in his arms. He cradled her in his arms crying heavily as he buried his face in her long black hair.

Midnight and Diana knelt beside Raven and placed their hands on his shoulder crying with him.

Raven backed away from Octavia. "You bitch! She was your sister!"

"Some sister. If she loved me so much, then why did she and you continue to keep Charlemagne away from me?"

"You still *don't* realize what he done to you when you were younger."

"I no longer wish to discuss why you and she hate Charlemagne." Octavia softly smiled and said, "Charlemagne and I will be renewing our wedding vows the day Marguerite makes me her underboss. I'm more excited over the wedding vow renewal then the ceremony that will make me her underboss. I'm finally having the wedding I've always wanted."

Raven lifted his arm and pointed his wand at Octavia. "We're taking you in to the police and you *will* tell us where Charlemagne is."

Octavia pointed her wand at him. "Give me Diana."

"She's not here. I've hidden her." Raven waved his wand at her only to have her escape the spell.

Octavia hit him with a powerful blast.

Raven fell onto the tarot reading table sending all 78 cards into the air. He slowly stood only to fall to his knees as his bones and muscles began to take on a new shape. His scream turned into a feline's screech.

Octavia walked towards the black cat and grabbed him by the scruff of his neck. "You're my prisoner now. I'm going to make you watch Diana die before I kill you." She left the tearoom with Raven in her arms.

Chapter 34

Discovering Diana curled up on the couch in one of the parlors, Giovanni sat beside her taking Raven's letter out from under her arm after discovering his name on the front. An uneasy feeling developed inside him as he tried to awaken her. Realizing she was under the witch's enchantment, he slowly opened the envelope. His hands trembled as he read:

'Giovanni,

At the tearoom, I received a call from Octavia requesting to come in to see me. She had some information about Lotus's death and who their child was. She and Charlemagne have been searching for the baby they were forced to give up.

She told me that if I give her Diana, she'll tell me everything.

I plan to lure her here so we can finally capture her. After I send Diana home, I'm calling Jason for back up since he and Caesar are still at the theater. They're closer. I wrote this letter after she called me in case I don't get the chance to notify Jason and Caesar.

Love,

Raven le Sorcère.'

In Italian, Raven wrote another paragraph explaining a secret he had been wanting to tell before he was hit with a memory altering potion. It was evidence that would prove

Giovanni and Charlotte's suspicions correct concerning Octavia and Charlemagne's lost child.

Chapter 35

The morning sun caressed the woods, statues, and plants in the mammoth Gothic garden as well as the ancient castle.

Giovanni phoned Valentina at work and sent for Lisa when he discovered Diana in the parlor while he was leaving an offering to the Egyptian Gods and Goddesses. Giovanni placed Diana in her bedroom until the sleeping spell wore off. He and Charlotte instructed Caesar and Michelle to guard her bedroom until her aunt was captured and Charlemagne executed. Charlotte wanted to question Octavia to see if there were anything else she was hiding.

Giovanni and Charlotte were now speaking to a private detective to instruct him to search for Raven after Charlotte showed him a photo of the witch during a family picnic.

"Raven loved his daughter. He would never abandon her. You've seen his letter to me. So that is proof that he had planned to return home."

The detective was a few years younger than Giovanni. His thin graying hair matched his gray suit and long black trench coat. The detective was a human-size faerie. He took the photo and said, "Have you reported her aunt to the police yet?"

"Yes. They questioned her, but could not charge her with attempted murder because of lack of evidence. They dismissed the case saying Raven left Diana and skipped town." Giovanni lit another cigar pulled out of a leopard's skull that sat on his desk.

The detective said, "Raven sounds like a very loving father from what you have told me."

"He is. He has done a lot for her since her mother died.   He still grieves for his late wife. I just wish he notified us right after she phoned. Charlotte and I have always loved Raven as though he were our real son."

"I will do my best to search for him.   I'll report to you once a week with any news."

"Thank you," said Charlotte.

"I will find him, even if it takes years."

#

Valentina entered Diana's bedroom holding Rosa's hand where Diana slept. Lisa was behind her holding Scarlet.

Viktor and Michael were seated in Victorian style chairs.

They sat at the edge of the bed watching Diana slowly lift her eyes. Diana woke from her father's spell around six in the morning and had been drifting out of sleep until nine o'clock.

The brass grandfather clock read fifteen after nine as Lisa asked, "How are you feeling?"

"Fine. Michael told me what happen to dad."

"Giovanni told us he and Charlotte has hired a detective to search for Raven," Lisa said as she and Valentina grasps Diana's hands in a sisterly way.

"We are sorry. I'm sure we will hear something," Valentina said.

"Thanks."

"We are always here for you." Valentina tenderly squeezed her hand.

"What else did the letter contain?" asked Diana.

Viktor said, "We don't know. Grandma told me she would tell us later."

"I bet it ties in with her mysterious past," said Michael.

"I hope she obeys great-grandma and informs us soon. I hate secrets," said Viktor.

"I have a feeling she will but only when she's ready. We shouldn't pressure her," said Valentina.

They spent most of the morning talking until they were called to lunch.

Chapter 36

Octavia sat on Charlemagne's lap kissing him softly on the mouth as his hands caressed her leg and back. She gave her husband a tight squeeze before she looked at the black cat she had caged on a stand. She smiled as Charlemagne kissed her lips a few times.

Octavia softly kissed Charlemagne's shoulder as she moved her gaze from his handsome old face to Marguerite standing in the center of the living room with Dante faithfully at her side. Octavia slid from his lap as he placed his arm around her waist. "I took care of Raven as you ordered."

Marguerite glanced at the cat pacing around in its cage and back at the two mobsters. "You didn't kill him?"

Octavia smiled. "I want to wait until we murder Diana. I want to see his heart break. I enjoy inflicting pain on those who have crossed me." She gently caressed Charlemagne's thigh.

Marguerite sat on a chair with Dante seated on the arm of her chair. She looks at

Octavia and Charlemagne. "Are you ready for tonight?"

Charlemagne tightened his hold on Octavia. "We can't wait." He gazed into Octavia's evil violet eyes.

Laying her head on Charlemagne's chest, Octavia said, "Me either." She gently kissed his mouth.

#

Marguerite's back yard was decorated with pink roses and white candles lit along the path through the garden.

Members of the DeMarco Crime family sat on stone benches in front of a white archway with moon flower vines twisting through the lattice work columns.

Ghosts of Delilah, Molly, and Jacqueline stood on the left side of Marguerite while Frank, Lucian, Tony, and Nikkolas stood beside Charlemagne.

White candles burned around the archway.

Pink and white roses decorated the benches.

When Marguerite rose from her seat, she approached her gangsters, those in attendance grew silent. Her gown was pale pink to match Octavia and Charlemagne's wedding colors.

She spoke to her people, "Family, friends, and associates; Octavia DeMarco will be made underboss tonight after her and Charlemagne's vow renewal. She is to be respected and honored as you honor and respect me." As Marguerite concluded her speech, she signaled for the bridal march to begin.

Charlemagne, dressed in a white tuxedo with a pink rose on the lapel and a pink comber bun, stood next to an altar under the arch.

The congregation rose when Octavia began to walk down the aisle in a white satin wedding gown and a long flowing veil. A tiara of pearls sat on her black hair. Pearls and sequins covered her corset style bodice.   Around her neck was a black rose with matching earrings. Her bouquet where made up of white and pink roses.

Octavia locked eyes with Charlemagne and smiled. When she arrived at the altar, she held his hand. She and Charlemagne faced Marguerite as she began the ceremony.

When they exchanged vows, they faced each other holding hands.

Charlemagne slid her wedding ring on her finger and said, "With this ring, I thee wed."

Octavia copied and after she said, "With this ring, I thee wed," Marguerite lifted a smaller version of her crown from the altar and placed it on Octavia's head after Octavia moved the tiara across her forehead.

Marguerite said, "I now pronounce you husband and wife and my underboss. Kiss your bride."

Charlemagne held her close and kissed her mouth slowly and passionately.

#

His hand moved to the front of her dress.

Octavia whispered, "Not here."

He kissed her across her forehead as he whispered, "Everyone 's on the patio dancing. No one will see or hear us. We'll join them in a moment."

Charlemagne tenderly led her into the gazebo after she and him spoke with friends and family.

Octavia looked at him nervously before he kissed her throat and neck.

While kissing her, Charlemagne led her towards a wooden bench that wrapped around the gazebo, removed his pants, sat on the edge of the bench, and drew her near.

Octavia stood in front of him with her back towards the entrance. Her wedding dress was temporally removed after he finished undressing himself. She wasn't wearing a bra or underwear. Only a pink lace garter.

Charlemagne kissed her stomach and hips before he entered her with his tongue. His hands caressed her ass.

Octavia moaned. Her fingers coiled around Charlemagne's hair while he licked and probed her clit.

Charlemagne tightened his hold around her waist as he brought her to her second climax. He opened her legs and sat her on his lap. He kissed her across her shoulders while she placed her legs around his waist.

Octavia laid her head on his chest. She wanted to moan louder but was still nervous with their family and friends outside.

Charlemagne pushed her as he covered her in deep passionate kisses. "Grind on my lap...oh...Octavia...don't be afraid to cry out for me." He loved the way she stroked him.

Octavia slowly began to return his passionate kisses while she grinded heavily on his lap. An intense wave of ecstasy rushed through her. She couldn't hold in her moans and cries. "Oh... Charlemagne, Charlemagne. I love you, I love you."

Charlemagne kissed her mouth and whispered in his raspy voice, "I love you." Still inside her, he rose from the bench and laid her on the bench and mounted her. He continued to move in and out of her before he moved deeper inside her.

Octavia moaned, cried, and screamed repeatedly. Her hands caressed his thighs before one hand caressed his chest. Her fingers clutched at the grey and blonde chest hairs. She gasped for breath.

Charlemagne grunted before he said, "Pull my chest hair........oh yes, Octavia. Harder... Harder." His hand reached to her thigh, caressed it, and moved to her clit. He stroked her clit with his finger.

Octavia began to buck in front of him. She screamed and pulled his chest hairs. "Oh God, oh God, Charlemagne, Charlemagne, Charlemagne!

Charlemagne bent over her and continued to stroke her. His hands caressed her thighs and breasts. Charlemagne brought her to her climax three times before he climaxed inside her. He tenderly pulled her into a seated position after she sat on his lap. He ran his fingers threw her hair.

Octavia trembled with ecstasy. She nestled his chest enjoying the sound of his rapid heartbeat. Her arms were around his neck. Her eyes closed when he caressed her arm and back.

Charlemagne nuzzled her neck and whispered in his low husky voice that turned her on, "Happy Anniversary. "

After a few moments in each other's arms, they stepped into their clothes. Charlemagne helped Octavia zip the back of her wedding dress.   They joined the rest of the party on the patio.

Chapter 37

The moon laid a thin blanket of silver light over the massive fenced in garden of Castle Olympia. Moonlight glittered through the cool water that flowed from the stone gargoyles, faeries, Goddesses, and Gods into ponds of every shape and size. The white moonlight caused the white roses to glow as if they were under a black light. The white beams caused an eerie light to form over the flying buttresses and the arched towers.

Nut's twilight gown was decorated with stars that depicted the many ancient constellations.

Crickets played their sorrowful symphony as the fireflies lit up the breeze.

Weeping willows gave a ghostly appearance with their veil-like branches sweeping the grass and cobblestone as if in mourning.

Bats were flying around the arched towers and around the towers on the hospital. The area where the outdoor altar sat was occupied by a dozen cats and kittens as Ari attempted to scry for Charlemagne.

Michael and Italia were making more silver bullets.

Diana and Michelle were in the kitchen brewing more potions.

The others sat in front of the crystal ball searching for Marguerite.

Ari wanted to search for Charlemagne and to step out of the castle to try out his new vampiric night vision. Filling the black scrying dish with water, he gazed into the blackness.

The bright crescent moon reflected in the black water.

In an incense burner stood a honeysuckle incense stick. Honeysuckle was one of many herbs used to aid psychic powers.

Meditating on the water, Ari saw,

'Charlemagne and Octavia stood behind a layered cake with the words 'Octavia and Charlemagne twenty-four years.' Together they cut their wedding cake.

The vision advanced to Octavia and Charlemagne slow dancing together. Charlemagne tenderly caressed her back while she rested her head on his chest. Charlemagne tenderly kissed her and said, "Before we leave for our honeymoon, I want to visit our son and see if he's ready to move in with us."

Octavia said, "I'll pack while you are gone."

"You don't want to come with me?"

"I'll see him at the apartment. He'll be more excited to see you then me."

"Alright."

For three hours, they danced and mingled with the other mobsters.

The vision moved foreword to show Charlemagne pulling into the Astredo Institution for Mental Health's parking lot.

Ari lifted his head from the bowl.

Demonique. He *was* their son.

Quickly, Ari rose from his knees. He didn't have time to run inside to tell the others about the vision. Instead he said, "Goddess Hecate, send Diana the vision You have just sent to me. So Mote it be."

He ran through the garden towards his car. He left the garden behind as he ran down the road until he stepped onto the gravel. He jumped in his car and tore off for the hospital.

The emergency room doors burst open as Ari quickly reached the elevator. He anxiously waited for the doors to open. He stepped in the elevator after a nurse stepped out. He hit the number for the third floor.

When the steel doors folded open, he ran down the vaulted hall towards

Demonique's room. He tore open the door, stormed in the room, and said to the faerie guards, "Where *is* he? Where the fuck is Charlemagne?"

Demonique lay in bed undisturbed by the witch's outburst. His breathing slow.

"Charlemagne, Mr. Astredo?" asked Nurse Collins as he checked Demonique's vitals.

Ari hadn't noticed the fifty-three-year-old nurse beside the young mobster. "Has there been anyone in here?"

"Only your mother, Nurses Stoker and Bernadette, as well as myself."

"Are you sure? Charlemagne's around grandfather and grandmother's age. Grey-blond hair. Handsome. Slightly psychotic."

"Yes, I'm quite sure. Is something wrong? You don't mean Charlemagne *DeMarco*, do you? He's been dead for sixteen years." Nurse Collins approached Ari and looked the handsome witch over. "Do you need to speak with someone?"

"No, I *don't* need to talk to anyone! What I need is to find is...Never mind!" Ari left the room and left the hospital. He noticed Charlemagne's car was pulling out of the parking lot. He felt foolish for bursting in on Nurse Collins and asking if Demonique was visited by a serial killer the world *thinks* is dead.

He drove towards home noticing Charlemagne stopping at the end of the garden. Ari stepped into the garden. He didn't understand why Charlemagne didn't stay. He arrived to the hospital to pick up his son. *'Perhaps Charlemagne saw me and hid somewhere. That makes sense. The old pervert was probably waiting for me to leave.'*

Ari stopped suddenly when he heard the chilling sound of a familiar low husky voice call out his name. For strength, he touched a statue of Hercules that stood beside a carved bench and an azalea bush. He slowly turned and confronted Charlemagne. At first he didn't know what to say to the vampiric serial killer. Finding the words, Ari asked, "Why did you follow me? I gave Diana the same vision that told me you were going to the hospital to pick up Demonique."

Charlemagne softly smiled. "Demonique. How is he? There are too many holy objects in the hospital for me to enter. I can barely stand to be in this garden."

"I won't allow you to take him home. He'll be placed in the jail cells in our catacombs until he is well enough to hand over to the police. And you, we *aren't* going to wait for the police to arrest you. We are going to *kill* you."

Charlemagne approached Ari, unarmed. He was suddenly knocked to the ground.

The two vampires fought on the ground.

Charlemagne moved Ari on his back and sat on his chest with his hands holding his wrists. "I *didn't* come to fight. Ari, listen to me..."

Ari lifted his leg and struck Charlemagne in the back with his knee. When his arm was free, Ari punched him and pushed him off him.

Charlemagne rolled on his back just as Ari kicked his side a few times.

"I know why you came. Your son, Demonique, you're taking that worthless asshole back to wherever the hell you and Octavia are. Is Candyce his mother? Why did she raise him instead of you and Octavia raising him?" Ari's foot rested on his chest. He wished he had his sword. Ari wanted to dismember him for killing Adrian and attacking Diana and Lisa.

Charlemagne said sounding offended, "*Don't* ever accuse me of sleeping with that whore! Octavia would *kill* me if I ever cheated on her."

"Is Octavia Demonique's mother?" Ari stomped on his chest.

"Ari, stop you're hurting me."

"*I'm* hurting you! You killed my great-grandmother and my friend Adrian. You almost raped Diana and attacked Lisa. Not to mention all those murders you've committed. You deserve to suffer."

"I can't believe you haven't figured out your visions. My memory blocking hex has been lifted." Charlemagne's face was kicked. Charlemagne grabbed Ari's leg and pulled him down on the grass.

They battled again.

Ari was thrown against a wall of vines before he was pinned to the wall by Charlemagne. As he struggled a vision appeared,

Salem, Ohio

1977

Charlemagne rose from the rocking chair with the baby in his tight embrace when Marguerite entered the nursery. "I told you mom, we are keeping him."

"It's too dangerous."

Charlemagne left the room and entered the bedroom where Octavia was seated in bed and feeling better.

"Can I see our baby now?" Octavia asked.

Charlemagne laid their son in her arms. He sat on the bed next to Octavia with his arm around her waist. It tore him apart that Marguerite wanted them to get rid of their creation. Tenderly, Charlemagne kissed the infant's forehead. Next, he kissed Octavia before resting his head on her shoulder. He loved his small family.

Octavia looked at the baby's face and said, "He's going to look like dad. I can see his Egyptian features." This was the first time she was able to hold him since she gave birth twelve hours ago. She looked at Charlemagne and softly smiled. "I think Marguerite is wrong. He'll grow up loving us. We can make it work out," said Octavia finally siding with Charlemagne.

Marguerite entered the bedroom and asked, "Have you looked at his shoulder, Octavia?"

Octavia removed the cream satin blanket from the infant's shoulder and gazed upon the God symbol with fear in her eyes.

"We can make it work out, Octavia," said Charlemagne. "He's ours. If he's around us long enough the tattoo will disappear. I want to keep him."

Octavia had a short vision of their child fighting against them with the rest of the Astredo family. The vision showed their child hating Charlemagne. "How did that happen? We can't keep him. He'll grow up killing you."

Tears filled his eyes. Charlemagne was handed the baby. He held his son close to him. "Octavia, you'll regret it."

Octavia gazed at the baby in Charlemagne's arms fearfully. "I don't know if I want to be a mother now."

"Octavia, you'll be a good mother. I'll teach you how to love him. Why don't you love him? I love him," said Charlemagne.

"He won't love us. He wasn't meant for us." Octavia continued to stare at the witch she just gave birth to. She didn't have any material instincts.

Charlemagne let a few tears fall from his eyes. "I don't understand why you don't want to give him a chance. You couldn't wait to have a baby."

Octavia just stared. Subconsciously, she recoiled from Charlemagne's touch. She shivered as he placed his arm around her waist again.

"Octavia, what's wrong?"

Marguerite entered the bedroom and said, "You, Esmeralda, and Amari traumatized her. Mostly you. She's too young to be a wife and a mother."

Charlemagne looked at Octavia and for the first time since he'd been dating her, realized the horror of what he did to Octavia. "Can we talk about this in the living room?"

Marguerite left the room.

Charlemagne gently kissed Octavia's forehead and said, "I'll be back. Get some sleep."

Octavia stared at him not understanding why she felt that having a sixty-nine-year-old man's child at her age was wrong. Her mother told her it was normal. Tears filled her eyes. She suddenly felt confused.

With one arm holding the baby, he helped her lay in bed. He pulled the blanket over her. He joined Marguerite in the living room.

"How could you be so fucking stupid? She doesn't even realize what you did to her was wrong. If I had known how old she was before you told me you were married, I would have moved her in with Dante, Gerard, and me until she was old enough to be your girlfriend. I thought Esmeralda was smarter than that to allow this to happen."

"Esmeralda was desperate to get Octavia away from Amari. Mom, please don't tell Octavia it was wrong. She's the first woman to accept me for what I am. I don't want to lose her or the baby." Charlemagne held his son tightly in his arms.

"She accepted you because she's too young to understand the monster you really are."

The baby began to cry from Marguerite's raised voice.

Charlemagne rocked him tenderly patting his back. He nuzzled his soft fragile neck. He didn't want to give this precious little boy up. "Mom, let me work this out. It may not be as bad as you predict."

"How are you going to raise him with a wife who hasn't grown up herself?"

"She's mature for her age."

"She doesn't seem like it. Octavia is too young for all this. I'm sorry Charlemagne. If we had taken her to the hospital, your child would have been taken away from you sooner once they would find out whom you are and that she was fourteen when she became pregnant and gave birth at fifteen. You will be sent to prison for statutory rape."

"I want to keep him."

"No. I'm putting her on birth control pills so this doesn't happen again. Why didn't you use protection?"

"Because we wanted to have a baby. I didn't think she wouldn't know what to do with a child. She was excited when she found out she was pregnant. We both were."

Next, the vision showed Charlemagne placing the baby in the wooden cradle before entering the bedroom. He crawled in bed next to Octavia. He pulled her into his arms.

She clung onto him and cried on his shoulder.

Charlemagne caressed her back and said, "I have to go now. Are you sure you don't want to hold him again?"

Octavia stopped crying and looked at him. "Can we try again for a better baby someday?" The question was asked as though she was talking about a car not *a human being.*

The question pained his heart. He couldn't understand why she had no feeling for their child. Had he done this to her? He felt terrible for making her his girlfriend at an age when she didn't fully understand the adult things everyone seemed to be making her do.

"Can we, Charlemagne?"

"We can. But, we have to wait until you're ready to have a baby."

"Why? Why is everyone against us being together? Why can't everyone see that I'm an adult?"

"Just get some rest. I won't be gone long."

"Hold me," she said.

"When I return I'll hold you. Marguerite will be in the next room in case you need anything." He kissed her a few times on the mouth, hugged her, and left the bedroom.

The vision advanced to show Charlemagne placing a basket in the Ohio River only to have Raven and Lotus pull it out and place the basket on the castle's doorstep.

Next, Brenda and Jason were seen signing adoption papers.

Ari woke from the vision and stared in shock at Charlemagne. He stepped back. "No. No. No! You *can't* be my father."

Charlemagne softly smiled. "I am. Ari, it *wasn't* my idea to give you up. I *tried* to fight Octavia and Marguerite to keep you. Octavia was too young. She *didn't* know how to be a mother. She regrets it now because she now understands how much it hurt me."

"She *was* too young you fucking pervert!"

"Don't call me that. I made a mistake. I should have waited until she was older."

"I hate you. I fucking *hate* you!"

"Don't hate me, Ari. I want to be a part of your life. That's why I came here. To take you home. Your mother and I will be gone for a while so you'll have time to adjust to your new home.   I love you. I *never* stopped loving you."

"You *don't* know how to love. I don't want anything to do with you!"

Charlemagne's heart shattered. "Ari, please understand. I didn't want to give you up."

"How can you tell me you love me when you spent all those two years posing as our butler trying to kill me and the others?"

"I had planned to murder Viktor, Michael, Diana, and Valentina. With you, I wanted to kidnap. It hurt so bad to hear you call Jason, dad. I wanted to take you back so bad. Octavia only wanted you back because it was what I wanted." He pulled Ari close to him with an arm around his waist. His hand touched his face. "You look like your grandfather Amari. You grew into a handsome man. Give me a chance, Ari. I love you and I want you back."

Ari stared at him in shock.   "No. Octavia is messing with my visions. You're *not* my father. You can't be." Tears filled his eyes.

"Haven't you ever wondered why you look like Lotus, Octavia, and Diana? You have my eyes. They were grey when I was younger." Charlemagne ran his fingers through his black hair. "I think I can get Octavia to fall in love with you again. She wanted you until she had the vision." Charlemagne embraced him tightly in his arms. He never thought he'd ever get to hold his son again.

"Get away from me. I hate you."

"How can you hate me? What have I ever done to you? I want you to give me another chance. Please." Charlemagne kissed his forehead and cheeks.

Ari stepped back and left the garden. He didn't want to look at him. He ran into the kitchen, through the dining room, and finally the living room where the others sat. He looked at his adopted gypsy family and suddenly felt guilty for every murder Charlemagne committed. He expected them to reject him for being the son of a rapist.

Brenda approached Ari and said, "Diana shared your vision of Marguerite arguing with Charlemagne after she received the vision you had earlier. We know." Brenda reached for him but he backed away.

"Stay away from me. I'm not worthy to be a part of this family. My parents are mobsters. Marguerite, my grandmother, is the Godmother. My father murdered your kind." Ari back towards the dining room.

Jason approached him and said, "You're *our* son now, Ari. We love you." He grabbed his arm.

Ari backed away. "How can you love me after this? Your enemy is my father. My *grandmother* murdered Cassandra and the others."

Jason, as well as the others, began to get tears in their eyes. "Ari, that doesn't matter. You're *not* Charlemagne or Marguerite."

Ari left the living room.

Jason began to go after him when Giovanni stopped him.

"Perhaps, I should go speak to him," said Giovanni.

Suddenly, the scent of lavender filled the living room before Athena appeared. "He's too upset to listen to *any* of you."

"We can't let him be alone now. He needs us," said Jason.

"He does. But, right now he needs to speak with someone who was Charlemagne's victim," said Athena. "Wait for us."

Holding Brenda's hand, Jason watched his grandmother leave for the garden.

Ari sat in front of a statue of the Goddess Hecate and cried. He felt a gentle hand gently caress his back. He noticed his head was laying in someone's lap.

Athena's maroon gypsy skirt flowed under him. The gold coins on her black hip scarf reflected the moon light. She ran her fingers through his raven black hair. "Ari, you belong here with us."

Hearing his great-grandmother's voice, he encircled his arms around her waist and continued to cry.

"Ari, you are *not* Charlemagne. You share his blood but that's all. You are *not* a killer and he being your father will *not* make you one. Your adopted family will never reject you. *Don't* place his guilt on yourself."

Ari lifted his head from her lap and saw compassion in her eyes.

She continued to run her fingers through his hair and caress his back.

"Grandmother Athena, I was hoping those visions of Octavia and Charlemagne would turn out that Demonique would be their son. I wouldn't have minded if Raven and

Lotus were my real parents. Even Jason and Brenda"

"You were in denial. A part of you knew the truth."

"I don't mean to sound disrespectful, but you don't understand. Charlemagne has been grandma and grandpa's enemy for years. He killed *gypsies*."

Athena softly laughed. "I wouldn't understand, eh? Did you forget how I died?"

Ari looked at Athena said, "You were murdered during a long fight with the DeMarco Crime family out here."

"By that hedge, near the waterfall, I was murdered by Charlemagne. We fought for twenty minutes before he stabbed and shot me. Charlotte was the first one who found me. I died in her arms. Ari; Octavia and Lotus were gypsies also. That makes *you* and Diana gypsies."

"I knew that but..." Ari paused to let what Athena said sink in. "Octavia and Lotus were sisters," he said.

"You and Diana are cousins. Raven is your uncle and Lotus is your aunt."

Ari softly smiled and said, "Diana's my cousin. My *blood* cousin. That's awesome. I love Diana and to have someone like Raven for an uncle would be cool."

"You see. It's *not* that terrible. Charlemagne *would* be a terrible father and a terrible role model if he would ever have the chance to become a father again."

"Would he? What about Demonique? Was that wishful thinking on my part?"

"The Gods will *never* allow Charlemagne to have another child. He and Octavia are too evil. Demonique loves Octavia and Charlemagne as though they were his true parents. They're not. Charlemagne was appointed Demonique's body guard and teacher the moment he was born. Charlemagne had once been appointed as Octavia's body guard as well.   Marguerite wanted to train her."

They continued to talk until they returned to the castle.

Chapter 38

Octavia closed her suitcase that sat on the bed. She carried it into the living room and sat it on the chair. She returned to their bedroom and opened Charlemagne's dresser drawer. She picked out a sexy pair of underwear for him to wear on their honeymoon. Octavia looked at his black thong and wondered if they should try again for a child. She would like to get pregnant again, but there was a part of her that was still hesitant to do so. Since the eighties, she has had four miscarriages. She placed the thong in the suitcase. Next, she went to the closet and pulled out one of her teddies he loved to see her in.

She was placing shampoo and soap into the suitcase when Charlemagne entered the house. She walked out from the bedroom, down the hall and stairs, and found him sitting on the couch brooding. She sat next to him and asked, "Are you alright?"

Charlemagne placed his arm around her waist and pulled her onto his lap. He needed to hold her. Tears still lingered in his eyes. "He doesn't want anything to do with us."

Octavia held him close and tenderly caressed his back. "I'm not surprised. Charlemagne, I'm sorry."

Charlemagne softly cried on her shoulder. "I wanted to bring him home to us. I wanted him back."   He softly caressed her back and her thigh.

"He doesn't belong to us anymore. You have to move on." Octavia hugged him tenderly.

Charlemagne's tears stopped. He kept his head on her shoulder and said, "Your vision was correct. He looked at me with so much hate. If we have kept him, do you think he would've stayed with us or would he left us for them?"

"I don't know." Combing her fingers through his hair, she said, "I'm almost finished packing. The suitcase is on the bed. Why don't you finish packing while I run to the store for a few things?"

"What type of things?"

Octavia softly laughed. "I want to purchase some incenses." She played with his hair, and said, "Maybe some oils, and perhaps some other things that will make our honeymoon more exciting."

Charlemagne softly smiled, kissed her shoulder, looked at her, and said, "I can't wait. Before I left for Castle Olympia, I picked up a few anniversary gifts I'll pack while you're gone."

Octavia kissed his forehead and said, "I have your gifts in the suitcase already." She slid off his lap and walked towards the dinette where her purse hung over a chair.

Charlemagne gave her another hug, kissed her, and watched her leave.

Chapter 39

Thick black rain clouds slowly devoured the mid afternoon sun as a faint roar of thunder sounded in the distance. The once bright orange and yellow light casts a pale light over the grand castle before it was replaced by darkness.

Rain began to seep from the black clouds sprinkling the mammoth Castle Olympia turning the dark gray bricks black.

Lightening lit up the black sky resembling flashbulbs on an ancient camera.

A mixture of light and dark green leaves danced on the cobblestone walkways as if faeries were ridding them to Summerland. The strong wind pushed the leaves into the air creating miniature cyclones throughout the Gothic garden.

Rain was splattered on the multi-colored stained glass window causing the raindrops to appear red, blue, yellow, and green.

Gathered around the dining room table, The Astredo's watched Michelle as she stood over a map of Salem with a pendulum in her hand.

The crystal dangled from the chain as Michelle tried to scry for Charlemagne and Octavia.

Charlotte held Giovanni's hand tightly as the crystal suddenly dropped onto the map.

"They're downtown," said Michelle.

They rose from their seats and in pairs; they searched downtown for the mobsters.

#

The tiny store carried a verity of scents from incenses and candles.

Octavia selected massage oils that spark sexual arousal. Ylang-ylang. Cinnamon. Rose. Mint. Ginseng.   Dragon's Blood. Next, she selected a variety of toys they didn't already have.

Looking at a pair of pink fuzzy leopard printed handcuffs, she debated purchasing them. She liked the style. Although, she couldn't picture the fearless Gypsy Killer using pink handcuffs on her or himself. She searched for a pair in a less nauseating color. A pair of red fuzzy handcuffs were in the back. She placed those in her basket.

Octavia looked through the many selections of editable underwear and didn't think Charlemagne would go for it. She didn't think she'd like it either.

She moved on to another aisle and purchased another teddy, this one purple lace, and then moved to the checkout counter.

She carried the bag to her car and drove towards their apartment. She looked forward to their honeymoon in Greece. He booked a bridal suite overlooking the Mediterranean Sea.

'Fernando' blared from her cell phone.

She opened her cell phone to reveal a picture of Charlemagne and her. "I'm almost home Charlemagne. I can't wait to show you what I bought."

"I can't wait either.   I love you so much Octavia."

"I love you too," said Octavia. A few moments later, she hung up.

#

Charlemagne hung up the phone after he placed their second suitcase beside the table.   He looked forward to taking her to exotic places and giving her the life she deserves. Charlemagne looked at a big photo of them taken during their wedding vow renewal celebration. He loved the way she looked in her wedding dress. He thought about having her wear it one night for him.

Marguerite and Dante went out for dinner and a movie.

A soft rap was heard on the door.

"Come in," he said. He stepped back in surprise when Ari and Valentina stepped into the apartment.   "What do you want?"

The black cat in the cage paced and let out a series of meows.

Ari said, "To talk, dad."

Charlemagne stared suspiciously at Ari who was holding Valentina's hand. He saw no indication of any weapons. He asked, "About what?"

"Valentina and I thought about what you said about me belonging with you and Octavia. You were right."

Charlemagne looked at Ari hopefully. He wished he had the power to read minds. He sat at the table and invited them to sit.

Valentina said, "He's serious. He's been an ungrateful grandson towards Marguerite. I'm hoping she will forgive him and give him another chance."

"Have you honestly switched sides?"

"We have. We don't have a choice. You're my father, I *have* to follow you. Valentina's my fiancée; I don't want to leave the castle without her. I'm sure you could understand. You would want mom with you wherever you went," said Ari.

"I would. I love her so much. Ari, this means so much seeing you here. I didn't want to give you up.   I'm sorry, Ari. I wanted you."

"I know, dad. Could you forgive me for attacking you earlier? I was in shock. I was scared and confused."

"I forgive you, Ari. When your mother returns home, she and I are leaving for our honeymoon so just make yourselves at home. We can talk when we return."

"I want to talk now," said Ari.

Charlemagne was anxious to leave with Octavia. The promise of a new teddy excited the old serial killer.

Reading his twisted mind, Valentina shuddered and her hold on Ari's hand tightened.

"Alright, Ari. What do you want to know?"

"If you loved me so much, why did you give me up?"

"Marguerite knew you were going to be born with the God symbol. From her experience with losing her sons and daughters during the 1940s, she didn't want Octavia to have her heart broken. Octavia was so young and confused. She didn't mean to hurt me."

The door to the apartment opened.

Charlemagne smiled when Octavia entered the apartment holding a bag in her hand.

Octavia set the bag on a stand and went to reach for her gun when Charlemagne grabbed her wrist. "What are they doing here?"

Charlemagne pulled her onto his knee and placed an arm around her waist. "Ari wants to come back to us." He tightly hugged her and kissed her neck.

Octavia read their minds and said, "Perhaps we should call Marguerite. She would be interested in this." She leaned her head on his shoulder and became intoxicated by his cologne. Her hand caressed his inner thigh. "I want to leave, Charlemagne."

Charlemagne kissed her neck and said, "We'll leave in a moment. Our little boy is here."

Octavia moved her hand to his crotch and softly caressed him. "I want to leave, *now*." Octavia thought Ari looked too much like Amari.

Charlemagne received an immediate erection. "Don't you want to see Ari? He's your son too." He moved his hand up Octavia's thigh and softly caressed her inner thigh.

"He looks like my father. Exactly. I want to leave."

"Whatever my Octavia wants." Charlemagne nuzzled her neck. He wasn't going to force her to accept Ari. He figured in time she'll love him as much as he does. "Ari, we have to leave. We'll continue this when we return."

Ari rose from his seat and said, "Since you're leaving, could I have a hug as a sign of your forgiveness?"

Octavia slid from his knee and watched Ari and Valentina closely. She didn't trust them.

Charlemagne rose from his seat and stood before the son he was forced to give up. He hesitated. "Why should I believe the two of you?" He felt Octavia's hand on his arm in a protective manner.

"Because, I now see my mistake. I want to be with grandma, grandpa, and you."

"You want to be with me and Octavia?"

"I do. I want to get to know you, dad. You too, mom."

Charlemagne hugged him tightly. "Welcome home, son." His happiness soon disappeared when he felt a stake entering his stomach. He looked at Ari with tears in his eyes.

Ari pushed him onto the floor and knelt beside him, "Charlotte asked Valentina and I to bring you in paralyzed with the stake so she and the rest of us could take turns torturing you."

Octavia started to attack Ari when Valentina attacked her. She and Valentina fought in the living room throwing punches at each other.

Charlemagne watched Octavia and Valentina fight. He couldn't move although he was able to hear, feel, and see. He could barely speak as the muscles in his mouth and throat began to stiffen. "Ari...Ari... don't... allow anyone... to harm Octavia...Octavia.

Harming Octavia...will result in a massacre. I'll kill everyone.   I have

connections...who'll kill for me if she dies. Kill my Octavia and everyone shall slowly

suffer." His voice was lower and raspier.

"What connections?"

"...If...any harm befalls...Octavia...Charlotte's past...will destroy all...I

have...powerful friends...Charlotte is going to wish she...had told you...," his mouth

stiffened.

Ari pounded on his chest. "Speak damn it!" Ari watched Charlemagne's face

stiffen as he continued to watch Octavia and Valentina. Ari stared at the features on

Charlemagne's face. He noticed the only resemblance were their eye color and the shape

of their eyes. He said, "Octavia is going in a jail cell in the catacombs until grandma calls

the police."   Ari continued to look at his father. His hand touched Charlemagne's hand

and noticed they were like his hands. Ari said, "If it weren't for you attacking my family,

we could have had a chance to reconnect. Perhaps even bonded. If it weren't for

grandma's request to tear you apart herself, I would have fucking killed you the moment

you allowed me in the apartment."

Hearing a body collapse onto the floor, Ari turned his head towards Valentina and

Octavia.

Octavia was on her knees with Valentina's arm around her waist and a gun

shoved on her throat.

Valentina's finger was on the trigger.

"*Don't* kill her!"

"She killed my parents."

"If you kill her we all die. He's watching and listening."

Valentina kept her finger off the trigger but focused the gun on Charlemagne. She looked at Octavia and said, "Don't struggle. I'll kill him if you try to fight me." Valentina recited a spell that tied Octavia's hands together.

"Let me sit next to Charlemagne."

Valentina hesitated.

"Go ahead, she can't remove the stake." Ari pulled out his cell phone and called the others.

Valentina moved Octavia towards Charlemagne.   Valentina focused the gun on his head.

Octavia knelt beside him and tenderly kissed his neck and whispered in his ear, "I love you." She was moved to her feet just as Lisa and Michael entered the apartment with Diana and Viktor.

The others were on their way as they were on the other side of town.

Viktor looked at Charlemagne lying motionless on the floor. "Too bad stakes don't kill vampires," he said. He kicked Charlemagne's waist and said, "That's for attacking Lisa, Adrian, and Diana. You deserve more and you shall receive more." Viktor kicked him again.

"Stop it," said Octavia.

"How could you love that piece of filth? You can have any man you want. Why did you settle for this worthless prick?" asked Michael.

"He was the only person who cared about me. I am the only person who ever cared about him." Octavia gazed at Charlemagne. She knew he was still alive although seeing him lay motionless bothered her.

The lights above the catacombs were left on after Octavia was placed in one of the jail cells

Next to a cot, sat a small nightstand with a large picture of Charlemagne and a few other personal items.

Raven paced around the cell with his ankle in a shackle.

Octavia had requested she be permitted to bring the cat.

Octavia sat on the cot and gazed at Charlemagne laying on a gurney staring into her cell. She rose off the cot and approached the bars. She noticed he was following her with his eyes.

Hung in each corner of the jail, were pentagrams that prevented her from using her magickal powers to escape.

Charlemagne was still on his back with his head turned to the side. He watched Octavia protectively.

The sound of someone walking down the stairs didn't distract their focus on each other.

Charlemagne heard a pair of dress shoes approach him before he felt a hand on his arm as that hand caressed his arm. Blocking his view of Octavia, Charlotte stood in front of him.

Charlotte slipped her hand through his hand. She felt Octavia watch her closely. "Before I take you to the police, I would like to speak with you."

Charlemagne watched as Charlotte removed her hand from his hand and ran her fingers through his grey and blonde hair. "I hate you, Charlemagne. Please don't misinterpret my actions. I'm simply planning where I want to burn you first. I wouldn't do it while you were lying there helpless anyway. It's not my style. I'm *not* like how Delilah was."

Charlemagne felt his scalp become warm from her stroking his hair. Soon he began to smell burnt hair. He saw the worried look in Octavia's eyes.

Charlotte said, "When our sister, Jacqueline, informed me that I would be her underboss, I was excited. Until I met Giovanni and learned about the Tattoo I was born with." Tears filled her eyes. "I loved you and our brothers and sisters. My love for you died the night you murdered our step-mother. I loved her more than our real mother. What the fuck was going through your mind?"

Octavia said, "Jealously. Charlemagne can be possessive. You and he were close until he thought you were giving your step-sister and step-mother more attention. He only wanted you in his life. Although, that is not the only reason. You know there's more to yours and Charlemagne's history. You weren't an angel."

Charlotte approached Octavia's cell and said, "I can see now why my children wish to interrogate you before calling the police. You know *everything*. You know what I've done."

Octavia smiled and said, "I also know that there are people who will kill your family if you tell them about your past and if you kill me...your family will die either way. Charlemagne wasn't happy when you left the mob to join the Astredos. That's why he's so protective of me, he won't lose family again. He fears being alone." Octavia moved her gaze towards Charlemagne and back at Charlotte. "Your family doesn't realize that when they interrogate me, I'll tell them *everything*."

"Charlemagne is to be executed by sunlight in a few days. I want him to suffer with the stake. Once he's dead, you don't have to carry out any order of his. You will be free."

"Do you *still* think I could be rehabilitated? Didn't my murders prove that I'm not as innocent as everyone thought? Charlemagne *never* forced me to murder anyone." She softly laughed and said, "When I committed my first murder, Charlemagne was startled to learn what I had done. He was horrified that I behaved calmly for someone my age."

"We don't think you're innocent. I just know the psychopath you married."

"He's *never* hurt me. There's another side of Charlemagne no one seems to admit exists. He's loving. He's gentle. He's understanding. He's affectionate. He's very romantic. We *all* have our light and dark sides."

"That *doesn't* excuse his crimes. He will be punished," said Charlotte.

"His death *won't* stop the terror. It will only make things worse. I have my own connections. I have a lot of friends in the criminal underworld as you once did. They've already been ordered to assassinate the Astredo family in the event of Charlemagne's death."

"I'm not a mobster anymore. We can defend ourselves and each other. I will not permit that monster to roam the streets again."

"And yet you refuse to tell your family about your side of the family. Very contradicting."

Charlotte hesitated for a moment before she said, "They deserve to know. I would rather wait until the two of you are in your graves. The ones I used to call family are dead."

"Killing us will be the death of the Astredo family."

"Fuck you," said Charlotte as she stepped away from the barred door and approached Charlemagne. She pushed the stake deeper into his chest causing a muffled scream to sound behind his closed mouth. "That was for attacking two of my girls. You should be thankful I didn't burn your dick off. Which, I may still do." She left the catacombs.

Octavia watched her before she sat on the cot. In her arms, she held his black satin robe sprayed with his cologne. She nuzzled her face into it. Still holding the robe as though it were a security blanket, she gazed at Charlemagne. She said, "We'll go on our honeymoon. Marguerite won't keep us here for long." She lay on the cot snuggled in the robe. She pictured she was laying in his arms. She kissed the satin material. Octavia softly smiled when she read his thoughts. He was picturing himself snuggled in her arms.

Chapter 40

A few days later.

The black and gray storm cloud disincarnated in the night sky leaving behind the sky mapped in sparkling white stars. The full moon hung brightly shinning down upon the Gothic garden.

Moonlit water fell out of the stone mouths and stone flowers on the gargoyle, faerie, and angel water fountains.

The white roses glowed in the moonlight while the other deep colored flowers and plants shut their delicate blossoms for the evening.

The Gothic garden was enchanted from spells performed by angels, faeries, gnomes, and wood nymphs.

Torches were set ablaze along the twisting cobblestone sidewalks in huge black cauldrons.

The tall green shrubs resembled walls in a house and the cauldrons were like Gothic style lamps as they created a maze throughout Giovanni and Charlotte's garden.

Large bats flew in and out of the belfries in the tall towers chasing insects that flew in the night air. A large three-story bat house sat on a tall pole beside a tiny pound with a statue of a gargoyle spilling water out of its mouth into the dark waters of the pond.

In one corner of the garden were cast iron benches placed in front of the circular wall. A huge torch was lit creating a warm glow on a life size statue of the Goddess Isis.

Two silver candelabrums holding five tall black candles were placed on two stone tables on either side of the benches.

On a night such as this, the white and bronze statues of angels, dragons, gargoyles, faeries, unicorns, and other creatures looked to be as head stones and decorations in a cemetery. The closed flowers looked as if death had overcome them during the change from day to night.

Nighttime sounds filled the air with the sounds of the bats flying above the castle and garden. Frogs sang in the watery ponds and fountains and the running water from the stone creatures added to the symphony of the night.

The atmosphere was perfect for a Gothic wedding.

Giovanni stood in his ritual robe. Behind him was a Wiccan alter. In his aging hands was his and Charlotte's worn out Grimoire they had read for Markus, Jason,

Aaron, and Caesar's weddings. Now, they were about to marry their older grandson.

Charlotte stood beside Giovanni as the High Priestess in her handfasting ritual robe.

Ari stood beside Giovanni wearing black pants with a white poet shirt with wide bell sleeves.

Caesar, Markus, Jason, Michael, and Viktor wore a black suit with a deep purple rose on their lapel.

Diana, Lisa, Brenda, Italia, and Michelle wore dresses made from black velvet with a deep purple lace shawl. They held long stemmed dark purple roses taken from a nearby rose bush. In their hair was a crown of purple rose buds mixed with ivy leaves with black and purple ribbons falling behind the circle of flowers.

Rosa stood between Lisa and Giovanni wearing a black gown with deep purple accents. She held a tiny basket filled with black and purple rose petals.

Scarlet was sitting on the cool grass beside her sister with Diana behind her. She had on a black sleeper with purple booties.

Jason closed the wrought-iron gate behind him and Valentina as he escorted her towards the Circle.

Valentina's wedding dress was a deep purple medieval style gown with a black corset. Her sleeves were long, bell shaped, and they nearly touched the ground as she walked. Her eye shadow was black and dark purple with black eyeliner under her hazel eyes. Her lips were the color of the roses her bridesmaids carried in black baskets. A pewter tiara exploding with diamonds rested in her dark blonde hair, which was pulled up in a bun. A long purple vial flowed behind her coming from her tiara. Around her neck was a pewter choker studded with tiny black roses that were made from onyx stones. A tiny chain hung from the center of the choker with a black and pewter pentacle resting on her neck. Onyx stones hung from her ears and her wrists. In her arm, she carried a dozen black roses. Her shoes were made from glass with small onyx studs lining the sides of them.

Valentina took Ari's hand as Giovanni and Charlotte began the handfasting ritual. They exchanged vows before Giovanni and Charlotte blessed the wedding rings. The star-crossed lovers stood facing each other, holding hands, while Charlotte wrapped a cord around their hands. Their hearts, minds, and souls were now bonded.

Charlotte said, "In the eyes of our Lord and Lady, Ari and Valentina Astredo are now one. So Mote It Be.'

The others repeated, "So Mote It Be."

Giovanni lay down a broomstick for Valentina and Ari to jump over while holding hands.

#

After the cakes and wine, Ari and Valentina left for their bedroom.

The scents of rose and jasmine perfumed the air from the candles and incenses burning on his dresser, nightstand, and shelves.

Their wedding clothes were lying in a heap on the black marbled floor. Valentina's veil lay on her vanity she had brought over from her house.

They lay under their black and deep purple satin sheets making love. Their moans and cries entwining together like their bodies.

Ari lay above her tenderly pushing her. He kissed her passionately from her lips to her chest. His hands explored her body stopping at her thighs where he heavily caressed the sides of her thighs.

Valentina softly moaned as she drug her nails across his back. She closed her eyes feeling a wave of ecstasy wash over her as he pushed faster and deeper into her. Her nails dug deeper into his back.

Ari moaned in pleasure from the deep scratches. Ari kissed her shoulder, neck, and nibbled on her earlobe. His fangs lightly scrapping across her skin. His hand traveled from her thigh to her breast caressing it and playing with her nipple. His mouth caressed her other breast deeply as she began to climax. He pushed her harder and faster wanting her to call out his name. He whispered, "I love you." He kissed her cheek still pushing her.

Valentina screamed his name in passion when his fangs sank into her neck. After he took her blood into him, she drank from a small cut he made on his neck.

Chapter 41

Two days later

Standing in front of the arched front door, Giovanni held Charlotte in a gentle embrace after he hugged her tightly. He gazed into her eyes and said, "Good luck."

Charlotte softly smiled and said, "Thanks." She planned to execute Charlemagne and Octavia when she and Viktor returned. She returned his hug.

Giovanni gave her a long passionate kiss.

Charlotte returned his kiss before she met Viktor at the door. "Let's place another asshole in jail."

#

The Cleveland Hopkins International Airport was the thirty-ninth largest airport in North America. It was founded in 1925.

In the busy terminal, Michael said, "Call me if you need me." Michael was leaving for his final semester of collage for acting and theater management. It was the same college Giovanni and other ancestors had attended.

"We will. Be careful." Ari gave his baby cousin a long hug.

Michael returned his hug and said, "I can't wait to return around Imbolic." He moved to Lisa, embraced her and said, "I'm going to miss you. I love you,"

Lisa returned his tight hug, "I'll miss you, too. I love you." She kissed him before he picked up his suitcases.

Lisa and Ari watched Michael board the plane before driving back to the family estate.

#

Raising from his coffin, he searched for his beloved Octavia. He left the bedroom and walked down the hall. Disappointment developed in him when he found the house empty.

Marguerite and Dante broke into the police station. With their vampiric powers of mind control, they removed Charlemagne's body from the police station.

Dante and Marguerite were figuring out a way to get Octavia.

Their suitcases were still by the table and the purchases from the porn store were still in their bag.

Charlemagne reached in the bag and withdrew the purple baby doll teddy. He softly smiled. He couldn't wait to see her in it.

"I've never cared for that style in lingerie. I don't like what it represents. That's just as disturbing as calling your lover 'baby' 'daddy'," said Dante appearing before Charlemagne. He looked at a picture of him and Octavia taken when they were first dating. "Your marriage disturbs your mother and me. What were you thinking? Couldn't you have waited until she was at least eighteen?"

"She was the first and only woman who loved me for who I was. I didn't want to be alone. Where's Octavia?"

"She's still in the catacombs of Castle Olympia. Marguerite and I are working out a plan to brake her out."

"Let me get her out. I don't want to leave her alone," said Charlemagne.

"Not now. They will be expecting you."

Charlemagne paced the room. "I don't want her there by herself."

"Octavia can protect herself. She's *not* a fragile child. "

Charlemagne said, "I know she's not fragile." Charlemagne hesitated. He didn't want to leave her there. "They wouldn't be foolish enough to harm her."

Chapter 42

Octavia sat on the cot stroking Raven's fur. She could tell the gypsy hated her touch.

Raven's meows of protest echoed throughout the catacombs. He stopped struggling when he heard someone walk down the stairs.

"Octavia, may I ask you some questions?"

His voice reminded her of her father's voice, only Ari didn't have an Arabic accent. Octavia wished he looked and sounded like Charlemagne. Maybe she would have fought Marguerite to keep him if he didn't look like her side of the family.

Raven leaped off her lap and stood on hunches at the barred door.

Octavia joined the cat at the door and looked at her son. "At least you have your father's eyes."

"What's that supposed to mean?"

"If you would have looked like Charlemagne's side of the family, sounded like my Charlemagne, I may have allowed Charlemagne to keep you."

"You would have *allowed* him to keep me? I was a *human* not a kitten."

"I'm not very maternal."

"I can't believe I'm about to ask this, but did you ever want me? Were you happy that you were pregnant?"

"I was very happy. Although I was very naive about love, marriage, and parenting.   I was too young to realize what I had done. I was too young and scared to permit Charlemagne to help me learn to be a mother."

"How did you get messed up with him?"

"I *didn't* get 'messed up with him.' I've always hated that phrase. People make it sound as though I'm stupid. He and my dad were close friends. The day I was born, the summer of 1960, Charlemagne was appointed my body guard. From birth, I was one of the chosen to be Marguerite's successor. The other chosen were Marguerite's daughters, but unfortunately, they died. Charlemagne and I became friends before we became lovers. I didn't fall in love foolishly. I knew about his crimes. My childhood had been surrounded by violence."

"Don't think I want you or Charlemagne in my life. I *don't* care about you or him.

I *hate* you both."

"You even sound like Amari. He never cared for me. Amari would always remind me how he *never* wanted daughters."

Ari said, "His and Esmeralda's neglect caused you to seek comfort in the arms of a child molester."   Ari looked at the picture of Charlemagne. "Sick fuck."

"I was *never* a child. If you hate us, then why are you here?"

"I wanted to ask you about grandmother. My first questions were just morbid curiosity."

"Esmeralda began her life of crime the same age as I was..."

"*Not* her! I *don't* consider you or Charlemagne my family. I am an Astredo."

Octavia softly laughed. "I hope Charlemagne never hears you say you don't consider us family. It'll break his heart. He loves you and he *didn't* want to give you up. Charlotte Astredo has a very interesting past. Charlemagne has told me everything. From growing up around Charlemagne and his friends, I heard stories and had psychic visions. What would you like to know?"

"Everything. What's her maiden name? Why must her past be a secret?"

"Ari! Come here!" Giovanni's voice was heard from the top of the staircase.

Ari moved his sexy grey eyes towards Octavia. "This isn't finished." He left the catacombs.

Chapter 43

Angel slept beside Rosa's head while an assortment of kittens slept among the maroon and black satin blanket.

Ari and Valentina sat on the edge of her bed and looked down at her. Tenderly,

Ari touched her cheek.

Ari kissed Rosa's forehead and said, "Good night, Rosa *Astredo*."

Valentina tenderly kissed their new daughter's cheek as Ari asked,

"Should we tell them they were your sisters before they became our daughters?"

"When they're older."

After they tucked the children in for the evening, they retreated to their room.

Ari held Valentina tightly in his arms before carrying her to their double coffin.

Three hours later, Scarlet's cries were heard through the baby monitor. Ari held Scarlet in his arms as he walked from the kitchen to the living room.

Valentina sat beside her husband on the couch. Placing her arm around his shoulder, she cuddled up to him. "Are you alright?"

Ari watched the infant gently suck on the nipple. He looked at his baby's light blue eyes as he leaned closer to Valentina and rested his head on her shoulder.

"I'm still shocked knowing that Charlemagne is my real father. That makes Marguerite my grandmother."

Valentina slid her arm around his waist and held his hand gently. "Ari, you don't have to have him be a part of your life. Jason and Brenda raised you and they love you."

Ari's smiled uneasily as he remembered the evening when Charlemagne announced that he and Octavia were his true parents. Having the Godmother of the DeMarco Crime family as his grandmother didn't disturb him as much as being the son of the Gypsy Killer did. He gently kissed her hand as he felt the blood flow underneath her skin. Ari felt himself begin to crave her blood again. He tenderly turned her hand up so he could look at her wrist. The long blue vein was enticing him. Ari kissed her wrist and felt her pulse. "When you and I researched his criminal records last night, I was still bothered with what I saw. For five years, he was in prison for multiple rapes and murders. When he got out in 1959, he began to rape and murder gypsies. In France, Egypt, and America he's a level three sex offender."

Valentina kissed the top of his hand. "There's a lot of wisdom in what Athena told you. That doesn't mean you will do what he has done just because he's your father." She softly smiled. "Don't look surprised. I read your mind. I know your fears. You have gypsy blood in you from Octavia and Lotus so there *is* good in you. Your adopted gypsy family will *never* hate you because of what Charlemagne has done."

"Thanks. I feel better from speaking with Grandmother Athena and you." Ari smiled, and kissed her wrist again. His eyes gently closed and felt her warm wrist against his lips.

Valentina watched him kiss her wrist before he released her hand. She knew what he wanted before he gave her the choice of dying a normal mortal death or joining him. She welcomed the vampire's kisses wanting to be by his side always. She still could feel his fangs slowly sinking into her neck to take her blood.

Scarlet fell asleep after she drank from the bottle. She nestled her tiny face against Ari's chest feeling his love and warmth.

The vampire lovers looked into each other's eyes loving each other.

Chapter 44

Octavia sat on their couch leaning against Charlemagne with his arm across her shoulders. On her lap sat the black cat.

With assistance from a shape-shifter, Octavia *never* appeared in the cell. Octavia managed to pull the stake from Charlemagne's chest. Marguerite was making it harder to capture her mobsters. She wasn't going to bury anymore of her children.

Charlemagne caressed her thigh and nuzzled her neck before he kissed her. "Why don't you put the cat in his cage?"

"I will." She began to stroke the cat as she gazed into the cat's copper eyes.

Charlemagne placed his hand on her knee and tenderly caressed her. He savored the feel of her warm, tender, young skin. "Just kill him, Octavia." He deeply kissed her neck as he moved his hand up her thigh.

"I want him to watch Diana die first."

"Put him away. We have a week to catch up on." He kissed her deeply on the lips.

His kiss still made her feel faint as he leaned her back against the couch. "You're making it hard for me to want to get up." She smiled just before he kissed her lips again.

Charlemagne softly bit her neck and tenderly released her from his embrace.

Octavia held Raven as she stood from the couch and walked towards a small cage that sat on a stand. The stand sat next to a small 1950's style dollhouse. After she tossed the cat in the cage and locked the door, she returned to Charlemagne's arms.

Charlemagne hugged her tightly while he kissed her passionately on the mouth. He missed the feel of her body next to his and her cries of ecstasy.

Octavia's hands heavily caressed his back and chest after she removed his shirt.

Charlemagne kissed her lips and gazed into her eyes. "I can't wait until we leave for our honeymoon. I renewed the reservations for the honeymoon suite."

"I can't wait to wear my new teddy for you. I purchased some toys and oils we can experiment with." She hugged him tightly while his hand unbuttoned and unzipped his pants.

"I'm looking forward to seeing you in it. We'll leave tomorrow morning. I love you so much." Charlemagne removed his pants and underwear. As he continued to kiss her, he removed her clothes.

"Charlemagne, Charlemagne, Charlemagne!" She lay on the couch with him above her.

His mouth explored her body in deep passionate kisses. He pushed her heavily as their moans, cries, and screams united.

Octavia's hands caressed his back and thigh. Ecstasy raced through her with each passionate thrust from Charlemagne. She kissed him along his shoulder, throat, and lips.

He held her tightly as she began to climax.

"Oh Octavia, call out to me." He pushed her harder and faster.

"Charlemagne, Charlemagne, Charlemagne."

"Yes Octavia yes." His psychotic eyes gazed at her closed eyes.

"Charlemagne, Charlemagne! Yes, yes, yes. CHARLEMAGNE!"

He loved to hear her scream. After her intense orgasm, he had his. He remained above her while he held her in a tight embrace.

"Oh Charlemagne, don't stop."

"I'm just resting. Remember I told you that I wasn't going to allow you to sleep when we arrived home," he said.

"I remember." Octavia ran her fingers through his blonde-grey hair.

"Are you honestly ok with me as a vampire?"

"Yes. I would *never* lie to you. It does *not* bother me."

"Good. I don't want to lose you."

"You won't."

"You belong to me."

"I don't want anyone else."

"I want to make you a vampire."

"Not yet."

"Why not?"

"I'm not ready."

"I want you to spend eternity with me."

"I will. Just give me some more time. Please."

"Alright. Octavia, I want you at my side."

"You have me. I would *never* leave you."

Charlemagne held her close.

"I love you, Octavia."

"I love you, Charlemagne." She kissed his lips a few times. "Make love to me again, Charlemagne."

Charlemagne entered her and began to push her.

#

Greece

So Charlemagne's coffin could easily be transported, they arrived by Marguerite's private jet.

While Charlemagne slept in his coffin during the day, Octavia explored the shops, and went to the beach. Mostly, she stayed on the beach.

Each evening, Charlemagne and Octavia saw plays, ate at expensive restaurants, danced, and explored some of the museums Octavia visited during the day.

The honeymoon suite was on the fourth floor in a ninth floor hotel. The walls were peach with white billowy curtains.

The king size bed was dressed in mint green satin sheets and blankets.

They experimented with the items Octavia purchased at the adult video store and made endless love until he had to retreat to his coffin.

After a quick breakfast at a small restaurant, Octavia entered a few bookstores and other stores before arriving at the beach.

The turquoise water glistened under the hot sun.

Octavia lay on a pink and purple beach towel reading a paranormal romance novel under a white umbrella. She wore a blue one-piece bathing suit and planned to save the two-piece when she and Charlemagne swam in the Mediterranean Sea at night. Before turning the page, she took in her surroundings. She wished Charlemagne were able to join her although it was nice to have some time to herself. She watched the many different people on the beach and in the ocean.

They were oblivious to the dangerous future Godmother enjoying the exotic location with them.

Among Marguerite's foot soldiers, associates, hit men and hit women, and other mobsters, Octavia was treated as the princess of crime she was. Even before she married Marguerite's son, Marguerite chose Octavia to be her successor the moment she was born.

Here, she was barely noticed. She was seen as another tourist with a husband who was on a business trip.

With Charlemagne at her side, she felt more like royalty.

Octavia read a few more pages before she swam in the warm sea. Her naturally tan Egyptian skin became darker in the sun.

She returned to the hotel an hour before the sun set. She showered and changed into a pale yellow gown and brushed her hair. As she applied make up, the lid on Charlemagne's coffin opened. She couldn't see his reflection; although, she felt his hands tenderly caress her shoulders. She shivered with excitement from his caresses.

Charlemagne tenderly kissed her cheek and asked, "How was your day?"

"Wonderful." She told him all the things she did and saw. She leaned back in his arms.

"You deserved to be pampered, Octavia." He hugged her tightly and nuzzled her black hair. She was the best thing that has ever happened to him. He didn't want anyone else.

Octavia rested her head on his chest and enjoyed just being in his arms. Their new station in life as the next to run the family business mattered not to her and to her relief to him.

Charlemagne hugged her again before he took a shower and dressed. He placed his arm around her waist and escorted her from the door.

After dinner and a walk along the beach, Octavia sat on his lap and slowly stroked him. She was dressed in a purple lace teddy. She just finished giving him a lap dance. Her arms were around his neck.

Charlemagne leaned against the headboard with his hands caressing her thighs.

He moaned a few times before he kissed her along her shoulder.

Octavia gazed into his blue eyes and said, "I don't want our honeymoon to end. Oh Charlemagne, Charlemagne."

He kissed her forehead and enjoyed the way her voice sounded when she was in ecstasy. "We have another week. We'll be traveling to exotic places again." His eyes closed and he softly moaned.

Octavia kissed his chest and found his nipple. Deeply, she sucked on him. She rode him. Her nails dug into his skin causing him to moan louder.

"I love you, I love you, I love you, Charlemagne." Octavia grinded harder in his lap.

Charlemagne moved his hand along her thigh before placing his finger on her clit and stroking it in circular movements. "*Je vous aime. Amoureux, Amoureux. Vous êtes ma vie.*"

Octavia kissed his mouth slipping in her tongue to explore his mouth. She scratched his thigh causing him to moan. After her passionate kiss, she breathlessly moaned, "*Mon Cheri, Mon Amour.*" She began to climax.

After he reached his long climax, he moved her onto her back. He sat astride her caressing her waist before moving his wrinkled hands along her arms until he reached her wrists.

Octavia trembled from her last climax as he clasped her wrists in the red fuzzy handcuffs. Earlier, she placed the cuffs on him and took him in her mouth before she lay on top of him. Octavia screamed when he began to probe inside her with his tongue.

Charlemagne devoured her bringing her to orgasm several times before he replaced his tongue with his penis. He lay on top of her and ravished her.

Chapter 45

2008

Salem, Ohio

Astredo Institution for Mental Health

Orange and Yellow fire danced from black cauldrons in the hospital windows.

Using spell that changed her appearance, Octavia walked down the long hallway towards a room in the psyche ward.

Earlier, a vision showed her Marguerite's assassin waking from a coma.

Octavia shot the faerie guards with silver bullets before approaching Demonique's bed. She lifted the spell to reveal her true face. Her beloved Charlemagne was waiting in the car since he couldn't enter the building due to all the religious Pagan decorations.

Demonique's eyes quickly opened for the first time in nine years.

Octavia updated him before she said, "Charlemagne can't wait to begin training you again."

Demonique smiled and said, "Are you taking me out of here?"

"Yes. Marguerite wants you to do a little job for her."

#

The thick blanket of dark clouds covered the setting midwinter sun causing the city to look as though it were a black and white photograph. Even the pine trees appeared dim from the freshly fallen fog.

Demonique pulled into the parking lot leading into the tiny police station. Raindrops the size of quarters fell from the clouds.

Demonique glanced at his beat up 1983 avocado green sedan. The dashboard lights had been burnt out for three years. The gas gage was stuck on E and the pale green leather seats were faded with fast food grease stains and dirt from dusty roads. The back window was cracked in a spider web design from a shot from a BB gun.

His mother gave him the car as a reward for completing a drug delivery for her.

On the passenger seat, his cell phone rang.

The caller ID read: Charlemagne DeMarco.

"Is the job done?"

"Not yet. I just arrived."

"Marguerite wants it done quickly."

"It will be." Bitter thoughts came to his mind. Demonique found himself not being able to wait to carry out his Godmother's orders. He softly laughed, "I have waited eight years for this job."

"Marguerite feels that you are now ready to become a made man. Octavia is now Marguerite's underboss."

"What are *you* to me now? Aren't you my bodyguard?"

He gently laughed and said, "I'm *still* your bodyguard. Marguerite doesn't want you out of *my* sight. She sees you as a son as she sees Octavia as a daughter."

Demonique smiled. He had gone from prostitute to a mobster. "Where are you Charlemagne?"

"I'm in the red pickup behind you."

Demonique glanced in his rearview mirror and saw Charlemagne in the driver's seat. He moved his gaze towards the back of the police station. "Are you following me or staying in the truck?"

"I'll be hovering over you in the form of a bat. Marguerite doesn't want me to help you. She only wants me to protect you."

"I won't let her down." Demonique stepped out of the car. Demonique cautiously glanced around the parking lot.

For a brief moment, he placed his hand on the lid of the trunk as if it were a headstone.

Inside the truck were a large supply of weapons and torture devices. Inspired by Charlemagne's stories.

He nervously gazed at a police car before he casts a spell that made his car appear to be invisible.

Demonique entered the police station using a spell causing him to become invisible. He slipped passed two policemen on his way towards a cell at the end of a long hallway. Seeing a woman standing by a bared window, he used another spell to make him step through the metal door.

Candyce de Obscuritè slowly turned from the window and felt a strange presence in the room. Her eyes widened in fear when she saw her dead son stand before her.

"Surprised to see me, mother?"

"I thought someone killed you."

Demonique took a step closer to her as she took a step back. "I was in a coma. Octavia and Charlemagne visited me every day along with Marguerite and Dante. Marguerite is my new bosses. I no longer work for you. You never visited me. Before you were arrested, you *never* asked how I was. I was *nothing* more than a *slave* to you!"

He withdrew a gun from his jeans. He placed his finger on the trigger and enjoyed seeing the terror fill from within her.

"Don't kill me! I'm your mother. I honestly *did* care for you."

"What mother would sell her only son into prostitution? Dante and the others have given me more love and affection then *you* ever did!"

"I'm sorry, Demonique. I'll change. I promise!"

Demonique fixed the gun on her forehead. "You'll *never* change! You've damage me in *many* ways!"

"I did those things out of love. I love you, Demonique."

"You don't love me! You didn't want a son. You wanted a sex object. Something you can make money on so you can buy more drugs."

Candyce trembled and the color drained from her face. "I had no choice to sell you into prostitution! Your father didn't leave me anything in his Will. He owed the Mafia everything.　If you help me escape, I promise I'll make it up to you. We can get back in the business again."

"I work for Don Marguerite. Octavia and Charlemagne are wonderful to me. I'm beginning to love them as if they were my real parents. Charlemagne has been the perfect father figure. I don't need you anymore."

Flesh, hair, and parts of the skull hit the wall leaving a bloody trail towards the dusty floor. She collapsed onto the floor when he fired the gun again blowing a hole through her chest. Red, yellow, and gray brain matter flowed from the opening in her skull onto the floor surrounding her corpse.

Demonique smiled at his work and turned to leave. Before he made himself invisible again, two policemen entered the hallway.

The two policemen quickly withdrew their guns and commanded Demonique to stop.

With a calmed reaction, the newly made mobster fixed the gun on the police officers and fired two shots. The first bullet entered the first policeman's heart causing it to explode. The second bullet blew the other officer's head off.

The sun disappeared as twilight began over the town.

Demonique returned to his car just as a group of policemen came out of the station firing guns. Demonique grabbed his machine gun from the back seat and began spraying police officers. From his truck, Charlemagne called for backup on his cell phone after watching four police cruisers and a car belonging to the Astredos join the battle.

Charlemagne stepped out from his truck with his machine gun.

In five minutes, two cars filled with Marguerite's foot soldiers arrived.

Ari and Valentina stepped out of the car with Michael, Lisa, Viktor, and Diana.

They used their elemental powers as well as their swords and guns.

Lisa and Michael conjured icicle spears and threw them into approaching mobsters.

Viktor tossed fireballs at another set of mobsters.

Demonique aimed his gun at Viktor and Diana. He placed his finger on the trigger finding out he ran out of bullets. He exchanged his gun for a sword. His blade reflected Viktor's fireballs as thought they were orange and red baseballs.

Viktor pulled Diana behind a police car to escape a ricochet fireball. They watched Demonique turn his attention towards two police officers approaching him. He grabbed Diana's hand and quickly walked towards their cousins.

Diana watched Charlemagne run out of bullets. She conjured a windstorm to knock his gun out from his grasped. She smiled as a police officer placed him against a car placing his hands in handcuffs.

Viktor looked at his wife of six-years, smiled, and said, "Awesome."

Diana smiled watching Lisa and Valentina finish off the last of Marguerite's gangsters.

Ari and Michael joined Viktor and Diana after using their elemental powers to capture three mobsters for the police officers.

Hearing a gun shot, Diana turned her attention to Demonique.

Demonique had a police officer's gun while the police officer lay in a pool of blood. His gun was pointed at Viktor.

Viktor collapsed to his knees with Ari, Michael, and Diana at his side. Pain exploded across his chest as Michael laid him on the black top, Ari's hand covered the wound, and Diana calling for Lisa.

Valentina and Lisa rushed over to their husbands and cousins as Demonique was getting arrested.

Ari's hand was covered in blood as Lisa quickly knelt beside Viktor placing her hands over his wound.

Valentina sisterly caressed Diana's back. She looked at Michael and said, "Call an ambulance."

Michael obeyed when Ari had a vision.

After the vision, Ari said, "Stop, Lisa."

The bullet was held at the surface inches from his skin.

Lisa asked, "What did you see?"

"A short message from the Gods. They want me to turn him."

Lisa quickly removed her hands and stood with Valentina and Diana. She placed her arm around Diana's waist.

Diana watched Ari hold his older cousin in his arms before sinking his fangs into his neck. Tears continued to fall from her eyes.

Viktor moaned when his blood left his body to mix with Ari's vampiric blood. His mouth was covered by Ari's wrist.

The bullet pushed through his skin and the hole closed.

Viktor went limp in Ari's arms while his body went through a change.

#

A few hours later

"How are you feeling?" asked Diana refilling Lisa and Michael's mugs with herbal tea. They were in Nefertiti's Tearoom seated at one of the round tables. Diana became the owner when she turned eighteen. Midnight worked for her.

Viktor said, "Better. I'm *not* as dizzy."

"Do you need more blood?" asked Valentina. She was seated between him and Ari.

"I think so."

Valentina opened another blood bottle and poured Viktor another glass full.

Viktor took a long drink before setting the glass down. He poured himself another glass.

After speaking with the police and the paramedics, they drove to the tearoom to recharge from the battle.

Ari called Giovanni while Diana was closing the tearoom.

Diana placed the tea kettle on the stove before joining the others.

Viktor placed his arm around Diana's waist while Valentina and Ari told him what to expect with his new lifestyle.

The sun and moon wind chimes rang from hanging in the open window above the sink.

A black cat jumped in the center of the table.

They softly laughed as Viktor said, "I think it's time we put a screen in that window."

Diana touched the velvet fur. A vision came:

'Marguerite set the black phone on its cradle. She was in the living room while Octavia sat on the couch with Charlemagne's black satin robe covering her like a blanket. "Charlemagne and Demonique are in jail."'

The vision showed Marguerite, Octavia, and Dante leaving the house.

'The caged cat pushed against the bars and fell onto the Victorian style rug. Raven quickly ran out an open window.'

Diana held the cat in her arms and said, "Its dad."

#

Diana, Viktor, Ari, Valentina, Lisa, and Michael entered the large black and burgundy hallway.

Diana was holding Raven in her arms when she entered the living room.

The elder Astredos rose thankful Viktor survived being gunned down and finding Raven.

Charlotte approached Diana and tenderly stroked Raven's fur. "I had Michelle grab the Book of Shadows. Let's get him on the floor."

Diana sat Raven on the floor.

Raven stood in a circle created by his family while they chanted a counter-curse. He quickly changed from feline to human.

Hugs were exchanged before they returned to their chairs, couches, and love seats.

Charlotte and the others filled him in on the nine years he was held captive.

Raven told them how he was kept in a cage observing the mobs activates.

Charlotte nervously listened to Raven's tales about her family. She had to figure out a way around her mother's threat.

#

Valentina, Ari, Lisa, Diana, Viktor, and Michael were in their gym practicing fighting techniques.

Charlotte and Giovanni were in the nursery placing the children in bed.

Caesar, Markus, and Raven sat across from Jason in Jason's study while Michelle, Italia, and Brenda were getting drinks and making popcorn in the kitchen.

They decided to spend the rest of the evening catching Raven up on the past nine years and looking at old home movies.

"I can't wait to watch those old 8 mm home movies I transferred on VHS. The guy at the video place said I sent those old movie reels in just in time because the film was starting to disintegrate," Caesar said.

"I can't wait to see them either. Can you remember what the videos consists of?" Jason smiled excitedly tapping a dark green marble pen onto the deep cheery desk.

"I believe it is our graduation: Aaron and Cassandra's wedding; Markus and Italia's wedding; mine and Michelle's wedding; Valentina and Ari as babies; Ari, Valentina, Lisa, Michael, Diana, and Viktor as children and teenagers; plays; anniversary parties; birthday parties; and I think, cast parties."

"Remember when they graduated; Valentina wouldn't sit with the rest of her class until Ari walked down the aisle. He wanted them to walk together to get their diplomas."

"I still have a picture of them sleeping in the same crib on our fireplace mantel. And their senior pictures where they had to pose together," Markus said.

"It's amazing how they all have grown into mature adults. I'm proud of them," Raven said.

"So are we," Caesar said.

Jason said, "They have never been apart. Ari told me that if he dies before her, he wants to wait on the astral plane for her and he still wants to be in a double coffin holding her hand."

"That's so romantic, wanting to be buried like that," Caesar said.

"That's how Brenda and I are going to be buried. Let's get settled in the living-room and wait for Brenda and Michelle."

The witches stood and walked out of the study. Jason sat on the couch as Caesar sat on the love seat and Raven sat on Giovanni's black leather recliner chair.

The tape was already in the VCR and the channel was turned to the preview channel. A preview for a mobster flick flashed on the large screen TV. Jason changed the station to an old black and white sit-com.

Raven, Markus, and Caesar understood why Jason wanted to change the channel. Even though the three witches loved Mafia movies, the recent battle and almost losing Viktor, caused them to not be in the mood for gun-carrying mobsters.

#

"Are you still troubled by the battle, Italia?" Michelle asked while Brenda poured butter out of a crystal cup in a circular motion into a pewter bowl of popcorn. She was dressed in a light blue sundress with her silver pentacle around her neck.

Brenda changed out of her uniform wearing a pair of skintight black shorts with matching top. The shorts were only knee length. The tiny bell sleeves rested on her upper arms. She had taken her ponytail out and allowed her long hair to come around her shoulders.

"You could always read me." Italia smiled slightly closing the silver door on the refrigerator. Italia placed five glasses on a Gothic designed cart that was in the form of a dragon beside three bottles of wine coolers and three coke cans. She watched as Brenda placed the bowl of popcorn next to the beverages.

Brenda stepped closer to Italia. "Italia, we are sisters-in-laws. It's all right to be frightened. Michelle and I are still shaken up over it."

Italia glanced at Michelle and Brenda and saw the concern in their eyes. She let out a short laugh. "I know. I hold my emotions in as mom does. It did frighten me. We almost lost Viktor and possibly Diana."

"Brenda and I are still bothered by it," said Michelle giving her big sister-in-law a hug.

"He's ok. Ari turned him in time."

Tears fell from Italia's Indian eyes for a moment. "He did. Our kids kicked ass."

Brenda placed her arm around Italia's waist. She smiled and said, "Two assholes are in prison thanks to them."

The three witches pulled away from each other and finished preparing the snacks.

Taking the popcorn off the counter, Brenda carried the bowl of popcorn while Michelle pushed the cart out of the restaurant size kitchen.

They walked down the long candle lit hallway towards the living room.

#

Brenda, Italia, and Michelle entered the living room and placed the drinks and bowl of popcorn on the coffee table.

Italia sat cuddled next to Markus.

Michelle sat next to her husband as she leaned into his embrace, holding his hand. His arm encircled her waist tenderly touching her thigh.

Brenda sat beside Jason with her arms around his waist and her head on his shoulder.

Raven opened his can of cola and poured it into a Gothic designed glass.

Jason had his arm lying across the couch gently touching Brenda's shoulder. Hitting the button on the remote, they watched the thirty-year- old home movie.

The screen showed lines and dust particles from the cracks and tares on the film.

They watched a few silent seconds on each of their high school graduations before Jason and Brenda's handfasting. Next, Raven and Lotus were hand fasted. Their eyes filled with tears watching their siblings and best friends, Cassandra and Aaron, standing in front of Giovanni and Charlotte while they performed their handfasting. Brenda, Italia, and Michelle stood beside Cassandra wearing a dark maroon bridesmaid gowns. Jason stood beside Aaron as his best man.

"During his bachelor party, Aaron tried to decide who to have as his best man over a card game," Caesar said.

After the scenes of Aaron and Cassandra's wedding were over, scenes from Caesar and Michelle's wedding were shown.

Jason gave her shoulders a tight squeeze. "I would marry you *every day,* if I could." He gently nibbled on her shoulder.

Raven softly smiled at the way Brenda tenderly kissed Jason's shoulder as he thought about the way Lotus used to snuggle close to him while they watched movies. He turned his attention back on the television.

The next ten minutes of film showed Cassandra holding Valentina and Brenda holding Ari. They were feeding the newborns in the castle. Every few minutes, Aaron would give his baby daughter a kiss on the cheek. Jason was doing the same thing with his newly adopted son.
Brenda felt tears in her eyes like the others as the camera was focused on their late friends.

As the film advanced, it showed Valentina, Ari, Viktor, Diana, and Michael surrounded by Yule paper and toys of the 80's. Valentina and Ari were three-years-old, Viktor was four-years-old, and Michael was a year-old and in Charlotte's arms as

Valentina, Ari, and Viktor chased each other around the tree Giovanni, Jason, Aaron, and Caesar had cut down and placed in the castle's living room. The next shot showed Valentina and Ari asleep on the floor innocently cuddled together underneath the pine tree. Jason carefully picked up Ari while Aaron lifted Valentina off the floor. Both men were seated on the couch next to their wives. Cassandra was feeding Valentina's new brother while Michelle was on a love seat beside Caesar talking to Brenda. Valentina and Ari were still sleeping on their father's laps.

When that movie ended, Jason stuck in another tape.

Everyone in the room was startled when sound finally came through the speakers. They let out a short laugh as Jason turned down the volume.

The home movie was shot during a picnic Cassandra and Aaron Russo held when Valentina and Ari were in fifth grade. The first ten minutes of the film consisted of their small family playing around by the above ground pool or playing bocce ball.

Their eyes filled with tears as they watched Valentina's late brothers play a quick game of bocce ball with friends and family.
Giovanni was noticed in the background watching his boys. A few minutes later, they heard Aaron express, "Come, and join us, dad!"

Giovanni rose to his feet and joined the others in the game as Charlotte was in the pool with Brenda, Cassandra, Italia, and the rest of the Astredo women.

Then the film advanced to Cassandra and Aaron's wedding anniversary party. The camera focused on Cassandra and Aaron embraced together on the dance floor. They renewed their marriage vows dressed in their original bridal clothes. Aaron was giving her small kisses across her shoulders while his hand rested on her newly rounded stomach. The next day, Cassandra gave birth to Valentina's brother, Dario. Brenda and Jason were dancing next to Cassandra, Aaron, Caesar, and Michelle. Brenda's head was on Jason's shoulder while he was lovingly caressing her back. The three couples were dancing to, 'Total Eclipse of the Heart'.

Michael and Raven were briefly heard making jokes and Viktor laughing along with Lisa and Diana.

Behind Brenda and Jason, was Valentina dressed in a silver medieval style gown dancing with Ari. Valentina had her arms around his neck resting her head on his shoulder. Ari held her tenderly as he developed a crush on his childhood friend. Ever since childhood, they were destining to be together. Soul mates, even after death.

The film cut to Aaron, Jason, and Caesar singing to Air Supply's, 'Every Woman in the world' to their wives on a large stage where a karaoke machine sat.

Next, the tape showed Italia belly dancing with the rest of the women in the Astredo family. They were at Deadly Nightshade during a private birthday party for Giovanni.

They couldn't help not to let the tears of happiness and sadness fall from their eyes as the home movies brought back some of the best times they had together.

Brenda and Michelle cuddled closer to their husbands as the camera centered on a theatrical stage in their theater. Their tear-filled eyes fell on their best friend in a dark maroon corset dress. In Cassandra's hand was a medieval style sword with a jewel-encrusted handle. The audience was silent as she approached her husband, whom was wearing a pirate costume. Aaron was seated in front of an old writing desk counting four tall stacks of gold coins. The fake blade ran across Aaron's neck as the tiny package of corn syrup hidden under the ruffled collar of the costume broke releasing the fake blood. As Aaron fell to the floor, Jason entered the cabin in a similar pirate costume taking Cassandra in his arms. The theater lights dimmed as the curtain closed.

"She was a wonderful actress," Brenda said.

"I always thought she did better than the other girls," Michelle said.

The others agreed. Raven said, "She was so excited to return to the stage after she had Scarlet."

"Marguerite killed her a day before her maternity leave was over," Italia said.

When the tape ended, they sat in silence letting the VCR rewind the movie. Brenda hit the mute button so the memories of their departed friends wouldn't be drowned out by the noisy television.

It was another silent moment before they slipped another video into the gray VCR. A shiver crept through them as they watched Octavia enter the castle holding Diana's hand during a picnic Giovanni and Charlotte were hosting.

As they watched Octavia talk with them, they began to see signs that she was merely acting as if she were their friend.

As the tape progressed, they noticed Charlemagne in the background serving drinks while staring at Octavia lustfully.

Jason paused the film after their family rose out of their seats to go into the garden after Charlotte announced that dinner was ready. As Octavia passed Charlemagne, Charlemagne discreetly touched Octavia's butt. While on pause, Octavia looked at Charlemagne as if she was about to quietly scold him for almost blowing their cover.

"One of them must have used a mind altering spell to cause us to forget we passed by him and the bar because, I was behind Octavia," Michelle said.

"I'm surprised Ari or I had not have received a vision of Octavia and Charlemagne working together," Raven said.

"They used strong magick to cover their tracks," said Brenda.

Raven looked at Charlemagne's hand resting on Octavia's butt as he said, "Do you know what is more disturbing than *that*?   When Giovanni had me chose a room the evening Diana and I moved in, I had visions of the many times Charlemagne would sneak Octavia into certain guest rooms, parlors, and make love to her. It took me a while before I found a room where they *didn't* have sex."

"That's creepy," Jason said.

"They never done it in any of *our* rooms have they?" asked Italia.

"No. After I told Giovanni and Charlotte the things I saw while choosing a room, they asked me to check their bedroom as well as all the bedrooms including the nursery."

"What did you find in the nursery?" asked Brenda wanting to tear Charlemagne's nuts off in case he and Octavia made love in the nursery.

"To my relief as well as Giovanni and Charlotte's relief, *nothing* sexual ever happened in the nursery."

"Thank the Gods," Caesar said.

"The only disturbing thing I saw was the way Charlemagne used to watch Ari sleep and plot ways to kidnap him and kill the others," said Raven.

"I hope he rots in prison," Jason said.

"I hate how he was near the children," said Brenda.

"It's very unsettling," Caesar agreed.

"He had no right expecting Ari to love him after he abandoned him," Jason said.

"If the situation was different, I'm sure Ari would've loved to start a relationship with him," said Caesar.

As they listened to the tape rewind, they sat in silence with the events of the tragic year of 1999 haunting their memories.

When the tape finished rewinding, Jason stood and walked towards the TV. He removed the last tape placing it in on a dragon carved shelf.

"While we were watching that last tape, I thought we should go into their old room and clean it out. It's been eight years and I doubt they would want it left as if it is a shrine. It may help us get closure," Michelle said.

Nervously, they thought it over.

Brenda said, "Let's do it."

#

Pulling out a black leather vest from inside a musty closet, Jason said, "Raven, I think you would like this. It is too small for me."

Raven placed the vest on his pile and said, "Thanks."

Jason and the others were gathered in Cassandra and Aaron's old bedroom going through their old clothes. They divided the items between them giving Valentina most of her mother's jewelry. At first, it bothered them to go through Cassandra and Aaron's things, but they knew it was the right thing to do. They had to move on and let Cassandra and Aaron rest in peace. They decided to give themselves closure after grieving for eight years.

They allowed the room to gather dust leaving everything the way it was the last time Cassandra and Aaron used it. Cobwebs and spider webs formed along the archways and among the gnarled pewter chandlers resembling Native American dream catchers. Some of their colognes and deodorants had dried up while some evaporated. The fancy perfume and cologne bottles were stained from the dried fragrance. Eight years of dust made the gnarled dark cherry wooded furniture appear as though it were dark gray. A blanket of dust even laid across the satin covers on the king size bed.

Italia took the dusty sheets and blankets to be washed along with the pillows and their dusty cases. They cleaned the rest of the furniture and placed fresh sheets and blankets on the bed. Even the large stained glass windows had to have the dust and cobwebs removed.

Brenda went through Cassandra's jewelry box. She left Valentina's share in the Gothic designed jewelry boxes planning to give Valentina her mother's castle designed ring and necklace jewelry box, her dragon and unicorn engraved Jewelry box, and her wizard and faerie jewelry box.

Raven looked through a pile of books on theater directing and said, "It is going to feel so strange reading these. He was a good director."

Caesar smiled and said, "I think Aaron would've liked you to carry on his role of being the director at the Dragon's Lair."

Tears filled their eyes as Raven said, "I think I'll have the first play I direct be dedicated in his and Cassandra's honor."

"I love that idea," Jason said.

"Do you think you may want to act in one of the plays?" Italia asked.

Raven softly smiled. "I may. It would be fun to act in a comedy with Michael and you two."

They softly laughed as Caesar said, "I should have asked Ari to write a spoof of old monster movies from the 1930's and the 1940's and have each of us have a part."

"That would be awesome," Raven said.

"I'll tell him about it when they finish in the gym. He's almost finished with his play about a haunted pirate ship," said Jason.

"That sounds cool," Markus said.

"It does. That's all he told me about it. He'll let me know more when he finishes it," said Jason.

They leafed through their memories of their departed friends. Looking through old record albums and eight tracks brought tears to their eyes remembering the many times they played poker or danced to the sounds of the 60's and 70's. They played certain songs on Cassandra and Aaron's old record player planning to leave the record player and the rest of the furniture in the room for guests.

They decided to place the records and eight tracks in the living room with the other records, 45 records, 8 tracks, cassette tapes, and CDs.

"I feel as though you and I are gaining another brother," Caesar said to Jason trying on a navy blue poet shirt over his dress shirt. Neatly, he folded the shirt and placed it on his pile after he had taken it off finding that it fit perfectly.

"It is more like that we have found our lost brother," said Michelle.

"I feel as though I have finally come home," said Raven.

"You have," Brenda said.

Jason pulled a few t-shirts from the closet that had a verity of pictures on them of dragons, wizards, faeries, and other fantasy creatures on the fronts. He tossed some on

Caesar's pile of Aaron's poet shirts after he tossed some on Raven's pile.

Michelle placed a black leather skirt in her pile. She caught a smile come across

Caesar's face when she laid the skirt down. She smiled back at her husband when he told

her that he couldn't wait to see her in the black leather skirt.

Brenda placed a pair of earrings among Valentina's pile as they continued to talk

about their deceased family members.

#

Alone in his new bedroom, Raven finished placing his new things away.

After he and the others went through the last of Cassandra and Aaron's things,

they retired to their bedrooms.

Raven sat the theatre books on a stool shaped like the God Anubis.

Raven's bedroom had dark blue velvet wallpaper with black accents. His bed had

black and dark blue satin sheets, pillows, and blankets.

The Pagan and Gothic decorations from his old apartment matched well with the

Gothic architecture of the room.

On his nightstand, sat a picture of Lotus in a long teal sundress with her long

black hair falling over her shoulders and a silver ankh hanging around her neck.

Raven changed into his black pajamas and sat on the bed with a book on play

directing on the bed beside him. Sitting in bed, he held the book in his hand while

looking at the picture of his late wife. He still felt empty without her. He brooded over

her heavily.

Raven lifted her picture off the nightstand for a moment and tenderly kissed her picture. "I miss you, Lotus. I love you." Tears formed in his eyes as he stared at her picture for a moment before he placed the Gothic designed frame on the stand. His heart felt as if it were breaking again. She meant everything to him.

Raven opened the book and began to read. He was four pages into it before he closed the book and placed it on his nightstand. He crawled beneath his cover, turned off the lamp, and cried himself to sleep.

#

The next evening

The evening sun began to peek through the trees creating orange and red light patches to be seen along the ground and on some of the trees.

Birds began to return to their nests for their nightly slumber while the nocturnal forest animals began to waken.

The half-melted snow glittered from the dying sunlight as if the small white drifts were home to faeries, gnomes, and wood nymphs.

A few rabbits passed by the witches unafraid that they would be hunted.

A tall deer with a large rack lifted his gaze from a large pond that he was drinking from as he watched the reunited father and daughter walk through the semi-dark Gothic garden.

"What do you think of Viktor?"

Raven couldn't cease from taking in the growing beauty of dusk. His eyes glanced at the waning moon and saluted Her as he said, "Hail Isis."

Diana copied and waited for her father's answer.

"I like him. I always had."

"Are you pleased I married him?"

"Very."

Diana smiled as Raven studied the crisp winter air, the bare branches on the trees and bushes, and the snow covered flowerbed. "You act as though you've never seen a garden that's ready to transfer from winter to spring." She smiled.

"After being captured for a week, all I saw were decayed corpses and skeletons. Since Octavia replaced my voice with that of a feline, it killed me each time I would see someone enter the catacombs. After Charlemagne freed her, I only saw their bedroom."

"Eight years of listening to her make love to that pervert must have been maddening."

"It was. I quickly learned to block it out."

"The thought of him making love to somebody makes me shudder."

Raven paused beside a statue of Hathor and gazed at Diana in the moon light. "Makes me shudder also." He gazed into her violet eyes and said, "You look like Lotus."

Diana smiled.

Raven escorted Diana to the back door of the castle.

#

Giovanni's private library

Moonlight covered the massive Gothic garden like a silver blanket. The moonlight fell over white statues of gargoyles, faeries, and Gods giving them a ghostly glow.

The crisp night wind carried the sound of ritual drums and Native Americans chanting in the woods and hills. Their deep voices and fast drumming seem to carry throughout the twenty- acre garden.

She walked through the high arched vaults passed life size statues of Gods, dragons, and gargoyles.

Walking up the stone staircases towards the North wing, Charlotte moved slowly. Entering the second floor of the North wing, she passed conference rooms and parlors that were draped in the shadows of night.

Opening a stained glass arched door, Charlotte slowly entered the massive library. She carefully entered the dark room and approached a gigantic fireplace. Lifting a matchstick that sat in a vase on a mahogany end table, she lit the charred tree truck, which lay on the ancient cobblestone.

The fire lit the room revealing one thousand books on every subject. Old newspapers lined a wall in glass dating from the 1500's to the present. Under the glass were yellowed articles and pictures of Castle Olympia and the generations of Astredos. Old articles from the 1970's told how Jason found Ari on his doorstep immediately wanting to adopt him; And various stories on Ari, Jason, Michelle, Lisa, Michael, Aaron, Cassandra, and a few other's careers at the Dragon's Lair Theater; Valentina on some paranormal investigations; Diana's tarot reading parlor as well as Italia dancing at Deadly Nightshade. Two columns displayed the obituaries of Cassandra and Aaron Russo. Cassandra and Aaron were placed in the mammoth catacombs under the sanctuary in a double silver coffin. Dario and Adrian 's coffins were on either side of their parent 's coffin.

Charlotte stood before a long glass case. She opened the top of the glass with a key Giovanni and Charlotte gave to each family member. In her other hand, she lifted her brother's fake obituary. She looked at the many paper clippings about the Gothic castle and the Astredo family. Most of the newspaper clippings were yellowed and brittle while some were recently placed in the long showcases. Laying Charlemagne's obituary beside a black and white photo of Michael and Lisa's handfasting, taking place during Lughnasadh, she took a moment to look at the other clippings. After she closed and locked the glass case, Charlotte stepped away from the glass case and found Giovanni standing by one of the bookcases as he gazed at her with desire in his old Italian eyes. She slightly smiled at him as she approached him.

"Are you ok," Giovanni asked.

"I'm not sure. Giovanni, I want to tell them everything. I 'm beginning to feel that Charlemagne was only messing with us when he said the entire family will suffer."

"The memory altering potion could have conjured many unrealistic fears and other psychological problems."

"That's possible. I want to put an end to their guessing game. It's not right. I don't know what to do."

"I could call Kathy and ask her advice," said Giovanni. He pulled her into his embrace kissing her passionately on the mouth, stripping her, before he explored her body. "You're a strong woman, you're going to get through this," he said before he kissed her again.

Charlotte peeled off his clothes as her mouth caressed his chest and shoulders deeply and passionately. She lightly shut her eyes as she enjoyed his tender kisses while he gently laid her on the dark grey carpet before he entered her. Charlotte softly moaned his name as he pushed her at a fast pace.

They rolled along the aisle in between the tall bookcases with her on top riding him until she climaxed screaming his name.

#

Dragon's Lair Theatre

A few nights later

Michael and Caesar were giving Raven a tour of the old family theater after they stalked the concession stand with popcorn tubs, plastic dragon shaped cups for drinks, straws in castle shaped holders, nacho containers, and other mediaeval themed plates, bowls, and cups for snacks.

The three witches spent the morning filling the soda fountain, stocking the shelves with a verity of chips, candy, trail mix, granola bars, and pretzels.

After they completed that task, they began working on Ari's play.

#

Jason sat at his desk and paid the theater's electric bill while listening to a Gothic rock band. He wore a black T-shirt with a picture of the Egyptian God Horus. His rings were Gothic and Pagan themed and a pewter ankh hung around his neck.

He lifted his eyes to his opened door. He smiled when he saw Brenda enter his office.

Since it was her day off, she had on a pair of black leather pants and a black gypsy-style blouse. She stood across from him. "Mom told me there's no bail on Charlemagne and Demonique. Marguerite and Octavia *can't* bail them out."

Jason gently pushed his computer chair away from his desk and welcomed her on his lap. Placing his arms around her waist, he held her closer.

Brenda placed her arms around his neck as he said,

"That makes me feel better."

"Me too."

Jason nuzzled her neck as his hand began to caress her thigh. Jason gazed at his wife of thirty-four years before he tenderly kissed her along her throat. He hugged her tightly.

Brenda moved her hands under his shirt caressing his back moaning as his caresses grew heavier touching places that immediately sent shocks of ecstasy through her. She kissed him passionately on the lips after removing his shirt after he removed her shirt. She removed her pants, sat on his lap, wrapping her legs around his waist. She kissed him again while she began to grind on his lap.

Jason kissed her neck and along her shoulders. His hand caressed her thigh while his other hand caressed her back. He pushed her harder moaning and crying out with her.

"Oh, oh, Jason!"

"I love you, Brenda," he said as his lips moved towards her chest cupping a breast with his hand before sucking hard on her erect nipple. After giving the other breast the same attention, he kissed her along her throat and mouth.

Brenda held him tightly against her as ecstasy busted through her. She screamed his name as he pushed her harder.

He was intoxicated by the way her passion-filled voice repeated his name. His hands caressed her back and thigh enjoying the soft touch of her skin. He nuzzled her neck before he kissed her along her throat and her lips again.

Her legs tightened around his waist as she moaned, "Jason, Jason, Jason!"

Jason brought her to orgasm a few more times before he arrived at his climax.

When they were finished, they went out to a Greek cafe until his lunch break was over.

Chapter 47

Salem, Ohio

Castle Olympia

2008

Charlotte lay awake staring at her large mahogany dresser sitting in the moonlight. She was tired, but couldn't return to sleep.

Ever since the amnesia spell Charlemagne placed on her family was lifted, she and Giovanni were remembering past battles with Marguerite and her crime family.

Charlotte turned toward Giovanni placing an arm around his bare waist. She kissed his natural tattoo of the God symbol.

Giovanni lay on his stomach unaware that his eighty-five-year-old wife was tenderly caressing his naked body. His beauty remained with him through the years. Streaks of silver were mixed through his black hair. The only traces of wrinkles were his crows-feet and two faint lines across his forehead. Charlotte hugged him gently before removing herself from the bed.

Removing her red satin nightgown from the floor, she stepped into it.

The nightgown reached her ankles with a slit on the right side with a low V-neck bodice.

It was Giovanni's favorite nightgown on her.

Charlotte lifted the matching satin robe from the floor next to his red satin pajama pants. After she slipped her robe over her nightgown, she quietly left their bedroom walking down the long dark hallway.

The castle was silent with their children, grandchildren, and great-grandchildren in their bedrooms.

Moonlight poured over the castle and garden.

The night carried the sound of nocturnal animals while constellations began to cover the sky.

Running water from fountains, garden ponds, and frogs joined the sounds of evening.

The many cats and kittens sharing the castle and the large Gothic garden were asleep on the Gothic and Egyptian carved furniture, arched windowsills, and some statues.

Stepping into their large Gothic kitchen, Charlotte walked towards a cupboard and pulled out a glass with red and black dragons engraved into the glass. Setting the glass on the counter, she moved to the refrigerator and pulled out a black and purple picture filled with chamomile tea.

Standing in front of the black sink, she gazed out the kitchen window at the moon soaked statues of Gods, Goddesses, dragons, unicorns, and other creatures. She slowly sipped her tea reflecting back to the nightmare.

Remembering the feel of his warm breath against her bare shoulder and the cool steel of his knife pressing against her throat caused her to shudder. Charlotte took another sip of her tea reminding herself that she was an Astredo now. A witch. A *fire starter*.

Movement in the large Gothic garden caught her attention. She watched a large shadow move closer to the bricked patio. A white and grey form appeared in front of the kitchen window. Recognizing the spirit, she stepped away from the window. Her eyes locked with the ghostly wolf before the spirit vanished.

The wolf was sometimes accompanied by a woman dressed in clothes from the nineteen thirties. The woman's ghost was Delilah DeMarco, Marguerite's oldest daughter and underboss. The wolf's ghost was alone this time still giving Charlotte a sense of protection. The man in her nightmares wasn't the werewolf 's ghost that was outside her window.

In the air, arose the sweet scent of lavender.

It filled the room as if it were a dense fog.

The kitchen was suddenly covered in a blanket of purple ice draping over the counter tops, cupboards, shelves, table, doors, appliances, and windows.

Charlotte felt someone behind her and for a moment forgot the familiar scent of lavender accompanied the phantom draft. She quickly turned expecting to find another ghost from her dark and tragic past. However, instead, her eyes fell on a ghost of a 46-year-old gypsy woman with long black hair and a 1940's style dress. Charlotte softly smiled at the family's matriarch, Athena Astredo.

"You have to tell them about your side of the family. They could benefit from yours and Giovanni's experiences. They're powerful witches. They know how to protect themselves and each other. Dante and Marguerite wish to have their family and friends reunited. Tell your children and grandchildren. Forget about her threat to kill them. She would have murdered them anyway."

"Tomorrow evening, Giovanni and I will tell them *everything*."

Athena smiled. "Italia and the others will be pleased. A family such as ours should *not* keep secrets."

#

In Giovanni's large kitchen, he finished preparing breakfast for their children and grandchildren.

Rosa and Scarlet Astredo wore gypsy style skirts and blouses.

After Charlotte helped Giovanni set the table, they sat at their marbled table.

Markus and Italia sat at the table after they closed Deadly Nightshade for the day.

Charlotte said, "After Valentina, Ari, and Viktor wake, there are some journals in the library I have to read to you."

Jason asked, "Are they written by *your* side of the family?"

Charlotte nervously smiled. "They are." She looked at her breakfast. She lost her appetite.

Italia reached for her hand and said, "Take your time, mom."

Feeling his grandmother's emotions, Michael said, "We *won't* hate you. We understand you and grandpa had spells casts at you to forget."

Charlotte looked at her family and said, "I was going to wait until the truth unfolds while reading my brothers and sisters' journals. Although, I think it won't be too shocking if I tell you now. Your attention should be focused on learning about the enemy."

Markus said, "*Enemy*?"

Charlotte's hand clasped tightly around her daughter-in-law's hand as though it were a security blanket. "Marguerite DeMarco is my mother. I was a lady mobster."

Charlotte and Giovanni's three sons, three daughters-in-law, and grandchildren stared in surprise.

After a few moments of silence, Brenda asked, "You are the daughter of the most famous mob boss in history?"

"I am. There's a lot you and the others have to know."

"I'll take the girls to the library so they can do their homework after I pick up the journals," said Diana.

When breakfast ended, Diana, Michael, and Michelle assisted Giovanni and Charlotte with clearing the table and placing the dishes in the dishwasher.

Gathered in the living room, they sat on carved Gothic style couches and chairs while Giovanni sat on his black leather recliner.

The patriarch of the Astredo family lifted a wand from a dragon shaped stand and enchanted the large scrying mirror that sat next to the television to check on the mob's current activities.

Chapter 47

A dark rainbow of red, blue, purple, orange, and green light poured through the arched stained glass windows in the north wing hallway.

Diana walked towards the family library.

The library carried the odor of musty antique books.

A long row of book cases shelved journals written by family members since the middle ages to the present along with journals belonging to Marguerite's mobsters.

Valentina was helping the girls with their homework after she found the journals Charlotte requested.

Rosa and Scarlet sat at their antique 19th century desks. With the mundane lessons, they were schooled in the family history. They used the old journals as textbooks.

On a round marbled table sat a stack of journals from 1918; 1920's to the 1940's.

"These should be an interesting read," said Valentina.

"I'm anxious to read them. Don Jacqueline DeMarco Tortelli's journal may be the most disturbing since she married a schizophrenic serial killer," said Diana.

"I'm looking forward to learning how he became so violent. I have a house to investigate after I finish with Rosa and Scarlet. I won't be long."

"Grandma wants to read them once we are all assembled. According to Michelle's tarot reading, Octavia will be become the next don."

"I shouldn't be too long."

After a few more minutes of conversation, Diana left the library with the old yellowed journals.

When she returned to the living room, everyone was discussing the new workday. Diana placed the journals on the coffee table and sat next to Charlotte.

As she gazed upon the tattered and worn covers, Charlotte said, "Giovanni and I will be the ones to read them out loud."

Diana removed a journal from the pile and looked at the faded name and year. Delilah DeMarco. 1918.

"It's hard to believe that we are related to the famous DeMarco crime family," said Diana.

"I know. It would be interesting to see how accurate all the movies have been," said Jason.

Valentina entered the large hallway and into the living room.

The rest of the family was already gathered into the living room.

Valentina sat beside Ari on a maroon velvet love seat.

Charlotte sat on the couch with Viktor, Diana, Jason, and Brenda.

Raven sat on another love seat with Caesar, Michelle, Michael, and Lisa on a black velvet couch.

Markus and Italia sat on maroon velvet chairs.

Charlotte looked at the supportive and patient expression her family was giving her. "Before I read these journals, I want to tell you about Marguerite's origins. You know why your ancestor, Olympia Astredo, casts the spell making them and future generations with the mark of the Gods. What you don't and *should* know is how and why Marguerite became a vampire." She picked up an old brown leather journal dated: 1509.

Chapter 48

Italy, 1509

Alexander Astredo I, owned a few vineyards. Alexander was the youngest son of Giovanni and Lynette Astredo. After he acquired wealth, he moved his vagabond family into the Gothic castle.

Alexander Astredo named Castle Olympia after his young wife, Olympia.

Dragons and other mystical beasts were carved in the dark wood furniture.

The Astredo family gathered in the temple room.

Life-size statues of Roman Gods and Goddesses filled the temple room.

Newly added, was a statue of Isis.

Olympia was Greek and brought with her the worship of the Egyptian and Greek pantheons. Her new in-laws worshipped the Roman Gods. Her gown was turquoise and around her neck, she wore the image of Hathor. Her long black hair was braided with a strand of turquoise beads weave through the braid. She was a psychic and controlled air.

With them, were Alexander's brothers and sister.

Draco Astredo was a fire starter. As the others, he was human, but had the spirit of the dragon within.

Alexander Astredo was the family alchemist with the power to heal. He controlled the element water.

Mariano was the oldest and looked like his father, Giovanni, although like his mother, he was born with the power to read minds and controlled earth.

Like her father, Deidre Astredo was an empath and controlled water.

With their weapons ready, they stood at different points of the room protecting Olympia while she casts a spell that would carry for many generations.

Olympia cast a Circle before she began to weave her spell. "Goddess bestow upon your chosen witches a symbol to mark them as your own and allow it to carry onto future generations. I pray that our powers will continue to be passed on throughout the ages to those who share our blood so they may continue to perform Your work long after we, the first generation of warrior witches, are resting within the catacombs of Castle Olympia. So Mote it be."

A warm sensation appeared on their right shoulders.

After she opened the Circle, she walked towards a mirror and studied her right shoulder.

A natural tattoo appeared. The Triple Goddess with a pentagram in the center of the Full Moon.

On the men's right shoulders, were the God symbol with a pentagram in the center of the Circle.

#

Marguerite DeMarco watched from her tower window as her grandmother's golden casket was lowered into the wet ground. Her expression didn't show sorrow like the other mourners. Instead, it showed rage.

Her hazel eyes looked past the family cemetery at the vast Apennine Mountains where the castle of her enemy sat with Mont Blanc behind in the far distance. A gray cloud hung over the snow-capped peaks like a canopy over a gnarled and distorted bed. Rain fell as tiny droplets of silver into the ground.

The cool rain was a slow and rhythmic drizzle accompanied by a faint rumble of thunder.

Earlier, she and her husband, Dante DeMarco, ended a brief battle with the Astredos.

A tear fell as Marguerite watched the circle of black umbrellas move away from her grandmother's grave. The black umbrellas were like large ravens feasting on a rotting corpse as they moved about in the cemetery. She recalled the moment during the start of the ceremony when she cried with grief. Not wanting any of her new foot soldiers and associates to see her, she fled for the castle.

Marguerite was now the leader of her grandmother's band of thieves. After becoming Elizabethan's protégée, she devoted her life to being her head assassin. She plotted revenge on the Astredos while the others mourned.

As she sat at the arched window watching the drizzle turn into a heavy downpour, her chamber door opened.

Dante entered wearing a dark green medieval style shirt, pants with chain mail netting around his neck, and sleeves. His long white hair was shoulder length and curly. He took Marguerite's last name when he married her. It was a DeMarco family tradition. His handsome tear-filled eyes gazed deep into his wife's, sorrow-filled eyes. He placed his hands on his beloved shoulders and said, "Let's join the others in the dining hall."

Marguerite allowed him to escort her where her new bandits were waiting.

#

Fireballs flew through the morning air landing on a few of Marguerite's assassins. Draco Astredo threw a few more fireballs.

Giovanni and Lynette fought with their children. They used their elemental powers against their enemies.

Mariano, the controller of earth, caused the ground around a trio of men to slip through the new crack.

Olympia created a cyclone as tall as she was with Alexander adding water into the cone.

The five-foot tornado began to spit out ice shards that impaled the enemy like razor blades.

Marguerite fought against Deidre after Deidre impaled many of Marguerite's bandits with ice spears.

Deidre conjured water, froze the stream, before throwing it at Marguerite.

The spear landed in Marguerite's hand before landing in Deidre's chest.

The battle ceased when the last bandit, was killed.

Olympia held her deceased sister-in-law while the others circled Marguerite.

Lynette approached Marguerite and said, "I could kill you, although, I would rather you experience the pain of losing a child. Marguerite, by the powers of Mother Earth, you *will* lose your children young either by death or born with our mark branding them as ours."

Later that evening, Marguerite lay snuggled in Dante's arms among their purple sheets.

Two puncture holes were on the side of her neck.

#

Charlotte lifted a journal from the coffee table and began to read aloud from its musty yellowed pages.

Chapter 49

Medea   Island 1928

Delilah DeMarco lived in the Gothic mansion with her husband, Lucian 'The Cobra' Phoenix. Marguerite's deceased friend's son, Tony Tortelli, live with them. She was the copy of her mother Marguerite. Dark Blonde hair. Italian-French features. Delilah was a fire starter.

After making Delilah her underboss, Marguerite gave her the mansion while she and Armand left for his place.

Delilah met Lucian through her oldest brother, Frank. After a two-week courtship, they married in a small twenty-four hour wedding chapel.

Over the phone, Delilah spoke with her sister-in-law Molly, Frank's wife, "Mom and dad are still having problems."

"What do you think will happen?"

"I'm not sure. I hope things will work out. I wish mom would leave Armand and Gerard and stay with Dante here."

"So do we. Charlemagne and Nikkolas were here with Jacqueline. She loves the way Charlotte and I decorated her room."

Delilah's brother Charlemagne was twenty-two and twins Nikkolas and Charlotte were five. Jacqueline was six.

"I can't wait to see it. Are Nikkolas and Charlotte staying with you and Frank also?"

"Nikkolas is just for the summer." There was a paused before Molly said, "Charlemagne: take Jacqueline and Charlotte outside."

Delilah held back tears hearing a back door close before Molly said,

"Frank and I are raising Jacqueline and Charlotte. Armand doesn't think Jacqueline's his and wants nothing to do with her. Mom doesn't like Charlotte's birthmark. It looks too much like the Astredo's mark."

"What does mom say about that? I can't see her following dad's orders."

"She's only going along with him just to keep Jacqueline safe. Marguerite is confused and heartbroken. She doesn't know what to do. It's not a good environment for Jacqueline and Charlotte. They'll be better off with us."

"Tony will be happy; Jacqueline 's closer," said Delilah. "What about Nikkolas and Charlotte? Will they be safe with dad?"

"He'll be fine. Armand *wanted* him. Dad doesn't care weather that is the Astredo's natural mark or not."

"Why doesn't mom just kill the prick? Why won't she take my offer and move the rest of our family back in *this* mansion?"

"I don't know. Perhaps she sees moving in with her daughters and sons as a sign of weakness or something. Let's just focus on our younger siblings and let Marguerite and Armand work on things. Frank is more concerned with Jacqueline, Charlotte, and Nikkolas. As long as Armand is alive Jacqueline is in more danger."

Delilah said, "If things get too bad, you can send the kids here for a while."

They talked for another hour before Delilah hung up.

Delilah tried to concentrate on the bills for her home and the casinos her parents owned on the island and in Ohio. She was dressed in her usual purple suit dress with matching fedora hat. Glancing up from her paper work, she watched six-year-old Tony Tortelli walk into her office speaking to his hallucinations and laughing loudly.

He had black hair and dark brown eyes like his father, Dominick Tortelli. Tony inherited his father's looks as well as his mental illness. His mother, Cara, died in childbirth and his father killed himself a few hours after he was born. Marguerite and Cara were close friends. Marguerite and Cara decided to betroth Jacqueline and Tony to help strengthen Cara's dying Mafia family. Cara requested that Marguerite become Tony's guardian. He was home taught by Lucian. Delilah was babysitting the mentally ill six-year-old while Marguerite is taking care of things between her and Armand. Tony had a wooden box filled with stolen knives he would spend hours staring at. He would make tiny cuts in the palm of his hand just to watch the blood rise to the surface. Lucian and Delilah tried to stop him from playing with the knives and from cutting himself.

Tony grabbed the back of one of the chairs that sat at the long table where Delilah was working. Violently, he began to rock it causing a tapping sound that echoed through the mansion. He laughed, liking the noise the chair made. He was suddenly stopped by Delilah's hand as she formed a tight grasp around his arm.

"I've told you before Tony; don't distract me while I'm working."

Tony's scared, pale blue eyes gazed into her angry brown eyes. "I was playing with my Jacqueline. She wanted me to rock her in the chair. I want my Jacqueline to be my girlfriend for ever and ever and ever."

Delilah removed her hand from his arm before she slapped his hand. "Jacqueline isn't here. Go somewhere else and play. I'm busy." As she returned to her seat, he quickly jumped in her lap placing his arms around her neck and said,

"When is dad coming home? When is dad coming home?" Tony hugged her tightly as she sighed in irritation.

Pulling him away from her, she held him by the arms. "Lucian's *not* your father. He's your future brother-in-law. Your father is dead." Too much was on her mind to deal with the schizophrenic little boy her mother's best friend left behind. Frank loved kids; she should've gifted him the burden of raising a serial killer's son. Dominick Tortelli terrorized the streets of Salem, Youngstown, and Boardman, Ohio while Cara was Marguerite's head hit-woman.

"What does dead mean? I want to play with my Jacqueline. Can you please ask Molly to bring my Jacqueline over here to my house?" Tony giggled and then let out a blood-curdling scream just to see Delilah's expression. Tony laughed at her terrified expression.

Delilah rolled her eyes at him and wondered if it was worth having him marry her baby sister. Charlemagne and others felt Tony would grow out of the destructive phase he was in. Causing him to look at her, she said, "I don't know if I want my little sister marrying you. Be satisfied with the pictures of her."

"No! I want my Jacqueline here with me! I want Jacqueline *now*! I wish you will allow me to touch my Jacqueline!" His young eyes glared murderously into her eyes.

Delilah wanted to strike him again, although, she was beginning to see that normal punishments were no longer working. She held his arms down and said, "Never talk to me in that tone again! Respect me."

Tony pouted, knowing Lucian and the others would give him anything he would ask for. He grabbed her arms, digging his nails into her skin, and said, "I want you to give me my Jacqueline! She belongs to me. I want her!"

Delilah pushed him off her lap and called for Lucian in irritation.

Entering the office, Lucian was wearing a black pinstriped suit. He was Italian and an incubus. He was bisexual. He had a dark complexion and raven black hair. He was handsome and very strong. His favorite murdering technique was strangulation. After Delilah told him what Tony said and did to her, Lucian approached Tony. "Tony, *never* disrespect women like that. If you want to marry Jacqueline someday, you have to learn that hitting women isn't right."

Delilah rose from her chair. "He's driving me fucking nuts."

Lucian took Tony's hand into his. "We promised your mother we would help watch him. He's just testing you. He doesn't act that way with Charlemagne, Frank, or I."

"Why? I don't punish him any different then the rest of you."

"Perhaps it's because you don't allow him to do what he wants once in a while. You're too strict with him."

"I'm keeping the little shit from getting hurt."

"He also knows you don't like him."

"I like Tony, just not when I'm trying to run the house for mom. I don't have the patience to deal with you and that brat. I'm going to the beach to be alone. I need to get away from him for a while."

Tony placed his arms around Lucian's waist.

Lucian tenderly caressed Tony's back. He watched her leave, he said, "Let's go play in the living room."

Chapter 50

1928

Salem, Ohio

One month later

Molly was dressed in a black beaded flapper dress. In her hair, she wore a black and gold sequined headdress with a black feather that stuck out from the side. She was human, but like Lucian, she was a succubus. She had the power to heal. Her long golden earrings dangled at the side of her neck as two long black and gold beaded necklaces hung around her neck.

Frank tightened his arms around her. The werewolf was dressed in a black pinstriped suit with a white shirt under the vest. On his thick, black curly hair rested his gray fedora.

They were slow dancing to a swing band in an Italian nightclub. Frank and Molly left Jacqueline with a babysitter so they could celebrate their seventh wedding anniversary before they left for Medea the next morning.

Molly placed her head on his chest, becoming mesmerized by his strong cologne. She softly moaned as he led a trail of deep passionate kisses down her throat.

Frank kissed her lips a few times. "Do you want to try again tonight?"

Molly gazed into his light gray eyes. "Why not? If we are lucky, perhaps I'll be able to go three months without losing the baby."

Frank gently smiled. "Molly, it'll happen. We just have to be patient." Frank nuzzled her neck, still saddened by their third miscarriage six weeks ago. He gently ran his fingers through her short, brown curly hair loving every moment of her.

#

After they performed oral sex on each other, Frank slowly pushed her with her lying under him. Frank caressed her mouth with his as he went deeper inside her.

Molly caressed his back and moaned as he continued to stroke her. She kissed him along his shoulders and neck before he sucked on her nipple, kissing it deeply. "Oh Frank!"

The car rocked violently as Molly began to scream his name.

Chapter 51

A middle aged woman sat in a green velvet chair with several bullets pumped into her head from a rival mobster who broke into Molly and Frank's two story century old home.

Wrapped around the pistol was a towel.

The mobster quietly crept up the stairs towards Jacqueline's bedroom. He walked down the dark narrow hallway towards the room at the end.

Jacqueline's bedroom was decorated in dark purples with a dark and light purple canopy hovering over her twin bed. A picture of Tony sat on her night stand.

The mobster pulled the lacy curtains back and placed a white pillow over her face which lay under the purple and white cotton blanket before he aimed the pistol at her forehead.

#

Frank's car pulled into their driveway with Molly leaning against him still kissing him along his neck and throat.

They walked into their home with their arms around each other's waists quietly laughing and kissing. Their laughter ceased when their terror filled eyes fell on the dead baby sitter. Molly and Frank ran up the stairs calling for Jacqueline. Molly was the first to open the door to her sister-in-law's room. She screamed as Frank gasped in shock.

Lying in a pool of blood was the mobster with his chest sliced open and organs exposed.

Jacqueline stood over him holding her bloody chef knife.

Chapter 52

Island of Medea

The same night as Jacqueline's first kill

"Molly, calm down. You and Frank should be praising her," Delilah said, talking on the phone. She stood in her large kitchen making supper while she listened to Molly and Frank explain Jacqueline's calm reaction to the way she handled the intruder. Delilah sent Frank to hide the two bodies.

"Delilah, we think Jacqueline was waiting for him. She took pillows from our room and her room and stuffed them under her covers. Then she hid in her closet with the chef's knife. When we discovered her, she looked at us and smiled," Molly said with tears streaming down her cheeks. Jacqueline was in the living room with Molly and was playing with her dolls as if nothing terrible had happened.

Delilah smiled. "I'm impressed. She'll make me proud someday. Is Charlotte ok? Have you told mom?"

"Charlotte's fine. Jacqueline locked her door. She saved her. Frank and I called mom after we cleaned everything. She was surprised and somewhat disturbed. She's coming into town to speak with her. She did mention that she was proud of the way Jacqueline defended herself and Charlotte."

"Are the others joining her?"

"She's not sure yet. She's thinking about having Gerard spy on the Astredos while she and Dante return to Italy."

Delilah softly smiled and asked, "Will she be staying with dad?"

"No, with us. Armand gets Nikkolas during spring and summer until he is eighteen. By his choice, Charlemagne is staying with Marguerite for a while," said Molly.

Delilah said, "Is it wrong for the future Godmother to wish her parents were still together?"

"No."

While she spoke, the doorbell rang. Tony was sitting in the small breakfast nook as he played with his toys.

"Get the door, Tony. Molly, it's time to tell Jacqueline who I am and that she's to become Godmother someday. It's obvious she's ready. I want you and Frank to relax. She did the right thing. Be happy she defended Charlotte and herself. Mom and I are proud of her," Delilah said.

Tony walked out of the kitchen, down the hall, and past the massive staircase towards an end table where another phone sat. He answered the door and looked into a police officer's eyes.

Speaking Italian and holding a map at his side, the policeman asked, "Hi, are your parents busy?"

Tony stared fearfully at his uniform remembering the few occasions when a policeman would come for Lucian and the others.

Seeing the fear in Tony's eyes, the policeman said gently, "It's alright. I'm new on this island and I just want to know if your parents could give me directions to Astredo's nightclub. I'm supposed to meet a few friends there."

#

Back in the kitchen, Delilah said, "Just watch her closely. Make sure she doesn't do that again."

"Delilah! Delilah!"

"Hold on, Molly." Delilah sat the phone on the counter before rushing into the hallway.

Holding his favorite chef's knife, he continued to stab and play with the organs that spilled out of the policeman's stomach.

Lucian looked at Delilah, fearfully. "Your mother created a monster. Delilah, he just stopped for directions. I overheard their conversation while I was in the casino."

"Go talk to your brother-in-law before the two of you have heart attacks."

Lucian looked at Delilah with a puzzled look as she approached Tony. "What is wrong with Molly and Frank? Is everything alright?"

Delilah knelt beside Tony and gently took him by the wrist. Tony giggled while staring at the blood covered corpse. She said, "Someone tried to hit Jacqueline and Charlotte a few hours ago. Thankfully Jacqueline saved Charlotte and herself by stabbing the bastard to death."

Lucian hurried into the kitchen and told Molly and Frank what Tony did.

Delilah escorted Tony over to a bench. She made him sit beside her as she called one of her body guards to take the body out back to where a huge cliff dropped off into the ocean.

She held Tony's blood covered hands.

"Did I do something bad?" His pale blue eyes filled with tears.

Running her fingers through his black hair, she said, "That depends. Why did you kill him?"

Tony slowly placed his arm around her waist resting his blood covered hand on her knee. "I didn't want him to take Lucian or you or Charlemagne or Molly or Marguerite or Nikkolas or Frank or Gerard or Dante away again. I love Lucian and you and everyone in our whole entire house."

"You were protecting us." Delilah encircled her arms around him to hold him in a motherly embrace.

She tenderly kissed his forehead as Lucian returned and kneeled in front of Tony. "He thought you were in danger. He was protecting you."

Lucian smiled uneasily. "Tony, thanks, but you can't kill like that. You and Jacqueline are too young. Please promise me and Delilah that you'll never do that again."

Tony gave Delilah a tight hug before he went into Lucian's fatherly embrace. "I promise." He kissed his cheek and asked, "What's my Jacqueline doing?"

"She's having the same talk you and I are having with Frank and Molly," Lucian said.

"Take him upstairs and clean him. I'll clean the hallway," Delilah said.

Lucian stood as Tony rose off the bench. He led him upstairs and Delilah left to grab the mop.

Chapter 53

1929

It was a few months after Jacqueline and Tony's first kill. After the police in Salem and on the Island of Medea discovered the murdered bodies, Jacqueline and Tony were sent to separate asylums for a month.

Screams of pain and terror echoed throughout the halls of Valletta Asylum. Blood and severed body parts intertwined with the antique torture equipment.

Bound in shackles and chains, Tony stood in cell number 83 screaming at his hallucinations in a mixture of English and Italian. He watched in terror as a hallucination of an asylum guard appeared to him and prepared to beat him. Tony aggressively struggled to break free of his imprisonment. Sweat drenched his small clothes. Blood flowed from his mouth and lip where a guard had hit him.

When a guard entered to calm him, Tony attacked the guard, kicking him with his leg that wasn't in a shackle. The guard was struck in the face by the swinging chains that draped between the shackles.

Tony's face was divided by a long cut from his hairline, down his forehead, his nose barely missing his left eye, down his cheek, and ending at his chin. He screamed for Jacqueline while he tugged at the shackle that was bolted into the white padded wall. When the guard attempted to call for assistance, Tony swung his arms to strike the guard in his face again, causing his face to bleed heavier. Tony glared murderously at the guard rambling, "Fuck you! I want to go to my house with my Jacqueline. I'm going to kill everyone in the whole entire world but my Jacqueline." Tony missed hitting the guard again when he stepped back and called for a doctor.

A doctor entered the cell and grabbed Tony by the arms. Pinning him against the white padded walls, he said, "You need to calm yourself or be tortured again."

Tony cried for Jacqueline glaring at the doctor. "I want to kill again and again and again and again! I liked it when the shiny red stuff came out. I want to show it to my Jacqueline. Jacqueline, Jacqueline, JACQUELINE!" Tony stopped struggling and cried as Lucian entered his cell.

As the doctor and the guard left, Lucian approached Tony. He hated the way the asylum still used barbaric methods to discipline prisoners. Lowering himself on his knees, Lucian fatherly embraced Tony. He wished he could take him somewhere to treat his schizophrenia. If such a place existed.

Tony placed his hand on Lucian's face. "When can I go home?"

Tears filled his gray eyes. He said, "Someday, Tony, we'll get you the help you need. Perhaps Jacqueline would be able to help me. She adores you." Lucian hugged him and wished he could adopt him.

Tony rested his head on his shoulder. He told him what they did to him. His tears ran down his bloody and bruised face.

When the guard returned to announce visiting hours were over, Lucian hugged and kissed Tony before he approached the guard.

The guard had a bandage over his forehead. He slowly backed away from Lucian, only to have Lucian's strong hands collapse around his throat.

"No one touches my kid!" Lucian snapped the guard's neck and tossed him onto the dirty floor, wanting to use his corpse as a warning to others of what would happen if they continued to beat Tony.

#

Youngstown, Ohio

Aesculapius Institution

The doctors in the large asylum, named after the Roman God of healing, weren't as corrupt and cruel as they were at *Valletta* Asylum. Like other asylums across Europe and the United States, the staff focused on treating mental patients instead of torturing them.

Jacqueline lay in a hospital bed with the restraints off and gazed at a recent picture of Tony. She was bored with the doctors and nurses' endless parade of questions.

"Jacqueline, please answer me. We are here to *help*," said a psychiatrist who sat next to the future lady mobster's bed.

Jacqueline looked at the psychiatrist. "I answered you yesterday. I was defending my sister." In boredom, she sighed. "I don't need help. I was protecting my family. Molly and Frank were proud of me and my big sister Delilah and my mother were impressed."

The psychiatrist tenderly shook her head. "Your sisters, brothers, and mom were proud of you for defending your sister and yourself, but they were concerned with the calm way you handled it."

Wishing her sister-in-law and brother would take her home, Jacqueline asked, "Would you guys rather I screamed my fucking head off and allowed him to kill Charlotte and I?" She remembered hearing how Molly gunned down four mobsters in a casino, Marguerite battling werewolves, other vampires, and how Delilah and the others praised her instead of sending her to an asylum.

"No, you did nothing wrong with protecting your sister and yourself. They don't think it's normal for a young girl to react so calmly to cutting an intruder into pieces," said the psychiatrist writing on a notepad.

"I wish my little sister could visit me and I wish I was in the same asylum and the same room with Tony. That would've been fun. Doctor, I've done nothing wrong. My sister was proud of me and Charlotte is safe. She's my best friend and sister."

"Charlotte is too young to visit.   Delilah isn't a good role model for you. Jacqueline, murder is a mortal sin. I don't want you to walk down her path. She's a cold hearted criminal."

Jacqueline kissed Tony's picture and said, "No, Delilah is a businesswoman. She doesn't have anyone killed unless it's deserved. It's just business. Someday I'm going to be her underboss and when she dies, I'll take over. I already have my betrothed waiting for me on the island. I can't wait until I'm old enough to work beside Delilah and Molly."

The psychiatrist rose from her chair as Molly and Frank entered Jacqueline's room. She left after stating that she would tell them when visiting hours were over.

They sat on the bed, each placing an arm around her. Frank tenderly kissed her cheek as Molly gave her a gentle hug.

"How is Tony?"

"He's disturbed and feels no remorse. He's still locked away. Lucian hates the place. You and Tony will be released in a few days," Molly said.

"I *don't* feel remorse, either. He deserved to die." Jacqueline wished they come to take her home.

"Molly and I want you to promise that you and Tony won't kill again until you're older. Just cooperate with the doctors and don't try to explain the family business to them. You frightened Molly and me."

"Why?"

"Because we love you and we don't want anything to happen to you," Molly said.

"Does Tony get to see Delilah and Lucian?"

"Not as often as we get to see you."

"I want to see Tony."

"You'll get to see him someday."

"I want to see him now."

"Delilah doesn't think you're ready."

"I know he has schizophrenia. I don't care. I'll love him anyway."

"Your sister can be a stubborn b- "

"Frank!" Molly said.

"What? I'm serious. She makes Capone seem like a saint."

The psychiatrist returned. "Visiting hours our over."

Molly and Frank kissed Jacqueline before they left.

Chapter 54

1930's

Island of Medea

Charlotte DeMarco sat in the back seat of a 1925 sedan.

In the passenger seat sat Charlotte's brother Frank with his girlfriend Molly at the wheel.

Underboss Delilah DeMarco Phoenix sat next to Charlotte.

They shared a bottle of wine.

Charlotte drank from the bottle and returned it to Delilah. She quietly giggled.

They recently pulled off a bank job.

Delilah looked at Charlotte. "When I become Godmother, I want you to be my head hit-woman while Molly becomes my underboss.

"I'm honored," said Charlotte.

Frank turned in his seat and said, "When she's sixteen. I was that age when mom made me a mobster." Delilah took another drink before she returned the bottle of Charlotte.

Chapter 55

Early 1940's

"Why, Giovanni?"

"To gain knowledge of our enemies." Giovanni stepped into a black suit with matching fedora hat.   His mobster appearance made her shudder.

"You're lucky I'm on speaking terms with Molly and that the rest of my family doesn't know you are a witch," said Charlotte. She was dressed in a black dress with her hair in a peek-a-boo style. She was the local pin-up girl for her family's two casinos. On her shoulder, she bore the Astredo's mark of the Triple Goddess. She recently discovered what that mark meant. She was anxious to learn about her new destiny.

"They know you have quit the mob?"

"Only Jacqueline does. She seems to understand. But I don't know who to trust anymore."

"You can trust me. I'm one of the good guys."

"I know. When Charlemagne received the invitation for Jacqueline DeMarco and Tony Tortelli's wedding, I was surprised my name was mentioned with him and Nikkolas."

"Remember what my mom said, 'take advantage of the situation. You don't know what you may learn. Even if its 10 years before the information is applied."

Charlotte looked at her made bed and couldn't understand why Giovanni wasn't pressuring her to have sex with him. She met Giovanni Astredo and the rest of his magickal family around the time she began to question the tattoo she was born with. His family owned a theatre in Rome, and America and a nightclub casino on the Island of Medea. She met him while she was working as an exotic dancer in her brother, Nikkolas' casino. That first night, she noticed he couldn't keep his eyes off the tattoo that made her mother disown her. He followed her to her dressing room, introduced himself, and told her he could provide her a better life.

A month later, she befriended the handsome witch and learned about her scared birth rite.

Giovanni gazed at her with his eyes full of desire. Along with magick, he hoped to teach her to allow herself to be loved. "You look beautiful."

"Thanks." She quickly smiled.

"Are you and Giovanni ready?" Scarlet Astredo entered the guest room she and Mariano let Charlotte have. "Kathy and Barbara have finished making an identity shielding potion."

Giovanni escorted her out of the Astredo family mansion and into his aunt's black limo.

#

Island of Medea

The DeMarco crime family mansion sat nestled in the jungle on the tropical island.

Charlotte sat next to Giovanni in Delilah's garden. She could tell her family was studying Giovanni. She was glad his suit covered his tattoo of the God symbol.

Giovanni placed his arm around her shoulders, leaned close to her, and said, "Listen to every conversation and take note of every action."

"What *are* we looking for?"

"Mom, Aunt Scarlet, and Uncle Mariano wants to know if Amari and Esmeralda are associates of Marguerite's or if they are her top assassins. Amari and Esmeralda deal in trafficking lycanthropes. This is a good opportunity for you to see what your unique power is. If you're psychic, you should receive a premonition from handling things or when you dance with someone. I hope they have a bride and groom dance liked they do in America. Jacqueline is the new Don since the police gunned down Delilah and it will be good to know if she'll be just as brutal as Delilah or worse. I'm leaning towards worse since Tony was in and out of asylums his entire life. He's schizophrenic and very dangerous."

"Charming couple. What do you know about them?"

"Testing my knowledge on your Mafia family?" Giovanni gave her that seductive smile that made her want to take him into a parlor and have her way with him. "According to newsreels, cops are referring to Jacqueline and Tony as the Caribbean's version of Bonnie and Clyde. Jacqueline admires Bonnie Parker. She cried on Tony's shoulder during the newsreel that reported her death. Jacqueline has been helping Tony with his schizophrenia ever since she moved in with him and the rest of your family at the age of sixteen. They lived together for 5 years before becoming engaged. If Delilah were alive, she would be giving them this wedding. Delilah liked Tony, although she was wary about him marrying Jacqueline. Charlemagne and the others liked Tony. Charlemagne is very protective with his sisters. Two months ago, Jacqueline and Tony became parents to a healthy baby girl named Angelique. Tony and Jacqueline became engaged two years ago. Delilah used to beat her husband Lucian and was secretly dating Chicago mob boss Python Diavolo. Since Stefano is an empath, he once felt Molly's lust for Lucian. Molly has been seducing Lucian ever since Frank died in a mob hit meant *for* Molly and Delilah's affair with Python."

"Impressive. How would Delilah feel about Angelique?"

"She would love her if she knew that Angelique *isn't* schizophrenic like Tony. She didn't want to create more 'retards as Delilah once phrased it," said Giovanni.

Charlotte said, "I wouldn't call Tony retarded. Disturbed, maybe."

"Psycho," said Giovanni.

"Pretty much."

Their conversation ceased when the wedding began.

Molly walked Jacqueline down the ales in a gold gown. She and Frank raised her sister-in-law Jacqueline when Charlotte was a year old and Jacqueline was a month old.

Jacqueline was dressed in her Marguerite's wedding gown from the 1800's. The young mob boss resembled Delilah.

Charlotte watched Tony's face brightened at the sight of his beloved.

In the black marbled gazebo, Tony took Jacqueline's hand after Molly gave her away.

Molly took her seat, took Angelique from a bodyguard, and held her while Jacqueline and Tony exchanged vows.

After the wedding, Charlotte and Giovanni joined the mobsters, foot soldiers, associates, and other family members in the ballroom. They sat at a table with Charlemagne, Nikkolas, and Armand.

Charlotte felt Giovanni didn't deserve her. He was one of those rare gentlemen that deserved better than her.

Giovanni placed his arm around her waist and whispered, "Do you feel any psychic vibes?"

"None."

After watching Jacqueline and Tony dance to a few slow songs; Tony dancing with Angelique and later dancing with Jacqueline and Angelique, Giovanni and Charlotte rose from their seats to dance with the bride and groom.

Molly and Lucian were dancing with Angelique.

Charlotte nervously waited for her turn to dance with Tony. She couldn't remove his gruesome murders from her mind. She wasn't surprised that Jacqueline was just as brutal.

Tony appeared just as nervous as Charlotte.   Even though he has seen her many times during his childhood. He watched Jacqueline dance with Giovanni. His attention was turned away from Jacqueline when Charlotte said,

"Hi, Tony. Do you remember me? Charlotte DeMarco? I'm your sister-in-law."

Tony shyly smiled and said, "Yes. My Jacqueline is pretty. I like to play with my knife, but Jacqueline won't allow me anymore since she's the Godmother now that Delilah went to sleep."

While Charlotte danced with Tony, she pieced together Tony's odd speech brought on by his schizophrenia. She understood that Jacqueline wanted him to retire from organized crime since he didn't realize he was killing people. He didn't understand the concept of death. He just assumed the people he murdered were asleep. It was something Lucian and Charlemagne taught him. Charlotte was glad Jacqueline treated Tony better and it appeared as if Jacqueline was helping him through his mental illness. She tried to sense a psychic vibration, although she didn't experience what Athena goes through during a psychic vision. One power ruled out. She decided to ask Athena to teach her how to use runes and tarot cards anyway. She softly laughed to herself when she realized she was enjoying her new life. She was still confused and afraid to allow

Giovanni to fall in love with her and to make love to her. She also couldn't understand

why the Goddess chose her to bare the sacred mark.

When the dance was over, Charlotte joined Giovanni in a dance. She watched

Tony hold Jacqueline tightly in his arms and tell her how much he loved her. He was the

only mob guy she knew who honestly loved his lover. She figured it was because he

didn't know how to be cruel, deceitful, or abusive. She felt that Jacqueline was lucky to

never go through what she went through with the many Mafia johns she had to deal with.

She hated all of them. Giovanni seemed different. He never lied to her, hit her, or forced

himself on her while they danced; she gazed into Giovanni's eyes and noticed that he

couldn't take his eyes off her. She laid her head on his chest. As he caressed her back, she

felt strangely comfortable in his arms.

Giovanni nuzzled her neck and hugged her tightly. "My brother has our yacht

anchored on the beach, would you like us to sit on the dock with me and look at the

stars?"

"Did we collect the information your mother and aunt asked for?"

"Yes. Jacqueline asked me if I was a gangster when she discovered I was with

you. I don't think the mob or anyone else knows about us. Are you ready? I have so much

to tell you about fighting evil and other things."

"What other things?"

He kissed her forehead. "You and me." He escorted her out of the ballroom

without her family realizing she was gone.

The warm tropical breeze moved the Italian and American flags that flew over the family yacht.

From the view on the beach, the tiny island looked as if it were all jungle.

The sounds of waves mixed with nocturnal animals.

After lying on a blanket and discussing the constellations, Charlotte stood by the aluminum railing and watched the waves caress the beach.

"Do you *still* think you're *not* good enough for me?" asked Giovanni. He placed his arm around her waist.

"I'm *not* worthy to fight for the God and Goddess. I'm a hooker. I once joined the Mafia with my family."

"You *were* a hooker. That's all behind you. Your new life began the day we met."

"You *don't* want me. You deserve someone like Athena. Or Scarlet. Or Kathy. Or Barbara."

"I want *you*."

"Why? I can't love anyone."

"You never experienced any type of love, have you?"

Tears filled her eyes. "I don't know how to love."

Giovanni pulled her close. "I don't believe that. I don't think you are used to being treated with respect. You have had sex, but *never* made love."

"I don't belong with your family. I *don't* deserve a decent man like you."

"You deserve a man who beats you and cheats on you, correct?"

"That's all I've known. You deserve someone who *doesn't* have a past like mine."

"No one is perfect, Charlotte. *I'm* not perfect. I've made mistakes also. I know you want this life. I know you love me and love that my brother, his boyfriend, and our cousins treat you with respect. I know you admire mom for being the strong independent woman she is."

"How could you know how I feel?"

"Beside the fact that mom and Barbara are psychic and Stefano and Luca can feel emotions, I can tell by your actions and your words. If you *didn't* want to better yourself, you wouldn't be here with me. You would be a mobster and your tattoo would transfer into Marguerite's black rose tattoo. You would no longer bare the Holy sign of the Goddess."

Charlotte was silent.

"Come away with me for a week," said Giovanni.

"I can't. I have another year before I become an adult. Charlemagne is my guardian. He'll be looking for me."

"I don't think he'd come or miss you. Spend a week on my yacht with me. You need a break from them to adjust to your new life."

Charlotte didn't want to return to her brothers and sisters. Although, she could keep her job as an exotic dancer to save money to move out when she became eighteen. She told Giovanni that. "I'll have you wait in my dressing room after each show in case I need your help to remind men I'm no longer a hooker. You'll help me through this, right?"

"I will. Since they served lunch at the reception, let's have dinner in a restaurant. When we return, I'll show you the difference between sex and making love. This could be our first date."

She tried not to smile. "It's been awhile since I've been on a real date. What is your idea of making love?"

"Cuddling, foreplay, oral sex: both ways, sometimes toys. Pleasing each other."

"Anything else?"

"Just as a warning, I've been known to moan or whisper 'I love you' and *mean* it." He smiled.

"No one has ever said that to me."

"That's because it *never* was out of love."

After dinner, they returned to the yacht and entered Giovanni's bedroom.

Stefano and Roman were already in bed as the boat pulled away from the shore.

Charlotte watched him strip before he began to remove her dress.

Giovanni's hands explored her body. His hand touched the crotch of her panties, caressed it before he removed them. He covered her face and neck in deep passionate kisses while his finger entered her.

Charlotte caressed his back and softly moaned. A rush of ecstasy traveled through her when he placed his other finger on her clitoris. She kissed his shoulder before she climaxed. She stroked his penis.

Giovanni held her close and enjoyed her screams and her pulsating body until he climaxed. He laid her on the bed and stroked her breasts with his mouth and sucking deeply on each nipple.

Charlotte moaned and softly cried out while he kissed her stomach, inside of her thighs, and went down on her. She came immediately from someone returning their love and passion for the first time. "Giovanni," she screamed. She climaxed two more times before she took him into her mouth and messaged his testicles in her hand. She sucked him until he released himself in her mouth. She swallowed him before he lay on top of her.

Giovanni passionately kissed her mouth after he entered her and pushed her.

Their passion intensified the faster, deeper, and harder he stroked her.

He brought her to several climaxes, each one intense and long. Her nails impaled his back. "Giovanni, Giovanni! Yes, yes, yes!"

While he pushed her, he stroked her clitoris with his finger.

His name was repeatedly screamed.

For hours, they made love in different positions.

When he lay on top of her again, he cried out, "Oh, oh, Charlotte, Charlotte, I love you. I love you, I love you!"

She held him tightly as he pushed her harder. Tears filled her eyes. "I love you, Giovanni."

After another hour of making love, they talked for the duration of the evening before they fell asleep in each other's arms.

Chapter 56

1942

Island of Medea

The sounds of a casino mixed with a local singer who performed on stage as a seventeen-year-old Charlotte DeMarco briefly gazed at a group of sailors that sat in a corner booth. Charlotte was dressed in a red, orange, and yellow beaded swimsuit.

Charlotte stood behind the small stage smoking a long cigarette while she continued to gaze at the table of sailors.

"You're brave for looking at him, Charlotte."

Charlotte turned to discover 36-year-old mobster Molly DeMarco Phoenix behind her.

Molly was dressed in a black suit with gold lamè blouse. Her chestnut curls reached the side of her neck and she bared a deep knife scar on her cheek. She was a succubus with healing powers. She and her husband, Lucian, seduced their victims before they killed them.

Charlotte nervously asked, "What are you doing here?"

"I miss my sister-in-law."

"Bullshit!"

"I *wasn't* the one who betrayed yours and Giovanni's secret. Delilah did that after she abandoned us a few months before she was gunned down. Lucian, Jacqueline, and I are in the booth across from the pool table. Please sit with us. I want to speak to you."

"I told you, Molly; I want out! I'm *not* doing it again."

"Once you pull off your first hit, you'll *love* it. Don't waste your time with those witches. Our Godmother can give you anything you desire."

Charlotte finished her cigarette and said, "I'm next. I'll meet with you."

Molly smiled and said, "Good. I'll be waiting." She left to join her husband.

Charlotte walked on stage and began her exotic dance routine. She locked eyes with one of the witches. She quickly smiled at Giovanni. She couldn't wait to meet him in their secret meeting place. Giovanni was with Stefano, Roman, Leonardo, Russell, and Luca. Charlotte watched him watch her. She wanted to be nestled in his arms where his passionate lovemaking would erase her shady past.

After her performance, she joined Molly at her booth. Charlotte sat across from Molly with the Astredo's protective gaze on her.

Molly sat next to her dark-haired husband, Lucian, and on her other side sat Don Jacqueline DeMarco Tortelli.

Jacqueline's best friend, Jasmine Khazzan, sat next to Jacqueline. She was Jacqueline's consigliere.

Charlotte looked at the young twenty-year-old Mafia Don and saw Marguerite and Delilah's features and black hair. Her twenty-year-old husband, Tony Tortelli was at their hotel with their daughter and two bodyguards. Charlotte said, "Molly, this is pointless."

Molly said, "It's not. How long have you been fucking the enemy?"

The casino cleared out leaving the witches and the mobsters as the only patrons since it was an hour before closing.

"He's *not* the enemy!"

"Return to your true family."

"No!"

Jacqueline's brooding eyes gazed into Charlotte's dark eyes. "Perhaps it's for the best she doesn't want in. Did you curse our family so that Delilah would abandon us for some sleazy Chicago mob boss?"

"I had *nothing* to do with our family dramas! I *don't* want this life anymore!"

"Don Jacqueline; Charlotte *didn't* use witchcraft on our crime family," said Nikkolas as he sat next to his twin sister. He didn't notice the Astredo's in the booth across from them since the lights were still low.   "Sorry we're late, Jacqueline. Amari and Esmeralda's flight was late."

With Nikkolas were Charlemagne, Amari, and Esmeralda.

Charlemagne sat on the other side of Charlotte.

Jacqueline asked, "Since when are you standing up for Charlotte? She turned her back on our sisters."

Nikkolas placed his arm around Charlotte's shoulders. "Charlotte was brainwashed by her lover and his band of witches."

Charlemagne touched her hair and neck before he slapped her thigh. "We could bring her back to us."

Nikkolas said to Charlemagne, "We could. Perhaps you or Amari could carve Marguerite's mark into her left shoulder while the other one removes their mark." Nikkolas tightened his hold on his sister's shoulder.

Charlemagne replied, "I wouldn't mind peeling that off with my knife."

Charlotte recoiled from their touches. She hated to be touched by them. She was drawn closer to Nikkolas when he wrapped his arm around her waist. A nozzle from a gun was suddenly stabbed into her side. "I *don't* want anything to do with the mob!"

"Return to organized crime. You haven't murdered anyone yet, so how do you know you don't like it," said Nikkolas.

"Fuck you!"

"Charlotte, you were a wonderful whore," said Lucian. "I miss you." His foot rubbed against her foot. He and Charlemagne laughed.

Charlotte glared at her first john and said, "You tricked me with your powers as an incubus. I *didn't* know you and Nikkolas had planned to *sell* me!"

"It was your punishment for leaving us. Marguerite organized it." Nikkolas shoved the gun further into her side. "You brought in a lot of money. I hate to see you go," said Nikkolas.

"I wouldn't have minded being one of your customers," said Charlemagne.

Charlotte glared at Charlemagne and said, "You are my *brother*. I would *never* sleep with you! I *hate* you!" Charlotte returned her gaze and on the lady mobsters. She noticed Jacqueline had the same repulsed expression towards Charlemagne. She could almost feel the hatred Jacqueline had for Charlemagne. She reasoned it was because of his over protectiveness and the way Charlemagne would control her every move. Charlotte was glad she wasn't the only person who hated their brother since it appeared that everyone the DeMarcos ran around with thought Charlemagne was the greatest thing since Dean Martin.

"Is that witch you're fucking better than me?" Lucian reached across the table and grabbed her hand.

"He's much better." She removed her hand from his hold.

Lucian's face brightened as he asked, "Could I barrow him some night?"

"He's straight. Even if he were gay or bisexual, he would *never* get involved with an asshole like you."

Molly placed her hand protectively on Lucian's arm. "He's *not* an asshole!"

Charlotte moved her gaze towards the Astredo's table and noticed that they were prepared to defend her. She turned her gaze to Nikkolas's evil stare after he buried the nozzle deeper into her side.

The mob withdrew their guns and aimed at her. Charlemagne shoved the nozzle into her neck. His fingers combed through her dark hair.

"I should arrange your marriage to one of my mobsters. That way I can keep an eye on you," said Jacqueline.

"I would rather die!"

"Be careful what you wish for," said Nikkolas.

"Return to our family," said Molly.

Charlotte said, "Go to hell."

Molly, Lucian, and Jacqueline bestowed upon her a cold stare. The mobsters reached for their guns. "It's a shame. You could have been one of us."

The mobsters were thrown across the room by Giovanni's powers of telekinesis.

Molly, Jacqueline, and Lucian were thrown into card tables while Nikkolas was thrown across the black jack table. Charlemagne and Amari caused a craps table to collapse and Esmeralda was thrown over the bar.

Giovanni took her arm and quickly escorted her out of the nightclub with the others behind them.

When they approached the two black sedans, Stefano jumped in the driver's seat while Roman climbed into the passenger seat.

Leonardo climbed in the second car.

Giovanni opened the back door for Charlotte just as bullets began to fly in the air.

Jacqueline's mobsters sprayed anything that moved with bullets.

Giovanni entered the car, slammed the door, before he waved his hand at the mobsters and warlocks causing them to be thrown across the parking lot.

The car ride towards the Astredo's old mansion was silent. Charlotte gazed out the window. The sound of the machine guns continued to thunder in her mind.

Giovanni placed his arm around her waist and tenderly pulled her close to him. "We can talk after the guys go home, if you want."

"We can," she said.

Giovanni and Stefano's family home was an old castle built in the 1500's. Scarlet and Mariano returned to the family home in the nineteen thirties. Giovanni, Stephano, and Roman accompanied Athena to the island after she received a vision of Marguerite having a daughter baring the Astredo's mark. Occasionally, they helped their family members whenever they needed it.

They were scheduled to leave in a few weeks to Castle Olympia.

As Stefano drove through the wrought-iron gates, Charlotte glanced at her work clothes and said, "I can't allow your mother, uncle, and aunt to see me like this."

The six witches laughed gently.

Stefano said, "Not to worry. Mom used to be a belly dancer in her old gypsy tribe."

"You're family, Charlotte. They *love* you," said Roman.

Charlotte's eyes misted over as she said, "I'm looking forward to seeing them again."

Inside the ancient foyer, the 46-year-old gypsy woman greeted Charlotte with a motherly hug. Athena wore a maroon gypsy style skirt with a black bodice. Her jewelry were a balanced mixture of gold and silver. A large gold ankh hung around her neck along with two beaded necklaces. Silver crescent moons hung from her ears and she wore many gold and silver rings with Pagan symbols. She was a respected tarot reader and the

High Priestess of their coven and the mother of two other covens. One in Italy, one on the Island of Medea, and one in America. Athena raised Giovanni and Stefano by herself after she became a widow. For a moment, Athena held Charlotte in her arms in comfort and said, "You belong with us."

"I do."

Leonardo was already in the drawing room when Athena led Giovanni, Charlotte, Stefano, and the others into the room.

Giovanni and Charlotte sat on a couch next to Roman and Stefano. With their family, they discussed the many plays Giovanni performed. "I can't wait to return to the Dragon's Lair. I think the first play I'll put on will be *Dr. Jekyll and Mr. Hyde* with me in the role of Dr. Jekyll."

"I think you should recite poetry again. I loved listening to you speak," said Charlotte.

"Perhaps I may," Giovanni replied.

"Recite something from classic Literature for us, Giovanni," said Mariano. Giovanni began to recite Robert Frost's 'Fire and Ice', "Some say the world will end in fire. Some say in ice. From what I've tasted of desire, I hold with those who favor fire. But if it had to perish twice, I think I know enough of hate to say that for destruction ice is also great and would suffice."

A short applauded sounded in the large room.

They continued to talk and joked around for a few hours before Scarlet, Mariano, Kathy, Russell, Barbara, and Luca left for the rooms.

Athena practiced a new tarot spread in one of the parlors while Roman and

Stefano left for their room after one of their favorite radio shows were over.

Charlotte and Giovanni were walking through the garden.

Charlotte savored every moment with him. She wasn't sure what her punishment would be when she returned to her home. She prayed to the Gods Charlemagne was not there. Charlemagne would beat her as he used to do to Jacqueline whenever she disobeyed him or Delilah. Charlotte was the only one he would try to touch sexually. Jacqueline had Tony to protect her and Charlemagne was afraid of Delilah. He was now becoming fearful of Jacqueline since she was becoming *crueler* and brutal than Delilah and Marguerite. Whenever he would spend the night in his old room, Charlotte would lay awake with her bedroom door locked with a small dresser in front of her door. She shuddered at the memory of his advances last night. She was ordered to make dinner for her brothers and their friends when Charlemagne approached her, placed his arms around her, and began to nuzzle her neck, while he described sexual acts he wanted her to perform for him. She pushed him away from her with a high kick in the stomach that caused him to fall onto the kitchen table. In return, Nikkolas and Charlemagne took turns beating her. For the duration of the evening, she remained in her bedroom. She phoned Giovanni and told him what Charlemagne and the others did.

Giovanni was furious with Charlemagne and the others. Athena, Scarlet, Kathy, and Barbara wanted to tear Charlemagne, Nikkolas, and Lucian's balls off.

As if he were reading her mind, Giovanni placed his arm around her waist, and said, "You *don't* have to return to Charlemagne or any of them."

"What choice do I have? Charlemagne is mine and Nikkolas's guardian since we're seventeen."

"Stay with me. I can magickally transport your belongings to the mansion in Salem. He won't harm you; the mansion is protected by magick."

Charlotte said, "I don't have your ancestor's powers. What good will I be?"

"You will be able to tap into them once you're not under stress. You were born with them. Powers or not, you mean everything to me. I want you to move in with me and the others."

"You can move objects with your mind, Athena is psychic, Roman can heal, and Stefano can feel the emotions of others. What unique power do I have?"

"You will know soon."

"Why was I a born with the Goddess's mark? I am the daughter of a mobster. I was one of them. I later became a prostitute. Aren't I evil?"

"No one is born good or evil. We have choices. There is *no* devil that made us do anything. No one is perfect. I used to have a gambling problem. That's why my second girlfriend left me."

"So, I made the right choice?"

"You made the right choice. If you did anything evil, your tattoo would have changed into Marguerite's tattoo."

Charlotte tenderly touched her tattoo and felt the warmth from the Goddess. Giovanni told her that only those outside the family who are meant to be a part of the Astredo family will be born with the Goddess and the God's mark. Her stubbornness caused her to be skeptical of her destiny.

Giovanni tenderly embraced her and said, "Don't worry, it's still there. She is always there for Her children."

"Even the ones that fall for a man who only seduces her just to help her brother turn her into a prostitute?"

"Lucian honestly loved you."

"I don't believe that."

"Stefano and Luca felt his love for you. Don't dwell on that now." Giovanni tenderly caressed her thighs.

"I don't understand how he could love me at the same time..."

"He thought it was *your* idea. Nikkolas told him you wanted to work in Nikkolas's brothel."

"He's still a creep for not doing anything *after* he discovered Nikkolas's plan."

For a moment, Giovanni saw a tiny spark in her eyes when she became angry at the memory of her deceptive former lover. He softly smiled and said, "We should work with magick some more. I can see something igniting in your eyes."

"What is it?"

"I am not sure yet. I think you are beginning to tap into your unique powers now that you are away from them. Our intense emotions will activate our powers. One of my uncles, as well as Russell, on my father's side had to be careful when he became angry since he was a fire starter. I am anxious to learn what power you have inherited from my ancestors. Have you begun your grimoire?"

"No. I don't want Charlemagne or anyone to know that I'm studying witchcraft. I think Jacqueline knows."

"Perhaps it would work to your benefit if they knew. Then again, it's really no one's business what you believe in."

Charlotte glanced down at her watch and said, "It's late. Charlemagne will be furious at me. I need to...."

"You're *never* going back," he said.

"But my things..."

Giovanni whispered an incantation before he said, "Your things are in my room." He wanted her miles away from her abusive brother and the rest of her Mafia family.

Charlotte stared at him with a puzzled expression. "Giovanni, I work in his casino."

Giovanni said, "Mom raised Stefano and me to respect women and to treat them as equals. I'm not better then you and you're not better than me. I don't believe in ordering a woman around or making them my slave. Although in this case since you are being stubborn, I must do everything for you."

"You don't have to do *everything* for me. I'm still just...I don't know. I don't know what I want."

"You *know* what you what. You're just scared."

Charlotte wanted to argue with him, although, she knew he was correct.

Giovanni tightened his hold on her and said, "It's alright for the future mistress of Castle Olympia to be frightened of her new life. Mom would never admit it either that she was frightened when dad brought her from Italy to Island of Medea and later to America."

"Future *mistress* of Castle Olympia?"

"When the mob war is over, you and I are going to get married and move into Castle Olympia and raise a family."

Charlotte laughed and said, "While we fight the mob and other criminals."

"I can't wait." Softly, he kissed her. "Was that an answer to my statement earlier? That you'll move in with me?"

Charlotte glanced at the ancient mansion and thought about the huge mansion her Mafia parents have. Giovanni's family mansion was more warm and inviting than her parent's mansion. Giovanni's family loved her and respected her. She hated the crimes her family committed and hated some of the things *she* did. Charlotte robbed a string of banks with Molly and Delilah when they were younger. She never killed anyone, although, she wounded a few. Molly and Delilah were more vicious. Molly and Delilah were sadistic. The DeMarco's new Godmother, Jacqueline, was more sadistic then her sisters. Even though he never realized the things he did were wrong, Tony was just as dangerous as Jacqueline was. Charlotte was happy with her choice to give up organized crime.

"Charlotte, say you will." He gently nuzzled her neck.

She moved her gaze into his eyes. "I will. I want to leave my past behind and begin my new life with you."

"You won't be disappointed." He escorted her back into the castle.

In his bedroom, Charlotte opened the large closet and liked the sight of his clothes mixed with her clothes. She looked through the clothes for her nightgown. She pushed aside one of Giovanni's shirts and discovered her black pin-striped suit. The sight made her stomach turn as she pulled the suit out from the closet. She was about to throw it away when Giovanni entered the room wearing nothing but a long black satin robe.

"Shouldn't you keep that in case you have a job interview when we move to

America?"

Charlotte was still holding the hanger with the suit hanging above the trashcan. "I haven't thought of that. Although, I could always purchase another one. I would feel like a mobster again in this suit. *Any* suit would make me feel like I'm *still* in the mob."

"Not if you create a better experience in one. I like that one on you. I don't think you look like a mobster in that. That suit makes you look professional. Seriously."

"I know you would never tell me what I want to hear instead of the truth. What job can I have when I'm not battling the DeMarco Crime Family and whatever else is thrown at us?"

Giovanni sat on the bed and shrugged. "Whatever calls to you? Perhaps you should meditate about it. Do a tarot reading."

"Perhaps I will. I want to do something meaningful that may blend with our scared job."   Charlotte turned from the trashcan and walked towards the closet. She would feel as though she were a victim if she threw the suit away. She couldn't allow her family to win. She placed the suit back in the closet. Charlotte stepped out of her exotic dancer's costume and hung it up. "Perhaps Athena could teach me how to belly dance."

"She will. She would love it. Why are you bothering with a nightgown?"

Charlotte pulled out a maroon satin robe and closed the closet door. She laid the robe over an antique chair in case she had to leave the room. With Stefano and Roman being gay, and the other men in the mansion, she knew she would be safe in the castle in a nightgown only. It was a relief to be around men who didn't touch her. She only wanted Giovanni to touch her. She joined him on the bed. She was wrapped tightly in his protective arms. She began to kiss him passionately on the mouth while she rode him.

Giovanni explored her body with his hands as he returned her passionate kisses.

Charlotte kissed him across his chest before she sat up on him. She heavily grinded on his lap while his hands caressed her breasts.

Giovanni moved her onto her back after she arrived at her climax. He stroked her deeply while he covered her body with his warm kisses.

Charlotte's nails dug into his back. She moaned several times before she cried out his name. Her worries and fears dissolved as he continued to make love to her.

Over the next couple of days, Charlotte meditated in the temple room.

The temple room was designed to look like an Egyptian temple.

After she meditated, she filled a black bowl with holy water, set it on a table beside a statue of the Goddess Renenutet. She scried in the water after she said, "Lead me to the path I am to take in a career. So Mote It Be." She gazed into the black water for ten minutes before she began to see a scarlet plume of an ostrich. Next, came the zodiac symbol for Libra. The vision disappeared. She rose from the table and studied each statue of Egyptian Gods and Goddesses mixed with the Greek and Roman Gods and Goddesses. She approached a large statue of the Goddess Maat in a seated position. Charlotte gazed at the red ostrich feather. She was new to the Egyptian pantheon. What did this Goddess have to do with her future career? Charlotte left the room and entered the large library.

She pulled out a book on Ancient Egypt.

At an oak table, she began to read the article on Maat. "Maat. Goddess of truth, justice, and cosmic order.' She closed the book and stared at a pentacle made into the stained glass window. Was she to be a policewoman?

Next to the stained glass pentacle was a stained-glass picture of a goat with a fish tail. It was Capricorn.

Charlotte rose from the chair and searched each stained glass window for Libra.

The picture in the stain-glass window portrayed many Goddesses of justice, truth, and cosmic order.

In the center, stood Maat holding an ankh in one hand and in her other hand, she held scales that weighed the deceased heart against a red feather.

Charlotte softly smiled. While she battled mortal and immortal criminals for the Gods, she could also help send criminals to jail. She couldn't wait until she told Giovanni and the others. *Attorney* Charlotte DeMarco. Or better; Attorney Charlotte *Astredo*. Mr. and Attorney Astredo.

Chapter 57

1946

Giovanni and Charlotte sat on old furniture with an arm around each other's waist.

Leonardo, Kathy, Russell, Barbara, Luca, Scarlet, and Mariano was in the living room.

Athena sat in a chair beside the loveseat where Roman and Stefano were seated. She was dressed in a light green gypsy dress. Her Pagan jewelry was silver with emeralds.

Before they were to return to America, Athena, Giovanni, Charlotte, Stefano, and Roman wanted to spend the evening with their small family.

Giovanni, Stefano, and Charlotte planned to stay a few weeks later to help their aunt and cousins take care of a few things left over from the aftermath of a long mob war.

When the party was over, they said goodbye and exchanged hugs with Scarlet and their others.

After he hugged Charlotte, Roman and Stefano embraced tightly. Roman nuzzled his face in Stefano's chest. He was afraid to release him from his embrace.

Stefano returned his tight hug and said, "I'll be fine. When I return to America, you and I will rent a cabin in the mountains."

"I'm looking forward to that."

Stefano kissed Roman's mouth in a deep passionate kiss. "I love you," he whispered.

"I love you, Stefano," said Roman. He hugged him tightly. He wished he could stay on the island and help, although, since he was a high school Literature teacher, he had to return. Since Athena was with him, Roman didn't mind keeping her company and looking after her. Not that *she* needed someone to protect her. Athena was a powerful witch with an I-can-take-care-of-myself attitude. None-the-less, Roman planned to protect and be company for the matriarch of the family. She would allow him to watch over her only because she loved him as much as she loved her sons. Charlotte, she already loved her like a daughter.

Charlotte, Giovanni, and Stefano watched Athena and Roman leave for America.

\#

1946

A few months later

Salem, Ohio

Silver bullets shot through the air-striking mobsters sent by Marguerite.

The Astredos used their elemental powers as well as mundane weapons to defeat Marguerite's mob.

With her firepower, Charlotte vanquished three mobsters before she and Amari battled in Giovanni's Gothic garden. Her weapon was now her sword.

Amari's sword struck her sword while they fenced around statues of Gods and Goddesses and fantasy creatures.

Their battle ended when Charlotte's sword struck Amari's arm causing a deep gash.

Before Charlotte could finish him off, Marguerite used a tree branch to knock her down.

Charlotte attacked back quickly exchanging her sword for her gun with silver bullets. She fired two in Marguerite's stomach.

Marguerite fell into Esmeralda's arms. The mobster quickly healed her.

Charlotte fought more mobsters.

Roman fired his pistol into the chest of a werewolf foot solider, also sent by Marguerite. After he killed the werewolf, he vanquished a few vampiric hit-men.

Giovanni and Stefano were beside Athena's herb garden fighting off human mobsters, vampiric, and werewolf hit-men.

Athena was further away from her children vanquishing a group of mobsters with her gun filled with silver bullets. After her gun ran out of bullets, she changed to her crossbow and driven wooden stakes into their hearts.

The mobsters were vanquished before they had a chance to attack Athena.

After the last mobster was destroyed, she backed towards a high bush that created a maze throughout the garden. As she refilled her gun, a bullet nicked her wrist causing her to drop the gun. She stepped towards an opening in the maze when her eyes locked with Charlemagne's psychotic blue eyes. She prepared to fight him with the power of air. Another bullet entered her arm before Charlemagne attacked her with his fists. She fought back. She kneed him between his legs after he punched her jaw. She was pulled on the ground from him grabbing her ankle in the middle of her kick.

He was on her as they fought on the ground.

Athena impaled his eyes with her fingernails before she drug them down his face.

Charlemagne screamed before his hands clamped around her throat. Blood streamed down his face.

Her nails dug into his wrists. His blood appeared under her fingernails.

Charlemagne released her neck from his hold before he quickly withdrew his gun and shot her in the chest twice. Hearing Charlotte call out Athena's name, he shot her again before he left.

Charlotte began to scream for Roman after she discovered Athena. She knelt beside the gypsy and held her in her arms. Tears filled her eyes as her hand searched for a pulse on her blood- covered wrist.

Roman and the others arrived. Roman quickly held his hands over Athena's wounds. Heavy tears filled his eyes he gazed into Athena's lifeless eyes. "I'm too late. I *can't* heal her."

Charlotte held her close while she cried on her shoulder.

Giovanni knelt beside Charlotte and placed his arm around her waist as he softly cried on her shoulder.

Roman stood and gathered Stefano in his arms. They cried on each other's shoulder.

Athena's gypsy funeral was held the next evening. Stefano and Roman stood among the Circle with the rest of the coven and family members from Island of Medea with an arm around each other's waists. Stefano rested his head on Roman's shoulder. Stefano and Luca's grief was double since they were able to feel their emotions.

Roman held him tightly and caressed his back.

Her glass coffin was placed in the family catacombs under the temple room.

From the Ancient Egyptian Book of the Dead, Charlotte read the hymn to Osiris while Giovanni sprinkled holy water in the form of an ankh and a pentagram over Athena's body.

#

1948

After three years of being engaged, Stefano and Roman stood in front of Giovanni and Charlotte with the rest of their coven standing in the scared Circle.

Charlotte was their coven's High Priestess ever since Athena died. She wore a turquoise robe and a headdress that resembled Isis's horns and solar disk. Around her neck was a large gold ankh.

Giovanni was her High Priest ever since she received her third degree that made her the coven's High Priestess. Giovanni was also in a turquoise robe.

Roman and Stefano faced each other while Giovanni and Charlotte performed their handfasting after Giovanni casts the Circle with his athame.

Roman and Stefano wore black suits with a blood-red rose on the lapel. They exchanged vows before their wedding bands, with their names carved on them, were blessed.

Stefano took Roman's hand, slipped the wedding band on his left ring finger next to Roman's engagement ring, and said, "With this ring, I thee wed."

Roman slipped the other gold band on Stefano's finger and said, "With this ring, I thee wed." Tears lightly filled his eyes.

Charlotte took their hands and tied a cord around their hands and wrists. From Athena's grimoire, she said, "Roman and Stefano Astredo are now one before the Gods, our ancestors, and our friends. May their love continue to be strong and blessed by the Gods and our ancestors? So Mote It Be."

After the witches repeated 'So Mote It Be,' Charlotte said to Stefano,

"You may kiss your groom."

After Giovanni removed the cord, Roman and Stefano embraced before they kissed long and passionately. Next, they stepped over the coven's broomstick to complete the ceremony.

#

1954

Throughout the years, they continued to battle Dante, Marguerite, Gerard, Amari, Esmeralda, and Charlemagne. Recently, Charlemagne placed a memory block on them to make them forget their battles.

The large Gothic garden became a battlefield once again.

Mobsters swarmed the garden.

Marguerite and Esmeralda ambushed Roman and Stefano. They fought the witches using their pistols.

Esmeralda fired at Roman striking him in the gut.

He dropped to his knees.

Stefano rushed towards him and was shot in the stomach by Marguerite.

Roman called out his name just as Esmeralda shot him in the chest and stomach a few times.

After the gypsy funeral performed by Charlotte and Giovanni, the double glass coffin sat next to Athena's coffin in the catacombs.

Laying a bouquet of blue roses on the lid of the coffin, Stefano bent to kiss the cool lid. His tears were endless.

Giovanni's arm circled Stefano's waist at the same moment Charlotte placed her arm around Stefano's shoulders. Giovanni placed his head on Stefano's shoulder and softly cried. Charlotte softly cried as Stefano placed his head on her shoulder.

Heartbroken, Stefano never remarried. He claimed that he could not love anyone else.

#

1956

Salem, Ohio

The full moon shone through the stained glass windows inside Giovanni and Charlotte's bedroom.

Charlotte changed into her nightgown as her husband of eleven years pulled back the covers. She watched him climb into bed. "Giovanni?"

"What?"

"What do you think Markus would say when we tell him that he's going to be a big brother?"

Giovanni shrugged as he set the alarm clock. "I don't know. Why?"

Charlotte smiled and sat on his lap after he placed the alarm clock back on the nightstand. "You weren't paying attention were you?"

"I'm sorry. I was thinking about opening night tomorrow night and if I printed out enough programs. With most of my staff sick, Markus and I were busy. What did you say?"

Charlotte gently laughed. "I'm pregnant."

Giovanni excitedly hugged her and laid her down among their red satin sheets.

#

2008

Valentina and the others stared at the master and mistress of Castle Olympia in surprise. For a few moments, they were speechless.

"The DeMarco Crime family? The one Hollywood has made so many movies about," asked Jason.

"Yes. My two sisters were Caribbean's famous mob bosses during the 1920s to the late 1940s."

"So, you and dad *danced* with serial killers Tony and Jacqueline," said Caesar.

"We did. I knew Tony since he was a newborn. Tony's mother, Cara, was Marguerite's head hit-woman until she died in childbirth after suffering from the flu. Delilah became his guardian just as Molly became Jacqueline's legal guardian when Jacqueline was a few months old," said Charlotte.

"Why weren't you ever mentioned in old news reels and other biographies about them?" asked Michael.

"I am now. Athena informed me last night that I was doing more harm for my family by not informing them about my family. When my mob family and Marguerite began their hunt for me, Giovanni and I used spells to clear my name and image from their history. I had to disappear for a while. I couldn't wait to go to law school."

"Is that all?" asked Brenda.

"No. There's more to tell. Much more then I can tell you now. Mostly concerning your Aunt Jacqueline and Uncle Tony."

Chapter 58

2008

Charlotte slowly gathered the musty journals after the others parted for the evening.

Giovanni placed his hands on her shoulders. "Do you feel better?"

"I do."

"Do you need help taking those to the library?"

"No, Thanks. Go ahead and finish work in your den. I'll meet you there when I'm finished." She gave him a quick kiss before she left the living room.

The walls leading towards the library was lined with family pictures form the 1509 to present.

"Mom, wait."

Charlotte turned to see Markus approaching her. "What's wrong?"

"I want to apologize for the others and myself for going behind your back and investigating you. We're sorry. We should've listened to the girls."

Charlotte said, "What you and the others did *was* wrong. Although, *not* telling the truth about who I was, *was* wrong also. I forgive you and the others."

"We forgive you and thanks for understanding."

Charlotte hugged her son before he left the second floor after crossing into the living room and hallway.

Charlotte passed pictures and arched stained glass windows before entering the library.

The sweet aroma of pineapple and roses mixed with the musty books.

Charlotte slowly walked towards the ceiling to floor bookcases holding family journals feeling a draft. With a key, she opened the glass door and placing the journals in their proper order.

Jacqueline DeMarco-Tortelli's journal was the last to be shelved.

Charlotte looked at the faded black leather journal. She opened the book at the first page.

It was yellowed and brown spots were sprinkled over the pages.

In cursive, were the words: This Book Belongs to…printed in red.

Jacqueline DeMarco-Tortelli's name was in black ink. The date was 1936 to 1945.

The place provided for a name, was a heart drawn by Jacqueline with the names Jacqueline loves Tony written in the center.

Charlotte skimmed through the journal before closing the musty book and with the book still in her hand; she closed the glass door and locked it. She turned finding

Tony's ghost holding his favorite chef knife.

"Tony, stop it," Jacqueline's ghost appeared next to Tony. She gently removed the knife.

Charlotte held Jacqueline's journal close. "Does he remember me?"

Jacqueline softly smiled and said, "He does. Even in death he hallucinates. He could have seen you as a long past rival gangster. We're ghosts. Ghosts *don't* normally harm the living."

"What makes Tony different?" Charlotte looked into his confused blue eyes and returned her gaze to Jacqueline.

Jacqueline placed her arm around Tony's waist. "It's complicated." She looked at the journal in Charlotte's arms. "Is that mine?"

"It is."

"Were you planning to read it to our family?"

"Yes, Jacqueline."

Jacqueline tenderly caressed Tony's back and said, "Tony *doesn't* understand death. He thinks it is still nineteen forty-six."

"Whose side are you on," asked Charlotte.

"Octavia's side. Charlotte, I missed you."

"Is that why you are here? Because you miss me?"

"Our spirits do *not* restrict ourselves to mom, Dante, Charlemagne, and Octavia. You *are* still family. You, your husband, sons, daughters-in-law, grandchildren, everyone is a part of the DeMarco family."

"You, Tony, and who else visits us?"

"Does that really need defined? Delilah, Nikkolas, Lucian, Frank, and Molly."

"Your spirits are *not* welcome. Leave."

"Spirits can come and go as they please, especially when family is concerned. We do *not* intend to harm anyone. They all family. Those protective spells you and Giovanni placed around the castle do *not* work with human spirits. No one is all good or all bad. Tony's illness does *not* make him evil. His actions do. I am *not* only protecting Tony, I am protecting you and the others as well."

"Mom created a monster," said Charlotte.

Jacqueline said, "My nephews and nieces cann*ot* stop what is coming. Learn from the mistakes made in the past."

"If you're on Octavia's side, why are you helping me?"

"This is not what it appears to be. Our mother created a monster. It is my job to control my monster."

Charlotte watched Tony place his arms around Jacqueline's waist clearly forgetting about what he tried to do earlier. Tony was still staring at her in confusion. "*Your* monster?"

"He *is* the love of my life. He is my equal. My soul mate. My everything."

Charlotte looked at the scars covering her sister and brother-in-law. "What's coming?"

"I cannot say." Jacqueline looked at Tony for a moment. "Ready?"

Tony softly smiled and kissed her mouth.

"For what?"

Jacqueline lay her head on Tony's chest and said, "For the beginning."

Charlotte looked at the place where her baby sister and brother-in-law stood. With the journal in her hand, she left the library.

She entered Giovanni's den, closed the door, and sat on the edge of his desk. She placed the journal on top of Ari's play and told him about Jacqueline and Tony's visit.

"When do we tell the others?" Giovanni asked.

"As soon as we can."

Made in the USA
Middletown, DE
31 August 2018